MESSAGE FROM CHINUA ACHEBE:

Africa is a huge continent with a diversity of cultures and languages. Africa is not simple — often people want to simplify it, generalize it, stereotype its ·ld is just starting to ge of European contact presented Africa in a ve fricans to tell their own

The Penguin African Writers Series will bring a new energy to the publication of African literature. Penguin Books is committed to publishing both established and new voices from all over the African continent to ensure African stories reach a wider global audience.

This is really what I personally want to see — writers from all over Africa contributing to a definition of themselves, writing ourselves and our stories into history. One of the greatest things literature does is allow us to imagine; to identify with situations and people who live in completely different circumstances, in countries all over the world. Through this series, the creative exploration of those issues and experiences that are unique to the African consciousness will be given a platform, not only throughout Africa, but also to the world beyond its shores.

Storytelling is a creative component of human experience and in order to share our experiences with the world, we as Africans need to recognize the importance of our own stories. By starting the series on the solid foundations laid by the renowned Heinemann African Writers Series, I am honored to join Penguin in inviting young and upcoming writers to accept the challenge passed down by celebrated African authors of earlier decades and to continue to explore, confront and question the realities of life in Africa through their work; challenging Africa's people to lift her to her rightful place among the nations of the world.

PENGUIN  CLASSICS

A GRAIN OF WHEAT

NGŨGĨ WA THIONG'O was born in Limuru, Kenya, in 1938. One of the leading African writers and scholars at work today, he is the author of *Weep Not, Child; The River Between; A Grain of Wheat; Homecoming; Petals of Blood; Devil on the Cross; Matigari; Decolonizing the Mind; Moving the Center; Writers in Politics;* and *Penpoints, Gunpoints, and Dreams,* among other works, which include novels, short stories, essays, a memoir, and plays. In 1977, the year he published *Petals of Blood,* Ngũgĩ's play *I Will Marry When I Want* (cowritten with Ngũgĩ wa Mĩriĩ and harshly critical of the injustices of Kenyan society) was performed, and at the end of the year Ngũgĩ was arrested. He was detained for a year without trial at a maximum security prison in Kenya. The theater where the play was performed was razed by police in 1982.

Ngũgĩ's numerous honors include the East African Novel Prize; Unesco First Prize; the Lotus Prize for Literature; the Paul Robeson Award for Artistic Excellence, Political Conscience and Integrity; the Zora Neal Hurston–Paul Robeson Award for Artistic and Scholarly Achievement; the Fonlon-Nichols Prize for Artistic Excellence and Human Rights; the Distinguished Africanist Award; the Gwendolyn Brooks Center Contributors Award for significant contribution to the black literary arts; and the Nonino International Literary Prize for the Italian translation of his book *Moving the Center.* Ngũgĩ has given many distinguished lectures including the 1984 Robb Lectures at Auckland University, New Zealand, and the 1996 Clarendon Lectures in English at Oxford University. He received the Medal of the Presidency of the Italian Cabinet for "his uncompromising efforts to assert the values implicit in the mulitcultural approach embracing the experience and aspirations of all the world's minorities." He has taught in many universities including Nairobi, Northwestern, and Yale. He was named New York University's Erich Maria Remarque Professor of Languages and Professor of Comparative Literature and Performance Studies. In 2003 Ngũgĩ was elected as an honorary member in the American Academy of Arts and Letters. Currently he is Distinguished Professor of English and Comparative Literature and Director of the International Center for Writing and Translation in the School of Humanities at the University of California, Irvine.

ABDULRAZAK GURNAH was born in 1948 in Zanzibar, Tanzania. He is the author of the highly acclaimed novels *Memory of Departure, Pilgrim's Way, Dottie, Paradise* (shortlisted for the 1994 Booker Prize), *Admiring Silence, By the Sea, Desertion,* and *The Last Gift.* He teaches English literature at the University of Kent at Canterbury, England.

NGŨGĨ WA THIONG'O

A Grain of Wheat

Introduction by
ABDULRAZAK GURNAH

PENGUIN BOOKS

PENGUIN BOOKS
Published by the Penguin Group
Penguin Group (USA) Inc., 375 Hudson Street, New York, New York 10014, U.S.A.
Penguin Group (Canada), 90 Eglinton Avenue East, Suite 700, Toronto,
Ontario, Canada M4P 2Y3 (a division of Pearson Penguin Canada Inc.)
Penguin Books Ltd, 80 Strand, London WC2R 0RL, England
Penguin Ireland, 25 St Stephen's Green, Dublin 2, Ireland (a division of Penguin Books Ltd)
Penguin Group (Australia), 250 Camberwell Road, Camberwell,
Victoria 3124, Australia (a division of Pearson Australia Group Pty Ltd)
Penguin Books India Pvt Ltd, 11 Community Centre, Panchsheel Park, New Delhi – 110 017, India
Penguin Group (NZ), 67 Apollo Drive, Rosedale, Auckland 0632,
New Zealand (a division of Pearson New Zealand Ltd)
Penguin Books (South Africa) (Pty) Ltd, 24 Sturdee Avenue,
Rosebank, Johannesburg 2196, South Africa

Penguin Books Ltd, Registered Offices:
80 Strand, London WC2R 0RL, England

First published by William Heinemann Ltd. 1967
Revised edition published by William Heinemann Ltd. 1986
Published with a new introduction in Penguin Books (UK) 2002
Published in Penguin Books (USA) 2012

PUBLISHER'S NOTE
This is a work of fiction. Names, characters, places, and incidents either are the product
of the author's imagination or are used fictitiously, and any resemblance to actual persons,
living or dead, businesses, companies, events, or locales is entirely coincidental.

10

LIBRARY OF CONGRESS CATALOGING IN PUBLICATION DATA
Ngugi wa Thiong'o, 1938–
A grain of wheat / Ngugi wa Thiong'o ; with a new introduction by Abdulrazak Gurnah.—
Rev. ed.
p. cm.
ISBN 978-0-14-310676-0
1. Kenya—Fiction. I. Gurnah, Abdulrazak, 1948– II. Title.
PR9381.9.N45G73 2012
823'.914—dc23 2012007184

Printed in the United States of America

Contents

Introduction

Note: In discussing this story, it has sometimes been unavoidable that crucial elements of the plot have been given away. Readers encountering this story for the first time, therefore, might prefer to read this introduction afterwards.

Ngũgĩ wa Thiong'o is now established as a major African writer and one of the continent's foremost intellectuals, among the few most important of that gifted decolonizing era. He achieved his greatest fame during and after his detention by the Kenya government in 1977–8, and later as a result of his arguments against African writers using English as their writing language. Although he did not initiate this debate about language, Ngũgĩ has become its most renowned and most determined advocate. His own fiction since the 1978 detention has been in Gĩkũyũ, followed by translation into English. His critical and political writing (and the two have overlapped from the beginning) has focused ever more sharply on issues of culture and language. *A Grain of Wheat* came at a crucial moment in the radicalization of Ngũgĩ's thinking, most dramatically evident here in the way the writing moves from the single-character focus of the earlier novels to the social epic mode of the later ones.

Ngũgĩ wrote *A Grain of Wheat* at Leeds University in England, in the years 1964–6, when he was a postgraduate student there on a British Council scholarship. In the event he did not receive the research MA he was working on (on the work of the Barbadian novelist George Lamming), because instead of completing revisions to his thesis, he read widely and wrote *A Grain of Wheat*. He was then twenty-eight and already the author of two novels, *Weep Not, Child* (1964) and *The*

River Between (1965), both of which were published while he was at Leeds. It was also during this period that he first read Frantz Fanon's *The Wretched of the Earth*, as well as Marx and Engels, and later cited these writers, and Engels in particular, as important to the writing of the novel. These influences became much more evident in his next novel *Petals of Blood* (1977) and beyond. Ngũgĩ revised *A Grain of Wheat* in 1987, to make the 'world outlook' of his peasants more in line with his ideas of the historical triumph of the oppressed. But if Fanon and Engels played their part in Ngũgĩ's thinking during the writing of this novel, then so did Joseph Conrad. Ngũgĩ's special subject for his undergraduate degree was the writing of Conrad, and one of the novels he studied was *Under Western Eyes*. There are parallels in method as well as subject between the two novels – we will return to these later.

The present-time of *A Grain of Wheat* is the four days leading up to Kenya's independence from British colonial rule in December 1963, although the unconfessed events which are the drama of the narrative mostly took place during the Emergency in the 1950s. The Emergency was declared in 1952 to suppress the Mau Mau, an armed rebellion against European settlements in the highlands of Kenya. European settlement in the central highlands, later to be called the White Highlands to describe the racial dimension of settler activity, had been preceded by the expulsion of the Gĩkùyũ people and their transformation into labourers and squatters on the land they had thought their own. Ngũgĩ's writing is never far from the subject, and it is not surprising that this should be so. Settlement began just before the 1914–18 war and reached a peak in the 1930s, the era of Happy Valley and Karen Blixen's *Out of Africa*. Ngũgĩ was born in 1938, and grew up in the rural areas of heaviest European occupation, where memories of expulsion and displacement were within the life-time of the people. His elder brother joined the Mau Mau, and another brother, who was deaf and dumb, was shot by security forces in exactly the way Gitogo dies in the opening pages of *A Grain of Wheat*, unable to hear an order to stop running. Ngũgĩ's first novel, *Weep Not, Child*, which is written from a child's perspective, ends with the beginning of the Mau Mau rebellion and the approach of the Emergency. In *A Grain of Wheat* the Emergency has been over for seven years, the rebellion triumphant despite its military defeat, and independence is just days away. But for the rural Gĩkũyũ community of Thabai, the time of rejoicing and optimism is also edged with suppressed anxieties and guilts, the people are troubled by what it means to be free.

One of the most striking aspects of *A Grain of Wheat* is the method of its narration. The framing voice is a third-person narrator, who at times speaks with a clear political awareness of the context of Kenya's colonial history, and at other times slides quietly into the inclusiveness of the oral story-teller speaking to listeners who are familiar with the main events of the tale. 'Many people from Thabai attended the meeting because, you'll remember, we had only just been allowed to hold political meetings,' the narrator says at one point, speaking as much to the reader as to invisible listeners presumed in the telling. Yet all the main figures tell their own stories in confessional encounters and in interior monologues, stories which intersect and challenge each other, and which in a formal sense are inaccessible to the narrator. In this way, the narrative frequently slips in and out of present-time and between narrating voices, creating some instability about what is known and what it means to know.

The novel opens with the figure of Mugo. He was orphaned at a young age, was brought up by a drunken distant aunt who loathed and tormented him, and whom Mugo loathed in return and fantasized killing one day. He has grown into a tormented and isolated man, morose and self-doubting, agitated for reasons we do not at first fully know. 'Mugo walked, his head slightly bowed, staring at the ground as if ashamed of looking about him.' Yet this is not how Thabai sees him. To Thabai he is a hero, a long-suffering though steadfast victim of colonial violence. He had been arrested during the Emergency for intervening to stop a policeman from beating up a woman who, it was said, had refused him sex. In detention he had been obsessively tortured and harassed by the District Officer John Thompson for refusing to confess 'the oath'. On his release from detention after the Emergency, he had come back, built himself a hut and farmed the piece of land leased to him by one of the elders. To his community Mugo is a hermit: a holy, quiet, self-sufficient, moral man. In reality he is as guilty as sin, although we have to wait until the last quarter of the novel before we know this for sure.

Mugo then is alone from the beginning, orphaned and unloved, inarticulate and prone to visionary fantasies of messianic heroism. He hears the voice of God in his lonely wanderings. He is, very deliberately, on the edges of the community, because one of the questions the novel is interested in asking is, what are our responsibilities to ourselves and what are our responsibilities to our community?

In contrast to Mugo is Kihika, who is loved by family and friends, and who has an articulate vision of his political and social responsibilities. Kihika understands the need to resist colonial violence, and when the time comes, he runs away to the forest to join the Mau Mau. He becomes renowned for daring and courage, a myth in the making. In time he is captured by the colonial authorities, perhaps betrayed, and he is publicly hanged from a tree in Rung'ei market as a demonstration of what Kipling calls holding the intransigent colonial 'to strict account'. As the day of independence approaches in the present-time of the narrative, the Party notables of Thabai decide to celebrate Kihika's 'sacrifice' on the very field where he had been hanged. And they ask Mugo, another hero of the Emergency, to speak in his praise.

One of these Party notables is Gikonyo, whose estranged wife is Mumbi, Kihika's sister. Gikonyo too was detained during the Emergency, but he so missed his wife that he confessed the oath in the hope of early release. He was not released as he had hoped, and so spent six unheroic years in detention, finally returning to Thabai, to find Mumbi the mother of a child who could not be his. The father, it turns out, was a youthful rival Karanja, who had joined the Home Guard, the colonial security force, and was now the Chief of the protected village which the authorities forced everyone to move to. Gikonyo ignored his wife after this, living in the same house but hardly speaking to her.

So on the one hand there are these figures whose lives are interwoven and complicated, who wound and hurt each other, and fret over how to resolve their miseries. On the other there is Mugo, an outsider whose silence and inarticulateness is taken for depth and courage, but whose dearest wish, as we know from our privileged access to his thought, is to be left alone. With a tragic irony that would be comic were the issue not so fraught, it is Mugo that these other figures select as confidante and confessor. While they explain that they select him for his silent strength and his steadfastness, to Mugo it seems like another intrusion into the quiet space he has fashioned for himself, another demonstration of his nothingness and isolation.

Gikonyo seeks out Mugo to tell him about the breakdown of his marriage to Mumbi, something he has not talked about with anyone else, not even his wife. Mumbi in turn confesses her adultery with Karanja, and touches a vital nerve in Mugo, as it turns out. But first there was Kihika, who, after he assassinated DO Robson, Thompson's immediate predecessor in Thabai, sought out Mugo to hide him. He could do this because he knew that Mugo lived on his own, was not part of any alliance, and had no one to tell. This one expedient act transforms Mugo's life, and ends Kihika's. In Joseph Conrad's *Under Western Eyes*, Haldin selects Razumov's lodgings as the place to hide after his assassination of de P- for similar reasons, though in both cases a stream of explanations by the assassins partially disguises the expediency of the choice. Mugo, like Razumov, is deeply repelled by his forcible implication in these heroics, and says of Kihika after he has gone: 'He is not satisfied with butchering men and women and children. He must call on me to bathe in the blood. I am not his brother.' Both Mugo and Razumov betray the hero to the imperialist authorities, and live a life of secrecy and sin, which is none the less misunderstood as one of quiet courage and humility.

Conrad points to a well-rehearsed suspicion of the language of redemption. Remember Kurtz's high-flown treatise on human progress in *Heart of Darkness* and its hollowness in the light of the degradations of colonial power. For Conrad all such language is duplicitous, a self-deceiving disguise of baser motives, or as Marlow puts it in *Lord Jim*: 'it is my belief no man ever understands quite his own artful dodges to escape from the grim shadow of self-knowledge'. Ngũgĩ's own use of this idea of redemptive language in *A Grain of Wheat* is more equivocal, not to point to its inescapable duplicity, but to demonstrate the unavoidable inhumanity of sacrifice. Mugo rightly insists on his human need to live as he chooses, but in the argument of this novel to live alone is a pathology, and to live in a community, especially one as historically oppressed as this, requires a sacrifice of those needs. So Kihika signifies an inhumane heroism which is necessary for freedom and justice. He is the 'grain of wheat' of the title, who must die for new life to begin.

A Grain of Wheat has its own Kurtz. DO John Thompson is an idealist of Empire, who starts off with a vision of 'one British nation, embracing peoples of all colours and creeds, based on the just proposition that all men are created equal'. He starts working on a book to be called *Prospero in Africa*, which will put forward an argument for this conception of human progress. Like Kurtz, Thompson is mocked for the 'artful dodges' language allows him. In an echo of Kurtz's 'Eliminate all the brutes' scrawled over his treatise on progress, Thompson writes 'Eliminate the vermin' in his *Prospero* notes. From idealist he becomes a torturer, forcing confessions out of the detainees by any means possible, because that is the true meaning of colonial rule. Like Kurtz, Thompson comes to learn that violence and coercion are his unavoidable means. When eleven detainees die under torture at Rira camp under his command, Thompson, the rising man in the administration, is quickly transferred out of sight. Thompson, then, is offered as not only a critique of colonial methods but of the whole narrative of imperialism, which prefers the grandiose lying language of progress to 'the horror' of its actual practice.

Ultimately Thompson is denied humanity in the novel, because I don't think Ngũgĩ is interested in him and his motivations, but in using him to demonstrate an argument. Not only is he an imperial tool, and the means of offering a critique of colonial method, but he is also shown as incapable of attachment or warmth. Imperialism's self-deception and cruelty has turned him into an unfeeling brute. His story ends with his imminent departure on the eve of independence, demoralized and disillusioned, the ambitions of a lifetime transformed into inadequacy.

Ngũgĩ is, however, deeply interested in Mugo, and how to resolve the consequences of his debilitating aloneness. Mumbi's confession of her adultery touches him in an unexpected way. She is beautiful, she is young, and her vitality and courage in speaking about what had happened to her shames Mugo. It reminds him of the futility of his life: 'he was at the bottom of the pool, but up there, above the pool, ran the earth; life, struggle, even amidst pain and blood and poverty, seemed beautiful'. And so begins the process of Mugo's reintegration into his community, as first he confesses to Mumbi that he betrayed Kihika, her brother, and then confesses to the whole of Thabai the part he had played in the execution of their hero.

A Grain of Wheat is a political narrative. It is political in its desire to show the development of an awarenes of a history of oppression. When the rebellion comes, the novel argues, it is the culmination of a long series of more restrained acts of defiance. The individual dramas become more prominent as the narrative progresses, but the rebellion is its point of reference. Mugo, Gikonyo, and Karanja betray the cause of freedom in their different ways, but they also betray themselves, as does Mumbi. Through the guilt they suffer, they arrive at a point of understanding and self-knowledge, and so in the end the novel offers a possibility of regeneration. In this sense, *A Grain of Wheat* is also a moral narrative.

Ngũgĩ has said of the 1967 version of *A Grain of Wheat* that his 'peasant and worker characters' had the 'vacillating mentality of the petite bourgeoisie'. A lot had happened to the author between 1967 and 1987. He changed his name from James Ngũgĩ to the more correct Gĩkùyũ form of Ngũgĩ wa Thiong'o (Thiong'o was his father's name). The change was not just a desire to be more culturally correct, it was also a rejection of that 'missionary' construction 'James'. The legal change of name took place in November 1977, but by then Ngũgĩ had already publicly and repeatedly repudiated the influence of Christian missionary teaching. By the mid-70s he was writing in Gĩkùyũ as Ngũgĩ wa Thiong'o, working on agitprop plays in collaboration with other writers and in 'peasant' workshops. The thrust of his work by now was to see how writing could intervene in social change, how it could be instrumental to progress. It was this that finally panicked the government into detaining him for a year in December 1977. It was a powerful demonstration of Ngũgĩ's argument about which writing language was appropriate for the African writer. It was not that the play *Ngaahika Ndeenda* (I Will Marry When I Want) was making unprecedented criticisms, but that it was written in Gīkùyū and was comprehensible to ordinary citizens, and was therefore 'subversive', that led to his detention. Only a few months before his detention, Ngūgī had published *Petals of Blood*, which was sharply critical of the governing culture of Kenya without appearing to cause the authorities any anxiety. It was even launched by the Vice-President of Kenya Mwai Kibaki, in a public demonstration of the government's commitment to 'free speech'. A critical play in Gīkùyū, though, was another matter.

On his release, the government dismissed him from his academic job, and finally harassed him out of the country in 1982. The government that did this was led by the same Jomo Kenyatta who is everywhere lauded in *A Grain of Wheat* as the saviour of his people. The muted warning against betrayal of independence that Ngūgī had sounded in *A Grain of Wheat* had been proved devastatingly correct, and not only in his personal case. As Ngūgī's work grew progressively more 'radical', it is only consistent that he should want the 'world view' of his peasants to reflect the historical triumph of the oppressed rather than a nagging conviction that progress comes at a heavy price. The 1987 revisions do not do very much to improve the novel, but nor are they deep enough to diminish the power and the subtlety of its narrative play and its compulsive drama. Ngūgī's work has been influential and provocative from the beginning, and in that impressive body of work, *A Grain of Wheat* is his most humane and persuasive novel.

Abdulrazak Gurnah
2002

For Dorothy

Thou fool, that which thou sowest is not quickened, except it die. And that which thou sowest, thou sowest not that body that shall be, but bare grain, it may chance of wheat, or of some other grain.

1 Corinthians 15:36

Although set in contemporary Kenya, all the characters in this book are fictitious. Names like that of Jomo Kenyatta and Waiyaki are unavoidably mentioned as part of the history and institutions of our country. But the situation and the problems are real – sometimes too painfully real for the peasants who fought the British yet who now see all that they fought for being put on one side.

Ngũgĩ wa Thiong'o
Leeds, November 1966

A Grain of Wheat

One

Mugo felt nervous. He was lying on his back and looking at the roof. Sooty locks hung from the fern and grass thatch and all pointed at his heart. A clear drop of water was delicately suspended above him. The drop fattened and grew dirtier as it absorbed grains of soot. Then it started drawing towards him. He tried to shut his eyes. They would not close. He tried to move his head: it was firmly chained to the bed-frame. The drop grew larger and larger as it drew closer and closer to his eyes. He wanted to cover his eyes with his palms; but his hands, his feet, everything refused to obey his will. In despair, Mugo gathered himself for a final heave and woke up. Now he lay under the blanket and remained unsettled fearing, as in the dream, that a drop of cold water would suddenly pierce his eyes. The blanket was hard and worn out; its bristles pricked his face, his neck, in fact all the unclothed parts of his body. He did not know whether to jump out or not; the bed was warm and the sun had not yet appeared. Dawn diffused through cracks in the wall into the hut. Mugo tried a game he always played whenever he had lost sleep in the middle of the night or early morning. In total, or hazy darkness most objects lose their edges, one shape merging with another. The game consisted in trying to make out the various objects in the room. This morning, however, Mugo found it difficult to concentrate. He knew that it was only a dream: yet he kept on chilling at the thought of a cold drop falling into his eyes. One, two, three; he pulled the blanket away from his body. He washed his face and lit the fire. In a corner, he discovered a small amount of maize-flour in a bag among the utensils. He put this in a sufuria on the fire, added water and stirred it with a wooden spoon. He liked porridge in the morning. But whenever he took it, he remembered the half-cooked porridge he ate in detention. How time drags, everything repeats itself, Mugo thought; the day ahead would be just like yesterday and the day before.

He took a jembe and a panga to repeat the daily pattern his life had now fallen into since he left Maguita, his last detention camp. To reach his new strip of shamba which lay the other side of Thabai, Mugo had to walk through the dusty village streets. And as usual Mugo found that some women had risen before him, that some were already returning from the river, their frail backs arched double with water-barrels, in time to prepare tea or porridge for their husbands and children. The sun was now up: shadows of trees and huts and men were thin and long on the ground.

'How is it with you, this morning?' Warui called out to him, emerging from one of the huts.

'It is well.' And as usual Mugo would have gone on, but Warui seemed anxious to talk.

'Attacking the ground early?'

'Yes.'

'That's what I always say. Go to it when the ground is soft. Let the sun find you already there and it'll not be a match for you. But if it reaches the shamba before you – hm.'

Warui, a village elder, wore a new blanket which sharply relieved his wrinkled face and the grey tufts of hair on his head and on his pointed chin. It was he who had given Mugo the present strip of land on which to grow a little food. His own piece had been confiscated by the government while he was in detention. Though Warui liked talking, he had come to respect Mugo's reticence. But today he looked at Mugo with new interest, curiosity even.

'Like Kenyatta is telling us,' he went on, 'these are days of Uhuru na Kazi.' He paused and ejected a jet of saliva on to the hedge. Mugo stood embarrassed by this encounter. 'And how is your hut, ready for Uhuru?' continued Warui.

'Oh, it's all right,' Mugo said and excused himself. As he moved on through the village, he tried to puzzle out Warui's last question.

Thabai was a big village. When built, it had combined a number of ridges: Thabai, Kamandura, Kihingo, and parts of Weru. And even in 1963, it had not changed much from the day in 1955 when the grass-thatched roofs and mud walls were hastily collected together, while the whiteman's sword hung dangerously above people's necks to protect them from their brethren in the forest. Some huts had crumbled; a few had been pulled down. Yet the village maintained an unbroken orderliness; from a distance it appeared a huge mass of grass from which smoke rose to the sky as from a burnt sacrifice.

Mugo walked, his head slightly bowed, staring at the ground as if ashamed of looking about him. He was re-living the encounter with Warui when suddenly he heard someone shout his name. He started, stopped, and stared at Githua, who was hobbling towards him on crutches. When he reached Mugo he stood to attention, lifted his torn hat, and cried out:

'In the name of blackman's freedom, I salute you.' Then he bowed several times in comic deference.

'Is it – is it well with you?' Mugo asked, not knowing how to react. By this time two or three children had collected and were laughing at Githua's antics. Githua did not answer at once. His shirt was torn, its collar gleamed black with dirt. His left trouser leg was folded and fixed with a pin to cover the stump. Rather unexpectedly he gripped Mugo by the hand:

'How are you man! How are you man! Glad to see you going to the shamba early. Uhuru na Kazi. Ha! Ha! Ha! Even on Sundays. I tell you before the Emergency, I was like you; before the whiteman did this to me with bullets, I could work with both hands, man. It makes my heart dance with delight to see your spirit. Uhuru na Kazi. Chief, I salute you.'

Mugo tried to pull out his hand. His heart beat and he could not find the words. The laughter from the children increased his agitation. Githua's voice suddenly changed:

'The Emergency destroyed us,' he said in a tearful voice and abruptly went away. Mugo hurried on, conscious of the man's eyes behind him. Three women coming from the river stopped when they saw him. One of them shouted something, but Mugo did not answer or look at them. He raised dust like a man on the run. Yet he only walked asking himself questions: What's wrong with me today? Why are people suddenly looking at me with curiosity? Is there shit on my legs?

Soon he was near the end of the main street where the old woman lived. Nobody knew her age: she had always been there, a familiar part of the old and the new village. In the old village she lived with an only son who was deaf and dumb. Gitogo, for that was the son's name, spoke with his hands often accompanied with animal guttural noises. He was handsome, strongly built, a favourite at the Old Rung'ei centre where young men spent their time talking the day away. Occasionally the men went on errands for the shop-owners and earned a few coins 'for the pockets only, just to keep the trousers warm', as some carelessly remarked. They laughed and said the coins would call others (man! their relatives) in due time.

Gitogo worked in eating houses, meat shops, often lifting and carrying heavy loads avoided by others. He loved displaying his well-built muscles. Whispers current in Rung'ei and Thabai said that many a young woman had felt the weight of those limbs. In the evenings Gitogo bought food – a pound of sugar, or a pound of meat – and took them home to his mother, who brightened up, her face becoming youthful amidst the many wrinkles. What a son, what a man, people would say, touched by the tenderness of the deaf and dumb one to his mother.

One day people in Thabai and Rung'ei woke up to find themselves ringed round with black and white soldiers carrying guns, and tanks last seen on the road during Churchill's war with Hitler. Gunfire smoked in the sky, people held their stomachs. Some men locked themselves in latrines; others hid among the sacks of sugar and beans in the shops. Yet others tried to sneak out of the town towards the forest, only to find that all roads to freedom were blocked. People were being collected into the town-square, the market place, for screening. Gitogo ran to a shop, jumped over the counter, and almost fell on to the shopkeeper whom he found cowering amongst the empty bags. He gesticulated, made puzzled noises, furtively looked and pointed at the soldiers. The shopkeeper in stupid terror stared back blankly at Gitogo. Gitogo suddenly remembered his aged mother sitting alone in the hut. His mind's eye vividly saw scenes of wicked deeds and blood. He rushed out through the back door, and jumped over a fence into the fields, now agitated by the insecurity to which his mother lay exposed. Urgency, home, mother: the images flashed through his mind. His muscles alone would protect her. He did not see that a whiteman, in a bush jacket, lay camouflaged in a small wood. 'Halt!' the whiteman shouted. Gitogo continued running. Something hit him at the back. He raised his arms in the air. He fell on his stomach. Apparently the bullet had touched his heart. The soldier left his place. Another Mau Mau terrorist had been shot dead.

When the old woman heard the news she merely said: My God. Those who were present said that she did not weep. Or even ask how her son had met his death.

After leaving the detention camp Mugo had several times seen the old woman outside her hut. And every time he felt agitated as if the woman recognized him. She had a small face grooved with wrinkles. Her eyes were small but occasionally flashed with life. Otherwise they looked dead. She wore beads around her elbows, several copper chains around her neck, and cowrie-like tins around the ankles. When she moved she made jingling noises like a belled goat. It was her eyes that most disturbed Mugo. He always felt naked, seen. One day he spoke to her. But she only looked at him and then turned her face away. Mugo felt rejected, yet her loneliness struck a chord of pity in him. He wanted to help her. This feeling warmed him inside. He bought some sugar, maize-flour and a bundle of firewood at one of the Kabui shops. In the evening he went to the woman's place. The hut was dark inside. The room was bare, and a cold wind whistled in through the gaping holes in the wall. She slept on the floor, near the fireplace. Mugo remembered how he too used to sleep on the floor in his aunt's hut, sharing the fireplace with goats and sheep. He often crept and crouched near the goats for warmth. In the morning he found his face and clothes covered with ashes, his hands and feet smeared with the goats' droppings. In the end he had become hardened to the goats' smell. Amidst these thoughts, Mugo felt the woman fix him with her eyes, which glinted with recognition. Suddenly he shivered at the thought that the woman might touch him. He ran out, revolted.

Perhaps there was something fateful in his contact with this old woman.

Today this thought was uppermost in his mind, as he again felt another desire to enter the hut and talk to her. There was a bond between her and him, perhaps because she, like him, lived alone. At the door he faltered, his resolution wavered, broke, and he found himself hurrying away, fearing that she would call him back with mad laughter.

In the shamba, he felt hollow. There were no crops on the land and what with the dried-up weeds, gakaraku, micege, mikengeria, bangi – and the sun, the country appeared sick and dull. The jembe seemed heavier than usual; the unfinished part of the shamba looked too big for his unwilling muscles. He dug a little, and feeling the desire to pass water, walked to a hedge near the path; why had Warui, Githua and the women behaved that way towards him? He found his bladder had pressed him into false urgency. A few drops trickled down and he watched them as if each drop fascinated him. Two young women dressed for church, passed near, saw a big man playing with his thing and giggled. Mugo felt foolish and dragged himself back to his work.

He raised the jembe, let it fall into the soil; lifted it and again brought it down. The ground felt soft as if there were mole-tunnels immediately below the surface. He could hear the soil, dry and hollow, tumble down. Dust flew into the sky, enveloped him, then settled into his hair and clothes. Once a grain of dust went into his left eye. He quickly dropped the jembe in anger and rubbed his eye which smarted with pain as water tossed out from both eyes. He sat down: where was the fascination he used to find in the soil before the Emergency?

Mugo's father and mother had died poor, leaving him, an only child in the hands of a distant aunt. Waitherero was a widow with six married daughters. When drunk, she would come home and remind Mugo of this fact.

'Female slime,' she would say, exposing her toothless gums; she would fix Mugo with a fierce glance, as if he and God had conspired against her. 'They don't even come to see me – Do you laugh, you – what's your penis worth? Oh God, see what an ungrateful wretch is left on my hands. You would have followed your father to the grave, but for me. Remember that and stop laughing.'

Another day she would complain that her money was missing.

'I didn't steal it,' Mugo retorted, withdrawing.

'There is only you and me in this house. I could not have stolen it. So who could have taken it?'

'I am not a thief!'

'Are you saying that I am telling lies? The money was here, you saw me bury it under this post. See the way he looks, he creeps behind the goats.'

She was a small woman who always complained that people were after her life; they had put broken bottles and frogs into her stomach; they wanted to put poison in her food or drink.

And yet she always went out to look for more beer. She would pester men from her husband's rika till they gave her a drink. One day she came back very drunk.

'That man Warui – he hates to see me eat and breathe – that sly – smile – he – creeps – coughs – like you – you – go and join him—'

And she tried to imitate Warui's cough; but in the attempt lurched forward and fell; all her beer and filth lay on the floor. Mugo cowered among the goats hoping and fearing she had died. In the morning she forced Mugo to pour soil on the filth. The acrid smell hit him. Disgust choked him so that he could not speak or cry. The world had conspired against him, first to deprive him of his father and mother, and then to make him dependent on an ageing harridan.

The more feeble she became, the more she hated him. Whatever he did or made, she would deride his efforts. So Mugo was haunted by the image of his own inadequacy. She had a way of getting at him, a question maybe, about his clothes, his face, or hands that made all his pride tumble down. He pretended to ignore her opinions, but how could he shut his eyes to her oblique smiles and looks?

His one desire was to kill his aunt.

One evening the mad thought possessed him. He raged within. Tonight Waitherero was sober. He would not use an axe or a panga. He would get her by the neck, strangle her with his naked hands. Give me the strength; give me the strength, God. He watched her struggle, like a fly in a spider's hands; her muffled groans and cries for mercy reached his ears. He would press harder, make her feel the power in his man's hands. Blood rushed to his finger-tips, he was breathless, acutely fascinated by the audacity and daring of his own action.

'Why are you staring at me so?' Waitherero asked, and laughed in her throat. 'I always say you are a strange one, the kind that would murder their own mother, eh?'

He winced. Her seeing into him was painful.

Waitherero suddenly died of age and over-drinking. For the first time since their marriage, her daughters came to the hut, pretended they did not see Mugo, and buried her without questions or tears. They returned to their homes. And then, strangely, Mugo missed his aunt. Whom could he now call a relation? He wanted somebody, anybody, who would use the claims of kinship to do him ill or good. Either one or the other as long as he was not left alone, an outsider.

He turned to the soil. He would labour, sweat, and through success and wealth, force society to recognize him. There was, for him, then, solace in the very act of breaking the soil: to bury seeds and watch the green leaves heave and thrust themselves out of the ground, to tend the plants to ripeness and then harvest, these were all part of the world he had created for himself and which formed the background against which his dreams soared to the sky. But then Kihika had come into his life.

Mugo went home earlier than usual. He had not done much work, yet he was weary. He walked like a man who knows he is followed or watched, yet does not want to reveal this awareness by his gait or behaviour. In the evening he heard footsteps outside. Who could his visitor be? He opened the door. Suddenly the all-day mixture of feelings distilled into fear and animosity. Warui, the elder, led the group. Standing beside him was Wambui, one of the women from the river. She now smiled, exposing a missing line of teeth in her lower jaw. The third man was Gikonyo, who had married Kihika's sister.

'Come inside,' he called in a voice that could hardly hide his agitation. He excused himself and went towards the latrine. Run away from all these men ... I no longer care ... I no longer care. He entered the pit lavatory and lowered his trousers to his knees: his thoughts buzzed around flashing images of his visitors seated in the hut. Several times he tried to force something out into the smelling pit. Failing, he pulled up his trousers, but still he felt better for the effort. He went back to the visitors and only now remembered that he had not greeted them.

'We are only voices sent to you from the Party,' Gikonyo said after Mugo had shaken hands all round.

'The Party?'

'Voices from the Movement!' Wambui and Warui murmured together.

Two

Nearly everybody was a member of the Movement, but nobody could say with any accuracy when it was born: to most people, especially those in the younger generation, it had always been there, a rallying centre for action. It changed names, leaders came and went, but the Movement remained, opening new visions, gathering greater and greater strength, till on the eve of Uhuru, its influence stretched from one horizon touching the sea to the other resting on the great Lake.

Its origins can, so the people say, be traced to the day the whiteman came to the country, clutching the book of God in both hands, a magic witness that the whiteman was a messenger from the Lord. His tongue was coated with sugar; his humility was touching. For a time, people ignored the voice of the Gikuyu seer who once said: there shall come a people with clothes like the butterflies. They gave him, the stranger with a scalded skin, a place to erect a temporary shelter. Hut complete, the stranger put up another building yards away. This he called the House of God where people could go for worship and sacrifice.

The whiteman told of another country beyond the sea where a powerful woman sat on a throne while men and women danced under the shadow of her authority and benevolence. She was ready to spread the shadow to cover the Agikuyu. They laughed at this eccentric man whose skin had been so scalded that the black outside had peeled off. The hot water must have gone into his head.

Nevertheless, his words about a woman on the throne echoed something in the heart, deep down in their history. It was many, many years ago. Then women ruled the land of the Agikuyu. Men had no property, they were only there to serve the whims and needs of the women. Those were hard years. So they waited for women to go to war, they plotted a revolt, taking an oath of secrecy to keep them bound each to each in the common pursuit of freedom. They would sleep with all the women at once, for didn't they know the heroines would return hungry for love and relaxation? Fate did the rest; women were pregnant; the takeover met with little resistance.

But that was not the end of a woman as a power in the land. Years later a woman became a leader and ruled over a large section in Muranga. She was beautiful. At dances, she swung her round hips this way, that way; her plaited hair rose and fell behind her in rhythm with her steps. This together with a flash of her milk-white teeth made men smack their lips and roll their tongues with desire. Young and old, they shamelessly hung around her court, and hoped. The woman chose for herself young warriors who became the target of the jealousy and envy of others less favoured. Still more men paid homage to her; they never missed a dance in which she was to appear, many desperately longed to glimpse at her thighs. Came a night when, no doubt goaded by the admiration she aroused, or maybe wanting to gratify their shameless longing, she overreached herself. Removing all her clothes, she danced naked in the moonlight. For a moment, men were moved by the power of a woman's naked body. The moon played on her: an ecstasy, a mixture of agony and joy hovered on the woman's face. Perhaps she, too, knew this was the end: a woman never walked or danced naked in public. She was removed from the throne.

About Jesus, they could not at first understand, for how could it be that God would let himself be nailed to a tree? The whiteman spoke of that Love that passeth all understanding. Greater Love hath no man than this, he read from the little black book, that a man lay down his life for his friends.

The few who were converted, started speaking a faith foreign to the ways of the land. They trod on sacred places to show that no harm could reach those protected by the hand of the Lord. Soon people saw the whiteman had imperceptibly acquired more land to meet the growing needs of his position. He had already pulled down the grass-thatched hut and erected a more permanent building. Elders of the land protested. They looked beyond the laughing face of the whiteman and suddenly saw a long line of other red strangers who carried, not the Bible, but the sword.

Waiyaki and other warrior-leaders took arms. The iron snake spoken of by Mugo wa Kibiro was quickly wriggling towards Nairobi for a thorough exploitation of the hinterland. Could they move it? The snake held on to the ground, laughing their efforts to scorn. The whiteman with bamboo poles that vomited fire and smoke, hit back; his menacing laughter remained echoing in the hearts of the people, long after Waiyaki had been arrested and taken to the coast, bound hands and feet. Later, so it is said, Waiyaki was buried alive at Kibwezi with his head facing into the centre of the earth, a living warning to those, who, in after years, might challenge the hand of the Christian woman whose protecting shadow now bestrode both land and sea.

Then nobody noticed it; but looking back we can see that Waiyaki's blood contained within it a seed, a grain, which gave birth to a movement whose main strength thereafter sprang from a bond with the soil.

Meanwhile, the missionary centres hatched new leaders; they refused to eat the good things of Pharaoh: instead, they chose to cut grass and make bricks with the other children.

So in Harry Thuku, people saw a man with God's message: Go unto Pharaoh and say unto him: let my people go, let my people go. And people swore they would follow Harry through the desert. They would tighten their belts around the waist, ready to endure thirst and hunger, tears and blood until they set foot on Canaan's shore. They flocked to his meetings, waiting for him to give the sign. Harry denounced the whiteman and cursed that benevolence and protection which denied people land and freedom. He amazed them by reading aloud letters to the whiteman, letters in which he set out in clear terms people's discontent with taxation, forced labour on white settler's land, and with the soldier settlement scheme which after the first big war, left many black people without homes or land around Tigoni and other places.

Harry asked them to join the Movement and find strength in unity.

They talked of him in their homes; they sang his praises in teashops, market places and on their way to Gikuyu Independent churches on

Sundays. Any word from the mouth of Harry became news and passed from ridge to ridge, right across the country. People waited for something to happen. The revolt of the peasant was near at hand.

But the whiteman had not slept. Young Harry was clamped in chains, narrowly escaping the pit into which Waiyaki was buried alive. Was this the sign they waited for? People went to Nairobi; they took an oath to spend their days and nights outside the State House till the Governor himself gave them back their Harry.

Warui, then a young man, walked all the way from Thabai to join the procession. He never forgot the great event. When Jomo Kenyatta and other leaders of the Movement were arrested in 1952, Warui recalled the 1923 Procession.

'The young should do for Jomo what we did for Harry. I've never seen anything to match the size of that line of men and women,' he declaimed, gently plucking his beard. 'We came from ridges here, ridges there, everywhere. Most of us walked. Others did not bring food. We shared whatever crumbs we had brought. Great love I saw there. A bean fell to the ground, and it was quickly split among the children. For three days we gathered in Nairobi, with our blood we wrote vows to free Harry.'

On the fourth day they marched forward, singing. The police who waited for them with guns fixed with bayonets, opened fire. Three men raised their arms in the air. It is said that as they fell down they clutched soil in their fists. Another volley scattered the crowd. A man and a women fell, their blood spurted out. People ran in all directions. Within a few seconds the big crowd had dispersed; nothing remained but one hundred and fifty crooked watchers on the ground, outside the State House.

'Something went wrong at the last moment,' Warui said, and stopped plucking his beard. 'Perhaps if we had the guns . . .'

The revolt of the peasants had failed; the ghost of the great woman whose Christian hand had ended the tribal wars was quietened. She would now lie in the grave in peace.

Young Harry was sent to a remote part of the country.

The Movement was temporarily dismayed. But it was at this time that the man with the flaming eyes came to the scene. Then few knew him. But later, of course, he was to be known to the world over as the Burning Spear.

Mugo once attended a meeting of the Movement held at Rung'ei Market because it was rumoured that Kenyatta, who had recently come from the land of the whiteman, would speak. Although the meeting was scheduled to start in the afternoon, by ten o'clock there was hardly any sitting-room at the market place. People stood on the roofs of the shops. They appeared like clusters of locusts perched on trees. Mugo sat in a place where he could command a good view of the speakers. Gikonyo, then a well-known carpenter in Thabai, sat a few feet away. Next to the carpenter was Mumbi. She was said to be one of the most beautiful women on all the eight ridges. Some people called her Wangu Makeri because of her looks.

The meeting started an hour later. People learnt that Kenyatta would not attend the meeting. There were, however, plenty of speakers from Muranga and Nairobi. There was also a Luo speaker from Nyanza showing that the Movement had broken barriers between tribes. Kihika from Thabai was one of the speakers who received a big ovation from the crowd. He talked no longer in terms of sending letters to the whiteman as used to be done in the days of Harry.

'This is not 1920. What we now want is action, a blow which will tell,' he said as women from Thabai pulled at their clothes and hair, and screamed with delight. Kihika, a son of the land, was marked out as one of the heroes of deliverance. Mugo, who had seen Kihika on the ridge a number of times, had never suspected that the man had such power and knowledge. Kihika unrolled the history of Kenya, the coming of the whiteman and the birth of the Party. Mugo glanced at Gikonyo and Mumbi. Their eyes were fixed on Kihika; their lives seemed dependent on his falling words.

'We went to their church. Mubia, in white robes, opened the Bible. He said: Let us kneel down to pray. We knelt down. Mubia said: Let us shut our eyes. We did. You know, his remained open so that he could read the word. When we opened our eyes, our land was gone and the sword of flames stood on guard. As for Mubia, he went on reading the word, beseeching us to lay our treasures in heaven where no moth would corrupt them. But he laid his on earth, our earth.'

People laughed. Kihika did not join them. He was a small man with a strong voice. Speaking slowly with emphasis on the important words, he once or twice pointed at earth and heaven as if calling them to witness that what he spoke was the truth. He talked of the great sacrifice.

'A day comes when brother shall give up brother, a mother her son, when you and I have heard the call of a nation in turmoil.'

Mugo felt a constriction in his throat. He could not clap for words that did not touch him. What right had such a boy, probably younger than Mugo, to talk like that? What arrogance? Kihika had spoken of blood as easily as if he was talking of drawing water in a river, Mugo reflected, a revulsion starting in his stomach at the sight and smell of blood. I hate him, he heard himself say and frightened, he looked at Mumbi, wondering what she was thinking. Her eyes were still fixed on her brother. Everybody's eyes were on the platform. Mugo experienced a twang of jealousy as he too turned and looked at the speaker. At that moment their eyes met, or so Mugo imagined, with guilt. For a split second the crowd and the world at large seemed drenched in silence. Only Kihika and Mugo were left on the stage. Something surged for release in Mugo's heart, something, in fact, which was an intense vibration of terror and hatred.

'Watch ye and pray,' Kihika said, calling on his audience to remember the great Swahili proverb: *Kikulacho Kimo nguoni mwako.*

Kihika lived the words of sacrifice he had spoken to the multitude. Soon after Jomo and other leaders were arrested in October 1952, Kihika disappeared into the forest, later to be followed there by a handful of young men from Thabai and Rung'ei.

The greatest triumph for Kihika was the famous capture of Mahee. Mahee was a big police garrison in the Rift Valley, the heart of what, for many years, were called the White Highlands. In Mahee too was a transit prison for men and women about to be taken to concentration camps. Situated in a central position, Mahee fed guns and ammunition to the other smaller police and military posts scattered in the Rift Valley to protect and raise the morale of white settlers. If you stood at Mahee at any time of day, you would see the walls of the escarpment, an enchanting guard to one of the most beautiful valleys in the land. The walls climbed in steps to the highlands; a row of smaller hills, some hewn round at the top while others bore scoops and volcano mouths, receded into shrouds of mist and mystery.

At night the valley was hidden in darkness, except for the light outside Mahee. It was quiet. The guards, following the example of their white officers, who were used to a life of indolence, for the name of Mahee itself was proof against any attack, had already drunk and gone to sleep, leaving a few guards to observe the convention. Suddenly the night was broken by the simultaneous sound of bugles, trumpets, horns and tins. From inside the prison came a responding cry of Uhuru. The officer in charge, aroused from the spell of whisky he had taken earlier by this commotion, instinctively reached for the telephone, trying the magic feat of pulling up his trousers and ringing at the same time. Suddenly, the hand that lifted the receiver let it fall, the trousers also rolled to the floor. The telephone wires had been cut, Mahee could not get help from the outlying posts. Caught unawares, the police made a weak resistance as Kihika and his men stormed in. Some policemen climbed the walls and jumped to safety. Kihika's men broke into the prison and led the prisoners out into the night. The garrison was set on fire and Kihika's men ran back to the forest with fresh supplies of men, guns and ammunition to continue the war on a scale undreamt of in the days of Waiyaki and Young Harry.

People came to know Kihika as the terror of the whiteman. They said that he could move mountains and compel thunder from heaven.

A price was put on his head.

Anybody who brought Kihika, dead or alive, would receive a huge sum of money.

A year later, Kihika was captured alone at the edge of the Kinenie Forest.

Believe the news? The man who compelled trees and mountains to move, the man who could go for ten miles crawling on his stomach through sand and thorny bush, was surely beyond the arm of the whiteman.

Kihika was tortured. Some say that the neck of a bottle was wedged into his body through the anus as the white people in the Special Branch tried to wrest the secrets of the forest from him. Others say that he was offered a lot of money and a free trip to England to shake the hand of the new woman on the throne. But he would not speak.

Kihika was hanged in public, one Sunday, at Rung'ei Market, not far from where he had once stood calling for blood to rain on and water the tree of freedom. A combined force of Homeguards and Police whipped and drove people from Thabai and other ridges to see the body of the rebel dangling on the tree, and learn.

The Movement, however, remained alive and grew, as people put it, on the wounds of those Kihika left behind.

Three

'We are not staying long,' Gikonyo said, after a silence. 'We have really come to see you about the Uhuru celebrations on Thursday.'

Looking at Gikonyo, you could not believe that he was the same man whose marriage to Mumbi almost thirteen years before had angered other young suitors: what did Mumbi see in him? How could a woman so beautiful walk into poverty with eyes wide open? Now four years after returning home from detention, Gikonyo was one of the richest men in Thabai. He had recently bought a five-acre farm plot; he owned a shop – *Gikonyo General Stores* – at Rung'ei; and only the other day he had acquired a second-hand lorry for trading. On top of this, he was elected the chairman of the local branch of the Movement, a tribute, so people said, to his man's spirit which no detention camp could break. Gikonyo was respected and admired as a symbol of what everyone aspired to be: fiercely independent, bending all effort to success in any enterprise.

'What – what do you want?' Mugo asked, raising his eyes to Warui.

Warui's life was, in a way, the story of the Movement; he had taken part in the meetings of Young Harry, had helped in building people's own schools and listened to Jomo's speeches in the 'twenties. Warui was one of the few who saw in that recent employee of the Nairobi Municipal Council, a man destined for power.

'He will do great things,' he used to say of Jomo. 'You can see it in his eyes.'

Warui looked at the hearthplace. An oil-lamp with soot around the neck and sides of the glass, stood on the stone.

'We of Thabai Village must also dance our part,' he started, his voice, though low, embracing the whole room. 'Yes, we must dance the song the way we know how. For, let it never be said Thabai dragged to shame the names of the sons she lost in war. No. We must raise them – even from the dead – to share it with us. Our people, is there a song sweeter than that of freedom? Of a truth, we have waited for it many a sleepless night. Those who have gone before us, those of us spared to see the sun today, and even those to be born tomorrow, must join in the feast. The day we hold Wiyathi in our hands we want to drink from the same calabash – yes – drink from the same calabash.'

Silence followed these words. Each person seemed engrossed in himself as if turning over the words in his mind. The woman cleared her throat, an indication that she was about to take up the thread from Warui. Mugo looked at her.

Wambui was not very old, although she had lost most of her teeth. During the Emergency, she carried secrets from the villages to the forest and back to the villages and towns. She knew the underground movements in Nakuru, Njoro, Elburgon and other places in and outside the Rift Valley. The story is told how she once carried a pistol tied to her thighs near the groin. She was dressed in long, wide and heavy clothes, the picture of decrepitude and senile decay. She was taking the gun to Naivasha. As luck would have it, she was suddenly caught in one of those sporadic military and police operations which plagued the country. People were collected into the square behind the shops. Soon came her turn to be searched. Her tooth started aching; she twisted her lips, moaned; saliva tossed out of the corners of her mouth and flowed down her chin. The Gikuyu policeman searching her was saying in Swahili: Pole mama: made other sympathetic noises and went on searching. He started from her chest, rummaged under her armpits, gradually working his way down towards the vital spot. And suddenly Wambui screamed, the man stopped, astonished.

'The children of these days,' she began. 'Have you lost all shame? Just because the whiteman tells you so, you would actually touch your own mother's . . . the woman who gave you birth? All right, I'll lift the clothes and you can have a look at your mother, it is so aged, and see what gain it'll bring you for the rest of your life.'

She actually made as if to lift her clothes and expose her nakedness. The man involuntarily turned his eyes away.

'Go away from here,' he growled at her. 'Next . . .' Wambui never told this story; but she never denied it; if people asked her about it, she only smiled enigmatically.

'It is like our elders who always poured a little beer on the ground before they themselves drank,' Wambui now said. 'Why did they do that? It's because they always remembered the spirits of those below. We too cannot forget our sons. And Kihika was such a man, a great man.'

Mugo sat rigidly on his stool. Warui watched the lamp that badly lit the hut into an eerie haziness. Wambui rested her elbows on her knees and wedged her chin into the cupped palms of her hands. Gikonyo looked abstractedly into space.

'What do you want?' Mugo asked with something like panic in his voice.

Suddenly there was a loud knocking. All eyes were turned to the door. Curiosity heightened the tension. Mugo went to the door.

'General!' Warui exclaimed as soon as the new guests entered. Mugo walked back behind the two men. One was tall, clean-shaven, with close-cropped hair. The shorter man had his hair plaited. They were some of the Freedom Fighters who had recently left the forest under the Uhuru amnesty.

'Sit down – on the bed,' Mugo invited them, and was startled by the sound of his own voice. So old – so rusty . . . today . . . tonight . . . everything is strange . . . people's looks and gestures frighten me . . . I'm not really afraid because . . . because . . . a man's life, like mine, is not important . . . and . . . and . . . God . . . I've ceased to care . . . I don't . . . don't . . . The arrival of the two men had broken the mounting tension. Everybody was talking. The hut was animated with a low excited murmur. Wambui was explaining something about the Uhuru preparations to the man with plaited hair. In the forest he was called Lieutenant Koina. The tall one was the General, General R.

'A sacrifice! A sacrifice!' Koina exclaimed, laughing. 'And let me eat the meat. A whole ram. In the forest we only ate bamboo shoots and wild animals —'

'What do you know of sacrifice?' Wambui interrupted, joining in the laughter.

'Oh, we did sacrifice – and ate the meat afterwards. We prayed twice a day and an extra one before any expedition to wrest arms from European farms. We stood up facing Mount Kenya:

> 'Mwenanyaga we pray that you may protect our hideouts.
> Mwenanyaga we pray that you may hold a soft cloud over us.
> Mwenanyaga we pray that you may defend us behind and in
>   front from our enemies.
> Mwenanyaga we pray that you may give us courage in our
>   hearts.
> Thai thathaiya Ngai, Thaai.

'We also sang:

> 'We shall never rest
> Without land,
> Without Freedom true
> Kenya is a country of black people.'

Everybody had stopped talking and listened to Koina's singing. And the plaintive note below his words was at odds with his apparent mirth. There was a sudden, almost an uneasy silence. None of this is real . . . I'll soon wake up from the dream . . . My hut will be empty and I'll find myself alone as I have always been . . . Gikonyo coughed, dryly. Warui burst in.

'Cold? I always say this. The young of these days have lost their strength. They cannot resist a tiny illness. Do you know in our days we would lie in the forest nights long waiting for Masai? The wind rubbed our necks. As for our clothes, they were drenched with dew. Yet you would not hear a cough in the morning. No, not even a small one.'

The two freedom fighters looked at Warui. They had been in the forest for more than seven years. But nobody challenged Warui's claim.

'What is a prayer?' General R. suddenly asked, as if continuing the previous conversation. 'It did not help Kihika. Kihika believed in prayer. He even read the Bible every day, and took it with him wherever he went. What I never understand is this: Why is it that God would not whisper a word – just one word – to warn him not to walk into a trap?'

'A trap?' Gikonyo asked quickly. 'Do you want to tell us that Kihika was betrayed?'

'The radio said he was captured in a battle in which many of his men were killed,' Wambui said.

General R. took his time to satisfy this awakened interest. He stared at the ground in absorption.

'On that day he was going to meet somebody. He often went out alone to spy or to finish off a dangerous character like DO Robson. Yet he always told me about his plans. On this day, he told me nothing. He seemed very excited, you might say almost happy. But he grew angry whenever anybody interrupted him. Again, he never forgot to take his Bible. But on this day he left it behind. Perhaps he never meant to be long.'

General R. fumbled in his pockets and took out a small Bible which he passed on to Gikonyo. Warui and Wambui craned forward, excited by this, like little children. Gikonyo shuffled through the small Bible lingering on verses underlined in black and red. His fingers were slightly shaking. He stopped at Psalm 72, where two verses were underlined in red.

'What are these red lines?' Wambui asked, with awed curiosity.

'Read a few lines,' Warui said.

Gikonyo read:

> 'He shall judge the poor of the people, he shall save the children of the needy, and shall break in pieces the oppressor.
>
> For he shall deliver the needy when he cometh; the poor also and he that hath no helper.'

Again this was followed by a profound silence. Then General R. continued.

'Actually Kihika was never the same person after the day he shot DO Robson. And that's why we have come here tonight.' All this time, General R. had stared in one spot. And he spoke quietly, choosing words as if he was directing questions at his own heart. Now he suddenly raised his eyes to Mugo. And every other person's eyes were turned to Mugo.

'I believe you were the man who sheltered Kihika on that night. That is why you were later arrested and sent to detention, is that not so? What we want to know is this. Did Kihika mention to you that he would be meeting somebody from the village – in a week's time?'

Mugo's throat was choked; if he spoke, he would cry. He shook his head and stared straight ahead.

'He did not mention Karanja?'

Again Mugo shook his head.

'That's all we wanted to know. We thought you might be able to help us.' General R. fell back into his former silence.

'Now, now, who would have thought—' Warui started and then stopped. Wambui seemed fascinated more with the Bible than with General R.'s news.

'A Bible! You might have thought his father a priest . . .' she moaned. 'Our son should have been a priest . . .'

'He was a priest . . . a high priest of this our freedom.' Warui said. Gikonyo laughed, uneasily. He was joined by Wambui and Lt Koina. Mugo and General R. did not laugh. Again the tension was broken. Gikonyo coughed and cleared his throat.

'General, you almost made us forget why we came here,' he announced, now the voice of a businessman who had no time for rituals. 'But I am glad you came for this also concerns you. It is like this. The Movement and leaders of the village have thought it a good idea to honour the dead. On Independence Day we shall remember those from our village and ridges near, who lost their lives in the fight for freedom. We cannot let Kihika's name die. He will live in our memory, and history will carry his name to our children in years to come.' He paused and looked straight at Mugo and his next words addressed to Mugo were full of plain admiration. 'I don't want to go into details – but we all know the part you played in the movement. Your name and that of Kihika will ever be linked together. As the General here has said, you gave Kihika shelter without fear of danger to your own life. You did for Thabai out here and in detention what Kihika did in the forest. We have therefore thought that on this important day, you should lead in the sacrifice and ceremonies to honour those who died that we might live. The elders will guide you in the details of the ritual. For you the main thing will be the speech. We are arranging a large meeting at Rung'ei Market around where Kihika's body hung from a tree. You will make the main speech of the day.'

Mugo stared at a pole opposite; he tried to grasp the sense of what Gikonyo had said. He had always found it difficult to make decisions. Recoiling as if by instinct from setting in motion a course of action whose consequences he could not determine before the start, he allowed himself to drift into things or be pushed into them by an uncanny demon; he rode on the wave of circumstance and lay against the crest, fearing but fascinated by fate. Something of that devilish fascination now seemed to light his eyes. His body was deathly still.

'What do you say?' Wambui asked slightly impatient with Mugo's intense look. But Warui was fascinated by people's eyes and he always said this of Mugo: He has a future, a great future. Shouldn't I know? You can see it in his eyes. He now said:

'You need not talk the whole day. I have seen many people ruin good speeches because they would talk till their mouths were drained of all saliva. A word to touch the hearts – that is all. Like the one you spoke that day.'

'I do not understand,' Mugo at last said.

'We of Thabai want to honour our heroes. What's difficult in that?' Warui asked.

'I know how you feel,' Gikonyo said, 'You want to be left alone. Remember this, however: it is not easy for any man in a community to be left alone, especially a man in your position. No, you don't have to make up your mind now. But we would like to know the answer soon, December 12 is only four nights away.'

Saying this, Gikonyo rose to leave. The others also stood up. Gikonyo hesitated a moment as if an undelivered thought lingered in his mind.

'Another thing! You know the government, now that it is controlled by the Movement, will allow chiefs to be elected by the people. The branch here wants you to stand for this area when the time comes.'

They went out.

A smile slowly spread from the edges of Mugo's mouth. It could have indicated joy, mocking or bitterness. The visitors had left the door ajar. He shut the door and sat on the bed. Gradually the meaning of what Gikonyo had said began to light the blank abyss of incomprehension. What do they want? What do they really want? he asked himself, holding his head in his hands to steel himself.

Outside Mugo's hut the forest fighters parted from Gikonyo, Wambui and Warui. The two shared a hut at the other end of the village. The hut had been bought for them by some ardent members of the local branch of the Party who then believed the Party was the reincarnation of the Movement.

'Do you think he will help us?' Koina suddenly asked.

'Who?'

'That man!'

'Oh, Mugo. I don't know. Kihika rarely mentioned him. In fact, I don't know if he knew him well.'

They walked the rest of the way without more words. Koina fumbled for matches to light the oil-lamp. He was small-boned, light-skinned, and had large veins that protruded on his face and hands. General R. sat on the bed, absorbed in thought. Koina stood and stared at the yellow flame.

'All the same, we must find out the traitor,' General R. said, as if continuing their earlier conversation. His voice was low and carried grim determination.

Koina did not answer at once. He remembered the day Kihika went out, never to return. Kihika commanded more than three hundred men, split into groups of fifty or even twenty-five men. The groups lived apart, in different caves, around Kinenie Forest, and only came together when going for a big venture like the capture of Mahee. Koina was always struck by Kihika's absolute disregard for personal danger. The way he had finished DO Robson was already a legend in the camps around Longonot, Ngong and even in Nyandarwa. Koina felt worshipful admiration for Kihika. At such times he would swear: 'I will never leave him. I swear to God above I'll never abandon Kihika. I was without faith. He has given it to me.' Yes, Kihika had given him, a mere cook, new self, by making him aware of black power. Koina had felt this the day they took Mahee. As they waited for Kihika to return, he keenly felt the imminence of that black power. Later they sent out scouts, who reported that a big operation was on. Word went round. General R. ordered his men to prepare for a quick retreat into Longonot, their other big hide-out. They learnt that Kihika had been arrested. Njeri had wept. And even he, too, a man, could not hide his tears.

'Do you think that he was going to meet a woman?' Koina now asked.

'No, I don't think so. Karanja is really our man if what you tell me about him is true.'

'Everybody in Githima tells me the same story. If you touch him from behind, he shakes uncontrollably. He never walks in the dark alone. He never opens his door to anybody after seven o'clock in the evening. All these are signs of a guilty man, but—'

'God! If the louse had anything to do with Kihika's crucifixion!' General R. said, jumping to his feet. He paced up and down the room. 'We all took the oath together. We took the oath together.'

Koina sat on the bed, surprised by the passion and vehemence in the General's voice. Koina had always feared him and even felt small in the other's presence. Both had been in the Second World War; the General had fought in Burma. But he, Koina, never rose beyond the rank of a cook. After the war, the General worked as a tailor. Koina moved from job to job. His last job was with Dr Lynd, an ugly white spinster, whom Koina hated at first sight. He and the General really knew one another in the forest. In the battles, General R. emerged without betraying emotion. When Kihika was arrested General R. had remained calm, had shown no surprise or any sign of loss. With years Koina, who had wept at the time, forgot Kihika's death and did not feel any urgency for revenge. Now it was the General who trembled with passion. Koina looked around the bare hut, avoiding the pacing figure. A sufuria, two plates, empty bottles and a water-tin lay on the floor, rather disconsolately. He cleared his throat:

'Perhaps it is no use. Perhaps we ought to forget the whole thing.'

General R. abruptly stopped pacing. He looked at Koina, weighing him up and down. Koina fidgeted on his seat, feeling the antagonism in the other's stare.

'Forget?' General R. asked in a deceptively calm voice. 'No, my friend. We must find our traitor, else you and I took the oath for nothing. Traitors and collaborators must not escape revolutionary justice. Tomorrow you must go back to Githima and see Mwaura about the new plan.'

The other three delegates walked some distance from Mugo's hut before anyone spoke.

'He is a strange man,' Wambui commented.

'Who?' Warui asked.

'Mugo.'

'It is the suffering,' Gikonyo said. 'Do you know what it was to live in detention? It was easier, perhaps, with those of us not labelled hard-core. But Mugo was. So he was beaten, and yet would not confess the oath.

'It was not like prison,' Gikonyo went on, surprised at his own sudden burst of feelings. 'In prison you know your crime. You know your terms. So many years, one, ten, thirty – after that you get out.'

As suddenly Gikonyo checked himself. He could not clearly see Wambui or Warui in the dark. It seemed to him that he had only spoken to empty air.

'Sleep well,' Gikonyo called outside the house he had recently built.

Warui and Wambui went away without answering. The empty silence harrowed Gikonyo. He did not want to enter the building. Light from the sitting-room showed through the curtains and glass windows. Mumbi, then, must still be waiting for him. Why can't she go to bed? He walked away from the light, without knowing where he was going. He resented his recent outburst in the presence of Wambui and Warui. Why could he not control his emotions in Mugo's hut? A man should never moan. And for Gikonyo, hard work had been a drug against pestering memories.

He had built a house, one of the best and most modern in the village; he had wealth, albeit small, and a political position in the land: all this a long way from the days of the poor carpenter. Yet these things had ceased to have taste. He ate, not because he enjoyed the food, but a man had to live.

The village was now far behind. Darkness had thickened. It struck him, like a new experience, that he was alone. He listened. He seemed to hear, in the distance, steps on a pavement. The steps approached him. He walked faster and faster, away from the steps. But the faster he walked, the louder the steps became. He panted. He was hot all over, despite the cold air. Then he started running, madly. His heart beat harder. The steps on the pavement, so near now, rhythmed with his pounding heart. He had to talk to someone. He must hear another human voice. Mugo. But what were mere human voices? Had he not lived with them for six years? In various detention camps? Perhaps he wanted a voice of man who would understand. Mugo. Abruptly he stopped running. The steps on the pavement receded into a distance. They would come again, he knew they would come to plague him. I must talk to Mugo. The words Mugo had spoken at a meeting two years before had touched Gikonyo. Lord, Mugo would know.

But by the time he reached Mugo's hut, the heat of his resolution had cooled. He stood outside the door, wondering if he should knock or not: what, really, had he come to tell Mugo? He felt foolish standing there, alone. Maybe he had better come tomorrow. Maybe another time he would know how best to tear his heart before another person.

At home, he found Mumbi had not yet gone to bed. She brought him food. This reminded him that he had hardly eaten anything the whole day. She sat opposite him and watched him. He tasted a little food and then pushed the rest away. He had lost his appetite.

'Make me a cup of tea,' he said between his teeth.

'You must eat,' Mumbi appealed. Her small nose shone with the light from the lamp. The appeal in her eyes and voice belied the calm face and the proud carriage of her well-formed body. Gikonyo stared at the new, well-polished mahogany table. Perhaps he should have called on Mugo for a talk between men.

'I don't want anything to eat,' he grunted.

'It's my food you don't want.'

Gikonyo kept quiet. In detention, he had longed to come back to Mumbi. Was this the same woman? He looked at her. She had turned her face to the door. Maybe she was crying.

'I don't feel like eating, that's all,' he said, relenting a little.

'It is all right,' she whispered. She went to another room in the house and brought cups, a pot, tea-leaves, milk and sugar. She added more charcoal into the burner and carried it out to have it wind-fanned into flames. She stayed out in the dark.

Gikonyo took out an old exercise-book from an inner pocket of his jacket. He fumbled for a pencil, got it, saw it was broken, and sharpened it with a penknife. He wrote down figures; he added, subtracted, multiplied, cancelled; they stole his concentration so that Gikonyo temporarily forgot other things outside the day's returns and prospects for business tomorrow.

Mumbi brought back the fire. She put the pot, full of water, on the fire, and sat again to watch her husband. She appeared expectant, a bird ready to fly at the first sign or word from the master. But Mumbi had learnt to school her desires, to accept what life and fate gave her.

'Did you see Mugo?' she ventured to ask.

'Yes.'

'Did he say he would lead us?'

'He will think about it.' Gikonyo did not raise his head from the exercise-book.

'Wambui told me about it.' She broke into his thoughts. He did not answer.

'Why didn't you tell me about it?' she continued. 'Don't forget that Kihika and I come from the same womb.'

'Since when did you and I start sharing secrets?'

Immediately he hated himself for adopting that tone. He had vowed he would always be polite to her, that he would never let this voice betray any bitter emotion or his inner turmoil.

'I am sorry,' she said, humiliated. 'I had forgotten that I am a nobody.'

Tea was soon ready. She poured him some and filled a cup for herself. Then, as if compelled by a great power within, Mumbi left her seat and stood in front of her husband. She put her small hands around his neck, resting them on his shoulders. Her eyes glowed. Her lips trembled.

'Let us talk about it,' she whispered.

'About what?' he asked, and raised his head.

'The child.'

'There is nothing to talk about,' he said with acid emphasis.

'Then, come to my bed tonight. I have waited for you only, these years.'

'What is wrong with you?' Gikonyo pulled her arms from around his neck and slightly pushed her away. 'Please go and sit down. Or better, go to sleep. You are tired.'

Mumbi stood there, cold. Her breasts heaved up and down. She opened her mouth as if to shout. Then suddenly she grabbed her knitting from the ground and ran to her bedroom. In fact, it was Gikonyo who felt tired, tired and aged. He propped his head with his left hand, the elbow planted on the table. He lifted the pencil with the right hand and tried to scribble a figure. But his hand was not steady, he let the pencil drop. With effort he rose from the seat, took the lamp and for a few seconds stood outside Mumbi's door. Then he resolutely moved away, towards his bedroom.

And the Lord spoke unto Moses,
Go unto Pharaoh, and say unto him,
Thus saith the Lord,
Let my people go.

Exodus 8:1
(*verse underlined in red in Kihika's personal Bible*)

Four

In the days when European and Indian immigrants wrestled to control Kenya – then any thought of a black person near the seat of power was beyond the reach of the wildest imagination – Mr Rogers, an agricultural officer, travelling by train from Nairobi to Nakuru one day, saw the thick forest at Githima and suddenly felt his planning mind drawn to it. His passion lay, not in politics, a strange thing in those days, but in land development. Why not a Forestry Research Station, he asked himself as the train rumbled towards the escarpment and down to the great valley. Later he went back to Githima to see the forest. His plan began to take shape. He wrote letters to anybody of note and even unsuccessfully sought an interview with the Governor. Mad they thought him: science in dark Africa?

Githima and the thick forest, like an evil spirit, possessed him. He could not rest; he talked to himself about the scheme, he talked about it to everybody. One day he was crushed by a train at Githima crossing, and he died immediately. Later a Forestry Research Station was set up in the area, not as a tribute to his martyrdom, but as part of a new colonial development plan. Soon Githima Forestry and Agricultural Research Station teemed with European scientists and administrators.

It is said that the man's ghost haunts the railway crossing and that every year the rumbling train claims a human sacrifice from the Githima settlement; the latest victim was Dr Henry Van Dyke, a fat, drunken meteorological officer, who had always sworn, so the African workers said, that he would kill himself if Kenyatta was ever set free from Lodwar and Lokitaung. His car crashed into the train soon after

Kenyatta's return home from Maralal. People in Githima, even his enemies, were dismayed by the news. Was this an accident, or had the man committed suicide?

Karanja, who worked at Githima Library dusting books, keeping them straight in their shelves and writing labels, remembered Dr Van Dyke mostly because of a strange game he sometimes played: he would come up to the African workers, put his arm around their shoulders and then suddenly, he would strike their unsuspecting bottoms. He used to let his hand lie on their buttocks feelingly, breathing out alcohol over the shoulders of his victims. Then unexpectedly he would burst into open and loud laughter. Karanja resented the laughter; he never knew whether Dr Van Dyke expected him to join in it or not. Hence Karanja always settled into a nervous grin which made him hate Dr Van Dyke all the more. Yet the news of the man's death, his car and body completely mangled by the train, had made Karanja retch.

Karanja picked a clean stencil from a pile on the table and started writing labels. The books recently bound at Githima belonged to the Ministry of Agriculture, Nairobi. Soon Karanja's mind lost consciousness of other things. Uhuru or Dr Van Dyke, and he concentrated on the label in hand: STUDIES IN AGRONOMY VOL. – Suddenly he felt a man's presence in the room. He dropped the stencil and swung round. His face had turned a shade darker. He tried, with difficulty, to control the tremulous pen in his hand.

'Why don't you people knock at the door before you rush in?' he hissed at the man standing at the door.

'I knocked, three times.'

'You did not. You always enter as if this was your father's thingira.'

'I knocked at this door, here.'

'Feebly like a woman? Why can't you knock hard, hard, like a man circumcised?' Karanja raised his voice, and banged the table at the same time, to emphasize every point.

'Ask your mother, when I fucked her—'

'You insult my mother, you—'

'Even now I can do it again, or to your sister. It is they who can tell you that Mwaura is a man circumcised.'

Karanja stood up. The two glared at one another. For a minute it looked as if they would fall to blows.

'You say that to me? Is it to me you throw so many insults?' he said with venom.

Mwaura's lower lip fell. His stomach heaved forward and back. His breathing was quick and heavy. Then he seemed to remember something. He held his tongue.

'Anyway, I'm sorry,' he suddenly said but in a voice edged with menace.

'So you ought to be. What do you want here?'

'Nothing. Just that Thompson wants to see you, that is all.' Mwaura went out. Karanja's mood changed from tension to anxiety. What did Thompson want? Perhaps he would say something about pay. He dusted his khaki overall, passed a comb through his mole-coloured hair and hurried along the corridor towards Thompson's office. He knocked boldly at the door and entered.

'What is it? Why do you people knock so loud?'

'I thought, I thought you sent for me, sir,' Karanja said in a thin voice, standing, as he always did before a white person, feet slightly parted, hands linked at the back, all in obsequious attention.

'Oh, yes, yes. You know my house?'

'Yes, sir.'

'Run and tell Mrs Thompson that I'll not be coming home for lunch. I am going – eh – wait a minute. I'll give you a letter.'

John Thompson had, over the years, developed a mania for writing letters. He scribbled notes to everyone. He rarely sent a messenger anywhere, be it to the Director, to the stationery office for paper, or to the workshop for a nail or two, without an accompanying note carefully laying down all the details. Even when it might be easier to see an officer personally he preferred to send a letter.

Karanja took the note and lingered for a second or two hoping that Thompson would say something about the pay increment for which he had recently applied. The boss, however, resumed his blank stare at the mass of paper on his table.

John Thompson and Mrs Dickinson used Karanja as their personal messenger. Karanja accepted their missions with resentful alacrity:

weren't there paid messengers at Githima? Mrs Dickinson was the Librarian. She was a young woman who was separated from her husband and she made no secret of living with her boyfriend. She was rarely in the office, but when she was in, men and women would flock to see her and laughter and high-pitched voices would pour out all day. An enthusiast for the East African Safari, she always took part, co-driving with her boyfriend, but she never once finished the course. Her missions were the ones Karanja hated most: often she sent him, for instance, to the African quarters to buy meat for her two dogs.

Today as he rode his creaking bicycle he was once again full of plans: he would certainly complain to John Thompson about these trivial errands. No, what Karanja resented most was not the missions or their triviality, but the way they affected his standing among the other African workers. But on the whole Karanja would rather endure the humiliation than lose the good name he had built up for himself among the white people. He lived on that name and the power it brought him. At Githima, people believed that a complaint from him was enough to make a man lose his job. Karanja knew their fears. Often when men came into his office, he would suddenly cast them a cold eye, drop hints, or simply growl at them; in this way, he increased their fears and insecurity. But he also feared the men and alternated this fierce prose with servile friendliness.

A neatly trimmed hedge of cider shrub surrounded the Thompsons' bungalow. At the entrance, green creepers coiled on a wood stand, massed into an arch at the top and then fell to the hedge at the sides. The hedge enclosed gardens of flowers: flame lilies, morning glory, sunflowers, bougainvillea. However, it was the gardens of roses that stood out in colour above the others. Mrs Margery Thompson had cultivated red roses, white roses, pink roses – roses of all shades. Now she emerged from this garden of colour and came to the door. She was dressed in thin white trousers and a blouse that seemed suspended from her pointed breasts.

'Come into the house,' she idly said after reading the note from her husband. She was bored by staying in the house alone. Normally she chatted with her houseboy or with her shamba-boy. At times she quarrelled with them and her raised voice could be heard from the road. Both boys had now left and it was during these few days that she had come to realize how they had been an important part of the house.

Karanja was surprised because he had never, before, been invited inside the house. He sat at the edge of the chair, his unsteady hands on his knees, and idly stared at the ceiling and at the walls to avoid looking at her breasts.

Margery felt a sensual power at the fear and discomfiture she inflicted on Karanja. Why did he not look at her? She had often seen him, but never thought of him as a man. Now she was suddenly curious to know what thoughts lay inside his head: what did he think of the house? Of Uhuru? Of her? She let her fancy flow. She warmed all over and stood up, slightly irritated by the thrill.

'Would you like some tea, coffee or anything?'

'I – I must go!' Karanja stammered out his thoughts.

'Sure you don't want some coffee? Never mind Mrs Dickinson,' she said, smiling, feeling indulgent, almost glad of a conspiracy.

'All right,' he said edging deeper into the seat with eyes longing for the door and the hedge beyond. Even now he had no courage to lean back and be comfortable. At the same time, he desperately wished one of the workers was present to see him entertained to coffee by a white woman, the wife of the Administrative Secretary.

In the kitchen, Margery played with pots and cups. Although she was still ashamed of the thrill, she would not let it go. She could only remember once before when she had experienced a similar flame. That was the day she danced with Dr Van Dyke at Githima hostel. This was soon after the Rira disaster. She was attracted, at the same time disgusted, by his drunken breath. When later in the evening he took her for a drive, she submitted to his power. She let him make love to her, and experienced, for the first time, the terrible beauty of a rebellion.

Waiting in the room, Karanja found his nervous unease replaced by a different desire. Should he ask her, he wondered. Maybe she would give him what he really wanted: to hear her contradict rumours that the Thompsons would be flying back to England. Many times Karanja had walked towards Thompson determined to ask him a direct question. Cold water lumped in his belly, his heart would thunder violently when he came near the whiteman. His determination always ended in the same way: he would salute John Thompson and then walk past as if his business lay further ahead. What Karanja feared more than the rumours was their possible confirmation. As long as he did not know the truth, he could interpret the story in the only way that gave him hope: the coming of black rule would not mean, could never mean the end of white power. Thompson as a DO and now as an Administrative Secretary, had always seemed to Karanja the invincible expression of that power. How, then, could Thompson go?

Margery came back with two cups of coffee.

'Do you take sugar in your coffee?'

'No,' he said automatically, and knew, at the same time, he lacked the courage to ask her about the rumours. Karanja loathed coffee or tea without lots of sugar.

Margery sat opposite Karanja and crossed her legs. She put her cup on the arm of the chair. Karanja held his in both hands afraid of spilling a drop on the carpet. He winced every time he brought the cup near his lips and nostrils.

'How many wives have you?' she asked. This was her favourite question to Africans; it began the day she discovered her latest cook had three wives. Karanja started as if Margery had tickled a wound that had only healed at the surface. *Mumbi.*

'I am not married.'

'Not married? I thought you people— Are you going to buy a wife?'

'I don't know.'

'Have you a friend, a woman?' She pursued, her curiosity mounting; her voice was timbred with warmth. Something in the quality of her voice touched Karanja. Would she understand? Would she?

'I had a woman. I – I loved her,' he said boldly. He closed his eyes and with sudden, huge effort, gulped down the bitter coffee.

'Why didn't you marry her? Is she dead or —'

'She refused me,' he said.

'I am sorry,' she said with feeling. Karanja remembered himself and where he was.

'Can I go now, Memsahib? Any message for Bwana?'

She had forgotten why Karanja had come into the house. She re-read the note from her husband.

'No, thank you very much,' she said at the door.

It was almost twelve o'clock when Karanja left Thompson's house. The wound that Margery had tickled smarted for a while. Then gradually he became exhilarated, he wished Mwaura had seen him at the house. He also wished that the houseboy had been present, for then news of his visit would have spread. As it was, he himself would have to do the telling: this would carry less weight and power. Being nearly time for lunch-break, he went straight to the eating-house at the African quarters, thinking about his visit and the bitter cup of coffee.

The eating-house was called *Your Friend Unto Death*, in short, *Friend*. The stony walls were covered with grease, a fertile ground for flies. They buzzed around the customers, jumped on top of the cups and plates and at times even made love on food brought on the table. Plastic roses in tins decorated each creaking table. The motto of the house was painted in capitals across the wall: COME UNTO ME ALL YE THAT ARE HUNGRY AND THIRSTY AND I WILL GIVE YOU REST. On another part of the wall near the cashier's desk hung a carefully framed poem.

> Since man to man has been unjust,
> Show me the man that I can trust.
> I have trusted many to my sorrow,
> So for credit, my friend, come tomorrow.

Friend was the only licensed eating-house at Githima.

There Karanja found Mwaura. It was not good to create enemies, Karanja always told himself after alienating any of the other workers.

'I am sorry about the incident,' Karanja quickly said, an affability that didn't come off. 'I hope you'll take it as a little shauri between friends. You see, some people don't understand that the work we do, you know, writing labels for all those books of science, requires concentration. If somebody flings the door open without warning, it upsets you and you ruin the letters. I tell you, if you knew that

Librarian woman as well as I do – you think she separated from her husband for nothing – Waiter, two cups of tea, quick . . . Now, what news from Rung'ei?'

John Thompson – tall, a leathery skin that stuck to the bone – did not go to Nairobi, but remained at Githima during the lunch-hour going through the motions of working: that is, he would stand, go to the cabinet by the wall, pull out a file, and return to the table, his face weather-beaten into permanent abstraction, almost as if his mind dwelt on things far away and long ago. His thin hands and light eyes went through each file carefully before returning it to the cabinet. Once or twice he sat up and his finger played with a few creases crowded around the corner of his mouth.

In turn, Thompson contemplated the clean blotting-paper on the table, the pen and pencil rack, the ink-bottle, the white-washed office walls and the ceiling as if seeking a pattern that held the things in the room together: but his mind only hopped from one thought to another. He then took the day's – Monday's – issue of the *East African Standard*, the oldest daily in Kenya, and leaned back on the chair. Glancing through reports on Uhuru preparations for Thursday, Thompson winced with a vague sense of betrayal. He could not tell what it was in the paper which since internal self-government in June, caused this feeling – whether it was in the Uhuru news, which he already knew, or in the tone, a too-ready acceptance of things. Once he saw the picture of the Prime Minister on the front page: he could not look at it twice, but hurried on to the next page: afterwards he felt ashamed of this reaction, but he could not bring himself to look at it again. Thompson already knew the Duke of Edinburgh would deputize for the Queen. Any news of Uhuru always reminded him of this knowledge. No matter how he looked at it, Thompson was pinched by sadness at the knowledge that the Duke would sit to see the flag lowered, never to rise again on this side of Albion's shore. This sadness was accentuated by his mind racing back to 1952 when the Queen, then a princess, visited Kenya. For a minute, Thompson forgot the newspaper and relived that moment when the young woman shook hands with him. He was then District Officer. He felt a thrill: his heart-beat had quickened as if a covenant had been made between him and her. Then, there, he would have done anything for her, would have stabbed himself to prove his readiness to carry out that mission which though unspoken seemed embodied in her person and smile. Recalling that rapture, Thompson involuntarily pushed away the paper and rose to his feet. There was a flicker in his eyes, a water glint. He walked towards the window muttering under his breath:

'What the hell was it all about!'

The momentary excitement died and a hardness settled in his belly. He leaned forward, his eyes vaguely surveying the scene: in front of him lay the low corrugated-iron roofs of the three laborat- ories – one for plant pathology and forestry, one for soil-physics and the other for soil-chemistry. To the left, hot-houses were scattered about in groups of two or three. He watched Dr Lynd, a plant pathologist at the station, cross the tarmac road; soon she disappeared behind the hot-houses; a few seconds later her dog, a brown bull- mastiff with black dewlaps, dashed from the laboratories and followed her. To the right, he could just see the library: a group of Africans lay on the grass below the eaves. Everything was so quiet, Thompson reflected, now looking from the green grass compound to the chemistry-block, the nearest laboratory. Test-tubes upon test-tubes were neatly arranged by the glass window. Would these things remain after Thursday? Perhaps for two months: and then – test-tubes and beakers would be broken or lie unwashed on the cement, the hot- houses and seed-beds strewn with wild plants and the outer bush which had been carefully hemmed, would gradually creep into a litter-filled compound.

The bull-mastiff emerged from the other side of the chemistry- block, sniffing along the grass-surface. Then it stood and raised its head towards the library. Thompson tensed up: something was going to happen. He knew it and waited, unable to suppress that cold excitement. Suddenly the dog started barking as it bounded across the compound towards the group of Africans. A few of them screamed and scattered into different directions. One man could not run in time. The dog went for him. The man tried to edge his way out, but the dog fixed him to the wall. Suddenly he stooped, picked up a stone, and raised it in the air. The dog was now only a few feet away. Thompson waited for the thing he feared to happen. Just at that moment, Dr Lynd appeared on the scene and, as the dog was about to jump at the man, shouted something. Thompson's breath came back first in a long-drawn wave, then in low quick waves, relieved and vaguely disappointed that nothing had happened.

He left the office and walked across the grass compound towards the library where a small crowd of Africans had gathered. Dr Lynd held her dog by the collar with the left hand and pointed an accusing finger at Karanja with the other.

'I am ashamed of you, utterly ashamed of you,' she said putting as much contempt as she could into her voice. Karanja looked at the ground; fear and anger were visible in his eyes; the sweat-drops had not yet dried on his face.

'The dog – dog – come – Memsahib,' he stammered.

'I would never have thought this of you – throwing stones at my dog.'

'No stones – I did not throw stones.'

'The way you people lie —' she said, looking round at the others. Then she turned to Karanja. 'Didn't I catch you holding a stone? I should have allowed him to get at you. Even now I've half a mind to let him —'

At this point John Thompson arrived at the scene. The Africans gave way, Dr Lynd stopped admonishing Karanja and smiled at Thompson. Karanja raised his head hopefully. The other Africans looked at Thompson and stopped murmuring and mumbling. The sudden silence and the many eyes unsettled Thompson. He remembered the detainees at Rira the day they went on strike. Now he sensed the same air of hostility. He must keep his dignity – to the last. But panic seized him. Without looking at anybody in particular, he said the first Swahili words that came into his mouth:

'I'll deal with this.' And immediately he felt this was the wrong thing to have said – it smacked too much of an apology. The silence was broken. The men were now shouting and pointing at the dog: others made vague gestures in the air. Karanja watched Thompson with grateful eyes. Thompson quickly placed his arm on the woman's shoulder and drew her away.

He led her through the narrow corridor that joined the library block and the administrative building, without knowing where he was going. Everything seemed a visitation from the past: Rira and the dog. Dr Lynd was talking all the time.

'They are rude because Uhuru is coming – even the best of them is changing.'

He wanted to tell her about the dog but somehow found it difficult. He knew he ought to have done something. What if Karanja had been touched by the dog? As the Administrative Secretary, he was supposed to deal with staff–worker relations; and he had received a number of complaints about Dr Lynd's dog from the secretary of the Kenya Civil Servants' Union (Githima branch). They had now come into a big tree-nursery surrounded by a wire fence. They sat down on a grassy part. He wanted to tell her the truth – but he would have to tell her about his own paralysis – how he had stood fascinated by an anticipation of blood.

'Actually, it was not the boy's fault . . .' he stared. 'I saw the dog run towards them.'

Like many other Europeans in Kenya, Thompson had a thing about pets, especially dogs. A year ago he had taken Margery to Nairobi to see *Annie Get Your Gun* staged at the National Theatre by the City Players. He had never been to that theatre before – for nothing really ever happened there – he always went to the Donovan Maule Theatre Club. The road from Githima to Nairobi passed through the countryside. It was very dark. Suddenly the headlights caught a dog about to cross the road. Thompson could have braked, slowed down or horned. He had enough time and distance. But he held on the wheel. He did not want to kill the dog and yet he knew he was going to drive into it. He was glued to the seat – fearing the inevitable. Suddenly there was a scream. Thompson's energy came back. He braked to a stop and opened the door and went out, taking a pocket torch. He went back a few yards; there was no dog anywhere. He looked on either side of the road but saw no sign of the dog – not even a trail of blood. Yet he had heard the thud and the scream. Back in the car, he found

Margery quietly weeping. And to his surprise, he too was shaking and could not comfort her. 'Perhaps it's under the car,' she said. He went out again and carefully peered under the car. There was nothing. He drove away sadly; it was as if he had murdered a man.

He had relived the chilling scene the moment he saw the bull-mastiff run towards Karanja; the incident was still close to the skin as he tried to tell Dr Lynd what had happened – the difficulty lay in separating what had occurred outside his office on the grass – only tell her that – from what had gone on inside him.

To his surprise and extreme discomfort, he saw that she was weeping, and looked away: the dog was wandering among the young trees; it stopped beside a crowd of camphor trees, raised its hind leg and passed water.

'I am sorry,' Dr Lynd said, suppressing a sniff, holding a white handkerchief to her eyes. She was a grey-haired woman with falling flesh on her cheeks and under her eyes. She daily flitted about the compound – between the hot-houses, the laboratories and the seed-beds – a solitary being, like a ghost.

'Don't let it worry you,' he said, his eyes vaguely following the dog.

'I tried not to, but – but – I hate them. How can I help it? Every time I see them I remember – I remember—'

He fidgeted on the grass, felt his ridiculous position in relation to this woman from whom he wanted to get away now that the urge to tell her about the dog had faded. But Dr Lynd was in that mood – a sudden upsurge of pure holy self-pity – when one feels closer to another person, even to a stranger, and ready to confide in him one's innermost dreads and burdens. So she told him about the incident that had plagued her life, had shamed her being. She had lived alone, at Muguga, in an old bungalow overgrown with bush on all sides to the roofs. She had loved the house, the solitude, the peace. It was during the Emergency. Many times the DO warned her to leave the lonely place and go to Githima or Nairobi where she would be sure of protection and security. She would not hear of it: the stories of women murdered in their remote farm-houses did not frighten her. She had come to Kenya to do a job not to play politics. She liked the country and the climate and so had decided to stay. She had never harmed anybody. True, she often scolded her houseboy but she also gave him presents, clothes, built him a little brick house at the back, and never worked him hard. He was a small Kikuyu man from Rung'ei who had apparently been a cook or something during World War II, but had been without a job for a long time before he came to her. Between the houseboy and the dog had developed a friendship which was very touching to see. There came one night, it was dark outside, when the boy called her to open the door rather urgently. On opening the door, two men rushed at her and dragged her back to the sitting-room, the houseboy following. They tied her hands and legs together and gagged her. She waited for them to kill her, for after the initial shock she had resigned herself to death. But what followed was no less cruel and barbaric than if they had killed her. Her dog had barked at the two men. But on seeing the houseboy it wagged its tail and held back its attack. But the houseboy hacked it to pieces. Blood splashed her clothes. She wished she could faint or die there and then. But that was the terrible part, she saw everything, was fully conscious . . . They took money and guns from the safe. Later two men were arrested and hanged; the houseboy was never caught. She had to buy and train another dog. She had never been able to outlive the heavy smell, the malicious mad eyes of those men – no – no, she would never forget it to her dying day.

Thompson looked at her, recoiling from her voice, from her body, from her presence. Both left the field, and took different paths, almost as if they were ashamed of their latest intimacy. He felt rather than knew the fear awakened in him. In the office, he tried to suppress the low rage of fear, but only thought of the dog. And he remembered the other dog as the headlight caught its eyes. What happened to it? What would have happened if the bull-mastiff had jumped on Karanja and torn his flesh? The hostility he saw in the men's eyes as he approached them. The silence. Sudden. Like Rira. There the detainees had refused to speak. They sat down and refused to eat or drink. The obduracy was like iron. Their eyes followed him everywhere. The agony, lack of sleep, thinking of how to break the silence. And in the dark, he could see their eyes. In the men at the library, he had recognized the eyes, the same look.

John Thompson had worked as a District Officer in many parts of Kenya. He worked hard and his ability to deal swiftly and effectively with Africans was widely recognized. A brilliant career in the colonial administration lay before him. During the Emergency he was seconded to detention camps, to rehabilitate Mau Mau adherents to a normal life as British subjects. At Rira, the tragedy of his life occurred. A hunger strike, a little beating and eleven detainees died. The fact leaked out. Because he was the officer in charge, Thompson's name was bandied about in the House of Commons and in the world press. He had suddenly become famous. A commission of inquiry was set up. He was whisked off to Githima, an exile from the public administration he loved. But the wound had never healed. Touch it, and it brought back all the humiliation he had felt at the time.

As he now stared at their eyes, he saw in them a new and terrible significance: would he have had to endure another inquiry, this time under a black government, had anything happened to Karanja?

He could not work and yet the afternoon passed quickly. Maybe he would come back tomorrow to finish the job. He shut the window and again relived the scene and his fear. At the end of the corridor, Karanja waited for him. What did he want? What did he want?

'Yes?'

'I took the letter.'

'So?'

'I want to thank you.'

Thompson remembered his lie; he stared at the boy and passed on. On second thoughts, he called Karanja.

'About that dog—'

'Sir?'

'Don't worry about it, eh? I'll deal with the matter.'

'Thank you, sir.'

And Thompson went away raging within. Did he have to pacify Karanja? What have we come to!

He felt tears at the edges of his eyes. Blindly he rushed to the car.

Five

John Thompson wanted to tell Margery about Dr Lynd; he was struck by the coincidence that she had told him about the death of her dog when he was thinking about the death of another dog; twice he had opened his mouth and only ended by complaining about the day's heat. He tried to fix his mind on to the future: the farewell party tomorrow; their flight home the day after; their new life in Britain. But his mind only dwelt on the past and the trivial side of it: like the dog incident earlier in the day.

'What were you doing in Nairobi?' she asked him, sensing his unease amidst her own thoughts.

'I didn't actually manage to get there,' he said.

'Why?'

'Too much work in the office,' he murmured, picking up an old issue of *Punch* as if to protect himself from her.

'I hope everything is all right now – I mean, in the office.'

'Yes. I was checking a few files. There are a few more to do tomorrow and a few urgent letters to answer. All set for the new man.'

'Have they found anybody?'

'Yes – no – I don't think so.'

'Maybe an African? I suppose they're Africanizing everywhere now?'

He put down the paper on his knees. He became stiff, as if a pin had pricked his buttocks. His earlier vision in the day came back now even more vividly: broken jars and test-tubes on laboratory floors now included his office filled with unanswered letters, with dust and paper on the floor. He felt jealous of his office, of the order he had created; felt hatred for the man who would follow him, and wished he could at least protect his chair from any abuse. Thompson felt that silent pain, almost agony that people feel at the knowledge that they might not be indispensable after all; that the school they have left, the university, the club, would accept new men, however reckless and irresponsible, without regrets, as if they had never existed, as if they had never made their mark on the things they used to call their own. And for no apparent reason, Thompson felt this anger turn against his wife; he wanted to ask her a question, throw a challenge at her, to find if she too was against him. What he really wanted to know was this: If he had died yesterday, at Rira, at Kinenie Forest, if he died today, would she turn to another man? Suddenly he put the *Punch* down and walked to the next room without answering the question Margery had asked him. A few minutes later, he came back with a file consisting of notebooks and papers and started going through them.

Margery rose to clear the cups and saucers. She lingered over his cup, looked at him, and remembered the days before they joined the colonial service when he used to open his heart to her, carrying her high on the waves of his moral vision and optimism. That was after John returned to Oxford from the African campaigns in the Second World War. Softened by this memory, she now saw the strain on his face and for a second wanted to smooth it away, gently, for ever. And then impatient thoughts and memories killed the desire: when, precisely, had they started moving along their separate ways? She hurriedly collected the remaining things and went to the kitchen. Perhaps it was the work that had taken him away. For as he became engrossed in the daily business of administration with his eyes on promotion, his vision seemed to fade and she had found it increasingly difficult to penetrate his inscrutable face till it became eventually painful to summon even a minimum of emotion and tenderness for him. During the Rira disaster she made excessive efforts to give him support and comfort. But where was the real sympathy she, as a wife, ought to have felt? She could not share in his agony. Instead, she had felt the shame of a child who sees a grown-up suddenly caught in the act of chasing a butterfly over fields and roads.

Margery never allowed one thought to dominate her for long. Now in the kitchen, washing dishes, she found herself reviving the warmth she had felt earlier in the day. How ridiculous, she told herself, recalling every detail of that brief encounter with Karanja. Perhaps it is because I am leaving Africa. No, maybe I'm growing old. They say the African heat does these things to women. She quietly laughed but abruptly stopped: was she really using this kitchen for the last time? Would she never, never see Githima again? Would her flowers mean anything to whoever would take her place in this house? Every corner of the house, the chairs, the table, the beds and even the walls, held a memory for her; in her wanderings from district to district all over Kenya, no other house, no other place was so intimately bound up with her. No other place had given her such a sense of release, of freedom, of power.

It was at Githima that she had met Dr Van Dyke and something in her, something she never knew she had, had been violently awakened. She felt weak, exhilaratingly weak, before the man. And yet how disgusting were his drinking habits, his excessively loud laughter. He was certainly a contrast to John, who was always correctly dressed, knew how to behave, and never allowed himself to get drunk. None the less, Margery was suffused with new energy; the secrecy, the daring, the anarchic joy of breaking a law, sharpened the excitement of their affair. The first night had been specially wonderful, a moment pregnant with fear and curiosity and wonder. She knew something would happen the second her husband excused himself from the dance. When Van had offered to take her home, she felt so grateful she could have squeezed his arm. In the car, parked in one of the many planted forests at Githima, she closed her eyes and his lips touched hers.

'Let's go to the back seat,' he breathed into her ear.

'Not today, Van, not today,' she whispered weakly.

'Today. Now,' he said almost pulling her clothes off as he climbed into the back seat.

She followed him obediently, hardly able to speak.

'Please let us be careful.' She found her voice, as she felt him.

'Yes, yes.'

'Be gentle—' she cried, and her words were interrupted by the

49

thrust of his body; she clung to him, fearing the car and the whole world would give way beneath her. The silence in the dark, the incessant buzz in the forest, added to the moment. After it, she wept, wondering how she could ever face her husband.

'Why are you crying?'

'My husband.'

'Hell!' He swore under his breath.

Theirs was never a happy affair. She became increasingly jealous. At parties she hated seeing him talk or laugh with other women. But she could not make a scene in public, or openly claim him. So their quarrels and fights occurred in private, in the precious moments, because stolen, when they ought to have been happy. One day, John Thompson went to a conference in Uganda. Dr Van Dyke came into the house and for the first time he talked to her about his work. He spoke soberly, without swearing, a streak of pride in his work.

'People don't realize what we are faced with in Kenya. You see, in a country like Britain, which is relatively flat, it is easy to determine the movements of, let's say, a low pressure area over the country. But in Kenya, where the high altitude tends to effect sudden and unexpected changes in the pressure areas, it is much more difficult to predict the weather.'

'But you must have compensations?'

'Oh, yes. With so many factors to be considered, it makes meteorology in places like Kenya or South Africa much more exciting . . .'

She entered a new world in which she saw there was more to what she had learnt at school about rain-gauges, wind-vanes, isobars, troughs of low pressure, air-masses. She knew he was born and educated in South Africa, that he had worked in Southern Rhodesia, that in each place he had felt himself haunted by things he could not understand; he kept on running away, so to speak, until he came to Githima, where only drink, so she had concluded, kept him reconciled to himself. But this was the first time he had spoken about his work. Gradually the talk drifted to their lives and she started probing into his affairs with other women. 'Hell! I am not your husband!' he shouted at her, and walked out in the middle of the night, leaving her on the sofa, lonely, miserable. 'I never want to see him again,' she told herself. The following day she sent a note to him, asking him to come back to her quickly.

Often she was in a mood of ruthless self-analysis. She would take a fresh look at her relationship with her husband. It could not be denied that John had a hold over her, that it was to him that she really belonged. Was this the sole meaning of marriage? At such moments, wading through the nightmare of guilt and self-hatred, she would feel tender towards him. The impulsive desire to confess, to clean her breast, was very strong. She hated Dr Van Dyke. But the more she hated him, the more she knew his power over her: she wanted his body, the wild plunge into darkness unknown, an orgy of revulsion, desperation and attraction. Jealousy and fear of what he was doing behind her back ate into her rest and peace.

And then, unexpectedly, the train claimed her lover: to her surprise, she felt neither sad nor anything; in fact, the first reaction was a vision of peace regained. Soon, however, she was restless, like a person who misses something without knowing, in particular, what he has lost. She started growing flowers (she had neglected this hobby during the affair) with a new vigour.

All these things streamed through her mind as she washed the dishes. The sadness melted into fatigue and impatience at her husband. They were on the brink of change, she reflected, and still he would not talk. Uhuru had brought their lives into a crisis and he behaved as if nothing was happening. Not that she knew exactly what she wanted him to say: but let a man and wife at least share their anxieties about everything: their past, the party tomorrow, their flight home on Wednesday.

Yes, she would compel him to talk, tonight, she resolved, and stopped wiping the dishes, walking back to the sitting-room with determination. John was peering into the mass of notebooks and papers before him, occasionally scribbling something with a hand that appeared to be shaking. She bent behind him, put her arm around his neck, and lightly touched the lobe of his left ear with her lips. She was surprised at herself, since she had not done this for years. Suddenly her grim determination to force their relationship into the open crisis subsided.

'Good night.'

'Good night.'

'And don't be late,' she called on her way to the bathroom and then to bed.

Thompson first came to East Africa during the Second World War, an officer, seconded to the King's African Rifles. He took an active part in the 1942 Madagascar campaigns. Otherwise most of his time was spent in Kenya doing various garrison and training duties. After the war he returned to his interrupted studies in Oxford. It was there, whilst reading history, that he found himself interested in the development of the British Empire. At first this was a historian's interest without personal involvement. But, drifting into the poems of Rudyard Kipling, he experienced a swift flicker, a flame awakened. He saw himself as a man with destiny, a man poised for great things in the future. He studied the work and life of Lord Lugard. And then a casual meeting with two African students crystallized his longings into a concrete conviction. They talked literature, history, and the war; they were all enthusiastic about the British Mission in the World. The two Africans, they came from a family of Chiefs in what was then Gold Coast, showed a real grasp of history and literature. This filled Thompson with wonder and admiration. His mind started working. Here were two Africans who in dress, in speech and in intellectual power were no different from the British. Where was the irrationality, inconsistency and superstition so characteristic of the African and Oriental races? They had been replaced by the three principles basic to the Western mind: i.e. the principle of Reason, of Order and of Measure. For days and weeks he thought about this with one recurring impression: the two Africans seemed proud of their British heritage and tradition. Thompson was excited, conscious of walking on the precipice of a great discovery: what, precisely, was the nature of that heritage? He woke up one night, elated, and saw his destiny dressed in the form of an idea.

'My heart was filled with joy,' he wrote later. 'In a flash I was convinced that the growth of the British Empire was the development of a great moral idea: it means, it must surely lead to the creation of one British nation, embracing peoples of all colours and creeds, based on the just proposition that all men were created equal.

'For me, a great light had shone in the darkness.'

Transform the British Empire into one nation: didn't this explain so many things, why, for instance, so many Africans had offered themselves up to die in the war against Hitler?

From the first, as soon as he set his hands on a pen to write down his thoughts, the title of the manuscript floated before him. He would call it: PROSPERO IN AFRICA. In it he argued that to be English was basically an attitude of mind: it was a way of looking at life, at human relationship, at the just ordering of human society. Was it not possible to reorientate people into this way of life by altering their social and cultural environment? *Prospero in Africa* was a result of an assiduous dive into English history, and the General History of Colonization from the Roman times to the present day. He was influenced by the French policy of Assimilation, but was critical of the French as he was of what he called 'Lugard's retrograde concept of Indirect Rule'.

'We must avoid the French mistake of assimilating only the educated few. The peasant in Asia and Africa must be included in this moral scheme for rehabilitation. In Great Britain we have had our peasant, and now our worker, and they are no less an integral part of our society.'

It was to Margery that he often revealed his ambitions. She was first attracted to him by the sadness and distance in his face. She admired his brilliance. His moral passion gave life a meaning. Once they went for a walk in London. They stood, for a time, at St James's Park, their eyes raised towards Westminster Abbey, the British House of Commons and beyond. Margery inclined her head on his shoulder as if she wished he would carry her with him to those lands he talked about. He did. A few years later, Mr and Mrs Thompson sailed for East Africa, to be at the centre of the drama in the Colonial administration.

'I am delighted,' he had written on arriving at Mombasa, 'to touch the red earth of Kenya. I was here during the war and I liked the climate. Then I never knew I would come back on a different mission.'

He always remembered those words. And even today, on the eve of his departure from East Africa, the touch of Margery's fingers had brought back a flicker of the faith that then imbued him. His faith in British Imperialism had once made him declare: To administer a people is to administer a soul. He was then talking with a group of officers at the New Stanley Hotel. After dinner, he had written the words in his diary – no, not a diary but a mass of notes he scribbled at various times and places in his career, hoping to incorporate them into a coherent philosophy in *Prospero in Africa*. These were the notes that were now in front of Thompson; he went through them, lingering over the entries that struck his mind.

> *Nyeri is full of mountains, hills and deep valleys covered with impenetrable forests. These primordial trees have always awed primitive minds. The darkness and mystery of the forest, have led him (the primitive man) to magic and ritual.*

> *What's this thing called Mau Mau?*

> *Dr Albert Schweitzer says 'The Negro is a child, and with children, nothing can be done without the use of authority.' I've now worked in Nyeri, Githima, Kisumu, Ngong. I agree.*

> *I am back in Nyeri. People are moving into villages to cut the connection between them and the terrorists. Burning houses in the old village, suddenly I felt my life was coming to a* cul-de-sac.

> *Colonel Robson, a Senior District Officer in Rung'ei, Kiambu, was savagely murdered. I am replacing him at Rung'ei. One must use a stick. No government can tolerate anarchy, no civilization can be built on this violence and savagery. Mau Mau is evil: a movement which if not checked will mean complete destruction of all the values on which our civilization has thriven.*

> *'Every whiteman is continually in danger of gradual moral ruin in this daily and hourly contest with the African.' Dr Albert Schweitzer.*

> *In dealing with the African you are often compelled to do the unexpected. A man came into my office yesterday. He told me about a wanted terrorist leader. From the beginning, I was convinced the man*

was lying, was really acting, perhaps to trap me or hide his own part in the movement. He seemed to be laughing at me. Remember the African is a born actor, that's why he finds it so easy to lie. Suddenly I spat into his face. I don't know why, but I did it.

Thompson woke to the present. He stared at the manuscript without seeing anything. Before Rira, his way to the top had been so clear, so open. Now at Githima he felt the irony of the words he had written, the irony accentuated by the fact that the Queen's husband would be the guest of honour at the Uhuru ceremony. His vision, vividly resurrected by his wife's touch, mocked him: what even if he had gone to the top, a DC, PC, or a Governor? All these would now go, like this house, the office, Githima, the country. Let silly fools like Dr Lynd stay. But eventually they would all be thrown out without ceremony. That is why Thompson had resigned, to get away before Uhuru. For why should people wait and go through the indignity of being ejected from their seats by their houseboys? And he remembered Dr Lynd and the story. His lie to Karanja. He wanted to talk to Margery. Tonight, anyway, because she had renewed her faith in him. Her softened eyes and voice would exorcize the hallucinations that plagued him. How we have grown old. He braced himself for the effort. His heart livened with hope and fear as he went into the bathroom to prepare himself for the great confession.

He opened the door to the bedroom cautiously and stepped in. He did not put on the lights, feeling that darkness would create the right atmosphere. A man was born to die continually and start afresh. His hands were shaking, slightly, and he felt darkness creep towards him, as he reached for the bed. But Margery was already asleep. Thompson saw this and felt enormous relief and gratitude. He got into bed but for a long time he could not sleep.

Six

God helps those who help themselves, it is said, with fingers pointing at a self-made man who has attained wealth and position, forgetting that thousands of others labour and starve, day in, day out, without ever improving their material lot. This moral so readily administered, seemed true for Gikonyo. People in Thabai said: Detention camps have taught him to rule himself.

Gikonyo was among the first group of detainees to pass through the pipe-line back to the village. (The pipe-line was the official euphemism for the chain of concentration camps all the detainees had to pass through.) When he returned his only companions were an old saw and a hammer. Fortunately he had come back during August and September harvests, when carpenters are in great demand to construct barns and stores for the maize and beans and potatoes. People in Thabai had known him before the Emergency. Now he worked harder and finished each barn on time. He got more orders. But if he promptly fulfilled his part of the contract, he expected no less from the other side. Thus he insisted on getting the money at the agreed day and time. He would not countenance a delay. He treated the poor and the rich alike. The only difference was that he could give a man who so requested a longer time in which to find the money. But on the date agreed, whether after one, two or three months, the money had to be ready. 'Detention has changed him,' they moaned. But they trusted and came to respect his scrupulous honesty. At least he did fulfil, on time, his own part of the bargain.

Instead of buying clothes for himself or his family, Gikonyo did what Indian traders used to do. He bought maize and beans cheaply during the harvests, put them in bags, and hoarded them in his mother's smoky hut. That's where he and Mumbi also lived. He argued: they (his wife and mother) have been naked and starved for the last six years. A few months of waiting won't make much difference. When the jobs-boom created by the harvest ended, Gikonyo did odd things here and there, waiting for an opportunity. At Thabai and villages around Rung'ei, most families finished their harvested food by January. Then there always followed one or two months of drought before the long rains started in March. Even then people had to wait for the crops to grow. That was the time Gikonyo gave up hack-work as a carpenter and entered the market. He went to the market very early in the morning, bought one or two bags of maize at a wholesale price from licenced, and at times black-market, maize suppliers from the Rift Valley. Later in the day his wife and mother would join him. Along with other market women, Mumbi and Wangari would sell the maize at a retail price using tiny calabashes for a measure. With the money obtained, Gikonyo would again haggle for another bag and the two women did the retail selling. The profit gained would be re-invested in the business on the next market-day. Sometimes Gikonyo would buy a bag of maize and then sell it there and then to another person at a higher price. He was never rude to customers. He talked with humble conviction and put himself at their service; always ready to apologize, he insisted on giving his customers prompt attention. This way, he coaxed in money. Women, especially, liked doing business with him. 'Such a tongue, and so honest too,' they said. So his fame spread through the market. All the time Gikonyo waited until the maize-grain was very scarce. The supply from the European farms in the Rift Valley was severely controlled. At the right time, he poured what he had hoarded on to the market at a high price.

It had been a life of struggle. At first other men derided him for doing a woman's job. Brushing sides with women's skirts. But when his fortunes changed, they started respecting him. Some even tried to follow his example with varying degrees of success.

The story of Gikonyo's rise to wealth, although on a small scale, carried a moral every mother in Thabai pointed out to her children.

'His wife and his aged mother need no longer go rub skirts with other women in the market. This is only so because their son was not afraid to make his hands dirty. He never slept to midday like a European.'

It's true that Gikonyo always rose early. He did not let the troubles of the heart or anything deflect him from the immediate purpose. On the morning following the visit to Mugo, for instance, he rose before the birds and went to Kiriita, beyond Uplands, where he bought vegetables which he would later transport to Nairobi. Supplying vegetables to Nairobi (Gikonyo had many orders there) was a lucrative job, especially if you oiled smooth with money your relationship with the traffic and market police who could always create trouble for African businessmen. Internal self-government had not changed preferential treatment for Europeans and Asians. Because Gikonyo could not drive, he had employed two men, a driver and a turn-boy, who looked after this side of his business. But Gikonyo kept a vigilant eye on everything. In any case, he liked to set the pace for his workers. At lunchtime, he held a meeting with the committee responsible for decorating the field where sports and dances would be held on Uhuru day.

In the afternoon he had an appointment with the MP for the area. About a month back, Gikonyo and five other men had decided to contribute and jointly buy a small farm belonging to Richard Burton. Burton was one of the earliest settlers, who, encouraged by the British Government to settle in Kenya after the railway line to Uganda was finished, came and got the land for a song. His children were born in Kenya, went to school there – the boys to the Prince of Wales School and the girls to Kenya High School (or as they called it, the *Heifer Boma*), and then went home to England for their university education. Most of them had stayed in England, but one son and a daughter had returned to Kenya. The son worked for one of the big oil companies in Nairobi. An old man, Burton really knew no other home than Kenya, and had never intended leaving the country (he never even went to Britain for leave or for health reasons) until he saw, beyond any doubt, that power was going to black hands. For, like many settlers and in spite of hints from their leader, Sir Michael Blundell, Burton had never believed that the British Government would abdicate. Now Burton wanted to sell the land he loved and in which he had put so much of his life and go home to Britain. Gikonyo had already contacted Burton and made preliminary arrangements. Because the five men could only raise half the amount (Burton wanted cash), Gikonyo had gone to see the MP to find out if he could recommend them, or use his influence behind the scenes, to get them a government-backed loan from a bank. The MP had gravely listened to their needs, noting down all the particulars about the farm, on paper. Then he had asked Gikonyo to return today. 'This is the real Harambee spirit. This is real self-help,' he told Gikonyo, shaking his hand firmly.

And Gikonyo was very hopeful as he hurried from the meeting to catch a bus for Nairobi. The bus, called A DILIGENT CHILD, belonged to one of those people in Rung'ei whose fortunes were made during the War of Independence. Those were men who through active co-operation with the colonial government had acquired trade licences and even loans to develop their business. Although Gikonyo was hopeful he was slightly bitter about having to go all the way to Nairobi. Few MPs had offices in their constituencies. As soon as they were elected, they ran to Nairobi and were rarely seen in their areas, except when they came back with other national leaders to address big political rallies. Before they reached Nairobi, the bus was stopped by two African policemen. One came in and counted the number of passengers, while the other one asked for the driver's licence. The bus had two passengers extra. The driver argued with the policemen. Then the cashier took the two policemen outside, and waved the driver to go on. The driver understood the sign. He drove a few yards and stopped. Soon the cashier came running, and got into the bus. 'They just wanted a few shillings for tea,' he said, and people in the bus laughed. A DILIGENT CHILD continued on its journey to the city. The Uhuru Highway (formerly Princess Elizabeth), was lined on either side with columns of the new black, green and red Kenya flags, and flags from other African countries. For a time Gikonyo forgot his mission to the city as his heart fluttered with the flags. He got out of the bus and walked down Kenyatta Avenue feeling for the moment as if the city really belonged to him. The statue of Lord Delamere that proudly dominated the Avenue (the Avenue previously bore his name) had been replaced by a fountain around which African men and women crowded, spilling into the grounds of the New Stanley Hotel, all pointing at, and talking about, the rotating jets of water. 'They are many penises spurting out water in competition,' Gikonyo heard a woman say. The others around her laughed. To Gikonyo, Nairobi seemed ready for Independence. He resolved that when he returned to Thabai he would try to inject new enthusiasm into decorating Rung'ei.

He crossed Government Road to Victoria Street and his business mind started to work again. He started wondering, he often did whenever crossing the two streets, why there was not a single African shop in the whole of the central and business area of Nairobi. In fact, Nairobi, unlike Kampala (at least, so Kariuki said) was never an African city. The Indians and Europeans controlled the commercial and the social life of the city. The African only came there to sweep the streets, drive the buses, shop and then go home to the outskirts before nightfall. Gikonyo had a vision of African businessmen like himself taking over all those premises!

A crowd of people waited outside the office of the MP because he was not in. But people were used to broken appointments and broken promises. Sometimes they would keep on coming, day after day, without seeing their representative.

'It is like trying to meet God,' one woman complained.

'Why, what do you want to ask him?'

'My son wants a scholarship to America. And you?'

'It's just troubles at home. Last Saturday, they came and arrested my man because he has not paid taxes. But how does he pay poll tax? He has no job. Our two children have had to leave school because no money . . .'

Some people had come for land problems, others for advice in their marriage problems, and yet others were a delegation to seek the support of the MP in applying for a secondary school in their ridge.

'Our children have nowhere to go after their primary schools,' one of the elders was explaining.

After an hour or so, the MP arrived; he was dressed in a dark suit and carried a leather portfolio. He smoked a pipe. He greeted all the people like a father or a headmaster his children. He went into the office without apologizing. People went in one by one.

Gikonyo's heart was beating with hope. If only they could get this loan! A vision of a new future unrolled before him. They would work the farm on a co-operative basis – keep grade cows, grow pyrethrum, tea, maize – everything. Later the co-operative might be broadened to take in more people. A new black brotherhood in business! At long last, his turn came. The MP seemed surprised to see him.

'Sit down, sit down, Mr Gikonyo,' he said generously pointing to a chair with his left hand while his right hand supported the pipe in his mouth. He took out a file from the drawer, opened it, and for a few minutes seemed really absorbed. Gikonyo waited in suspense. The MP raised his face from the file and leaned back against the chair. He removed the pipe from his mouth.

'Now, about these loans. They are difficult to get. But I am trying my best. Within a few days I may have good news for you. You see, these banks are still controlled by whites and Indians. But some are already realizing that they cannot do without *help* from us politicians. Gikonyo, my brother, they *need* us!'

'When can I come back?' Gikonyo asked, unable to hide his disappointment.

'Aah! Let us see. Today is . . .' He fumbled through his diary and then looked up at Gikonyo.

'Let us leave it like this: suppose I come to see you, or even write to you, when I've got results? You have a shop in Rung'ei, haven't you?'

'Yes.'

'That will save you a lot of trouble. Shall we leave it like that?'

'All right,' Gikonyo said as he rose to go. At the door, Gikonyo turned round.

'Do you think it possible to get the loan, or should we go ahead and find other means of getting the money?'

Gikonyo thought he detected alarm on the other's face.

'Oh, no, no,' he said, and stood up. He walked with measured steps to where Gikonyo was standing. 'There is no real difficulty about that. The loans are there. It is just a question of knowing the ways. I have told you: the whites cannot do without us! . . . just leave it with me. All right?'

'All right!' Gikonyo said, resolved to go and see Mr Burton tomorrow. If Mr Burton could accept half the money now, they could surely give him the rest when the loan came or else raise the money by some other means. Before Gikonyo had gone a few yards, he heard people whistling behind him. He turned his head and saw people beckon to him. The MP wanted him back. So he again ascended the steps into the office.

'It's about these Uhuru celebrations at Rung'ei. Please thank the branch and the elders for inviting me. But on that day all the Members of Parliament have been invited to various functions here in the *capital*. You see, we have so many foreign guests to look after. So apologize to the people for me and say I can't come.

'Uhuru!'

'Uhuru.'

Two days later, people were to talk about Mugo in the eight ridges around Thabai: they told with varying degrees of exaggeration how he organized the hunger-strike in Rira, an action which made Fenna Brokowi raise questions in the British House of Commons. His solitary habits and eccentric behaviour at meetings marked him as a chosen man. Remember also that the years in detention and suffering had enhanced rather than diminished his powerful build. He was tall with large dark eyes; the lines of his face were straight, clearly marked, almost carved in stone – one of those people who induce hope and trust on the evidence of their looks.

But neither on Sunday nor on Monday had Mugo any premonition that general worship was coming his way. In fact, the sudden proposal from the Party threw him off his balance. He woke up in the morning hoping that last night's experience was another dream. But the sight of the stools on which the delegates had sat dispelled such illusions. The words spoken passed through his head with a nightmarish urgency. Why did they want him to lead the Uhuru celebrations?

Why not Gikonyo, Warui, or one of the forest fighters? Why Mugo? Why? Why?

He thought of going to the shamba. No, he could not do any work. Besides he did not want to walk through the village. He did not want to meet Warui, Wambui, Githua or the old woman. A walk to Rung'ei would be better. It was another hot day; the sand burnt his bare feet; dust collected and stuck to his sweating toes. The heat accentuated the feverish excitement and confusion in his head. Yes . . . they want me . . . me . . . to make a speech . . . praise Kihika and . . . and all that . . . God . . . I have never made a speech . . . oh, yes! . . . I have . . . they said so . . . said it was a good one . . . Ha! ha! ha! . . . told them lies upon lies . . . they believed . . . Anybody . . . why me . . . me . . . me . . . want to trap me . . . Gikonyo – Kihika's brother-in-law . . . General R. . . . Lt Koina . . . Oh yes . . . a speech . . . speak . . . words . . .

Mugo had made only one real speech in his life. That was at a meeting which took place outside the Kabui shops near Thabai. The Movement convened the meeting to introduce returning detainees to the public. Mugo agreed to attend because, then, he had thought he could settle down to a normal life in the village: why draw attention to himself by refusing to attend? Many people from Thabai attended the meeting because, as you'll remember, we had only just been allowed to hold political meetings; other people came, hoping to be diverted with escape stories and other heroic deeds. The situation in Kenya was then like this: the state of emergency had officially ended (almost a year before) but Jomo Kenyatta and his five compatriots of the Kapenguria trial were still detained in prison. Also the many wounds which our people had suffered were too fresh for the eye to look at, or the hand to touch.

Party leaders from the district were the first to speak. They said Jomo Kenyatta had to be released to lead Kenya to Uhuru. People would not accept any other person for the Chief Minister. They asked everyone to vote for party candidates in the coming elections: a vote for the candidate was a vote for Kenyatta. A vote for Kenyatta was a vote for the Party. A vote for the Party was a vote for the Movement. A vote for the Movement was a vote for the People. Kenyatta was the People! The meeting had, however, really been called to introduce the men whose sacrifice and loyalty to the country had made these elections possible.

The rhetoric tone was seized by the detainees who rose to speak. They talked of suffering under the whiteman and illustrated this with episodes which revealed their deep love of Kenya. In between each speaker, people would sing: Kenya is the country of black people. These speeches were summed up by one detainee who said: 'What thing is greater than love for one's country? The love that I have for Kenya kept me alive and made me endure everything. Therefore it is true, Kenya is black people's country.'

It was at this stage in the proceedings that a few detainees who had heard of Mugo's case in Rira pushed him forward. Among these was Nyamu (later to be elected the secretary of the local branch of the Party) who had also been at Rira the week the eleven detainees were beaten to death. Mugo stood before the crowd. His voice, colourless, rusty, startled him. He spoke in a dry monotone, tired, almost as if telling of scenes he did not want to remember.

'They took us to the roads and to the quarries even those who had never done anything. They called us criminals. But not because we had stolen anything or killed anyone. We had only asked for the thing that belonged to us from the time of Agu and Agu. Day and night, they made us dig. We were stricken ill, we often slept with empty stomachs, and our clothes were just rags and tatters so that the rain and the wind and the sun knew our nakedness. In those days we did not stay alive because we thought our cause strong. It was not even because we loved the country. If that had been all, who would not have perished?

'We only thought of home.

'We longed for the day when we would see our women laugh, or even see our children fight and cry. When we thought that one day we would return home to see the faces and hear the voices of our mothers and our wives and our children we became strong. Yes. We became strong even in days when the cause for which blood was spilt seemed – seemed—'

At first Mugo enjoyed the distance he had established between himself and the voice. But soon the voice disgusted him. He wanted to shout: that is not it at all; I did not want to come back; I did not long to join my mother, or wife or child because I did not have any. Tell me, then, whom could I have loved? He stopped in the middle of a sentence and walked down the platform towards his hut.

After the meeting, Mugo took refuge in reticence. People went on with their daily work, reconstructing that which had been broken. Elections came. People voted the Party into power and resumed their toil. Mugo thought Thabai had forgotten him. But legends have thrived on less fertile ground. People in the meeting said the man was so moved he could not speak any more. And whenever Warui commented on this meeting he never forgot to say: 'Those were words from no ordinary heart.'

Mugo walked determinedly, as if intent on reaching his destination early. His mind would suddenly see his whole past in a flash – like when lightning cuts the night in two. His whole life would be compressed into the flash. Then he would single out events trying to skip over the ones that brought him pain. He remembered that meeting – then his mind reverted to last night's gathering. 'He shall judge the poor of the people, he shall save the children of the needy, and shall break down in pieces the oppressor.' The words thrilled him; a flicker once more danced within him. He stood, transfixed. Then, as suddenly, other thoughts rushed in and blew out the flicker. Unless they had suspected him could General R. have asked those pointed questions? Meeting somebody after a week? Karanja? Yes, could they really have asked him to carve his place in society by singing tributes to the man he had so treacherously betrayed?

Mugo was weighed down with these fears, hopes and doubts when in the evening Gikonyo said 'hodi' at the door and entered. For a time they stood, each embarrassed by the other's presence.

'Take a seat.' Mugo offered him a stool near the fire.

'I'm sure you did not expect me,' Gikonyo started awkwardly after he had sat down.

'It is nothing. I suppose you have come to hear my decision.'

'No. It is not that which brought me here tonight.' He told Mugo about his visit to Nairobi and his meeting with the MP.

Mugo, who sat on the bed opposite Gikonyo, waited for him to continue. The fire contained in the hearthplace by three stones glowed between them.

'But it is not that which brought me here. It is my troubles, troubles of the heart.' Gikonyo smiled and tried to sound casual. 'I was really coming to ask you a question,' he finished with a dramatic pause.

Mugo's heart sagged between fear and curiosity.

'Do you know that you and I were once in the same detention camp?' Gikonyo said, feeling his way into a talk.

'Were we? I can't remember.' Though slightly relieved, Mugo was still suspicious. 'There were so many people,' he added quickly.

'It was at Muhia camp. We knew you were to be brought there. We had, of course, heard about you in connection with the hunger-strike at Rira. The authorities did not tell us. It was supposed to be a secret, but we knew.'

Mugo vividly remembered Rira and Thompson, who beat him. Of Muhia, he could only recall the barbed-wire and the flat dry country. But then most camps were in such areas.

'Why do you tell me all this? I don't like to remember.'

'Do you ever forget?'

'I try to. The government says we should bury the past.'

'I can't forget . . . I will never forget,' Gikonyo cried.

'Did you suffer much?' Mugo asked with sympathy.

'No, I did not. I mean . . . Do you know I was never beaten, not once. Does that surprise you?'

'There were some who were not beaten, I know.'

'Were you?'

'Yes. Many times.'

'You were brave not to confess. We admired your courage, and hid our heads in shame.'

'There was nothing to confess.'

'We confessed. I would have done anything to come back home.'

'You had a wife. And a mother.'

'Yes. You understand.'

'No, I don't understand, I don't understand anything,' Mugo declared in a raised voice.

'Why did you speak like that, then?'

'When?'

'At that meeting! Remember? Many of us talked like that because we wanted to deceive ourselves. It lessens your shame. We talked of loyalty to the Movement and the love of our country. You know a time came when I did not care about Uhuru for the country any more. I just wanted to come home. And I would have sold Kenya to the whiteman to buy my own freedom. I admire people like Kihika. They are strong enough to die for the truth. I have no such strength. That's why in detention, we were proud of you, resented you and hated you – all in the same breath. You see, people like you, who refused to betray your beliefs, showed us what we ought to be like – but we lacked true bones in the flesh. We were cowards.'

'It was not cowardice. I would have done the same.'

'Why didn't you?'

'You want to know, do you?' Mugo said, forgetting himself. Then the temptation fleeted away.

'I had no home to come to,' he said quietly, without emotion. 'I suppose I did not want to come back.'

'No, it is not that,' Gikonyo said in a gale of genuine admiration. 'You have a great heart. It is people like you who ought to have been the first to taste the fruits of Independence. But now, whom do we see riding in long cars and changing them daily as if motor cars were clothes? It is those who did not take part in the Movement, the same who ran to the shelter of schools and universities and administration. And even some who were outright traitors and collaborators. There are some who only the other day were singing songs composed for them by the Blundells: Uhuru bado! or Let us carve Kenya into small pieces! At political meetings you hear them shout: Uhuru, Uhuru, we fought for. Fought where? They are mere uncircumcised boys. They knew suffering as a word. They should have listened to your speech that day. All of them. As you spoke, I felt you were reading my heart . . .'

'Was it hard waiting, for you?' Mugo spoke abstractedly as if he wanted to change the subject of conversation. Gikonyo needed only small encouragement.

'Yes. Because I thought I would never come back. You see with the experience of hardship in detention, I knew that if I could get out I could make something great out of my life with Mumbi.'

Gikonyo talked of a world where love and joy were possible. Why was he now troubled, then, Mugo wondered. He had all that a man needed to be happy: wealth, position, and relations who cared for him.

'You love your wife,' Mugo observed.

'I did!' Gikonyo said slowly and emphatically. The hut was silent. The fire still glowed between them. The oil-lamp went on fluttering.

'She was my life, all my life,' Gikonyo declared, staring fixedly at the hearth. 'Do you know,' he went on in the same quiet tone, 'do you know that when I finally came back, well for me everything had changed; the shambas, and the villages, and the people . . .'

'Mumbi?'

'She too had changed,' Gikonyo said, almost in a whisper. 'God, I sold my soul, for what? Where is the Mumbi I left behind?'

Seven

Then, as now, Thabai Ridge sloped gently from the high ground on the west into a small plain on which Rung'ei Trading Centre stood. The centre was a collection of tin-roofed buildings that faced on another in two straight rows. The space enclosed served as a market where women from various ridges congregated to sell and buy food and exchange gossip. Indian traders from Nairobi had also discovered this market, where they often came, haggled over prices with the women, let slip one or two dirty words which sent the women into fits of dirty laughter, and then took the vegetables and other wares to Nairobi where they disposed of them to the city people at a much higher price. Other Indians had settled in the area; a few minutes' walk from the African shops brought you to the Indian place, where buildings, also in two straight rows, were made of corrugated-iron sheets. These Indians also brought potatoes, peas, beans, and maize grain from Rung'ei Market during the harvest. But they stored them at the back of their shops, and later sold them during the hard times.

The African shops, though often roofed with rotting tin, had the unsurpassed virtue of having stone or brick walls. People claimed that Rung'ei was the first centre with such buildings in all Gikuyu country. Rung'ei had other virtues, too. The iron snake had first crawled along this plain before climbing up the escarpment on its way to Kisumu and Kampala; for a long time Thabai was the envy of many ridges not so graced with a railway line. Even people from ridges bordering the Masai land paid visits once in a while just to see the train coughing and vomiting smoke as it rattled along. Thabai was proud of Rung'ei. They felt the centre belonged to the ridge, that even the railway line and the train had a mystical union with Thabai; were they not the first to welcome the rail and the train into the heart of the country? Of the story, current to this day in other ridges, which told how men, women and children deserted Thabai for a whole week when the iron snake, foreseen by the Gikuyu seer, first appeared on the land, they kept discreet silence. They ran for refuge to the neighbouring ridges, so the story goes, and only trickled back, and that cautiously, after the warrior spies, armed with spears and simis, brought news that the snake was harmless, that the red strangers themselves were touching it.

Later, the railway platform became the meeting place for the young. They talked in groups at home, they went for walks in the country, some even went to church; but in their minds was always the train on Sunday. On Sunday afternoon, the passenger train to Kampala and the one to Mombasa met at Rung'ei station. People did not go there, as it might be thought, to meet friends arriving from Mombasa, Kisumu or Kampala – they just went there to meet one another, to talk, to gossip, to laugh.

Love-affairs were often hatched there; many marriages with their attendant cry of woe or joy had their origin at the station platform.

'Will you go to the train today?'

'Oh, yes.'

'Leave me not behind, friend.'

'Then you must be ready on time. It takes you a whole day just to put on your clothes.'

'That's a lie in clear daylight.'

Girls normally went to the river on Saturday to wash their clothes. Sunday morning was the time for pressing the clothes and also making their hair. By lunchtime, they were ready to walk or run to the station. Men had no such rituals. They were ready all the time, and in any case, most of them spent their time at the Rung'ei shops, only a short distance from the station.

The train became an obsession: if you missed it, sorrow seized your heart for the rest of the week; you longed for the next train. Then Sunday came, you went there on time, and immediately you were healed.

From the station they normally went to dance in Kinenie Forest overlooking the Rift Valley. Guitar players occupied a place of honour in this community; beautiful girls surrounded them and paid tribute with their eyes. Men bought dances. When a person bought a dance, the guitarist played for him alone, praising his name, always the son of a woman. The man danced to the rhythm alone or invited his friends to join him while others only watched. Nobody else could come in. The conventions governing the dances in the wood were well understood.

Often the dances ended in fights. Again this was well understood and men came prepared, at times courting danger with provocative words and insulting songs. The men organized themselves in groups according to the ridges of origin. Thabai was famous because men from there successfully fought other groups and took away their women. Girls loved men from Thabai, anyway, so that taking them captive was not exactly a difficult feat.

At the platform things were different. Nobody thought of starting a fight. There, the man who beat you the previous Sunday and took away your woman, was a friend. You talked and laughed together. But he knew later in the wood you would look for a chance to stab him and take away his woman.

'I rarely missed the train,' Gikonyo now remembered, years later, when this was only a myth. 'I loved to rub shoulders with the men and the women.'

'Yet the day I missed the train was the happiest in my life,' he told Mugo.

Then Gikonyo worked as a carpenter in Thabai. Though an immigrant to the ridge, he and his mother had been absorbed into the community and its daily rituals. He came to Thabai, a child strapped on the mother's back, from Elburgon area in the Rift Valley province where his father, Waruhiu, worked as a squatter on European farms. Being a hard-working man, it was not long before Waruhiu found himself the centre of attraction to many women. He got new brides and complained that the thighs of the first wife did not yield warmth any more. He beat her, hoping that this would drive her away. Wangari stuck on.

Eventually, Waruhiu ordered her to leave his home and cursed mother and son to a life of ever-wandering on God's earth. But Wangari did not wander for long; surely she could find welcome in Gikuyu land? 'Waruhiu thinks I will die because I am poor and have nothing to eat,' she one day said to herself sitting on a stone near Elburgon station. 'But there is no home with a boy-child where the head of a he-goat shall not be cooked,' she said, and holding the child to her breast she hurled an unspoken challenge to Waruhiu by boarding a train which took her to Thabai.

Wangari sent her son to school. But Gikonyo did not stay there for long because the woman had not enough money for fees. Fortunately at school he had learnt a little carpentry, and this he determined to use and make a living.

He loved carpentry.

Holding a plane, smoothing a piece of wood, all this sent a thrill of fear and wonder through the young man. The smell of wood fascinated him. Soon his senses developed sharp discrimination, so that he could tell any type of wood by a mere sniff. Not that the young carpenter made it appear so easy. In fact, Gikonyo used to act out a little ritual the performance of which varied depending on who was present. The drama went like this:

A woman has brought a piece of wood – she wants to know what type of wood it is. The carpenter takes it, gives it a casual glance, and then carelessly flings it onto a pile of other pieces. He continues with the job in progress. The woman stands there admiring the movement of his muscles. After a while, he lifts the piece of wood, its far end resting on the table. He shuts the left eye and peers at the wood with his half-open right eye. Then he closes his right eye and repeats the performance with the other eye. This finished, he knocks at it swiftly, rhythmically, with the knuckle of the right front finger as if he is exorcizing spirits from the wood. Next he takes the hammer; strike, listen, strike, listen. Then he sniffs the wood carefully (that is, professionally), and gives it back to the woman. He resumes the other job.

'What is the wood? It is podo—?' the woman ventures to ask, overwhelmed by the professional sniffs and pauses.

'Podo? Hmm. Bring it.' He sniffs at it again, slowly turns the wood round and round, nodding his head knowingly. Then he spends a few minutes explaining why the piece of wood is not podo.

'It's camphor. Have you ever heard of it? Grows mostly in the high ground in the Aberdares and around Mount Kenya. Very good timber. Why else do you think that the white people appropriated that land to themselves?' the carpenter pronounces with quiet wisdom.

The workshop was a small table set against the wall of Gikonyo's hut. Towards sunset, Wangari always came to the workshop, rummaged through the wood shavings, hoping to collect one or two unwanted pieces for the fire.

'Do you need this?' she asked, smiling.

'Oh, leave that, mother. You can never see a piece of wood without wanting to burn it. It costs money you know. But that is what a woman will never understand.'

'What about this?' Wangari was not easily daunted. She loved to hear the voice of the son admonishing her.

'All right. But don't come again.'

On the following day, at about the same time, she would be there. She picked a saw or a hammer and examined it carefully as if it was a mysterious object. Gikonyo would be forced to laugh.

'I believe you would have made a good carpenter, mother.'

'Whatever we say, these people are truly clever. How did they think of such tools which can cut anything?' Wangari always referred to white men as these people.

'Go and cook. These things are beyond women.'

'Do you need this piece here?'

'Oh, mother!'

Gikonyo's secret ambition was to own a piece of land where he could settle his mother. But this needed money. The ambition to acquire wealth increased whenever he saw or thought of Mumbi, a girl whose voice and face caused an anguished throb in him. But he thought his heart was beating in the wilderness. Surely Mumbi, the most beautiful girl on the ridge, would never deign to bring him a calabash filled with cool water and say: drink this for me. Nevertheless, he waited and groped his way slowly. He saw Mumbi moving in the country paths among the pea-flowers, and green beans and maize plants, and he braced himself to make his desires known. But courage failed him. He greeted her and passed on.

Mumbi's father, Mbugua, was a well-known elder in the ridge. His home consisted of three huts and two granaries where crops were stored after harvests. A bush – a dense mass of creepers, brambles, thorn trees, nettles and other stinging plants – formed a natural hedge around the home. Old Thabai, in fact, was a village of such grass-thatched huts thinly scattered along the ridge. The hedges were hardly ever trimmed; wild animals used to make their lairs there. Mbugua had earned his standing in the village through his own achievements as a warrior and a farmer. His name alone, so it is said, sent fear quivering among the enemy tribes. Those were the days before the whiteman ended tribal wars to bring in world wars. But Mbugua's reputation survived the peace. His word, in disputes brought to the council of elders for settlement, always carried weight. Wanjiku, his only wife, always called him her young warrior. She was a small woman, a striking contrast to her big-limbed warrior. Her voice was vibrant with warmth and kindness. It was her voice (she used to sing at dance gatherings in her day) that first captured Mbugua's heart. Of their two sons, Kihika and Kariuki, Wanjiku liked Kariuki mainly because he was younger and the last born. Mbugua secretly admired Kihika as the one most likely to take after him in courage and a well-regulated arrogance.

Kariuki also admired and looked up to Kihika. The boy longed for the time when he would join the ranks of men and be free to touch the sharp breasts of the initiated girls who often came to their house at night. Kariuki attended school at Manguo, one of the earliest Gikuyu Independent schools in the country. He loved books and in the evening read by the light from the wood fire. But how could he concentrate when all the young men and women of his brother's rika played and told wicked jokes and stories? He was not supposed to see or hear anything. 'You'll be thrown out of this house, you Kihii,' the men would warn him when they caught him laughing. Gikonyo often brought him sweets and things. For this, Kariuki liked the carpenter. Gikonyo used to tell funny stories which Kariuki really enjoyed. But as months and years went on, Gikonyo became increasingly quiet and rarely spoke if Mumbi was present. It was Karanja, in fact, who took the stage and always sent women into fits of ribald laughter. Karanja had a way of telling stories and episodes so that even without saying so he emerged the hero. As a result Kariuki had come to admire him for bravery, wisdom, and versatility.

Homes, like Mumbi's, with beautiful girls, were popular with young men and women. Wanjiku had to keep a regular supply of food. A home full of children is never lonely, she always said. When men arrived she excused herself and discreetly left the hut. 'Give them food,' she would tell Mumbi.

Mumbi often went to the station on Sundays. The rattling train always thrilled her. At times she longed to be the train itself. But she never went to the dances in the forest. She always came back home, after the train, and with one or two other girls, would cook, or undo and re-do their hair. Her dark eyes had a dreamy look that longed for something the village could not give. She lay in the sun and ardently yearned for a life in which love and heroism, suffering, and martyrdom were possible. She was young. She had fed on stories in which Gikuyu women braved the terrors of the forest to save people, of beautiful girls given to the gods as sacrifice before the rains. In the Old Testament she often saw herself as Esther: so she revelled in that moment when Esther finally answers King Ahasuerus' question and dramatically points at Haman, saying: The adversary and enemy is the wicked Haman.

She enjoyed the admiration she excited in men's eyes. When she laughed, she threw back her head and her neck would gleam in the firelight. At such a time, Gikonyo would not trust himself to speak. It was said that Richard, son of the Rev. Jackson, had proposed to Mumbi. Jackson was a leading clergyman in Kihingo. It was also rumoured that Richard, who was then in his last year at Siriana Secondary School, would later go to Uganda or England to complete his learning. Anyway, Mumbi declined the offer without hurting his pride so that they remained good friends. Richard often stole from home at night to go and see Mumbi at Thabai. So Gikonyo would ask himself: if she has refused such a man, what chance have I?

He threw himself into work. He made chairs for Thabai people; he repaired their broken cupboards; he fixed new doors and windows to their huts. A woman brought him a broken chair: she wanted a new leg fixed. He looked at it carefully, whistling a popular tune.

'Three shillings,' he said.

'What, three shillings, my son?'

'We cannot make it for nothing, you know.'

'My son. I am your mother. Let me give you a shilling.'

'All right,' he said, knowing that she probably would not pay him, even a shilling.

And the woman would go away knowing that he would eventually repair the chair (it might take him two months or more) and she would probably only pay him half the amount quoted. If she paid him at all, she would spread out the paying over a number of months.

'At this rate, I shall die poor,' he would complain to his mother.

'It's nothing,' Wangari often told him. 'You know if they had money, they would pay you.'

Feeling tired, he one day brought out his guitar and started to play. He had spent the morning and afternoon making furniture for a couple recently married. The man had promised to pay at the end of the month. Gikonyo liked his guitar. It was an old one, but he had paid quite a lot of money for it to the Indian trader.

He played softly, singing to himself, trying a new tune. Soon he was absorbed in his voice and playing, and the hardness began to leave his muscles. The sun was settling, the lengthened shadows of trees and houses were slowly merging.

Then the shavings rustled. Gikonyo started, and was a little embarrassed and excited at seeing Mumbi: she was working a piece of knitting tucked under her arm.

'Why did you stop?' she smiled.

'Oh, I didn't want you to hear my carpenter's voice and see my hands destroying both the song and the strings.'

'Is that why you never speak when you come to our place?' There was a malicious twinkle in her eyes.

'Don't I?'

'*You* should know . . . Anyway, I stood there all the time and heard you sing and play. It was good.'

'My voice or hands?'

'Both!'

'How do you know whether my playing is good or bad? You never come to the dances on Sunday.'

'Aah, true I never do. But do you think all other men are as mean as you? Karanja often plays to me alone at home. I sit. I knit my pullover, he plays. He is a good player.'

'He is a good player,' Gikonyo agreed curtly. Mumbi did not notice Gikonyo swallowing something in his throat. For at that time her mood had changed from playfulness to seriousness.

'But you also played – I never knew you could play so – and it was moving perhaps because you were playing to yourself,' she said with a frankness that pleased Gikonyo.

'Maybe sometimes I can play for you.'

'Play now, please play it to me,' she said eagerly. Gikonyo took this for a challenge, he feared strength would desert him.

'Then you must sing as I play. Your voice is so nice,' he said, and took the instrument.

But he found his hands were shaking. He strummed the strings a little, trying to steady himself. Mumbi waited for him to play the tune. As his confidence rose, Gikonyo felt Thabai come under his thumb. Mumbi's voice sent a shudder down his back. His fingers and heart were full. So he groped, slowly, surely, in the dark, towards Mumbi. He struck, he appealed, he knew his heart fed power to his fingers. He felt light, almost gay.

And Mumbi's voice trembled with passion as she weaved it round the vibrating strings. She felt the workshop, Thabai, earth, heaven, felt their unity. Then suddenly her heart was whipped up, she now rode on strange waves: alone defying the wind and the rain; alone fighting hunger and thirst in the desert; alone, struggling with strange demons in the forest, bringing glad tidings to her people.

The song ended. Gikonyo could almost touch the solid twilight calm.

'How is it the country is so quiet and peaceful now?' she asked.

'It is always so before darkness falls.'

'You know, I felt like Ruth gathering sheaves to herself in the field.'

'I believe you'll go to heaven. You always talk the Bible.'

'Don't mock,' she went on seriously. 'Do you think it will always be like this, I mean the land?'

'I don't know, Mumbi,' he answered, catching the solemnity from her. 'Haven't you heard the new song?'

'Which? Sing it.'

'You know it too. I believe it is Kihika who introduced it here. I only remember the words of the chorus:

'Gikuyu na Mumbi,
Gikuyu na Mumbi,
Gikuyu na Mumbi,
Nikihiu ngwatiro.'

It was Mumbi who now broke the solemnity. She was laughing quietly.

'What is it?'

'Oh, Carpenter, Carpenter. So you know why I came?'

'I don't!' he said, puzzled.

'But you sing to *me* and *Gikuyu* telling us *it* is burnt at the handle.'

At that point Wangari, who had gone to fetch water from the river appeared on the scene. She was pleased to see Mumbi.

'You should have born a girl instead of having a lazy male,' Mumbi teased her.

'It's my misfortune,' Wangari answered back, laughing. 'But it's nothing. The needs of an old woman are few. And that man is so lazy that he never wastes water in washing himself or his clothes.'

'You are unfair to me, mother. You'll make all the girls run away from me.'

'Shall I make you a cup of tea?'

'No,' Mumbi said quickly. 'I must be home before darkness falls.'

She turned to a small basket she was carrying and took out a panga.

'You see this panga needs a wooden handle. The old one was burnt in the fire by mistake. My mother wants it quickly because it is the only one she has got for cultivating.'

Gikonyo took the panga and examined it critically.

'How much?' Mumbi asked.

'Don't break your heart over that. This is nothing.'

'But you cannot work for nothing?'

'I am not an Indian shopkeeper,' he said irritably.

Karanja, Kihika and Gitogo and one other man came. Gikonyo's workshop was another place where young men used to gather for gossip. Karanja called out to Wangari.

'Mother of men, we have come. Make us tea.'

'Wait a little,' Wangari's voice reached them from the hut. 'Water is already on the fire.'

Mumbi, who was chatting with Gitogo, using hand signs, said she was going home. The men protested in chorus. But she insisted on getting away.

'All right. I will see you off,' Karanja offered gallantly.

'Come, my faithful,' Mumbi sang out to him. Soon Karanja and Mumbi were lost in the gathering darkness.

'Let us go into the hut,' Gikonyo told the others, his voice unusually low. He was envious of Karanja's ease and general assurance in the presence of women. Even the thought that Karanja played his guitar to Mumbi gnawed at him unpleasantly.

When Karanja returned, everyone noticed that he was quiet and thoughtful.

'Heh, man,' the man sitting next to him teased him, 'have you fallen in love with that girl?'

Everybody, except Gikonyo, laughed. Even Karanja grinned.

Early the next day Gikonyo started work on the handle. Low waves of excitement left his heart in a glow as he chose a piece of wood on which to work. The touch of wood always made him want to create something. But now he felt as if his life depended on giving himself wholly to the present job. His hands were firm. He drove the plane (he had recently bought it) against the rough surface, peeling off rolls and rolls of shavings. Gikonyo saw Mumbi's gait, her very gestures, in the feel and movement of the plane. Her voice was in the air as he bent down and traced the shape of the panga on the wood. Her breath gave him power.

And now he exerted that power on the podo-wood. He chiselled and scooped out the unwanted parts to make two pieces of the right shape. He took particular pains over boring the holes. Worms of wood wriggled along the cyclic grooves of the drill-bit and heaved themselves on to the table. The holes were ready. Next he cut three nails with which he riveted the two pieces of wood to the panga. As he hammered the thin ends of the nails into caps, another wave of power swept through him. New strength entered his right hand. He brought the hammer down, up, and brought the hammer down. He felt free. Everything, Thabai, the whole world was under the control of his hand. Suddenly the wave of power broke into an ecstasy, an exultation. Peace settled in his heart. He felt a holy calm; he was in love with all the earth.

He thought of taking the panga on Sunday morning. Came the time and doubts began to stab his complacency. He found faults; the smoothness and the fitting had fallen short of the vision in his mind. The handle appeared ordinary, the sort of thing that any carpenter could make. And the wood? It would surely blister a woman's hands within a few minutes of use. He changed into a defiant mood. What did it matter if Mumbi liked it or not? If she did not like the clumsy offering, she ought to do the carpenter's work herself or ask Karanja to help her. In any case she might not be at home. Yes. He would love to find her absent. But as he came to the narrow path leading into the yard through the hedge, he began fearing that she might not be at home; his work would not be complete without her participation.

He found her sitting on a four-legged stool outside her mother's hut. Gikonyo affected a nonchalant air.

'Is your mother in?' he asked casually, his hands itching to show the panga to Mumbi.

'What do you want with mother? Don't you know that she has got a husband?' Her eyes were laughing at him. Gikonyo would not respond to her smile. He became more solemn, with difficulty.

'Sit down,' she said, rising to give him her seat. Then she saw the panga. She rushed forward and took it from his hands. For a moment she stood there, admiring the new handle. Suddenly she pranced towards the hut shouting, 'Mother! Mother! come and see!'

Sweet warmth swelled up in Gikonyo. Joy pained him. His work was done. For Mumbi's smile, for that look of appreciation, he would go on making chairs, tables, cupboards; restore leaking roofs and falling houses; repair doors and windows in all Thabai without a cent in return. He would never make money, he would remain poor, but he would have her.

He was still standing, revelling in the vague resolutions, when Mumbi came out with another chair and again invited him to sit.

'I am in a great hurry,' he protested without conviction.

'Are you going to a wedding?'

'No, not unless yours!' he laughed, but remembering Karanja, he stopped and sat down without another word.

'Why all the hurry? We are not going to eat you,' she said, vainly attempting to summon anger to her voice, which pleased Gikonyo.

He watched Mumbi make her hair: how he longed to touch it, and at the thought blood rushed to his finger-tips. A small mirror was propped between Mumbi's knees; her hands, bent at the elbows, met over her head and the fingers played with the hair. Occasionally she gave Gikonyo a quick under-glance and a smile. Gikonyo drank all in.

Then Kihika and Karanja arrived at the scene, and Gikonyo hated them for challenging his monopoly over Mumbi's attentions: why did they have to appear at that moment? Resigning himself to the inevitable, Gikonyo joined in the talk which unerringly led to politics and the gathering storm in the land.

Kihika's interest in politics began when he was a small boy and sat under the feet of Warui listening to stories of how the land was taken from black people. That was before the Second World War, that is, before Africans were conscripted to fight with Britain against Hitler in a war that was never their own. Warui needed only a listener: he recounted the deeds of Waiyaki and other warriors, who, by 1900 had been killed in the struggle to drive out the whiteman from the land; of Young Harry and the fate that befell the 1923 Procession; of Muthirigu and the mission schools that forbade circumcision in order to eat, like insects, both the roots and the stem of the Gikuyu society. Unknown to those around him, Kihika's heart hardened towards 'these people', long before he had even encountered a white face. Soldiers came back from the war and told stories of what they had seen in Burma, Egypt, Palestine and India; wasn't Mahatma Gandhi, the saint, leading the Indian people against British rule? Kihika fed on these stories: his imagination and daily observation told him the rest; from early on, he had visions of himself, a saint, leading Kenyan people to freedom and power.

Kihika was first sent to Mahiga, a Church of Scotland school not far from Thabai, on the advice of the Rev. Jackson Kigondu. Jackson, as he was popularly called, was a friend of Mbugua, who liked visiting people's houses and in the course of an evening talk, would slip in a word or two about Christ. Whenever he came to Thabai, he would call on Mbugua, and preach to him about the Christian faith. 'Ngai, the Gikuyu God, is the same One God who sent Christ, the Son, to come and lead the way from darkness into the light,' Jackson would reason out, trying to show that the Christian faith had roots in the very traditions revered by the Gikuyu. Mbugua would listen carefully, then he would go into a corner, bring out a calabash-pot of beer and offer it to Jackson.

'And now that we have talked,' he would say, 'let us settle into old men's water to quench our thirst.'

Laughing at this temptation, Jackson would go out, resolved to come back again and continue the unfinished game of words and actions. He was small and thin with a tight-skinned face and hollow eyes that seemed to carry years of wisdom. He always wore a pastor's collar and a hat that covered his shining bald head. Jackson was a respected elder among the ridges that surrounded Rung'ei; often the village council of elders invited him to participate in important issues affecting the ridges. They saw him as an elder among elders and he too carried himself as one.

'Reverend here will read the word from his book and tell us what he thinks about this,' an elder would say. All this went on for many years before the revivalist movement reached Kenya and swept through the ridges like a fire of vengeance. The movement was of those Christians, irrespective of denomination, who had seen the light. By publicly confessing their sins, they became the saved ones. It is said that this evangelical movement (its remnants survive in the villages to this day) was started by a white missionary in Ruanda and quickly spread to Uganda and Kenya. A few months after the State of Emergency was declared, Jackson suddenly became converted to this movement. He stood in front of the congregation at Mahiga and like a man possessed, trembled and beat his breast, saying: 'I had called myself a Christian. I had put a white collar around my neck and thought this would save me from the fire to come. Vanity of vanities, saith the preacher, vanity of vanities. All was vanity. For my heart harboured anger, pride, jealousy, theft and adulterous thoughts. My company was with drunkards and adulterers. I walked in the darkness and waded through the mud of sins. I had not seen Jesus. I had not found the light. Then, on the night of the 12 January 1953, I was suddenly struck by the thunderbolt of the Lord, and I cried: Lord, what shall I do to be saved? And he took my hands and thrust them into his side and I saw the print of the nails in his hands. And I cried again: Lord, wash me in thy blood. And he said: Jackson, follow me.' Then he confessed how he used to minister unto the devil: by eating, drinking and laughing with sinners; by being too soft with the village elders and those who had rejected Christ; by not letting Christ's blood water the seed so that it could take root. He was now a Christian soldier, marching as to war, politics was dirty, worldly wealth a sin.

'My home is heaven: here on earth I am a pilgrim.'

Brothers and sisters in the Lord rose and started singing and jumping about in the church: others went to the front and embraced Jackson and kissed him a holy kiss. Jackson tore the collar and his hat – a sign of humility and a heart broken to pieces by the Lord. The revivalist movement was the only organization allowed to flourish in Kenya by the government during the Emergency. Jackson became the leader in the Rung'ei area.

He was among the first group of Christians to be killed in Rung'ei.

His body was one morning found hacked with pangas into small pieces: his house and property were burnt to charcoal and ashes. His wife and younger children were not touched. But they were left without a home! Richard was then away in England. News of Jackson's death spread into people's hearts in Thabai and the surrounding ridges.

Which other traitors would be struck down next by the Mau Mau, people wondered, remembering Teacher Muniu (another revivalist, also reputed to be a police informer) who had been killed in a similar method only a few days before? The revivalists praised God and said that Jackson and Muniu, by their deaths, had only followed in the footsteps of the Lord. What greater honours could befall a Christian? But the people prayed a different prayer: yes, let all the traitors be wiped out!

Few would have foreseen this turmoil in the days when Kihika was going to school and discovering the world of the printed word. The boy was moved by the story of Moses and the children of Israel, which he had learnt during Sunday school – an integral part of their education – conducted at the church by the headmaster. As soon as he learnt how to read, Kihika bought a Bible and read the story of Moses over and over again, later recounting it to Mumbi and any other person who would listen.

Kihika left Mahiga school a little disgraced. It happened like this. During a session one Sunday morning, Teacher Muniu talked of the circumcision of women and called it a heathen custom.

'As Christians we are forbidden to carry on such practices.'

'Excuse me, sir!'

'Yes, Kihika.'

The boy stood up, trembling with fear. Even in those days Kihika loved drawing attention on himself by saying and doing things that he knew other boys and girls dared not say or do. In this case it was his immense arrogance that helped him to survive the silence and blurt out:

'That is not true, sir.'

'What!'

Even Teacher Muniu seemed scared by the sudden silence. Some of the boys hid their faces, excited yet fearing that the wrath of the teacher might reach them.

'It is just the white people say so. The Bible does not talk about circumcising women.'

'Sit down, Kihika.'

Kihika fell into his seat. He held on to the desk, and regretted his impulsive outburst. Teacher Muniu took a Bible and without thinking asked the pupils to look up 1 Corinthians, 7, verse 18, where St Paul discussed circumcision. Muniu triumphantly started reading it loudly, and only after a couple of sentences did he realize the mistake he had made. Not only was there no mention of women, but circumcision of the flesh was not even specifically condemned. He closed the Bible, too late. For Kihika knew he had won the contest and could not help trying to seek approval from the eyes of the other boys, who secretly rejoiced to see a teacher humiliated by one of themselves. Muniu rather awkwardly explained the verses away and then dismissed the children. Kihika was the centre of attention, a little hero, as the boys argued and commented, and puzzled out what the teacher would do next. On Monday, Teacher Muniu said nothing. On Tuesday morning he assembled the whole school (pupils and staff) in the church building. In a voice trembling with emotion, he warned them to be aware of blasphemy against the sacred word.

'For who are we to say that the word from God's own mouth is a lie?' his deep voice boomed across the building.

However, after discussing Sunday's incident with the church elders, he had decided to give the boy a chance to save his soul. The teacher had therefore decided to whip the boy ten times on his naked buttocks in front of the whole assembly – this for the sake of the boy's own soul and of all the others present. After the beating, Kihika would have to say thank you to the teacher and also recant his words of last Sunday. The church was absolutely still. One or two coughs only increased the tension. Muniu turned to a fellow teacher and asked him to get the two sticks that lay prominently on the altar.

'Kihika, stand up.' Until that moment, the teacher had not mentioned Kihika by name, he had talked of a certain pupil. Now many boys including those who had proudly identified themselves with Kihika in his moment of triumph on Sunday, looked at him with hostile eyes that disassociated themselves from his guilt.

'Come forward!'

Kihika's feet stuck to the ground. His inside was hollow as if all the contents had been removed. Even before he had started to move, others had cleared a path for him.

'I said, come forward.'

He made as if to move. His eyes rolled to the roof, to the teacher, the sticks, the altar.

'You will hit me only after you have told me exactly the wrongs that I have done!' Kihika said, trembling with anger. Muniu lurched towards him. Suddenly Kihika clambered on to the desk, jumped to another, and before people knew what was happening, had reached the nearest window and climbed out of the church to freedom. He never stopped running until he reached home, where he fell down crying with fear.

'I would rather work on the land,' he told his father, who had suggested another school.

For a long time the incident boiled in his mind. He read more; he even taught himself how to read and write Swahili and English. Years later, soon after the end of the war, he went to work in Nairobi, attended political meetings and discovered the Movement. He had found a new vision.

'You ask what is needed,' Kihika was now saying. 'I will tell you. Our people have talked for too long.'

'What can we do?' asked Karanja whose eyes kept on moving from Kihika to Mumbi. 'They have got the guns and the bombs. See how they whipped Hitler. Russia is the only country now that makes the British tremble.'

'It's a question of Unity,' Kihika explained excitedly. 'The example of India is there before our noses. The British were there for hundreds and hundreds of years. They ate India's wealth. They drank India's blood. They never listened to the political talk-talk of a few men. What happened? There came this man Gandhi. Mark you, Gandhi knows his whitemen well. He goes round and organizes the Indian masses into a weapon stronger than the bomb. They say with one voice: we want back our freedom. The British laughed; they are good at laughing. But they had to swallow back their laughter when things turned out serious. What did the tyrants do? They sent Gandhi to prison, not once, but many times. The stone walls of prison could not hold him. Thousands were gaoled; thousands more were killed. Men and women and children threw themselves in front of moving trains and were run over. Blood flowed like water in that country. The bomb could not kill blood, red blood of people, crying out to be free. God! How many times must fatherless children howl, widowed women cry on this earth before this tyrant shall learn?'

His words and his slightly broken voice told on those present. Their effect was captured in the silence that followed. Mumbi was always moved by her brother's words into visions of a heroic past in other lands marked by acts of sacrificial martyrdom; a ritual mist surrounded those far-away lands and years, a vague richness that excited and appealed to her. She could not visualize anything heroic in men and women being run over by trains. The thought of such murky scenes revolted her. Her idea of glory was something nearer the agony of Christ at the Garden of Gethsemane.

'I would hate to see a train run over my mother or father, or brothers. Oh, what would I do?' she quickly exclaimed.

'Women are cowards,' Karanja said half in joke.

'Would you like a train to run over you?' Mumbi retorted angrily. Karanja felt the anger and did not answer.

'Take up my cross, is what Christ told his people,' Kihika resumed in a more lighthearted tone. 'If any man will come after me, let him deny himself, and take up his cross, and follow me. For whosoever will save his life shall lose it: and whosoever will lose his life for my sake shall find it. Do you know why Gandhi succeeded? Because he made his people give up their fathers and mothers and serve their one Mother – India. With us, Kenya is our mother.'

Gikonyo was touched more by the voice of Kihika and the glint in his eyes than by the argument which he did not follow anyway.

'I would faint at the sight of blood,' Mumbi commented.

'What we want in Kenya are men and women who will not run away before the sword,' Kihika told her.

'How do we unite the people?' Gikonyo said, just to contribute to the discussion.

Wanjiku came to the door and announced that tea was ready. They said they wanted it outside in the sun. Soon, two girls from Thabai joined them.

'Have you become Europeans, taking tea outside in the wind?' Wambuku asked.

'Yes, yes, true Europeans but for the black skin,' Karanja replied, imitating a drawling European voice. Everybody laughed.

'You do it well,' Njeri said.

Wambuku and Njeri were Mumbi's friends and often teased her about Karanja's love for her.

At the sight of Wambuku, Kihika's face brightened. Kihika nearly always partnered Wambuku at dances and generally liked talking to her. The two girls joined in the tea-drinking. Karanja's eyes rarely left Mumbi. Gikonyo watched to see if Mumbi would give Karanja a smile similar to the one she had bestowed on him. Njeri's eyes turned to Kihika who was sharing a joke with Wambuku. Left in the cold, Njeri tried to amuse herself by watching the rivalry between Karanja and Gikonyo. The carpenter attempted to engage her in a talk but his heart was not in the words. Mumbi, whose hair was now done, left them and went inside the hut to change into her Sunday clothes. Njeri walked away lazily and climbed onto a small hill near the hedge. Suddenly she started shouting: 'The train! the train!'

She ran down the hill: 'We are late for the train.'

The others too could hear the rumbling noise. Wambuku stood up, and taking Kihika's right hand, jerked him up. She let go his hand and started running down the path, through the hedge, towards the station. Kihika followed her. He was a small man with a rather sad face. Mumbi! Mumbi! the train! Njeri was shouting as she swooped on the kerchief she had left on the chair and followed the other two. Karanja and Gikonyo hesitated a little as if each expected the other to take the lead. Both had stood up at Njeri's first mention of the train and now glanced, in comic unison, at the hut and then at the running figures. Mumbi came out adjusting a belt around her small waist. Wanjiku's voice reached her: Here, you have left your handkerchief. She dived back into the hut. Karanja and Gikonyo still waited, pretending they were on the run.

'Let us go,' Mumbi called, already ahead of them by many yards. Gikonyo followed her, Karanja held the rear. The Kisumu train could be heard urging them: run and run, run and run. The path from

Mumbi's home to the station passed through a small forest at the far end. Njeri was approaching the wood. Wambuku and Kihika were already hidden from view.

Slightly the taller, Karanja soon outdistanced Gikonyo. The carpenter summoned his strength in the race for Mumbi. Karanja overtook Mumbi and strode ahead; already he could see leaves of victory on his head. Gikonyo's heart sank with fear of humiliation as he too overtook Mumbi; he panted hard, realizing, bitterly, that he would not catch up with Karanja, who had already disappeared into the wood.

Mumbi stopped running; she called out to Gikonyo who slowed down and waited for her.

'I am tired,' she said.

'Why do you stop? We shall miss the train.'

'Is it so important to you? Would you die if you didn't see it today?'

Gikonyo was surprised: why was she angry with him?

'I don't want to go there today,' she continued, more gently.

They walked side by side. Gikonyo smarted under the defeat in the race to the station. But as they came to the wood, the resentment melted away when it suddenly occurred to him that he was alone with Mumbi, the real object of the race. He groped for words, hoping, at the same time, the girl would not hear the loud beat of his heart. Mumbi, leaned against a tree trunk and Gikonyo saw that laughter had come back into her eyes. The wood made a cool shelter from the sun. The grass and the thick underfoliages teeming with flowers had grown higher, tree-tops and branches seemed to have dropped closer to the ground. Mumbi said:

'You must have put a lot of hard work into fixing the handle to that panga. It was light and smooth; my mother was so pleased.'

'It's nothing.'

'Nothing?'

'I mean it was a small piece of work and I liked doing it.'

'And you say it is nothing?' she laughed quietly. Her cheeks were full; her voice stabbed into his flesh pleasantly.

'I am sure,' she went on, 'it must be wonderful to be a carpenter, to work in wood. Out of broken pieces of timber, you make something.'

'You knit pullovers, too.'

'It is not the same. I once watched you in your workshop and it seemed – it just seemed to me you were talking with the tools.'

'Let us explore the wood,' Gikonyo suggested in a voice vibrant with subdued emotion. They came to an open place at the centre of the forest. Green Kigombe grass reached up to their knees. He stood facing Mumbi and surrendered himself to a power he knew drew them together. He held her hands and his fingers were full, so sensitive.

'Mumbi, —' he tried to say something as he held her to himself. She lay against his breast, their heart-beat each to each. It was all quiet. Mumbi was trembling, and this sent a quiver of fear and joy trilling in his blood. Gradually, he pulled her to the ground, the long grass covered them. Mumbi breathed hard, but could not, dare not, speak. One by one, Gikonyo removed her clothes as if performing a dark ritual in the wood. Now her body gleamed in the sun. Her eyes were soft and wild and submissive and defiant. Gikonyo passed his hands through her hair and over her breasts, slowly coaxing and smoothing stiffness from her body, until she lay limp in his hands. Suddenly, Gikonyo found himself suspended in a void, he was near breaking point and as he swooned into the dark depth he heard a moan escape Mumbi's parted lips. She held him tight to herself. Their breath was now one. The earth moved beneath their one body into a stillness.

At the station, Karanja found the crowd and the train dull. He was tired, his stomach was empty. The exciting possibilities he had felt alive when Mumbi was present had fallen from the air. In vain, his eyes searched for Mumbi in the restless crowd.

The women, as usual, were more colourfully dressed than men, in fashions that differed from ridge to ridge. Those from Ndeiya and ridges miles away from Rung'ei had bright blue, green or yellow calicoes passed under their armpits and ending in complicated flower-shaped knots over the right shoulder. Thin wool or cotton belts hung loosely from their fat waists. The long belt-tails flapped and rippled behind as the women walked along the platform, parading themselves before the men. Most of the girls from Thabai, Kihingo or Ngeca had cotton printed frocks in styles two or three years behind the current fashion in Nairobi.

Not so the men.

Some came in baggy trousers and jackets bought second-hand at the Indian or African shops in Rung'ei. The knees, small black heads, popped through the holes in the trousers as the men walked along the platform, flinging their legs carelessly but firmly, each step an unnecessary emphasis of their manhood.

Karanja stood apart from this moving throng. Jealousy crept into him, a surprise because he had always refused to consider Gikonyo a serious rival: how could the carpenter, without wit or any suavity, even dare? But now he knew that Gikonyo and Mumbi were together, alone, somewhere. He was angry at the knowledge. How could Mumbi make him pant and sweat in the sun, all for nothing? How could she make him trot ahead, like a child, so that she might remain behind with Gikonyo? He thought of rushing back, seek her out, humiliate her, force her to her knees in public, till she cried to him to save her. The impulse to effect this was so strong that he started walking away from the platform even as the thought was forming. Then he stopped, stood, debated whether he ought to run or not, as if the manner of his retreat from the platform would determine the degree of success in his self-appointed mission. What if he should find her in Gikonyo's arms? He traced the carpenter's rough hands on Mumbi's body beginning from the breasts down to the navel and— No! He dare not, must not contemplate it; he swore, torturing his mind with more sordid images. No, not the carpenter, he shuddered, calling upon the Lord. Else let heaven fall, the earth tremble, people tumble, break their hips and moan (oh, the terrible moaning) down to the gaping vaults to suffering and death.

The violence of his own reactions surprised him and he tried to control the shuddering, reasoning that he had never, in any case, told Mumbi his love. And nothing perhaps had passed between Gikonyo and Mumbi. This reflection comforted him. He clung to it, elaborated it and supported it with numerous reasons. He even attempted to laugh to drive out the unease hovering at the edges of his new-found calm.

He moved to join a group of men a few yards away. He had made up his mind to act quickly and open his heart to Mumbi. The men crowded around Kihika and with animated faces listened to him speak. Further down the platform other men and women were strolling or standing in groups of varying sizes: the sight of men and women laughing together made Karanja miss Mumbi terribly.

Suddenly the whistle shrilled, the train pulled out of the station, and Karanja, who was watching it intently, had a strange experience. First the whistle shrilled and the coaches clinked into his flesh. (This sensation in fact tickled through him long after the train had gone.) Then he was standing on the edge of the platform and staring into a white blank abyss. He saw this clearly, he could swear afterwards. The rails, the people at the platform, the Rung'ei shops, the whole country went in circles, faster and faster, before his eyes and then abruptly stopped. People stopped talking. Nothing moved or made noise. Karanja was frightened by this absolute cessation of all motion and noise and he looked about him to confirm the truth of what he saw. But nothing had stopped. Everybody was running away as if each person feared the ground beneath his feet would collapse. They ran in every direction; men trampled on women; mothers forgot their children; the lame and the weak were abandoned on the platform. Each man was alone, with God. It was the clarity of the entire vision that shook him. Karanja braced himself for the struggle, the fight to live. I must clear out of this place, he told himself, without moving. The earth was going round again. I must run, he thought, it cannot be helped, why should I fear to trample on the children, the lame and the weak when others are doing it?

A man standing next to him quickly put his arms around Karanja preventing him from falling on the hard surface.

'What is wrong, man? You drunk?'

'I – I don't know,' Karanja said, rubbing his eyes like a man from sleep. Everything on the platform was normal. The train was just disappearing at the far corner. 'It's my head,' he explained to the man who had helped him. 'It was going round and round.'

'It's the sun. It makes people feel dizzy. Why don't you sit under a shade and rest?'

'I am all right,' Karanja laughed uneasily and walked away to join the group around Kihika. Few had witnessed the little drama. Karanja found Kihika explaining something about Christ.

'No struggle for Wiyathi can succeed without such a man. Take the case of India, Mahatma Gandhi won freedom for people and paid for it with his own blood.'

Karanja, slightly shaken by his recent vision, suddenly felt irritated with Kihika.

'You say one thing now. The next hour you say another,' he said, addressing Kihika. 'This morning you said Jesus had failed. And now you say we need Christ. Are you becoming a revivalist?'

Karanja's contemptuous tone of unbelief and slightly derisive laughter hurt Kihika. He hesitated a little, not knowing how to react to this public challenge from a friend. People came closer and nodded their heads to see if Kihika had really been silenced. Kihika controlled his anger with difficulty and went on:

'Yes – I said he had failed because his death did not change anything, it did not make his people find a centre in the cross. All oppressed people have a cross to bear. The Jews refused to carry it and were scattered like dust all over the earth. Had Christ's death a meaning for the Children of Israel? In Kenya we want deaths which will change things, that is to say, we want true sacrifice. But first we have to be ready to carry the cross. I die for you, you die for me, we become a sacrifice for one another. So I can say that you, Karanja, are Christ. I am Christ. Everybody who takes the Oath of Unity to change things in Kenya is a Christ. Christ then is not one person. All those who take up the cross of liberating Kenya are the true Christs for us Kenyan people.'

Njeri and Wambuku, with a few other girls, came and joined the group. The political talk ended, most of the young men impressed with Kihika's mind. The intensity on their faces broke as they smiled and laughed with the girls.

Karanja and Kihika, however, remained abstracted, for different reasons, and without either of them planning it, mutually avoided one another. They remained quiet all the way to the dance in the wood.

It was quiet and cool in Kinenie Forest. Again the men and women fell into groups and laughed and buzzed, animating the wood. Somebody thrust a guitar into Karanja's hands. 'Play,' the girls shouted. When he played his own guitar, Karanja always felt the strings' immediate response to the touch of his fingers. Today he had not brought his own instrument, but he was excited as he tried to establish similar dominion over this guitar. The excitement, caught in the strings, reached the people who had already started dancing. The first few dances were free.

Wambuku and Kihika danced together. The music thrilled her and she moved closer to Kihika, her head hung back, looking at him with eyes that sparkled. Her pointed breasts heaved back and forth, rippled into Kihika so that he forgot the incident at the station. Seeing them dance so closely, Karanja remembered Mumbi. He had once or twice played to her at her home. Now he wanted to play to her again and this desire awakened wires in the blood whose delicate vibration went to his fingers. The strings would say his heart. The appeal of pregnant desire would surely go beyond the forest, to the village, to Mumbi.

Karanja played differently from Gikonyo. Gikonyo went into the instrument with a kind of dark fury. At times the instrument possessed him and his playing had crude power. But Karanja stood above the instrument; he controlled it, like the carpenter with his tools, so that his playing was more sure and more finished.

A man walked to where Njeri was standing. She declined to dance with a dreamy shake of the head. Her eyes followed Kihika and Wambuku weaving their way round the silent trees, their feet shuffling through the fallen leaves. The tree-trunks also seemed to move among the dancing couples. Karanja sang in sad exultation. Now the men and the forest belonged to him. But he only wanted Mumbi to hear him; she would hear the mad desire in his voice. She would run to him, she must surely follow him. For how could she throw herself on the carpenter? This brought back the pain, and Karanja's voice and guitar ended in mid-air, and to an abrupt profound silence. Then big applause and exclamations of delight tore the silence into shreds.

Kihika and Wambuku found an open place in the sun. The thick part of the forest, the dancers in the wood, and the hungry eyes of Njeri were behind them. Here green wattle trees and bush sloped steeply into the valley below. The valley sprawled flat for a distance and then bounced into the ridge of small hills. Beyond, and to the right, Kihika could just trace the outlines of Mahee Police Station, a symbol of that might which dominated Kenya to the door of every hut.

'Destroy that, and the whiteman is gone,' Kihika thought. 'He rules with the gun, the lives of all the black people of Kenya.' A light danced in Kihika's eyes, his heart dilated with the intensity of this vision, exulting in it, for a time forgetting the woman beside him. But he was aware of her breathing, and it seemed she had come here so that he might show her this thing. He took her hand in his hand his eyes still fixed on Mahee and the Rift Valley.

'And this road, too, this is the road the whiteman followed into the heart of the land,' he said slowly, thinking of the railway line which could just be seen running along the slopes of the Escarpment into the Valley.

'Do you never forget politics, Kihika?' Wambuku asked impatiently, the question poised between angry warning and desire.

Wambuku was not beautiful, except when she laughed or was animated with passion. Then, with her eyes dilated, her lips parted in expectation, and with her dark face glowing, she could be irresistibly attractive. A woman gifted with tremendous capacity for life, she lived for the moment, exploring and devouring its alluring possibilities. She really wanted life with Kihika, but he always stood on the edge of declaration. When alone together, she would wait expectantly, her heart beating with fear of unrevealed knowledge. Kihika would not take the plunge. He was a man following an idea. Wambuku saw it as a demon pulling him away from her. If only she understood it, if only she came face to face with the demon, then she would know how to fight with her woman's strength. Had the demon not assumed the rival woman to her? But how could she fight with a demon who never put on the flesh of a woman? How could she fight with things hidden in darkness?

'It is not politics, Wambuku,' he said, 'it is life. Is he a man who lets another take away his land and freedom? Has a slave life?'

He now spoke in a tortured voice, articulating words as if he sought answers to questions inside him. Wambuku impatiently removed her hand from his as if she would not link her fate with his.

'You have got land, Kihika. Mbugua's land is also yours. In any case, the land in the Rift Valley did not belong to our tribe?'

'My father's ten acres? That is not the important thing. Kenya belongs to black people. Can't you see that Cain was wrong? I am my brother's keeper. In any case, whether the land was stolen from Gikuyu, Ukabi or Nandi, it does not belong to the whiteman. And even if it did, shouldn't everybody have a share in the common shamba, our Kenya? This soil belongs to Kenyan people. Nobody has the right to sell or buy it. It is our mother and we her children are all equal before her. She is our common inheritance. Take your whiteman, anywhere, in the settled area. He owns hundreds and hundreds of acres of land. What about the black men who squat there, who sweat dry on the farms to grow coffee, tea, sisal, wheat and yet only get ten shillings a month?'

Kihika spoke with his hands as to a large audience in front of him. Wambuku suddenly felt she had to grapple with the demon now. She took his hand and gently pressed, so that Kihika looked at her. But words would not form in her mouth to express her heart.

'Let us not talk about these things now,' she said, sensing her failure. Kihika returned the pressure of her hand, experiencing the exquisite delight of a man who has found a comforting soul in his set course of action. He wanted to tell her his gratitude: had she not alone among all the people believed wholly in him, in his ideas? If she had not said as much before, she had now said everything, spoken in that gentle pressure of her hand.

'You'll not go away from me. You'll not leave me alone,' she said in desperation.

'Never!' Kihika cried in ecstasy, seeing Wambuku at his side always. When the call for action came, he alone among the other men would have a woman he loved fighting at his side.

His one word like a knife stabbed Wambuku, thrilling her into a momentary vision of happiness now and ever; would Kihika now leave the demon alone, content with life in the village like the other men?

They walked back to the dancers in the wood, hands linked, their faces lit, both happy, for the moment, in their separate delusions.

Gikonyo never forgot the scene in the wood; while in detention, yearning for things and places beyond the reach of hope, he lived in detail every moment of that experience, a ritual myth of a forgotten land, long ago.

'It was like being born again,' he recalled in the presence of Mugo, speaking in a low, even voice, groping for the word which would contain the reality of his experience. The fire in the hearth marked off by three stones, had ebbed into a dull glow; the oil-lamp fluttered, playing with shadows in corners, without clearly lighting the faces of Mugo and Gikonyo.

'I felt whole, renewed . . . I had made love to many a woman, but I never had felt like that before.'

He paused, puzzled in wonder, as if words had suddenly eluded him. Slowly he lifted his right hand from his knee, the fingers a little spread, and then let it slump back into its former position.

'Before, I was nothing. Now, I was a man. During our short period of married life, Mumbi made me feel *it* was all important . . . suddenly I discovered . . . no, it was as if I had made a covenant with God to be happy. How shall I say it? I took the woman in my arms – do you know a banana stem? I peeled off layer after layer, and I put out my hand, my trembling hand, to reach the Kiana coiled inside.

'Every day I found a new Mumbi. Together we plunged into the forest. And I was not afraid of the darkness . . .'

Wangari, his mother, was also happy. She had found a daughter in Mumbi with whom, even without the medium of speech, she could share a woman's joys and troubles. The two went to the shamba together, they fetched water from the river in turns, and cooked in the same pot. The soul of the mother warmed towards the young woman crossing the abyss of silence no words could reach, revelling in the tension of new recognition. Together they looked beyond the hut to the workshop, where the man held a saw or a plane. They listened to the carpenter's voice singing with the tools and their hearts were full to bursting.

Soon, however, Wangari and Mumbi, like the other women in Thabai, noticed a change in the man. He now sang with defiance, carelessly flinging an open challenge to those beyond Thabai, to the whiteman in Nairobi and any other places where Gikuyu ancestors used to dwell. Karanja, Kihika and others joined Gikonyo and they sang sad songs of hope. They laughed and told stories, but their laughter was no longer the same; it carried mocking and expectation at the corners of their mouths. They went less to the train, the dance sessions in the forest turned into meetings where plans for the day of reckoning were drawn. They also met in huts in dark places late at night, and whispered together, later breaking into belligerent laughter and fighting songs. The hearts of the women fluttered; they caught the sadness at the edge of the songs and feared for their children.

The air was pregnant with expectation.

One night it happened. Jomo Kenyatta and other leaders of the land were rounded up; Governor Baring had declared a State of Emergency over Kenya.

A few months after the declaration, Mumbi stood outside her hut looking dreamily at the land. Gikonyo was not at the workshop and Wangari had gone to the river. The untrimmed hedges surrounding the scattered homesteads made the ridge appear one endless, untamed bush, but for the curling wisps of smoke from the many huts which made the land homely and peaceful. The sun was about to set. The small hedge outside Mumbi's new home rippled with the breeze. She silently revelled in the scene before her.

She saw Kariuki, her younger brother, walking in the fields. Mumbi was suffused with warmth; she felt happy the boy was coming to visit her. She loved Kariuki and before her marriage always washed and pressed his clothes with care. In the morning she always woke up early and made tea for him before he went to school. Though she liked Kihika, admired him and leaned on him, the stronger, without understanding him, it was on Kariuki that she poured a sisterly care.

She and Kariuki often went for walks in the country together. She listened to the boy's prattles about anything, from school to women. She would rebuke him, without conviction, whenever he made comments on grown men and women. Then Kariuki would make comic faces and Mumbi's secret smile would break into open laughter.

Kariuki had his school clothes on, and as he came near, Mumbi was alarmed by the solemnity on his face. The light in her eyes faded, the revelry inside melted into anxiety and she was all set for activity.

'What is it, Kariuki? Has anything bad happened at home?'

'Is Gikonyo in?' Kariuki asked, avoiding her eyes, and her question.

'No, he is not in. But what's wrong? How your face alarmed me!'

'Nothing. Only my father sent me to tell Gikonyo to come home with me. You too.'

The boy was looking down. His voice had faded into a whisper though it could be seen he was trying to keep it strong. Now Kariuki looked up at Mumbi and something like tears glittered in his eyes.

'It is our brother, Kihika . . . Oh, Mumbi, Kihika has run to the forest to fight,' he added, and fell into Mumbi's arms. For a moment sister clasped brother; Thabai went round and round beneath Mumbi's feet. Then the earth became still again, and almost peaceful.

'What is to be done?' she asked.

It was dark outside. Wambuku and Njeri left Mbugua's hut and set out for home. They walked in silence each preoccupied with her own thoughts. Wambuku remembered the scene in the hut which for a time had driven out her own heartache. Mbugua sat with a bowed head, listening to Wambuku's story without interrupting. Only when she had finished did he look at her.

'He said his place was in the forest?'

'Yes.'

'What has come into his head? Don't I have enough land to last him all his life, he and his children's children?' It was left to Mumbi to put the particular grief into perspective.

'With the arrest of Jomo, things are different. All the leaders of the land have been arrested and we do not know where they have been taken. Do you think Kihika, who was the leader of the Movement in his region, was going to escape the heavy arm of the whiteman? He had to choose between prison and forest. He chose the forest.'

'Let God do with him as he sees fit,' Mbugua said. Wanjiku nodded her head in sympathy with her husband.

Wambuku had with difficulty prevented tears from showing, but now, in the dark, she wept silently. Her grief overflowed into words.

'It is the demon.'

'Will you go to him?' Njeri asked.

'No!' she cried with passion into the night. 'He went away from me, he broke away from my arms. Njeri, I begged him to stay, with tears. Yes. We were alone, outside my home. He came to tell me he was going. Would I wait for him? I reminded him of a promise he once made to me at Kinenie, that he would never leave me. But he went away—'

'Don't you love him?' Njeri asked in a tone that carried contempt and superiority.

'I do – I did – I kept myself from other men for his sake. At night I only thought of him. I wanted him. I could have saved him. He was a man, Njeri, strong, sure, but also weak, weak like a little child.'

'You did not love him. You only wanted him when he slept with you.' Njeri said with unexpected venom, which took Wambuku by surprise.

'You cannot teach me what's in my heart.'

'Some people don't know what's in their hearts.'

'I know. You are jealous.'

'Of you? Never!'

They separated without another word. Though Njeri was a short girl, her slim figure made her appear tall. But there was something tough about that slimness. She despised women's weaknesses, like tears, and whenever fights occurred at Kinenie, she always fought, even with men. A cat, men called her, because few could impose their physical will on her. Now she felt superior and stronger and she could not help her contempt for Wambuku. She stood alone in the dark outside her home, peering in the direction of Kinenie Forest.

'He is there,' she whispered to herself. Then she addressed him directly with a passionate devotion. 'You are my warrior.' She raised her voice, letting loose her long-suppressed anger. 'She does not love you, Kihika. She does not care.' She walked a few more steps and then wheeled round, willing the waves of the dark to carry her declaration of eternal devotion to Kihika.

'I will come to you, my handsome warrior, I will come to you,' she cried, and she ran into her mother's hut trembling with the knowledge that she had made an irrevocable promise to Kihika.

Gikonyo always returned in the evening to a secret he could only share with Mumbi. This he guarded jealously. He went on with the workshop, Karanja and others collected there in the evenings, hurled curses and defiance in the air, and reviewed with pride, the personal histories of the latest men to join Kihika. Wangari and Mumbi saw the carpenter's hand was not steady as he flung his plane along the surface of the wood. This, Wangari thought she understood and feared. But how could she explain the glow in his eyes, the animation in the voice, as if the fire of guns in the air, the bugle that told people to lock their doors at six, could not touch his manhood? Only Mumbi felt she could understand, because she knew the man's hands and fingers on her body; she knew the man's power as his limbs fixed her helpless to the ground. And her body would wait, wings beating in readiness. Those were the moments one experienced terror and tenderness; and she wanted him too, now exulting in her woman's strength for as the man swooned into her, it was her tenderness and knowledge that saved him and gave life back to him.

She did not want him to go and hated herself for this cowardice.

More men were rounded up and taken to concentration camps – named detention camps for the world outside Kenya. The platform at the railway station was now always empty; girls pined for their lovers behind cold huts and prayed that their young men would come quickly from the forest or from the camps.

One day the arm of the whiteman touched Mumbi's door. She had fearfully waited for the day, indeed had armed herself against its deadliness. But when the time came, she found herself powerless to save her man. She collected all her will and strength into a cry that went to the hearts of many present: Come back to me, Gikonyo. For the cry was like a shriek of terror. And this feverish terror seized the whole of Thabai as later in the night they learned that Gitogo, the deaf-and-dumb son of the old woman, had been shot dead by those messengers of whiteman's peace.

Perhaps they did not know that it was fitting that such an important campaign should open with blood on Thabai's own soil.

Gikonyo walked towards detention with a brisk step and an assurance born in his knowledge of love and life. This thing would end soon, anyway. Jomo would win the case, his lawyers having come all the way from the land of the whiteman and from Gandhi's India. The day of deliverance was near at hand. Gikonyo would come back and take the thread of life, but this time in a land of glory and plenty. This is what he wanted to tell his mother and Mumbi as the soldiers led him to the waiting truck. Let the whiteman then do anything; the day would come, indeed was near at hand when he would rejoin Thabai and, together with those who had taken to the forest, would rock the earth with a new song at the birth of freedom.

Six years later, it was the image of the thread that still appealed most to Gikonyo's imagination as he walked along a dusty road back to Thabai. He pulled down his hat (he had picked it up from the side of the road) to hide the tufts of hair sprouting over the otherwise bare convict's head, an impotent gesture, since the hat itself was so badly torn. His heavily patched coat, once white – daily use had now turned it yellow and brown – hung loosely from the slouching shoulders. His face, which six years before glowed with youth, had developed tiny lines creating, around the mouth when shut, the effect of a permanent scowl as if Gikonyo would flare up into violence at the slightest provocation.

The bumpy battered land sloped on either side; sickly crops just recovering from a recent drought, one more scourge which had afflicted the country in this period leaving the anxious faces of mothers dry and cracked, were scattered on the strips of shamba on either side of the road. Gikonyo, however, did not notice the sickliness around as he pressed on, the image of the Mumbi he had left behind leading the way. The image beckoned him, awakening in him emotions almost cracked by physical hardships and pains of waiting. Bare, disillusioned in his hope for early Independence, he clung to Mumbi and Wangari as the only unchanging reality.

Soon he would meet them. The thought seemed to give strength to his tired limbs, noticeable in the way he tried to walk faster, the hurrying steps leaving a thin train of dust behind him. Gikonyo had longed for this moment with increasing despair as each day came and went. The longing was bearable in the first few months of detention. Then the detainees used to sing defiantly at night and in the day, and laughed scornfully into the face of the whiteman. Some detainees were beaten, all of them were rigorously questioned by the government agents whose might lay in the very mystery of their title – Special Branch. The detainees had agreed not to confess the oath, or give any details about Mau Mau: how could anybody reveal the binding force of the Agikuyu in their call for African freedom? They bore all the ills of the whiteman, believing somehow that he who would endure unto the end would receive leaves of victory.

For Gikonyo, these would be given to him by Mumbi, whose trembling hands, as she held the green leaves he could so clearly picture. His reunion with Mumbi would see the birth of a new Kenya.

Despite this optimism, or perhaps because of it, the first setback had violently shocked Gikonyo. He went to his own cell and tried to puzzle out the implications of what had happened. Failing, he joined the other detainees for a collective attempt at reaching the depth of this devil's trickery. Jomo had lost the case at Kapenguria. The whiteman would silence the father and the orphans would be left without a helper.

At first, of course, they did not believe it. The Camp Superintendent, a fat man with a skin that looked bloodstained in the sun, had called them out of their tiny rooms into the compound and gave them a radio, their first contact with the outside world. The Superintendent, hands in his pockets (he was fond of khaki shorts), stood at a distance and with a satisfied smile studied the shocked faces.

'I will tell you something. Believe it or not, but the whiteman just wants to break us with lies,' declared Gatu, a detainee from Nyeri, who always instilled them with strength and hope. Gatu had a way of telling jokes and stories which compelled everyone to listen. The corners of his mouth were set in a satiric smile which tickled many detainees from sadness to laughter and warmth. Even the way he ordinarily walked could be irrepressibly comical, as he nearly always mimed the gait and mannerisms of the white officers and camp warders. His jokes and stories carried a moral. His laughing face and eyes had certain lines of unmistakable wisdom. But on that day his voice was broken and carried little conviction. Nevertheless, the detainees of Yala hung on to his words, and countered the silent taunts of the whiteman with open disbelief, ill-carried by their half-hearted grins and jarred laughter.

Each detainee slunk into his bed on the floor. In the day they avoided talking about Jomo or speculating about the outcome of the case in Kapenguria. They refused to look into one another's eyes in order not to read what the other was thinking. Long ago, Young Harry had also been detained, and sentenced to live alone on an island in the Indian Ocean for seven years. He had come back a broken man, who promised eternal co-operation with his oppressors, denouncing the Party he had helped to build. What happened yesterday could happen today. The same thing, over and over again, through history.

And one night, suddenly, they believed the news, all of the detainees to a man. They did not say their belief to one another, it was only that they gathered together in their compounds and sang:

> Gi-i-kuyu na Mu-u-mbii
> Gi-i-kuyu na Mu-u-mbii
> Gi-i-kuyu na Mu-u-mbi
> Nikihiu ngwatiro.

The day of deliverance had receded into a distant future. The Camp Superintendent came with a megaphone and surrounded with armed guards ordered them back to their cells. They dispersed without murmur (except the sound of their feet), and without laughter.

They were abandoned in a desert where not even a straying voice from the world of men could reach them. This frightened Gikonyo, for who, then, would come to rescue them? The sun would scorch them dead and they would be buried in the hot sand where the traces of their graves would be lost for ever. This thought brought more despair to Gikonyo, remembering Mumbi and Wangari: that his identity even in death would be wiped from the surface of the earth was a recurring thought that often brought him into a cold sweat on cold nights. At such times, words formed in prayers would not leave his throat.

In spite of this, the detainees of Yala held on to their vows. They would not say anything about the oath. Gatu remained their good spirit. He had joined the Movement early in his life and was active in the fever for Independent schools in Nyeri. His faith lay in the Movement; only through it could he see any prospect of Independence and the return of the lost lands. He was a great oath administrator in Nyeri and travelled from village to village on foot. Gatu knew about political parties and freedom movements in other countries. He often delighted the other detainees with stories of India and the trials of Nehru and Gandhi. He also told them about the American War of Independence and how Abraham Lincoln had been executed by the British for leading the black folk in America into a revolt. Napoleon had been a warrior, in fact one of the biggest warriors in history. His voice alone made the British urinate and shit on their calves inside their houses. These stories cheered them. They felt Gandhi, Napoleon, Lincoln were watching the black folk of Kenya in their struggle to be free. Even the African warders were impressed with Gatu's stories; they listened, their delight mixed with fear, and putting an unconcerned look on their faces, they taunted Gatu for his wild tongue. But their hearts were not in the rebuke and they did not stop him.

The men drew out plans of action after detention. They discussed education, agriculture, government, and Gatu had elaborate stories for all these subjects. For instance, he told them a wonderful story of what once happened in Russia where the ordinary man, even without a knowledge of how to read, write or speak a word of English, was actually running the government. And now all the nations of the earth feared Russia. No amount of beating could silence Gatu. He would come back to the others and re-enact the recent drama in the office, mimicking the English voices and miming their features. In the end, they confined him in a cell, all by himself. For days he was not allowed to see the sun or speak to anyone. He was given food once a day, which he ate in the dark. Later they let him out and he joined the men in his compound.

'What happened?' the detainees asked him eagerly, a confession that they had missed him.

'Forget these people. They are thick, thick like darkness. Instead I'll tell you the full story of my life. I was born in a valley. The grass in the valley – man, it was big and green-rich. The sun shone daily. And the rain also fell and fruit trees sprung from the earth. I often lay in the sun on the grass, a piece of fruit in my hand, and listened to the running stream and the wild animals. Nobody knew of this valley and I knew no fears. Then one day I was surprised to get an unexpected visitor. Can you guess who? Anyway, you can imagine my surprise when I saw the famous Queen – Queen of England. She said (mimicks her voice): "Why are you living in this dark place? It is like a cold, dark cell in prison." I lay there on the grass. I could see she was quite surprised, naturally, because I was not impressed with her blood-stained lips. "I like it where I am," I told her and went on lying on the ground. She said (mimicks her): "If you sell me your valley, I'll let you . . . once." Women are women you know. "In my country," I told her, "we do not buy that thing from our women. We get it free." But man, my own thing troubled me. I had not seen a woman for many years. However, before I could even say anything more, she had called in her soldiers who bound my hands and feet and drew me out of the valley. I have just come from there, and that's why, gentlemen, I am back with you here in case you are surprised.'

'Man,' he said after the laughter. 'I wish I had agreed at once to satisfy my thing which troubles me to this day.'

They went on laughing. 'Show us how she walked,' one of the men called out. Gatu stood up and mimed the whole drama amid appreciative murmurs and comments.

The Camp Commandant warned him, 'We shall get you!' Gatu had become the symbol of their collective resistance.

Gikonyo could never understand how Gatu remained so strong despite being singled out for torture. Was it his fantasies? Or was the man made of iron?

They went to break stones in a quarry five miles from Yala. The stones were for building houses for new officers and warders. Yala camp was expanding. More detainees arrived, the only contact with the outside world. Gikonyo and the others walked through hot sand in a flat land spotted with cactus bush and tiny thorny trees without leaves. Gikonyo raised and lowered the huge hammer until he entered into a mechanical rhythm. It was hot. Sweat rolled down, his shirt stuck to his clammy body. The unbroken flat land stretched wide from the hill towards the coast, fading into a grey shimmering. Suddenly Gikonyo found himself dwelling on a subject that transported his heart and mind to a world different from the one of the quarry and the Yala country. Soon after marrying Mumbi he had wanted to give her a gift, a creation of his own hands. He had thought of many things he could make for her but could not decide on any. Then one day he had overheard Mumbi and Wangari discussing traditional Gikuyu stools. 'These days there are no wood-carvers left,' Wangeri was saying. 'So you only get chairs and seats joined together with nails.' And immediately Gikonyo had itched to carve a stool. He wanted to carve one which would be different from any others. And for a whole year the desire often possessed him at odd times and places. He would become very excited but could never think of a motif. Now in the quarry he found himself thinking about the stool, dwelling on all sorts of motifs. He was still in this mood when their few minutes of rest came, and Gikonyo sat next to Gatu. Gatu's face was weary.

'What is it, man?' Gikonyo asked him.

'It's nothing.' His gaze went beyond the quarry to a land far away.

'You seem to be thinking of something,' Gikonyo pursued, dwelling on a motif which had just occurred to him.

'What's there to think about now?'

'Freedom!' Gikonyo said triumphantly.

'Freedom! Yes, freedom,' Gatu said slowly, in a subdued voice that sounded like a suppressed cry. The tone destroyed the motif and Gikonyo was depressed inside. Suddenly Gatu turned his eyes on Gikonyo. Gikonyo felt the terrible bond being established between them. He struggled against this but in the end gave up, so that it was he who first opened his heart to Gatu. He told him of Thabai, of Wangari, of Mumbi. He told him of his physical and spiritual union with Mumbi. And finally Gikonyo told Gatu of his one desire to see Mumbi just once.

'Why, I did not even say farewell to her when the soldiers carried me away.'

For a time, it was as if a load had been lifted from his heart; but immediately Gikonyo felt slightly ashamed at letting himself go. Gatu's silence following his own gush of words and feeling was like a rebuke. Gatu then turned his eyes from Gikonyo, and as he gazed into the shimmering distance, spoke in a voice clear, colourless, and not raised above a whisper.

'A certain man, the only son of his parents, once wanted a woman. And the woman also wanted to marry him and have children. But the man kept on putting off the marriage because he wanted to build a new hut so that children would be born in a different hut. "We can build it together," she often told him. In the end, she was tired of waiting and letting life dry in her. She married another man. The first man went on trying to build the hut. It was never finished. Our people say that building a house is a life-long process. As a result the man never had a woman or children to continue his family fire.' He then rested his eyes on Gikonyo and continued as if he was talking straight into Gikonyo's heart. 'So, you see, we all have our separate losses . . . for the cause. We have to, we must remain strong together!'

As soon as he had finished his story, Gatu stood up, and walked away from Gikonyo. 'Weak, weak like any of us,' Gikonyo at first murmured inside, filled with pity. Gatu had seemed so sure, so secure, so able to laugh at himself and others. Then suddenly Gikonyo's pity changed into hatred, so strong he could not understand it. 'So that's why he's so strong. He has no woman like Mumbi. How dare he talk to me about collective strength?'

The soldiers came for Gatu in the quarry. That very evening the others found his body hanging against the wall of his cell. 'Hanged himself . . .' the commandant told them, laughing. 'Guilt, you see! Unless you confess, you'll end up like him.' Gloom fell on Yala. They could not agree on a common united response to Gatu's murder. The event shook Gikonyo. 'I should have known it was coming,' he told himself, scared of his own weakness.

Nights followed days with a severe regularity. So Gikonyo started walking round the compound in the evenings before the sun set. The walls of each compound into which the camp was divided were buttressed with barbed-wired; the wall around the whole camp was covered with barbed-wire. In the morning they went away from the barbed-wire to the roads and quarries; in the evening they returned to the barbed-wire. Barbed-wire, barbed-wire everywhere. So it was today, so it would be tomorrow. The barbed-wire blurred his vision. 'There was nothing beyond it. Human voices had stopped. The world, outside, was dead. No, perhaps, he thought as he went towards the wall of barbed-wire, it was his ears that had gone dumb, his eyes blind. For days he went without food, he lived on water, and did not feel hungry or weak.

He blankly stared into the wire one evening, and with sudden excitement, wanted to cry or laugh, but did neither. Slowly and deliberately (he stood outside himself and watched his actions as from a distance) he pushed his right hand into the wire and pressed his flesh into the sharp metallic thorns. Gikonyo felt the prick into the flesh, but not the pain. He withdrew the hand and watched the blood ooze; he shuddered and enjoyed a strange exhilaration.

The warder held the gun firmly, waiting for Gikonyo to attempt to break, and seeing that he did not, called him. Gikonyo heard the voice, a distant echo, and walked towards it, elated by his new experience. He suddenly stood before the warder, stared insolently into his face and then raised the hand for the warder to see the blood and perhaps become envious. The warder (one of the few gentle ones) saw the glaze in Gikonyo's eyes. 'Go in and rest,' he told him and abruptly turned and walked away, almost running from Gikonyo's weird laughter. In his cell, Gikonyo found that everything – the barbed-wired, Yala Camp, Thabai – was dissolved into a colourless mist. He struggled to recall the outline of Mumbi's face without success, there was only a succession of images each one cancelling out the one immediately preceding it. Was he dead? He put his hand on his chest, felt the heart-beat and knew that he was alive. Why then couldn't he fix a permanent outline of Mumbi in his mind? Perhaps she too had dissolved into the mist. He tried to relive the scene in the wood and was surprised to see he could not experience anything; the desire, the full manhood, the haunting voice of Mumbi, the explosion, no feeling came even as a thing of the past. And all this time, Gikonyo watched himself act – his every gesture, his flow of thought. He was both in and outside himself – in a trance, considering everything calmly, and only mildly puzzled by the failure of his memory. Maybe I'm weary, the thought crossed his mind. If I stand up, everything that makes me what I am will rush back into activity. So he stood up and indeed things seemed to rush back into activity. The room for instance went round and round – he attempted to walk; panic suddenly seized him, he staggered against the wall, a grunt emitted from his mouth as he slumped back on to the floor, into total darkness.

Gradually he heard a faint sound of feet rustling through dry leaves in a forest. He strained his ears to catch the sound, which turned into Mumbi's voice. He raised his head and saw her angel's smile and her hands carried a flaming torch that dispelled the darkness in front of her. She wanted to lift him up, she who appeared so pure, an incorruptible reality in a world of changing shadows. Her purity crushed him, tumbled him, awed him. I know my redeemer liveth, he cried to her, kneeling before her, when suddenly new ecstasy swept through him and he desired to die into her as on that day in the wood, so that dying he might live. Surely she would receive him, he thought, as, still possessed by the ecstasy, Gikonyo sank into heavy sleep.

He woke up in the morning and found that he was extremely hungry. His right hand, swollen at the wrist, ached. He could not clearly remember what happened the night before. He only knew that he had woken from an unreal dream in which he had walked and walked ever since Gatu was hanged. His desire to see Mumbi was there. His mind was clear and he knew without guilt, what he was going to do. Word went round. All the detainees of Yala crowded to the walls of their compounds and watched him with chilled hostility. Gikonyo fixed his mind on Mumbi fearing that strength would leave his knees under the silent stare of all the other detainees. He walked on and the sound of his feet on the pavement leading to the office where screening, interrogations and confessions were made, seemed, in the absence of other noise, unnecessarily loud. The door closed behind him. The other detainees walked back to their rooms to wait for another journey to the quarry . . .

As Gikonyo left the road and took a path into the fields, he could still hear the echo of his steps on the cement pavement four years back. The steps had followed him all through the pipeline, for in spite of the confession, Gikonyo was not released immediately. Screened, he had refused to name anybody involved in oath administration. Would the steps always follow him, he wondered, suddenly scared of meeting someone he had known in the old days. He did not feel victorious, less so a hero. The green leaves were not for him. But then, Gikonyo did not want them. He only wanted to see his Mumbi and take up the thread of life where he had left it.

In the streets, naked and half-naked children played throwing dust at one another. Some of the dust entered Gikonyo's eyes and throat; he rubbed his eyes with the back of his hand (water streamed from his eyes) and he coughed with irritation. He stopped women whose faces he could not recognize and asked them for Wangari's hut. Some stared at him with open hostility and others shook their heads with indifference, making him both impatient and angry. At last a small boy pointed the way to the hut. Walking towards it, Gikonyo wondered what he would do when he stood face to face with Mumbi. Doubt followed excitement; what if Mumbi was at the river or the shops when he arrived. Could he possibly wait for another hour or two before he could see her?

Actually he almost hit into her at the door. She looked at him for a second or two, gave an involuntary cry, almost hoarse, and with her mouth still parted, moved back a step as if to let him in. Gikonyo saw a child securely strapped on her back. His raised arms remained frozen in the air. Then they slowly slumped back to his sides. A lump blocked his throat.

'Really you?' Mumbi was the first to speak.

'Yes. Whom did you expect?' he whispered. Smoke gushed from

the hut into his face so that he had to back a step from the door widening the gap between him and Mumbi. The child started to cry. Mumbi gave it a quick mother's glance, before looking back at her husband.

'You?' She asked again. 'I knew you would come, but I did not expect you so soon.'

'So soon?' Gikonyo echoed her words, his inner eye scanning the distance of six years. Nothing seemed real. He could not grasp the significance of what she said.

Aroused by the voices, Wangari came out of the hut and rushed to Gikonyo.

'My son!' she cried, her arms round his waist, tears running down her emaciated face.

Gikonyo felt his body stiffen at his mother's embrace. He knew without being told that the child strapped on Mumbi's back was from another man's seed. Mumbi had gone to bed with other men in his absence. The years of waiting, the pious hopes, the steps on the pavement, all came rushing into his heart to mock him. Kill her and the child . . . end all misery, he thought. He actually disengaged himself from Wangari's embrace to do this in the heat of the moment. But he remained rooted to the ground. Wangari glanced in the direction of Mumbi, who had already gone into the hut, where her voice could be heard trying to hush the weeping child.

'Come into the hut,' Wangari invited him. Gikonyo allowed himself to be led into the smoke-filled hut as if his own will to act had been drugged. Inside, Mumbi held the child in her arms and fed him from her breasts. Gikonyo sat on a chair. Now and then she stole glances at him. She is mocking me, he thought.

His eyes rolled from Wangari to Mumbi and then around the hut, trying to pick an object which might capture his concentration. The quick, bitter pang he had experienced a few minutes earlier was now replaced by a heavy dullness. Life had no colour. It was one endless blank sheet, so flat. There were no valleys, no streams, no trees – nothing. And who had thought of life as a thread one could continue weaving into a pattern of one's choice? He was remotely conscious that he was tired. And somewhere in that remote region of his mind, hidden, words formed. Gikonyo mechanically moved his lips and the words came out, clearly, carrying no emotion except perhaps disinterested curiosity:

'Whose child?'

Mumbi just looked at Gikonyo and the wall opposite. Wangari felt the pain of the son and the misery of the daughter. She searched her own heart for the healing word. She had always known that the knowledge would be hard to bear: now, she willed a mother's strength and tenderness go to him as she let out the truth.

'Karanja's child!' she said bluntly. She waited calmly for the thing to happen. She had prepared herself for a groan, a scream or an attempt on Mumbi's life. But not this, not this animal dumbness.

'Karanja, my friend?' he asked in the same detached voice, more puzzled than pained.

'Yes. These things happen,' she again said, and waited.

The child now slept on Mumbi's thighs, Mumbi leaning forward, her left hand delicately but firmly supporting the child's back and head. Her right arm bent at the elbow, rested on her knee, her small finger slightly pressing down the lower lip, revealed her milk-white teeth.

Gikonyo did not move. He only sat, leaning backwards, against a post behind him, his eyes now immobile, now rolling, without registering anything. Even the thought that Mumbi had been to other men's beds every night for the last six years seemed not to disturb him. As if drugged, Gikonyo did not feel the wound; and could not tell what caused this terrible exhaustion.

'I'm tired, Mother. I have come a long way and I want to sleep,' he said. Wangari did not understand. And now Mumbi wept.

He failed to sleep. Gikonyo lay on his back and stared into the darkness, every minute conscious of the heavy breathing from the two women. Six years he had waited for this day; six years through seven detention camps had he longed for it, feeling, all the time, that life's meaning was contained in his final return to Mumbi. Nothing else had mattered: the camps, mountains, valleys, everything could have been wiped from the face of the earth and Gikonyo would have watched this, without flinching, if he had known that he would, in the end, go back to the woman he had left behind. Little did he then think, never thought it could ever be a return to silence. Could the valley of silence between him and the woman be now crossed? To what end the crossing since he would reach the other side to find a woman who had hardly waited for him to disappear round the corner, before she rushed back to bed with another man? No, this silence was eternal. In his workshop he used to hold without words a dialogue with Wangari; he looked at her eyes and understood her fears and anxieties, and ambitions for him. She moved in the old hut with a mother's pride and assurance, which he trusted. He knew when she went to the river, to the shops or the shamba. Mumbi had come and fitted into the scheme, bringing into the dialogue, into the life of the home, a new vitality. It was Mumbi, in bed, her head on his breast, or breathing near him, who had taught him, who had made him understand there was nothing like the touch of a woman. What was there beyond this touch, this communion, which, for him had given life a meaning, a clarity? Then wealth and power were not important unless they enriched that silent communion from which living things heaved and opened to the sun. The silence to which he had now returned was dead. He lay thus in bed and watched the endless images tossing from his heated brain. Perhaps daylight would show the way.

But the sun did not bring relief. Early in the morning the child shrieked for attention, Mumbi lit the fire and again held the child to her breasts. The child went on whimpering, tearing into Gikonyo's nerves. Smash the child on to the floor, haul the dirty thing into silence, he thought, without attempting to rise from the bed. He did not want to see Mumbi's eyes, nose, mouth – and yet how that face had pleasantly tortured him in detention? Now he recoiled within, at the passing thought of Mumbi's hands on his body. The child stopped crying and whimpering as it suckled its mother's breasts. Perhaps it was not right to kill the child; the situation that had created the child would always gnaw at his mind: Mumbi had walked to another man's bed, had allowed, actually held another man's dangling thing between her thighs, her flesh, had rapturously welcomed the explosion of that man's seeds into her. And this not once but every night for the last six years. She had betrayed the bond, the secret, between them: or perhaps there had never been any communion between them, nothing could grow between any two people. One lived alone, and like Gatu, went into the grave alone. Gikonyo greedily sucked sour pleasure from this reflection which he saw as a terrible revelation. To live and die alone was the ultimate truth.

He went out of the hut – how it reeked with heavy smoke – and wandered through the New Thabai village where one street led into another and dust trailed behind at his heels. The very air choked him; Thabai was just another detention camp; would he ever get out of it? But go where? He followed the tarmac road which led him into Rung'ei. The Indian shops had been moved into a new centre; the tall buildings were made of stones; electric lights and tarmac streets made the place appear as a slice of the big city. The sewage smelt; it had not been cleaned for a year. He went on and came to the African shops in Rung'ei; they were all closed; tall grass and wild bush clambered around the walls of the rusty buildings and covered the ground that was once the market place. Most of the buildings had battered walls with large gaping holes, smashed and splintered doors that stared at him – ruins that gave only hints of an earlier civilization. At the door of one building, Gikonyo picked up a broken plank; the fading letters on it, capitals, had lost their legs and hands; but after careful scrutiny he made out the word HOTEL. Inside was a mound of soil; bits of broken china, saucers and glasses were scattered on top. He tapped, pecked and poked the wall with the sharp end of the broken plank; suddenly cement and soil tumbled down, hollow, in increasing quantity, it seemed the wall would break and fall. Gikonyo rushed out, afraid of the building, of ghost-ridden Rung'ei and did not stop running until he entered the fields. The African shops, as he learnt later, had been forced to shut as a collective punishment to the ridges. Gikonyo followed the paths in the neatly hedged fields – a result of land consolidation – but Gikonyo tried to shut his eyes to any more changes. Whenever anything touched him, shrubs or grass, Gikonyo would start and shiver. At the ridge he stopped and again looked at the new village – huts, grass, lives crammed together. Blue smoke from a few huts was lost in the bright midday sun. Last night it was different; then, smoke curling from the roofs of the various huts had gathered into a still, unruffled canopy above the village. Beyond, the blood-red streaks from the setting sun had spread out from the centre and broken into varying shades of brown and yellow at the edges, further on dissolving into dark grey. Nothing in the new village now attracted him; the huts did not make his heart rise and flap as on the night before. Was there anywhere else to go, could he go to another country? The steps in the pavement, the weeping child, and the image of the mother suckling the child, would always haunt him.

Gikonyo suddenly remembered that he was expected to report his arrival in the village to the Chief. The State of Emergency was not yet over: the whiteman still coughed and people everwhere danced to the tune, however rough. He had no difficulty in finding the Chief's house. It was inside the compound of the Thabai Homeguard Post. On the other side of the post, below it, ran the long tarmac road from Nakuru to the big city.

He stood at the door of the Chief's house and the ground below him began to move. Gikonyo stared at the stern face of the Chief. Fate was mocking him. This could not be.

'Come right in,' Karanja said. Gikonyo was shaken with bitter incomprehension – Karanja, a Chief, Karanja sitting erect behind a table, now lowering his eyebrows, the frown adding severity to his face.

'I said come in,' Karanja repeated in a voice, unnecessarily loud.

Gikonyo walked in, gingerly, conflicting thoughts passing through his mind. He sat on a chair and bit his lower lip to steady a bitterness close to tears as whispers went, simultaneously, through his head and heart: God was cruel, else, why didn't he spare him this humiliation? And he saw Karanja, his old friend, was watching his every reaction, Karanja, who now talked to Gikonyo coldly as if he did not know him, as if Gikonyo was a criminal.

'Let me see,' Karanja was saying, pulling out a printed sheet of paper hanging from the wall. 'You are – eh – Gikonyo, son of – eh – Waruhiu,' he continued, ticking something on the paper. Gikonyo watched this, his head bowed like an aged person's, and bit deep into his lower lip.

'Listen carefully. You have now come back into a normal life in the village. People here obey the law, hear? No meetings at night, no stories about Gandhi and Unity and all that. The whiteman is here to stay.'

Gikonyo unexpectedly stood up, and without knowing what he was doing, started for the door. Karanja let him go up to the door and then shouted: 'Stop!' Gikonyo stopped, as if paralysed by the voice, and then turned round, waiting.

'Where are you going?'

'To you!' he hissed back, rushing towards the table, hands spread, reaching for Karanja's throat. At the table, he stopped short and emitted a cry of fear: Karanja pointed a pistol at Gikonyo's heart.

'Sit down, Gikonyo.'

Gikonyo sat back in the chair, his body shaking visibly; everything assumed the character of a dream, but he spat on the floor, forcing as much disgust as he could manage in the act.

'You may spit on the floor,' Karanja said, in obvious triumph, leaning on his chair and placing the pistol on the table. 'But let me tell you this as a friend – you have to learn your lesson. Do you see the watchtower outside? A word from me, for what you tried to do just now, and the tower would be your home for a week or two.'

Everything had happened so quickly that Gikonyo could not sort out the feelings and thoughts that whirled through his head: he only knew that the man with whom he had taken an oath to fight the whiteman was talking to him about the power of the white people, the man with whom he used to play the guitar, who often came to the workshop for gossip, was now shouting at him.

And no sooner was he outside the Chief's house and office, than he remembered Karanja was the man who had slept with Mumbi, for whom she had carried a child in her womb for nine months. Somehow Karanja's name had not registered in Gikonyo's heated brain: all last night and all today he had thought of Mumbi as only going to bed with other men. Not once, not even in the office did he bring Karanja into his other torture, which lay, as it were, in a different compartment of his mind. But now the image of Mumbi moaning with pleasure as her naked body bore Karanja's heavy weight, corroded him everywhere. He recreated the scene in its sordid details: the creaking bed;

Karanja's fingers touching Mumbi everywhere; their heavy breath merging into one – and, oh, Lord, the sighs, those sighs! He went through a long, continuous shuddering, then tottered towards a small tree by the road and held on to it. But the images did not stop corroding his mind. Karanja on top of Mumbi. He found himself dwelling on irrelevant details, worrying himself, for instance, over whether Mumbi had whimpered with pleasure at the orgasm. . . . Before he could finish the details of the scene, he groaned and emitted a hoarse cry. He let go the tree. He ran down the street towards his mother's hut. The woman who had sighed under Karanja's sweating body could not live. Passers-by would look at him once and quickly clear out of the way. Gikonyo ran on. He would kill her. He would strangle Mumbi. The distance was too long. His imagination had shot ahead; Mumbi was gasping for mercy, saliva flowed out of her mouth, her eyes bobbed out. But fate lay in his way. The hut was locked. Perhaps they had locked themselves inside. He threw his weight against the door, shouting: 'Open the door. Open the door you who auction your bodies on the market.' The door did not open. He gathered force and crushed into it again and again. Suddenly the wooden door gave way. Gikonyo fell on to the floor and hit his head against the hearthstone. Foam tossed from the sides of his mouth. For a time the carpenter made incoherent noises through the foam, ending in one prolonged moan: 'God, oh, oh, God, my God.'

Eight

Gikonyo could never remember in detail his experience on the first few days of his return home. Everything remained like a misty dream and he found it difficult to tell Mugo a coherent account of what really happened. Again he groped for words and occasionally threw his despairing arms in the air.

'Anyway, I must have gone mad. I suppose there is nothing so painful as finding that a friend, or a man you always trusted, has betrayed you. Anyway, when later I woke up, I found myself in bed and a blanket covered me. The oil-lamp, just like this one here, was burning feebly, like something diseased, know what I mean? Even the smell of everything reminded you of a scene in hospital. My mother sat beside the bed. Mumbi stood a few feet away. I could not see her face clearly, but I thought she had been crying. For a moment, a minute, you might say, something rippled in my heart. Mumbi, the woman I knew, could not let Karanja into her bed. She was the same as I had left her. Then I saw the child. And I knew that what I had thought impossible had happened. My teeth started clattering and I shuddered all over, as if I had caught a cold and a fever, malaria. Yet now I had lost all desire to kill her. It was then that I made a decision: I would never talk about the child. I would continue life as if nothing had happened. But I would never enter Mumbi's bed. What more was there for me to do but to give myself wholly to work, hard work?' Gikonyo searched Mugo's face. He could not discern anything. The silence made him uncomfortable. It seemed as if the whole thing was a repetition of a familiar scene.

'Yes . . . I gave myself, heart and body, to work,' he said again. And still Mugo did not say anything, Gikonyo felt vaguely disappointed.

The weight had been lifted. But guilt of another kind was creeping in. He had laid himself bare, naked, before Mugo. Mugo must be judging him. Gikonyo felt the discomfort of a man standing before a puritan priest. Suddenly he wanted to go, get away from Mugo, and cry his shame in the dark.

'I must go,' he said, rising to his feet. He went out into the night. His heart's palpitations frightened him. He was scared of facing Mumbi, of being kept awake by the steps on the pavement. Darkness pressed him on every side as he hastened towards home that was no home. Mugo's purity, Mumbi's unfaithfulness, everything had conspired to undermine his manhood, his faith in himself, and accentuate his shame at being the first to confess the oath in Yala Camp.

As soon as Gikonyo had gone, Mugo rushed to the door, flung it open and cried out: Come back. He waited for an answer, and getting no response went back and sat down to think. His mind lightly hopped from one episode to another. Gikonyo had wanted him to say something. He felt he should have said something. Twice he had moistened his lips with spittle and cleared his throat ready to speak. But his mouth was dry; thoughts and words refused to form. What could he have told him? Gikonyo's outburst against Karanja's betrayal and his unforgiving anger at Mumbi had made Mugo recoil within. Every time Gikonyo talked about Mumbi and Karanja, Mugo felt sharp irritation as if acid was eating away at an ulcer in his stomach. He now shivered at the recollection. He became restless. He stood up and walked about the room. Suppose I had told him . . . suppose I had suddenly told him. . . . Everything would have been all over . . . all over . . . the knowledge . . . the burden . . . fears . . . and hopes. . . . I could have told him . . . and maybe . . . maybe . . . Or is that why he told me his own story? At this thought he abruptly stopped pacing and leaned against the bed. A man does not go to a stranger and tear his heart open. . . . I see everything . . . everything . . . he pretended not to look at me . . . yet kept on stealing eyes at me . . . see if I was frightened . . . see . . . if. . . . No. He recalled the agony on Gikonyo's face. His voice had sounded sincere and trusting.

Mugo went out. Perhaps the cold air and anonymous night would still his nerves on edge. A cup of tea at Kabui shops seemed the best plan. As he walked through the night, many scenes in his life flashed across his mind; he would be frightened, thrilled, repelled, etc., in turns at each succeeding scene. And strangely everything ended in last night's saying from the Bible: he shall judge the poor of the people, he shall save the children of the needy, and shall break in pieces the oppressor. The words tickled something in him, they disturbed a memory.

The memory was of a day in May 1955. Kenya had been in a State of Emergency for about two years. Mugo went to his shamba, another thin strip of land, near Rung'ei Railway Station. Then Emergency regulations and troubles had not touched him. Beyond the station was the tarmac road which went through the settled area to Nairobi, to Mombasa and into the sea. Mugo had never travelled beyond Rung'ei, to the settled area, or to the big city. Once or twice when he was a boy he saw a group of white people smoking, talking and laughing, while black people carried bags of maize and pyrethrum from standing lorries into the railway trucks. When all the lorries had been emptied, the goods train rattled away. Mugo had watched the scene from a safe distance. In after years, whenever he thought of a whiteman (even John Thompson) he always pictured a man smoking a cigarette and a standing train that vomited out smoke. On this day he had tied his shirt, unbuttoned, to the waist, so that the collar and the sleeves brushed against his calves and the back of his thighs as he bent over the crops. The sun burnt the bare black torso pleasantly. Light on the sweating body made the skin gleam brown. The crops – young maize plants, potatoes, beans, peas – opened out and spread their leaves to the sun. Mugo used a small jembe to turn the soil over in the bare and weedy patches between the plants, his fingers for earthing up the crops. As he disturbed the plant stems, the dewdrops on the leaves would break and melt away. The air was fresh and clear and sharp. The fields around, all covered with green things – long, wide leaves hiding the dark earth – appeared beautiful to look at. The sun became increasingly hotter; the moisture on leaves evaporated; leaves dropped, so that at noon the greenness had waned, slightly ashy, and the fields appeared tired. Mugo lay on his back under the shade of a

Mwariki and experienced that excessive contentment which one feels during a noon rest from toil. A voice, then he always heard voices whenever he lay on his back at rest, told him: Something is going to happen to you. Closing his eyes, he could feel, almost touched the thing, whose form was vague but, oh, so beautiful. He let the gentle voice lure him to distant lands in the past. Moses too was alone keeping the flock of Jethro his father-in-law. And he led the flock to the far side of the desert, and came to the mountain of God, even to Horeb. And the angel of the Lord appeared unto him in a flame of fire out of the midst of a bush. And God called out to him in a thin voice, Moses, Moses. And Mugo cried out, Here am I, Lord.

Whenever he thought of this day, he always saw it as the climax of his life. For a week later DO Robson was shot dead, and Kihika came into his life.

Mugo was in a feverish excitement when he burst into the tea-shop at Kabui. Previously the place was called *Mambo Leo*, but since self-government, the owner had renamed it: *Uhuru Hotel*: sub-titled: *Bar and Restaurant*. A group of men were shouting and singing at the counter. Other groups were scattered about the creaking tables. Mugo went into a corner and sat down. His head thrilled round and round: he was in a reverie, the ground on which he walked, the people in the bar, were all unreal. A minute, and they would vanish. Suddenly a voice rang out above the drunken noise. There was silence, profound in its abruptness. Githua on his crutches detached himself from the group at the counter and hobbled towards Mugo. He stood in front of Mugo, at attention, saluted, removed his hat and cried out:

'Chief! I salute you!' Githua exhaled a drunken breath, through his discoloured teeth. Then his posture metamorphosed into that of a fawning slave.

'Remember us, Chief. Remember us. Do you see these tatters? Do you see the lice crawling on my shoulder? I was not always like that. I swear by my mother's aged cunt, or that of the old woman. Ask anybody here.'

He raised his finger up in a swearing fashion and looked around the place as if for witnesses. By this time people had left their places and crept near the two men. Mugo was scared, at the same time, was thrilled, by the unreality of the whole spectacle.

'I was a driver – known from Kisumu to Mombasa. Me.' Again he was the proud man, defiantly beating his chest, for show. 'Money was nothing to me. I was negotiating for a farm in Kerarapon, near Ngong. At home here I had poultry – a lot – oh you should have seen the eggs. Waiter – give us a drink here – bring a drink for the Chief. Before the Emergency I could have bought the whole bar.'

Although people were used to Githua's bragging, nobody laughed. They listened to him seriously at one time nodding or shaking their heads in sympathy with the tears in Githua's voice. Mugo said he wanted nothing to drink. People started talking about Kenya, the land of conflicts. 'The Emergency hit us hard,' some were saying.

'Me! When the Uhuru war came, I knew I had to fight. Didn't think twice about it. General! General! Where is the General?'

Every eye looked around for General R. He was quietly drinking at the counter, bemusedly looking at the scene. Githua was still talking. He told of his exploits during the Emergency: how he used to supply bullets to Kihika and the freedom fighters. People loved good stories. And even those who were drunk forgot their beer as they let themselves be lured into heroic realms by Githua's stories.

'Then one day, the whiteman struck. Wheeeee! The bullet caught me here!'

He pointed to his cut leg, and Mugo recoiled from the dangling stump. Yet, like everybody else, he felt his sympathies now drawn to this man who was more worthy of praise than he.

'The government has forgotten us. We fought for freedom. And yet now!'

Again his voice vibrated with tears before it changed into that of a supplicant.

'So, Chief. Remember me. Remember the poor. Remember Githua. Waiter – Waiter – Bring Tusker beer here. The Chief will pay – the Chief will not deny a drink to Githua – poor Githua.'

Mugo searched his pockets and took out two shillings. All the time he was aware of the General's eyes on him. Suddenly he rose to his feet, pushed his way through the crowd and went out. And Githua's voice reached him in the street. 'Thank you, Chief! Thank—'

Before Mugo had crossed the road into the village, he heard running feet behind him. Then a man came and walked beside him. It was General R.

'A funny man! Isn't he?'

'Who?'

'Githua.'

Mugo was quivering: thoughts crowded into his head.

'I am not coming with you,' General R. was saying. 'I will see you tomorrow.' Then he vanished as quickly as he had come. Mugo was now alone in the darkness. He felt he could embrace the whole night, could contain the world within his palms. For he walked on the edge of a revelation: Gikonyo and Githua had brought him there. He remembered the words: he shall save the children of the needy. It must be him. It was he, Mugo, spared to save people like Githua, the old woman, and any who had suffered. Why not take the task? Yes. He would speak at the Uhuru celebrations. He would lead the people and bury his past in their gratitude. Nobody need ever know about Kihika. To the few, elect of God, the past was forgiven, was made clean by great deeds that saved many. It was so in the time of Jacob and Esau; it was so in the time of Moses.

In bed that night, he dreamed that he was back in Rira. A group of detainees were lined up against the wall, naked to the waist. Githua and Gikonyo were among them. From another corner, John Thompson came holding a machine-gun at the unfortunate men against the wall. He was going to shoot them – unless they told what they knew about Kihika. All at once, Githua shouted: Mugo save us. The cry was taken by the others: Mugo save us. The suppliant voices rose to a chanting thunder: Mugo save us. And John Thompson had joined the condemned men and he was crying out louder than all the others: Mugo save us. How could he refuse, that agonized cry. Here I am, Lord. I am coming, coming, coming, riding in a cloud of thunder. And the men with one voice wept and cried: Amen.

And the Lord said, I have surely seen the affliction of my people which are in Egypt, and have heard their cry by reason of their taskmasters; for I know their sorrows.

Exodus 3:7
(verse underlined in red in Kihika's Bible)

Nine

Learned men will, no doubt, dig into the troubled times which we in Kenya underwent, and maybe sum up the lesson of history in a phrase. Why, let us ask them, did the incident in Rira Camp capture the imagination of the world? For there were other camps, bigger, scattered all over Kenya, from the Manda Islands in the Indian Ocean to the Magata Islands in Lake Victoria.

When Mugo was arrested he was taken to Tigoni Police Station and then to Thika detention camp, where captured forest fighters were taken. Many of the fighters came from Embu, Meru and Mwariga. Here he was kept for six months, and at one stage he thought this his final place of rest. Then one cold morning they were all herded into waiting lorries, without warning, and rushed to the railway station. The coaches which took them to Manyani were covered with barbed-wire at the windows to bar any escape. Soldiers waited for them at Manyani. As soon as they got out of the train, they were made to squat in large queues with their hands on their heads. The soldiers beat them with truncheons, cynically encouraging one another: strike harder it's the whiteman, not we, who brought them here. Manyani was divided into three big camps: A, B and C. Compound C into which Mugo was hustled, was for the hardcore. Every compound was then subdivided into smaller compounds, each enclosing ten cells. One big cell housed about six hundred men.

It was after a series of screenings that Mugo and a few others were chained hands and feet and taken to Rira.

Rira camp was in a remote part of Kenya, near the coast where no rain fell and nothing grew except sand, sand and rocks. Detainees taken there consisted of a few who had sworn never to co-operate with the government as long as Kenyatta was in prison. They refused to answer questions and often would not go to work.

Here Mugo found conditions worse than those in Manyani. Food rations were small.

Meat: 8 oz. per week.
Flour: 7 oz. per day.

It was here that Mugo was destined to meet John Thompson again.

Thompson's sudden success in Yala was so impressive that he was immediately transferred to Rira. Thompson brought fresh breath to Rira. A common game in Rira had been to bury a man, naked, in the hot sand, sometimes leaving him there overnight. Thompson put an end to this means of extorting confessions. Instead he lectured the detainees in groups about the joys of home; they could go home to their wives and children as soon as they confessed the oath. This method had weakened resistance in other camps. Thompson hoped it would work the same magic. In his first month of reign, sanitation in Rira improved. Previously detainees suffering from typhoid were left to die. Now they were rushed to hospital.

When he considered the moment ripe, Thompson started calling them in singly into his office. His theory which had matured into a conviction over the years in administering Africans was: Do the unexpected. But here he met different men; men who would not even open their mouths, men who only stared at him. After two weeks he was driven by the men's truculence to the edge of his patience. He went home and cried to Margery: These men are sick.

He hoped the third week would prove different. He leaned back in his chair and waited for the African warders to usher in the first man. Beside Thompson sat two other officers.

'What's your name?'

'Mugo.'

'Where do you come from?'

'Thabai.'

Thompson was relieved to find a man who at least agreed to answer questions. This was a good beginning. If one man confessed the oath, others would follow. He knew Thabai. He had been a District Officer in Rung'ei area twice; the last time being when he went to replace the murdered Robson. So for a few seconds he tried a friendly chat about Thabai: how green the landscape was, how nice and friendly its inhabitants. Then he resumed the questioning.

'How many oaths have you taken?'

'None.'

This sent Thompson to his feet. He paced up and down the room. Suddenly he faced Mugo. The man's face seemed vaguely familiar. But then it was difficult to tell one black face from another: they looked so much alike, masks.

'How many oaths have you taken?'

'None.'

'Liar!' he shouted, sweating.

As for Mugo, he was indifferent to his fate. He was in that state of despair when a man perceives that all struggle is useless. You are condemned to die. Let the sword come quickly.

One of the officer's whispered something to Thompson. He studied the man's face for a while. Light dawned on him. He sent Mugo out of the room and carefully dived into the man's record.

Thereafter things went from bad to worse. Many detainees never spoke. In fact, Mugo was the only one who consented to answer questions. But he only opened to repeat what he had said in all the camps. Thompson, like a tick, stuck to Mugo. He questioned him daily, perhaps because he seemed the likeliest to give in. He picked him up for punishment. Sometimes he would have the warders whip Mugo before the other detainees. Sometimes, in naked fury, he would snatch the whip from the warders and apply it himself. If Mugo had cried or asked for mercy Thompson might have relented. But now it seemed to him that all the detainees mocked and despised him for his failure to extort a cry from Mugo.

And that was how Mugo gained prestige among the other detainees. Beyond despair, there was no moaning; the feeling that he deserved all this numbed Mugo to the pain. But the other detainees saw his resignation to pain in a different light; it gave them courage; they came together and wrote a collective letter listing complaints. Among other things they wanted to be treated as political prisoners not criminals. Food rations should be raised. Unless these things were done, they would go on hunger-strike. And indeed on the third day, all the detainees, to a man, sat down on strike.

Thompson was on the edge of madness. Eliminate the vermin, he would grind his teeth at night. He set the white officers and warders on the men. Yes – eliminate the vermin.

But the thing that sparked off the now famous deaths, was a near-riot act that took place on the third day of the strike. As some of the warders brought food to the detainees, a stone was hurled at them and struck one of them on the head. They let go the food and ran away howling murder! Riot! The detainees laughed and let fly more stones.

What occurred next is known to the world. The men were rounded up and locked in their cells. The now famous beating went on day and night. Eleven men died.

This was foremost in the mind of Mugo as on the following day after his vision he walked towards Gikonyo's home. In his miraculous escape from death, he now saw the guiding hand of fate. Surely he must have been spared in order that he might save people like Githua from poverty and misery. He, an only son, was born to save. The exciting possibilities of his new position agitated him and lured him on. He would tell Gikonyo his decision to lead the people of Thabai in the Uhuru celebrations. Thereafter, as a chief, he would lead his people across the desert to the new Jerusalem.

A song from the radio drifted to Mugo. A woman's voice, live, full, almost drowned the soloist in the radio. The song moved slowly, sadly, a strange contrast to the vigorously bright morning. For a time he stood, hesitant, near the neatly cropped hedge surrounding the house. The L-shaped house was roofed with new shining corrugated-iron sheets, and the outside walls were made of thick cedar slabs. He stood there, letting Mumbi's voice disturb him pleasantly, refusing to believe that discord could be hidden beyond the hedge. Wangari left the house, a sufuria in her hand, and walked towards a smaller house, also newly built, at the far corner of the compound. A small boy, whom Mugo took for the child in dispute, pranced ahead of Wangari, and this sight, for no apparent reason, gave him pain.

Mumbi welcomed him with a smile, her face lit up as if she had been expecting him. He looked back over the many years past and saw the young girl who once met him and expressed sympathy because of his aunt's death. Now her face appeared tired and hardened. Maybe weary inside, he thought. He became conscious of her well-formed body; her dark eyes, infinitely deep, swallowed him, unsettled him, and he feared her.

'I just wanted to see Gikonyo,' he said, refusing the seat she offered. 'Is he not in?'

'He goes to work very early.' Her voice was well controlled and clear, though Mugo detected a slight flow of lamentation below the surface of her words.

'Will you not sit down?' she went on. 'You must. I shall quickly make you a cup of tea, it will be ready in a minute.' Her voice grew animated, alive, he sat down in instinctive deference to her powerful presence. Studying her face, it occurred to him as odd that he rarely thought of Mumbi and Kihika as brother and sister. Her brows had the same Kihika curve, and her nose, though smaller, had a similar shape.

'How is your brother – I – I mean your younger brother, you have one, haven't you?' He stirred the tea in the cup to hide his confusion.

'Kariuki?' She sat on a chair facing him.

'That is the name, is that not so?'

'You know he finished his secondary school about two years ago. Then he worked in Nairobi for a bank before going to Makerere College.'

'That is in Uganda, Obote's kingdom?'

'Yes, he goes there by train. He says it takes a whole night and day to get there. How I feel envious . . . travelling by train all night and day. . . . I have never been on such a long journey by train.' She laughed quietly; her eyes lit as if with the thought of travelling, her whole body expressive of a resilient desire for life despite suffering. 'But he did not come home for the holidays this time, which is bad, because he will miss all the celebrations on Thursday.'

Mugo did not join in the talk about the celebrations, and the conversation ended abruptly. He searched for another subject, and failing, said he would leave. He stood up.

But Mumbi remained sitting, her face set, as if she had not heard him.

'I wanted to see you, and I would have come to you,' she said. Though not above a whisper, her words reached him as a command. He sat down and waited.

'Do you ever dream?' she suddenly asked, a sad smile playing on her lips. The question startled Mugo, again raised the thrilling fear which lasted a few seconds before subsiding.

'Yes, sometimes, that is, everybody dreams.'

'I don't mean ordinary dreams at night when you are asleep. It is when you are young in a clear day and you look into the future and you see great things. Your heart beats inside because you want the days to come quickly. Then Life's sorrow cannot touch you.'

Her voice increased the tremor in Mugo. She was recreating his dream, dressing it in live words, breath.

'Did you ever dream like that?'

'Perhaps, sometimes,' he started vaguely, but she quickly seized his answer.

'And it came true. You dreamt – yes, I knew it could come true for some people. I used to have so many of those dreams, and all so real,' she said, her voice and eyes and face digging into the past.

'It happens . . . happens with . . . eh, people . . . when they are young.' He risked the general comment.

'It was there,' she went on, 'when my brother talked. My heart travelled with his words. I dreamt of sacrifice to save so many people. And although sometimes I feared, I wanted those days to come. Even when I got married, the dream did not die. I longed to make my husband happy, yes, but I also prepared myself to stand by him when the time came. I could carry his sheath and as fast as he shot into the enemy, I would feed him with arrows. If danger came and he fell, he would fall into my arms and I would bring him home safely to myself.'

He saw the light at the bottom of the pool dancing in her eyes. He felt her dark power over him.

'Yet when they took him away, I did nothing, and when he finally came home, tired, I could no longer make him happy.'

She was still young, vulnerable; but it was he who was scurrying with hands and feet at the bottom of the silent pool. It was terrible for him, this struggle: he did not want to drown.

'I sometimes wonder,' she went on after a pause, 'whether Wambuku dreamt. And yet, she – she – you remember her?'

'Wambuku?'

'Yes.'

'No, I don't think so.'

'But you must. Don't you remember the woman you tried to save, the woman being beaten in the trench?'

'Yes . . . yes.' He could not recall her face except her dress torn by the whip and the impression of agony.

'She died.'

'Died?'

'Yes. Later. People say she was pregnant, you see, about three or four months. She had been Kihika's woman before he ran away to the forest. She never forgave him. But somehow she hoped he would come back to her and rarely went with anybody. But when Kihika was arrested and hanged on a tree, something strange came over her. For a few days she never left her home, and when she did so, eventually, well, she only destroyed herself with soldiers and home-guards, any man. But she refused, so it is said, the advances of this particular homeguard, who got his chance for revenge during the trench. She never recovered from that beating and died three months later, in pregnancy.'

She took out a handkerchief to rub something from her eyes. Just then her son came running into the room. He briefly looked at the man and then ran to his mother's knees.

'Why are you crying?' he blurted out to his mother, and looked at Mugo with open hostility. Mumbi pressed the boy to herself as if she would protect him from all harm and destructive knowledge. She tried to smile and whispered words to him.

'Run back to your grandmother, quick. You don't want to leave her alone, do you? She may be stolen by an Irimu and then what will you say?'

The boy glanced at Mugo and back at Mumbi and ran out of the house.

'You might say she died for my brother,' Mumbi resumed, as if there had been no interruption, but her voice was less intense, was more hesitant. 'A sacrifice. . . . And then there was Njeri.'

'Who was she?'

'She was also a friend, my friend. Wambuku and Njeri and I often went to the train together. But how could we tell that Njeri's heart really ached for my brother? She often quarrelled and fought with both men and other girls. None of us, however, knew that she had secret dreams. Anyway, not until she ran away to the forest to fight at Kihika's side. She was shot dead in a battle, soon after Kihika's death.'

Mugo's face was a shade darker, his lower lip had slightly dropped. He did not want to look at those things. He was already at the door when Mumbi's startled voice called him, jerking him back to the present. He stood at the door recollecting himself with difficulty. As he slowly turned round, he felt ashamed that he could still be powerless before his impulses. Mumbi too had stood up and was barely able to cover her own surprise and confusion.

'I have never talked these things to anybody,' she said, sitting down again. 'You make me feel able to talk and look at these things . . . strange, now that I remember. . . . Do you know my brother once, no, he said it often when angry with his friends, you make me remember it so well, he said that if he had something really secret and important, he would only confide in somebody like you.'

Mugo stood still, staring at her with vacant eyes. Leave me alone, he wanted to tell her, but he only whispered in a barely audible voice:

'These things . . . painful . . .'

Mugo sat down, succumbing to her seductive power, weak before her eyes and voice. He waited while she struggled with words.

'I wanted to talk to you about my husband,' she said bluntly, looking straight at him. Gradually the defiant challenge in her eyes melted into silent, almost submissive pleading. Her parted lips trembled slightly.

'I want him because, because I want him above everything else,' she said. After a pause she seemed to ease. She asked: 'You know about the child?'

Suddenly Mugo wanted to hurt her intensely. He revelled in this mad desire to humiliate her, to make her grovel in the dust: why did she try to drag him into her life, into everybody's life?

'Your husband told me.'

'He told you?'

'Yes.'

'When?'

'Last night.'

'Everything?'

'Everything . . . the child . . . Karanja.' He spoke bluntly, inwardly laughing with pain as he saw her wince, once or twice. The house was silent. Mugo's eyes were hostile. Even if she wept openly, he would not leave, he would not move, and he would not say a word of comfort. But the next minute Mumbi broke into the charged atmosphere, excitedly, as if she had just remembered something big and important.

'Did he tell you about the house, I mean our two huts? Did he?'

'House – which house?' he asked, genuinely puzzled.

'Where we lived before they took him away – aah, I see he did not tell you,' she went on with a sad triumph. 'Who could have told him but me? But he does not want to know. . . .'

Mugo remembered that those who did not move into the new village in time were ejected from their old homes; their huts were burnt down.

'Even now, at night, in bed,' she started. 'I remember the red flames. There were two huts. One belonged to my mother, the other was mine. *They* told us to remove our bedding and clothes and utensils. They splashed some petrol on the grass-thatch of my mother's hut. I then idly thought this was unnecessary as the grass was dry. Anyway, they poured petrol on the dry thatch. The sun burnt hot. My mother sat on a stool by the pile of things from our huts and I stood beside her. I had a Gikoi on my head. The leader of the homeguards struck a match and threw it at the roof. It did not light, and the others laughed at him. They shouted and encouraged him. One of them tried to take the matches from him to demonstrate how it could be done. It became a game between them. At the fourth or fifth attempt the roof caught fire. Dark and blue smoke tossed from the roof, and the flames leapt to the sky. *They* went to my hut. I could not bear to see the game repeated, so I shut my eyes. I wanted to scream, but I must have lost my voice because no sound left my throat. I suddenly remembered my mother beside me, and I wanted to take her from the scene, to prevent her from seeing it all to the end. For those huts meant much to her because she had built them after Waruhiu, her husband in the Rift Valley, had divorced her from his side. Anyway, she pushed my hands away and she shook her head slightly and she went on staring at the flames. The roofs were cracking. I remember the pain as the cracking noise repeated in my heart. Soon the roofs of the huts fell in, one after the other, with a roar. I heard my mother gasp at the first roar. But she never let her eyes from the sight. . . . Something gave way in my heart, something in me cracked when I saw our home fall.'

The breakup at the old Thabai Village followed the fall of Mahee Police Post to Kihika and his band of Forest Fighters. The blow at Mahee had incensed the government. It is said that the black man in Nyeri, Mwangi Matemo, who, in a forgetful moment of enthusiasm, heard the news of the capture over the radio was instantly taken to Manyani, the most famous and the largest concentration camp in the country. The item had been censored; but the radio only confirmed what people all over Gikuyuland knew. The government retaliated. All African trading centres like Rung'ei were to be closed 'in the interests of peace and security'. People were to move into fewer and less-scattered villages. At first this was a distant rumour; people shrugged their shoulders in disbelief and went on mourning the fate of those who had gone to detention or to the forest: would they ever return? Thomas Robson, then a District Officer, held barazas in every ridge, giving people two months within which to demolish the old and build new homes.

Mumbi was depressed because there was no man of the house. In the end, she tied a belt around her waist and took on a man's work. Together with Wangari, they cleared the site. Karanja came and helped them draw the plan of the hut on the ground. He was quiet and distant, but Mumbi was too busy to notice the reserve of a man undergoing a crisis. Within a few days the site was ready. Next she went to her father's small forest and cut down black wattle trees for posts and poles. These were days when no smoke rose from any of the huts in Thabai because men and women only returned to their homes with the dark. And the following day they would be back to the site: overnight children grew into men, women put on trousers; but the babies strapped on the backs of their mothers kept on howling for food and attention. Kariuki left school every day at four and ran home to help his sister with the building.

Men, finding women like Mumbi on the roof hammering in the nails, stopped to tease them: it was all because a woman – a new Wangu – in England – had been crowned: what good ever came from a woman's rule?

'Aah, but that is not true,' the women would reply at times, glad for the interruption. 'Doesn't Governor Baring, who rules Kenya, have a penis?'

'Aah, it's still the woman's shauri. See how you women have sent all the men to detention for their penises to rot there, unwilling husbands to Queen Elizabeth?'

'And to the forests, too,' the women would burst out, the raillery turning into bitterness. And without another word the men would hurry back to their own sites to continue the metallic cries of the hammer and the nail.

Karanja's intermittent help, though added to Kariuki's, was not enough, and Mumbi's hut had yet to be mudded when the two months' grace ended. Mumbi and Wangari stayed on in their old huts, preparing to mud the walls of their new hut in a day or two. But on the second day, the homeguards arrived. Mumbi opened the door, saw their eager faces, and rushed back inside, to prepare Wangari for the truth.

'I knew they would come, child,' Wangari wearily said, and started removing utensils and other things from the doomed place.

The homeguards went away solemnly as if they had just performed a ritual act; their eyes searched for approval on Robson's face. Robson drove off. There were more huts to burn down and the day was short.

Before night fell, the last walls of the old Thabai Village had tumbled down: mud, soot, and ashes marked the spots where the various huts once stood.

'On that night my mother and I slept in our new unfinished hut. My father broke the curfew order and came in the dark to take us to his own place. But my mother-in-law refused to go and I could not leave her alone. The roof was thatched with grass, but the walls were without mud. All night long cold wind rushed through the empty walls and lashed us on every side. I had wrapped myself with an old blanket and a sisal-sack and still I shivered. I don't think I closed my eyes even once. I knew my mother was not asleep, either, but we did not talk. Really, it was a long night.

'From that day, Karanja came to our place often and asked after our health, and sometimes he brought us food. He was quiet, though, and he seemed troubled by something. At first I did not notice this; I did not even particularly notice that his visits were becoming more and more frequent. I was too busy nursing my mother, for after our old home was burnt down, she kept on complaining of aches in the stomach, in the head, in the joints. One day he found me splitting wood outside. He stood there without speaking and only looked at me. I hate being watched when I am working, because I feel uneasy and I cannot control my hands properly. So I told him: "Come and help a woman split the wood." He took the axe from me and did the work. And still he did not speak. "Come inside for a workman's cup of tea," I told him. As I bent down to collect the pieces of wood, he put out his hand and touched me on the head and whispered: Mumbi. Anyway, I looked up quickly and saw he wanted to tell me something. I was frightened. You see, Karanja had once proposed to me, a week or so after I had already accepted to marry Gikonyo. I then had laughed him out of that passion and reminded him that Gikonyo was his close friend. He never proposed to me again and he had kept on coming to visit my husband. He must now have seen the fright in my eyes, for he went away immediately without saying anything. He did not even look back. I suppose if he had, I would have called him back, for I was struck with remorseful thoughts: something perhaps weighed heavy in his heart. Besides, he had been kind to me and my mother as befits a friend.

'He did not come again. Soon after this, Kihika was caught at the edge of Kinenie Forest and later hanged on a tree. Do you know that my father, once a warrior whose name spread from Nyeri to Kabete, urinated on his legs? He wept the night long, like a child, while Wanjiku, my real mother, comforted him. From that day, the two were broken parents. I believe that but for their faith and hope in Kariuki, they would have died. I also became sick and for two nights I would vomit out whatever I ate or drank. And then, as you know, the punishment came. Thabai was going to pay for my brother's actions. You know about the trench. At least the beginning. It was soon after you were arrested trying to save Wambuku, that I first heard Karanja had joined the homeguards. I could not believe it. He had been a friend of Kihika and Gikonyo; they had taken the oath together; how could he betray them?

'These thoughts soon gave way to the work at hand. The trench was to surround the whole village. After you were taken away, beating was not isolated to one person here, another one there. Soldiers and homeguards entered the trench and beat anybody who raised their back or slowed down in any way. They drove us into it, for, you see, there was a time limit. Women were allowed out two hours before sunset to go and look for food. Nobody else was allowed out: even school-children had to remain in the village. Within days, the two hours of freedom were reduced to one. And as the time neared, even one hour of freedom was taken away. We were prisoners in the village, and the soldiers had built their camps all round to prevent any escape. We went without food. The cry of children was terrible to hear. The new DO did not mind the cries. He even permitted soldiers to pick women and carry them to their tents. God! I didn't know how I escaped from that ignominy. Every night I prayed that such a thing should never happen to me. Wambuku died in the trench. They took her body and threw it into a grave dug a few yards from the trench.

'Do you know that we all thought the end of the world had come?

'Then one day we started singing. More soldiers and homeguards were added into the trench. They came with whips and sticks, but somehow these could not stop our voices. A woman or a man from one end of the trench would start and all of us joined in, creating words out of nothing.

> The children of Israel
> When they were in Misri
> Were made to work
> Harder than that done by cows and donkeys

'But the one that moved us most was sung on Wambuku in the grave.

> When I remember Wambuku
> A woman who was beautiful so
> How she raised her eyes to heaven
> Tears from the heart freely flow.
> > Pray true
> > Praise Him true
> > For He is ever the same God.
> Who will forget the sun and the dust today
> And the trench I dug with blood!
> When they pushed me into the trench,
> Tears from my heart freely flowed.'

Mumbi had stopped her narrative to hum the tunes for Mugo, trying to fit in two words she had forgotten. The tunes were slow, defiant yet mournful, the tears clearly stood at the edges of her eyes. Her breasts rose and fell with the songs, and Mugo was rooted to his seat, painfully reliving a scene he never saw, for by that time he had been detained.

'Invalids and old people like my father and children were not forced to dig. But they had to sit around the trench to watch their wives and sons and daughters or mothers work and bear the whip. Every day the DO came with a loudspeaker to remind us again and again why we were being punished. Thabai was a warning to other villages never to give food or any help to those fighting in the Forest.

'Two more women died. Another hole was dug by the trench.

'All this time I had not seen Karanja. People said they saw him at this end or that, but he never came to where I worked. By now our store of food was finished. I could not go to the neighbours because many were in the same condition. At that time, you hated anybody who came to visit you during a meal; no, we never visited one another. Came a day when I felt I could not endure it. I must say that my mother-in-law and my parents seemed to bear it better than I. For me I felt I could not live another day. And that night Karanja called at our place. He would not come inside, so I went outside. Under cover of the dark, he had brought us some bread. Saliva filled my mouth. (Have you ever seen a hungry dog's mouth at the sight of food?) But at the sight of the gun he carried, strength and appetite left me and I could not take the food he offered. I went back into the hut. (Then rumours had started that it was Karanja who had betrayed my brother.) I did not tell Wangari what had happened and she did not ask me any questions, but at the sight of her emaciated body, I felt guilty for having refused the bread. I thought she would die, we all would die, and I wept silently. I knew that my parents and Kariuki were equally stricken with hunger.

'Two men died.

'Our singing ended abruptly. There was no longer any sound of human voices and it seemed that even little children had stopped crying for food. The sound of jembes, spades, pangas and whips went on. A strange day: I was not feeling anything. And again that night Karanja came. I could not see him clearly in the dark, but I gathered my declining strength and moved my lips to let the word "Judas" escape from my mouth. When he spoke, his voice seemed many miles away from where I stood. "Take this maize-flour and bread, or else you will die. I did not betray Kihika, I did not. As for carrying a gun for the whiteman, well, a time will come when you too will know that every man in the world is alone, and fights alone, to live." He went away. Somehow I believed him, what he said about my brother. But even if I had not, I would still have taken the food. I am sure I would – though his words made it easier for me. When I went inside, I felt ashamed, even in the midst of my hunger and I could not tell Wangari where I got the food. She did not ask me any questions. Neither did my parents and younger brother when I gave them the food the following day. For many days I went with a head bowed down. You see at that time a number of women secretly and voluntarily offered themselves to the soldiers for a little food, and I felt no different. To this day I've never told anybody about the food which saved us. For, to tell you the truth, I still feel ashamed.

'Altogether, twenty-one men and women died. They were buried beside the trench. The strange thing is that not a single child died during that period.

'After the trench, I started work in the settled area. Those who worked for the white people in the farms or in their houses were given cards exempting them from forced communal labour which was the lot of those who remained in the village. And again it was easier for them to get pass-books. Your pass-book had to be stamped by the DO before you could move from the Reserve to the European farms or from one location to another. On the whole, I was lucky, because I was paid nine shillings a week while others in different farms only got six or four shillings a week. We worked in their large tea-plantations, sometimes digging at Muthangari grass and at times gathering the tea-leaves. With the money I earned, I bought flour which kept the five of us alive. I was determined not to accept any more help from Karanja, who by now had worked his way up and was the leader of the homeguards. Kariuki was doing well at school – I paid his school-fees. In him we saw the hope for the future. There is nothing like education.

'And all this time I never stopped thinking of my husband. It seemed to me that if only he was present, everything would be right. Months and years went. We never heard of those who went to detention. The radio said they would never come back. We did not believe this, but in public we told one another that our men would never come back. If anybody expressed a different opinion, we would look at her with angry eyes – and requested her to shut her mouth: how did she know? But in our hearts we hungrily ate these words of hope and we wanted such a person to go on insisting that those who had gone to detention would one day come back.

'At this time, something happened to Chief Muruithia which made us all fear another trench. Chief Muruithia, in charge of this area, was known everywhere for his cruelty. He was especially harsh to those

Gikuyu squatters repatriated to the Gikuyu Reserves from the Rift Valley Province, from Uganda and from Tanganyika. One day we heard that he had been shot on his way to Ndeiya, in broad daylight. The man who shot him wore a military coat and hat and had followed behind the Chief and his bodyguard at a safe distance. If the Chief stopped, the man too stopped and bent down to lace up his shoes or pass water. Then he entered the forest, ran ahead, and shot at the Chief. They say that he laughed openly as the Chief's bodyguard, homeguards and policemen, ran for cover. But before they could shoot back, the man had disappeared into the forest. The Chief did not die, and he was taken to Timoro hospital. A week later, two men carrying a basketful of food went to visit the sick Chief. Their papers were in order and they were allowed to his bed. There, they shot him dead and jumped through the window and went back to the forest.

'That is when Karanja became a Chief. Soon he proved himself more terrifying than the one before him. He led other homeguards into the forest to hunt down the Freedom Fighters. It was also during his rule that even the few remaining fit men were taken from the village to detention camps. He became very strict with curfew laws and forced communal work. I met him one day as I was coming from work. He stopped and called me. I went on. Two homeguards ran to me and threatened to beat me. But Karanja told them to leave me alone, and told them to move ahead, he would follow.

' "Why didn't you let them kill me?" I burst out.

' "Please, Mumbi."

' "Don't you call me Mumbi, Mumbi."

'I was angry and I did not want him to remind me of the gift of food. I longed for anything that would break that knot of guilt that tied me to him.

' "Mumbi, why do you hate me so?" he went on and broke into words of passion. He loved me, he said, and he wanted only me, that he had saved himself from detention and forests for me.

'Strange, isn't it, how we give many motives to our actions to fit an occasion. Anyway, I was no longer angry. Now I despised him. He really appeared contemptible in his khaki uniform, and a big rifle slung on his shoulder, and talking of love in the middle of the road. I even

A Grain of Wheat

managed to laugh, a little. This seemed to hurt him, but it did not stop the flow of words from his mouth. The words did not touch me. I wanted to hurt him, to strike a blow for Kihika and Gikonyo and everybody.

' "Why don't you wear your mother's skirt and Mwengu? When others went to fight, you remained behind to lick the feet of your white husbands." I said this clearly, and I thought he would beat me. This did prick him. His lips moved and he struggled to say something. His face changed shades from light to dark, and then he also spoke slowly and clearly.

' "You don't understand. Did you want us all to die in the Forest and in Detention so that the whiteman could live here on this land alone? The whiteman is strong. Don't you ever forget that. I know, because I have tasted his power. Don't you ever deceive yourself that Jomo Kenyatta will ever be released from Lodwar. And bombs are going to be dropped into the forest as the British did in Japan and Malaya. And those in detention will never, never see this land again. No, Mumbi. The coward lived to see his mother while the brave was left dead on the battlefield. And to ward off a blow is not cowardice."

'This frightened me.

' "Leave me alone, why don't you leave me alone!" I cried, feeling weak. He went away. My stomach was heavy, my heart dark. It was cruel of him to say Gikonyo would never come back.

'And yet towards the end of the year I had gone to seek out Karanja in his house at the Homeguard Post. Kariuki was with me, because he had passed KAPE and he was the only boy in these ridges to get a place in Siriana Secondary School. This had made many people angry: why, they asked, should a boy whose brother was in the Forest, be allowed to go to a government school, while the sons of loyalists could not? But they could not stop him unless they proved that he had taken the oath. That is why we went to the Chief's house. Karanja did not raise any questions. He gave us a letter stating that Kariuki had been screened and found not to have taken the oath. I felt ashamed of my sharp words to Karanja.

'It's when Kariuki went to Siriana that life came back to my parents.

144

Mbugua even started talking about the future, while Wanjiku wept because she was happy. I was also happy, but I could not forget, for a moment, Karanja's words, that those in detention would never come back. Maybe Gikonyo and the others had already been shot dead. The thought would keep me shivering in the night and I could not pray, or sleep. Wangari noticed my restless looks, and it was she who now became my warmth and comfort. In those years of waiting, we came closer together, not just a mother and a daughter-in-law, but as something else, I cannot describe.

'Karanja always pointed out to me that my faithfulness was vain. The government forces were beating the Freedom Fighters. We never got a letter or heard a word from those in detention. The radio no longer mentioned them. And with years, Karanja became arrogant towards me. He did not humble himself in front of me as he used to do. Instead, he laughed to hurt me, and I hung on to Gikonyo with all my heart. I would wait for him, my husband, even if I was fated to rejoin him in the grave. I completely lost hope of meeting him again on this earth, and lived on the memory of happy days before the State of the Emergency.

'Let me not tire you with a long story, though I might tell you it already makes me feel better to have opened my heart to you. One day Karanja sent for me to his house. It was on a Thursday, I remember. I felt tired and bored with living. For what is life unless you live for a person you love, a man who is breathing, whom you can see, and touch? Gikonyo was dead. And the Emergency was never going to end. Anyway. I went there and I swore that if he tried anything on me, even a word, I would get a piece of wood and strike him hard on the head or neck. I found him alone. I stood at the door for a while. He did not look at me directly. He seemed to have changed. He appeared worried and slightly aged. This surprised me – I thought he was ill or something. So I went in and asked him what he wanted with me. He did not answer me for a little while. Then he said:

' "Your husband is coming back."

' "What?"

' "Your husband is coming back," he repeated and tried to smile.

145

'Something that caused pain rippled in me, as if, as if I had been paralysed all over and blood and life was now entering into me.

' "Please, Karanja, don't play with me," I stammered. My voice was broken. My heart was full of fear and hope. I would have done anything to know the truth.

'He came to where I was standing and showed me a long sheet of paper with the government stamps. There was a list of names of those on their way back to the villages. Gikonyo's name was there.

'What else is there to tell you? That I remember being full of submissive gratitude? That I laughed – even welcomed Karanja's cold lips on my face? I was in a strange world, and it was like if I was mad. And need I tell you more?

'I let Karanja make love to me.'

She paused. The light still played in her dark voluptuous eyes. She was young. She was beautiful. A big lump blocked Mugo's throat. Something heaved forth; he trembled; he was at the bottom of the pool, but up there, above the pool, ran the earth; life, struggle, even amidst pain and blood and poverty, seemed beautiful; only for a moment; how dared he believe in such a vision, an illusion?

'When I woke and realized fully what had happened, I became cold, the whole body. Karanja tried to say nice things to me, but I could see he was laughing at me with triumph. I took one of his shoes and I threw it at him. I ran out, and I could not cry. Although a few minutes before, I had been so happy, now I only felt sour inside. I went to Wangari and this time I cried and I could not clearly tell her what had happened. But she seemed to understand, and she held me to her and tried to remove my shivers with words.'

Listening to Mumbi's story had drained Mugo of strength. He now searched for fitting words to break his silence.

'What do you want me to do?' he cried, weak with pain and longing.

She was about to say something when there was a hurried knock at the door and 'hodi'. General R. entered, closely followed by Lt Koina. The General's face beamed with satisfaction, which Mugo had not seen on Sunday night or the night before. Koina, on the other hand, looked pensive, aged.

'We are not staying for long,' General R. said after taking a seat.

He then turned to Mugo. He appeared more friendly and more voluble than usual.

'I came to your place. When I did not find you there, well, I thought I would come this way. I told you I would visit you? Remember last night? You appeared worried, or very excited. Didn't see anybody. I spoke to you outside but you only answered in a borrowed voice. A strange man, Githua? Did you hear what he said about bullets?'

'I can't – I can't remember—'

'You see! I said your mind was not on this earth. Githua is always telling people how he used to supply us with bullets. Do you know that he never once gave us bullets (Maize grains as we called them in the forest).'

'Didn't he?' Mumbi asked.

'Never. I've also learnt that he was never shot by anybody.'

'How did he break his leg?' Mumbi asked.

'His leg? The lorry he drove overturned in Nakuru. Githua's left leg was smashed to bits.'

'Why, then—'

'It makes his life more interesting to himself. He invents a meaning for his life, you see. Don't we all do that? And to die fighting for freedom sounds more heroic than to die by accident.'

Mugo felt let down by Githua. He was again alone, his vision disrupted by Mumbi and General R. He winced from the direct gaze of the General. Where was the warmth which had enveloped him last night, this morning, before he entered Mumbi's house?

'But let's leave Githua alone. We came to see you,' General R. said to Mugo.

'Shall I leave the room?' Mumbi asked, making ready to rise.

'Not unless you want to. This concerns your brother.'

'Kariuki? Has anything happened?

'No, Kihika!'

'Oh!'

'As I said on Sunday night, we believe that Kihika certainly walked into a trap. He was going to meet an important contact. Now, there are only three people he could have gone to meet. One of them is Wambui. But Kihika had already sent Wambui to Nakuru with messages to our agents. The other man is you!' he said, fixing Mugo with a glance. Mugo's belly tightened.

'But every child knows what you did for Kihika and what the whiteman did to you.'

'Who is the man?' Mumbi asked, relieved.

'A friend and not a friend. What was it Kihika used to say? Kikulacho kiko nguoni mwako.'

'Who is he?' she insisted, impatiently.

'You see Kihika had once or twice said he wanted to meet Karanja.'

'Ngai!' she exclaimed and looked at Mugo.

'And it was soon after Kihika's arrest that Karanja became a home-guard. His behaviour at Githima points to his guilt. Koina here was there yesterday.'

Koina started and looked at the General. His face looked weary, a little pained.

'And I'll never go back there. Never. Never,' he said in a voice totally unlike his lighthearted self. Mumbi and the General looked at him.

'What is the matter?' the General asked.

'Nothing. Nothing.' Koina said. 'It is only that I am puzzled about the meaning of what I saw there. But don't mind me. I am not feeling well.'

'You must go to bed,' Mumbi said anxiously. 'Do you want some Aspro?'

'Oh, it's only a small headache!'

'What did you see at Githima that makes you ill?' Mumbi asked. 'Ghosts?'

'Yes . . . Some kind of ghosts. But they were ghosts that make me wonder about what we are really celebrating!'

General R. thought of asking him to talk less mysteriously, but Mugo spoke first.

'What – what do you – did you want with me?' Mugo, who had been following his own thoughts, released his breath slowly.

'It is about the celebrations on Thursday. Let me first of all tell you that I never prayed to God. I never believed in Him. I believe in Gikuyu and Mumbi and in the black people of this our country. But one day I did pray. One day in the forest alone, I knelt down and cried with my heart. God, if you are there above, spare me and I'll find Kihika's real murderer. The time has come. The season is ripe for harvest. On Thursday people will gather in Rung'ei Market to remember Kihika. At Githima we have set Mwaura to persuade Karanja to attend this meeting. So what will you do? At the end of your speech, you'll announce that the man who betrayed Kihika should come forward – and stand condemned before the people. For in betraying Kihika, to the whiteman, Karanja had really betrayed the black people everywhere on the earth.'

The General's impassioned speech was followed by an uneasy silence. Each man in the house seemed absorbed in his own life – in his own fears and hopes. The atmosphere was tense – like a taut rope. Suddenly Mugo stood up, trembling, in the tension of a sudden decision.

'That cannot be,' he said. 'I came here to tell Gikonyo and the Party that I am not a fit man to lead them. The Party should look elsewhere for a leader.'

His voice was choked. He struggled to bring out another word, and then unexpectedly rushed out.

Ten

The decision to persuade, or failing that, compel Karanja to attend the big ceremony at Rung'ei had been taken the previous night after Lt Koina had met Mwaura.

Mwaura's reports had only confirmed what General R. had always suspected: Karanja was the man who had betrayed Kihika. That Karanja should die on Independence Day seemed just: that he should be humiliated in front of a huge crowd, if he gave himself up, or else be made uncomfortable, was only a necessary preparation for the ritual.

General R. was a man of few words, except when he was excited. 'I can't use my tongue,' he used to say with a streak of pride, 'but I can use my hands.' Kihika would pray and agonize over a problem, General R. acted. Kihika talked of oppression, and injustice, and freedom; General R. saw oppressed persons, or a cruel or a good man. He was something of an adventurer. Before the War of Independence he had lived in Rung'ei centre working as a tailor. Nobody knew of his origins: some said that he had come from Nyeri and others said his home was in Embu. Although he had lived in Rung'ei for many years, people in Thabai regarded him as a stranger in their midst. 'These from that side of Nyeri and Embu,' they would say, 'are people to be feared; you never know what they may carry in their fingernails or under their armpits.' People did not even know his real name: they all called him Ka-40, because once or twice, in one of his sudden but rare moments of self-revelation, he would sing his own praises thus: 'See me, a young man of '40. I was born in 1940, circumcised in 1940, went to fight Hitler in 1940, and married in 1940. So me, I am a young man of '40.' (To people's knowledge, he had no wife, but he had fought for the British in the Second World War.)

Otherwise he was quiet, rarely talked about himself or about his political beliefs, and noticeably avoided wild scenes and brawls that so often flared up in eating-houses and drinking places. Ka-40 was a good and successful tailor, specializing in clothes for women and children; his prosperity was attributed to 'something under the armpit'.

Yet this man, who clearly shunned quarrels and violence and mostly kept alone, became one of the most fierce of Kihika's band of Forest Fighters, feared in the village and even among his followers. General R. never forgot a friend or enemy. R. stood for Russia.

At the time that General R. was talking excitedly about the little drama to be enacted on Independence Day, Karanja, the main actor, was preoccupied with a problem which, three months before seemed small – viewed, of course, as a distant possibility – but which, Independence being only two nights away, had now assumed monstrous proportions: would Thompson really go? Today Karanja was determined to find out the truth, an inkling of which he had once tasted, when, as a Chief, he had been told that Gikonyo and other detainees were coming back to the village. Now he would go to Thompson and say: Sir, are you really abandoning Kenya? Not that between Karanja and John Thompson there had developed a relationship that might be called personal; nor was the consciousness of dependency mutual; only that to Karanja, John Thompson had always assumed the symbol of whiteman's power, unmovable like a rock, a power that had built the bomb and transformed a country from wild bush and forests into modern cities, with tarmac highways, motor vehicles and two or four legs, railways, trains, aeroplanes and buildings whose towers scraped the sky – and all this in the space of sixty years. Had he himself not experienced that power, which also ruled over the souls of men, when he, as a Chief, could make circumcised men cower before him, women scream by a lift of his finger?

So Karanja waited for the terrible knowledge. Twice he had gone along the corridors past Thompson's office, his ears set for any movement inside. Back in his own workroom, Karanja remembered that he could tell whether John Thompson was in or out by checking if his 'Another Morris' was stationed at its permanent place in the Staff Car Park. He rose from the chair like a man who unexpectedly sits on a drawing-pin, only instead of examining the seat, he craned his neck and peered at – at an empty place normally occupied by the Morris. Was the man not coming to work today? He found it difficult to write labels for any of the books on the table. It was lucky that Mrs Dickinson was not there today. He went to the bindery to kill time with the men there. Karanja always went there with this or that pretext whenever he was tired. Most of the binders came from Central Nyanza and Karanja always felt freer in their presence. He did not feel, as he did with the Gikuyus, that they were probing into his past. He also despised them and said so when talking with Mwaura or any other men of his tribe. 'These Jaluo!' he would say, 'they always stick together: once you put one of them in charge of a place, he invited all his tribesmen whenever a vacancy occurs.' They on their part were suspicious of him. 'These Wakikuyu – never trust them. A Kikuyu will embrace you as a friend today and tomorrow knife you in the back.' In his presence, they were friendly.

He found them talking about the late Dr Van Dyke. Had his death been an accident? What did that little Thompson woman (my God, she's pretty – her buttocks, man – wouldn't mind giving her the works myself) see in that pot-bellied Boer? Did Thompson know he was being double-crossed? He must have known. That's why he was always so sad. Did he himself taste other women, like Dr Lynd? Ha! Ha! Ha! They changed to the dog incident. They became angry. They sympathized with Karanja. Man! Thompson saved you. But he won't punish her. Karanja found the smell of the boiling glue, the men's talk and laughter, did not soothe his restless nerves. He went out and walked between the Soil Physics Laboratory and the main administrative block, affecting business-purposefulness, but really hoping to catch sight of John Thompson in the office through the window. Had the man gone, Karanja wondered? He should have asked him yesterday. Yesterday after the dog incident. Karanja recalled his terror as the dog approached him. He shuddered. Thompson had saved him from shame. Thompson. And he was going. He strolled back to his room, heavy with a sense of imminent betrayal.

He had once before experienced a similar feeling. That was the day, soon after the State of Emergency was officially lifted, that the reigning DO advised him to resign his post as Chief. Then new Party political leaders like Oginga Odinga were agitating for Independence and the release of Jomo Kenyatta. Karanja arrested a man who had not paid poll-tax for two years. The man had been without a job since he left detention. He was so angry that instead of answering questions, he spat on the dust. The Chief did exactly what he was used to doing: he had the man beaten by his bodyguard, and locked him up at the Homeguard Post until morning. The matter was taken up by men connected with Odinga, and in this way reached the courts. Karanja was compelled to pay a fine and make a public apology. This had cut him to the quick. Why should he be punished for doing exactly what he had been praised for doing a month or so before? Later Karanja was demoted. The DO, however, gave him a letter of recommendation listing Karanja's qualities of faithfulness, integrity and courage. 'You can wholly depend on him.' Armed with the letter (it bore a government seal) Karanja had drifted to Githima, where he again met John Thompson. Karanja had confessed his oath and registered as a homeguard when Thompson was the DO in the District (soon after Robson died), and although Thompson did not seem to remember the old days, Karanja felt the 'government' letter was itself a live link. He got a job at Githima. And soon his qualities of faithfulness, integrity and courage revealed themselves, and he quickly became a trusted servant of the white people at Githima.

Was the dog's threat a prelude to disaster, thought Karanja? In his consciousness of an imminent disaster, Karanja did not know whether to be pleased or angry when later Mwaura came into the room.

'Hey, man. Is it true?' Mwaura started in a subservient, conspiring whisper which said: you know all the secrets of the powers that rule above us. Throw me a few crumbs of your mighty knowledge.

'What?' Karanja asked, slow to respond to the affected adoration.

'Well, that the boss, you know, Ka-Thompson, has gone?' Whenever

Mwaura wanted to conspire against any man in authority, he always put the diminutive 'Ka' before his name.

'Who told you?' Karanja was startled, but tried to appear cool.

'Oh, just rumours. And I said to myself, the only person who would know is Karanja. He is in these people's secrets. Especially the boss. That man loved you, you know – always sent for you – oh, yes, and I could see he feared you. Is it true?'

Karanja knew he was being flattered, it made him feel good.

'You people and your rumours. Didn't you see him at work yesterday?'

'Yes, but. . . . Couldn't that have been the last day? That's why he called for you, is that not so? To say good-bye. Did he give you some money? And people say – well, do you know I often agree with you when you say that people's tongues are wild?'

'What do people say?' Karanja was suspicious and curious.

'That an African, a man with a black skin like you or me, is coming to replace him.'

'No!' Karanja said firmly, expressing more what he would not want to see happen than what he knew would happen. 'You may think what you like, but Thompson is not going anywhere. It was only yesterday that I was having a chat with his wife. She gave me coffee.'

'Really! Mm,' Mwaura said, nodding his head several times. 'I see, I understand. You know, I would not be surprised to hear that you have tasted that woman. Do you know how my mouth waters when I look at her smooth buttocks and her breasts that cry to you: touch me, touch me. And her voice, it is like a song, makes you think of her thing itself. Lucky man. How did you start her?'

'What are you talking about?' Karanja had warmed to the talk, but was uneasy, unable to deny or confirm what Mwaura was suggesting.

'Come, man. You must have tasted her. How do her goods taste?'

'You people. Why do you think Europeans have anything special? They are like everybody else, you or me.'

'A confession! Anyway, I knew you had done it. By the way, what are you doing on Thursday, on Uhuru day?'

'I don't know. Nothing . . .' he added, the inner warmth melting.

'Nothing? Aren't you going to this thing?'

'What thing?'

'The ceremony at Rung'ei. Don't you know they are organizing games and dances to celebrate Uhuru?'

'I don't know,' he said vaguely.

'But you can't stay here all alone! Everybody from the camp here is going to hear Mugo speak.'

'Who is Mugo?' he asked, more uncertainty creeping into his voice. Mwaura seized it.

'People say the man talks with God and receives messages from spirits of the dead. Or how do you explain that at Rira he escaped alive while ten of those involved in the hunger-strike died? And remember, he was the leader?'

'Nonsense. People are full of wild tongues,' he said without conviction. He had not thought what he would do on the day. But could he go back to Thabai and meet people who would mock him? What about if he went to see Mumbi just once? Couldn't he make a last attempt to wrench her from Gikonyo?

'You may call it nonsense. Anyway, I would rather go and see for myself. The man Mugo is a true hermit, has kept to himself, has never spoken to anyone, since he left detention camp. And there'll be plenty of women. You know how they go free (even married ones) on such occasions.'

'Are you going?' he asked, tempted by a desire to see Mumbi.

'Me, left behind?'

'Let me know when you decide to go,' Karanja said, looking at the window. John Thompson was just parking his Morris outside.

'There is *your* Thompson,' he told Mwaura, barely able to disguise his triumph. He stood up, quickly dusted the khaki overall, passed his hands over his hair and rushed out, hoping to meet Thompson along the corridor. Then he would put the awful question. A watery lump leapt to his throat as soon as he saw Thompson's abstract face: should I ask him or not?

'Excuse me, sir!' he called out, wanting to cry. John Thompson walked as though he had not seen Karanja. 'Excuse me, sir,' Karanja raised his voice, gathering courage in despair. Thompson turned round to face Karanja.

'Yes?' The voice was clear, cold, distant.

'You—' Karanja swallowed some lumpy liquid. '—you are going!' he made a statement instead of the intended cool question.

'What!'

'You are – you are—' he swallowed some more lumpy liquid; it made a noise as it went down his throat. But he stood his ground.

'—are you going back to – to your country.'

'Yes, yes,' the whiteman answered quickly, as if puzzled by the question. Panic seized Karanja. He played with his fingers behind his back. He would have loved to suddenly vanish from the earth rather than bear the chill around. Thompson was about to move, but then he stopped.

'What can I do for you?' he asked, in a brusque manner.

'Nothing. Nothing, sir. You have been very kind.'

Thompson hastened away.

Karanja stood in the corridor for a while and took a dirty handkerchief to rub off the sweat from his face. Then he went back, his gait, to an observer, conjuring up the picture of a dog that has been unexpectedly snubbed by the master it trusts. Karanja did not seem to see Mwaura, who was still waiting in the room. He sat on the chair, his hands limply on the table, and uncomprehendingly stared at the world outside the window.

'Is he going back, then?' Mwaura asked, tentatively.

'I don't know,' Karanja answered in a thin, colourless voice. Then suddenly he seemed to see Mwaura for the first time.

'What are you doing in the office?' he shouted at Mwaura, who quickly backed to the door. The tooth was aged and broken; it could not bite. As if exhausted by the gesture, Karanja resumed his deathly posture at the table. It was Mwaura's turn to feel triumphant and, for a time, forgot that his mission was to befriend Karanja and lure him to the Uhuru ceremony.

'Angry that master is leaving you, eh?' he taunted, standing safely at the open door. 'Not even decent enough to say farewell? I once worked for a whiteman in Nairobi. When he left Kenya, he at least shot dead all his pets – cats and dogs. Couldn't bear to leave them alive without a kindly helper.'

Karanja apparently did not hear him. He did not make the slightest stir from his position at the table.

Eleven

The farewell party held at Githima hostel was to start at eight. John and Margery Thompson went early but found some guests had already arrived. Dr Brian O'Donoghue, the Director of Githima Agricultural and Forestry Research Station, could not attend the party because he had gone to an International Forestry Commission in Salisbury. He was a tall thin man with big-rimmed glasses, who was never seen walking across Githima ground without a book under his arm. His wife, however, made a brief appearance. The official contingent was later strengthened by the arrival of the Deputy Director, his wife, and the heads of the various departments. Within an hour or so, the common room at the hostel was full of men and women, diversely dressed, clinking glasses, cracking little jokes, laughing.

At first, Mr and Mrs Thompson were the monopoly of the official contingent. Envious and deprecating glances were cast at the wives of the two Directors; they always dominated the scene, couldn't they give other people a chance to say a word to Mr Thompson (poor John, a real dear, liked him so much, such manners, such dedication: could a man be worse treated by his government?). They searched their hearts and suddenly discovered that they had always admired John, that Margery had been their special friend, and what wouldn't they do to help them settle down in their next home!

Thompson's imminent departure and the Independence tomorrow night brought back in their hearts the man who had been at the centre of scandal at Rira. Thompson was therefore a martyr, had been so received at Githima, was so regarded now on the eve of his departure from a country he had served so well.

As soon as the official contingent had gone, the party jumped to new life and commotion. Women fussed over Thompson: What was he going to do? Had he found a job? Wasn't it a shame the way the British Government abandoned men she had encouraged and sent abroad? It came from her yielding to African violence and International Communism. Didn't you see what was happening in Uganda and Tanganyika? The Chinese and the Russians had rushed to establish embassies. Mrs Dickinson, the Librarian, was always the more out-spoken in politics and predicted a holocaust after Uhuru. She and Roger Mason, her boyfriend had already booked a flight to Uganda, where they would stay to escape the violence that would be unleashed on all white people in Kenya. Now she was saying: 'I tell you, I can see it all, in ten years these countries will be Russian satellites or worse still, part of the Chinese Empire —' Another woman broke in: 'You resigned, didn't you? Now, think of that, and I —' Some wanted to know why he had taken such a step. Others withdrew fearing to embarrass John (poor John, they moaned again, casting deprecating glances at Margery, surrounded by men. The way she had carried on with that alcoholic, it wouldn't be surprising if really John wanted just to get away from the scene of shame).

Dr Lynd was talking to Roger Mason about her work, but kept on casting anxious glances towards John Thompson. She talked incess-antly and Roger Mason, a tall man with a red moustache, looked bored though he made no effort to get away.

'Githima area? Oh, it's all right, because though most potatoes here suffer from Fungus blight, they can be treated with copper sulphate. But potatoes suffering from bacterial blight can't. And it is this blight which affects most parts of Kenya, especially the African areas. Oh, yes, we do all sorts of experiments, like, for instance, the one I am doing now – injecting a specific bacterial strain to trace the path of infection through the plant. But – oh, excuse me —'

She hurried to where Thompson was standing and just managed to hold him to herself. Gradually she led him into a corner and compelled him to sit down. She looked agitated and he expected her to tell him about the dog.

'You remember the incident I told you about yesterday?'

'The dog?'

'Yes . . . the murder of my dog!'

'Yes.'

'You remember I told you about the houseboy.'

'Yes.'

'He was never caught.'

'Yes, I believe you told me so.'

'I am frightened. I don't know what to do.'

'Why, what's happened?'

'Because – because, I saw him again—'

'When?'

'Yesterday.'

'Yesterday . . . Do you think it is going to be safe for us who remain?' she asked him. But before he could answer, she added defiantly, 'No! Safe or not, I'll not leave this place. I'll not leave my property to them.'

'Then you'll have to get better homeguards!' he said, rather savagely. But Dr Lynd did not get the irony. She clung on to the idea. 'Yes . . . many more mbwa kalis to protect our lives and property,' she said and started talking about the qualities of the most loyal and the most ferocious guard dogs.

By eleven o'clock people were getting drunk. A few couples were dancing. The African waiters stood aside, like posts, dressed in white Kanzus, a red band round the waist, and a red fez on the head.

Men clustered around Margery, caressing her figure with their eyes. One by one they were pulled on to the floor by their wives, until only one fat man with a long unkempt beard and bushy eyebrows was left talking to her. She kept on stealing SOS glances at her husband, who did not see because he was now engaged in a group that was discussing politics, Independence Day, and the fate of the whiteman under a black government.

'It's logical, isn't it?' the bearded man was saying, as he pulled her to the floor for a dance.

'What's logical about that?' she yawned, unable to disguise her boredom. The man reminded her of the worst aspects of her lover.

'That we are all drunk, eh? I don't know why I act like this today –
hiccup! – and it follows that – hiccup – you—'

Suddenly she heard the sound of a broken glass on the floor.
Everybody stopped dancing and talking. Margery looked at the group
behind her husband. His empty hand was in the air as if holding a
glass to his mouth. Everybody's eyes were now turned on him.
Margery quickly walked across and linked her hand in his and bravely
smiled at nowhere. An African waiter rushed in with a dustpan and
brush and collected the broken pieces. The silence was over. The
conversation resumed as if nothing had happened.

John and Margery drove back in the dark slowly. The consciousness
that she was seeing Githima for the last time drew her closer to her
husband.

'Before the party I didn't feel that we were really leaving. Now it
seems that all this belongs to our past.'

He drove on, avoiding their home. At the very edge of the forest,
he stopped the car and lit two cigarettes. Suddenly Margery realized
that this was the very spot where Van had made love to her. She
started smoking furiously, waiting for him to accuse her.

'Perhaps this is not the journey's end,' he said, at last.

'What?'

'We are not yet beaten,' he asserted hoarsely. 'Africa cannot, cannot
do without Europe.'

Margery looked up at him, but said nothing.

Twelve

When Gikonyo came home in the evening, Mumbi could tell that he was in a bad mood. First he did not talk to her. This was not unusual. Then, when she gave him food, he only glanced at it once and then continued staring at the wall. Again this was not unusual. But it was the way he was breathing, as if suppressing a groan, that convinced her that something had happened. Though scared of him, of his moods, she could not help but probe into his affairs.

'What is the trouble?' she asked with submissive concern.

'Since when did I start discussing my affairs with you?' he answered. She withdrew, ashamed. What had come over him these last few days? She did not know which was worse: the previous formal, polite talk, or this recent attempt to hurt her with words.

'Mugo was here today,' she said coldly, after a while. 'He said that he would not take part in the ceremony.'

'What!' he shouted at her as if she was responsible for Mugo's actions. She did not answer.

'Have you no ears? It's to you that I am speaking. What did he say?'

'You seem to be seeking a quarrel tonight. Didn't you hear what I said? Mugo said that he would not lead the Uhuru ceremonies.'

'You should open your mouth wide and not speak with your teeth closed. Nobody is interested in seeing your teeth,' he added, resuming his previous posture.

Things might have returned to normal (politeness and all that), but then the boy in dispute came running into the room from Wangari's place. Previously, Gikonyo also treated the boy politely, showing neither resentment nor affection. For, as he argued in his heart, a child was a child and was not responsible for his birth. The boy had sensed his coldness and instinctively respected the distance. Today, however, he propped himself in between Gikonyo's knees, and started chattering, desiring to be friendly.

'Grandma has told me such a story – a good one – about – about— Do you know the one about the Irimu?'

Gikonyo roughly pushed the boy away from the knees, disgust on his face. The boy staggered and fell on his back and burst into tears, looking to the mother for an explanation. Mumbi stood up, and for a minute anger blocked her throat.

'What sort of a man do you call yourself? Have you no manly courage to touch me? Why do you turn a coward's anger on a child, a little child . . .' She seethed like a river that has broken a dam. Words tossed out; they came in floods, filling her mouth so that she could hardly articulate them.

'Shut your mouth, woman!' he shouted at her, also standing.

'You think I am an orphan, do you? You think the gates of my parents' hut would be shut against me if I left this tomb?'

'I'll make you shut this mouth of a whore,' he cried out, slapping her on the left cheek, and then on the right. And the flow of words came to an abrupt end. She stared at him, holding back her tears. The boy ran out of the house crying to his grandmother.

'You should have told me that before,' she said quietly, and still she held back the tears. Wangari came hurrying into the hut, her face contorted with pain, the boy following behind at a safe distance. Wangari stood between Gikonyo and Mumbi.

'What is it, children?' she asked, facing her son.

'He calls me a whore, he keeps me in this house as a whore, mother,' Mumbi said, in a choked voice, and now sobbed freely.

'Gikonyo, what's all this about?' Wangari demanded from the son.

'This does not concern you, Mother!' he said.

'Does not concern me?' She raised her voice, slapping her sides with both hands. 'Come all the earth and hear what a son, my son, answers me. Does not concern me who brought you forth from these thighs? That the day should come – hah!— Touch her again if you call yourself a man!' Wangari had worked herself into an uncontrollable fury. Gikonyo wanted to say something; then, suddenly he turned round and walked out of the house.

'And you now, stop crying, and tell me what happened,' she said gently to Mumbi, who had already sat down and was heaving and sobbing.

A river runs along the line of least resistance. Gikonyo's resentment was directed elsewhere; it was only that Mumbi happened to be near. And her face and voice found him at a time when the walls that carefully guarded his frustrated life from the outside world were weakest.

Following yesterday's talk with the MP, Gikonyo called on the five men concerned with the scheme. They reviewed their position and decided to enlarge the land company, raise the price per share, and invite people to buy the shares. In this way, they would raise enough money for Burton's farm. In the afternoon they went to see Burton, to see if he would accept a large, first instalment. Then they would pay the rest at the end of the month. If the loan promised by the MP came, they would use it to develop the farm. The first thing they saw at the main entrance to Green Hill Farm (as Burton's farm was called) was a new signpost. Gikonyo could not believe his eyes when he read the name. They walked to the house without a whisper among themselves, but all dwelling on the same thought. Burton had left Kenya for England. The new landowner was their own MP.

Gikonyo tried not to think of the day's experience or his quarrel with Mumbi as he went to Warui's hut. His first duty was to the Party. Besides he wanted the Uhuru celebrations to succeed, for this would add to his power and prestige. Warui was in the hut alone, taking snuff at the fireside. What made such a man as Warui contented with life in spite of age and loss of a wife, Gikonyo mused, taking a seat and listening to Warui's delighted words of welcome. Was it because he had lived his own personal life fully as a man, a husband and a father, or was it because he had lived his life for the people? 'I have got my heart's earliest wish: my mother has a good house in which to live. I have a bit of land and money enough to buy me food and drink. But now the money gives me no pleasure, the wealth tastes as bitter water in my mouth. And yet I must go on seeking for more.'

Warui was not as contented with life as his outer frame suggested to Gikonyo. It was only that he took delight in active living, and refused to bow to disappointments. His wife had died the year before. Mukami had been a wife who admired her husband and enjoyed singing his praises among other women. Warui on his part always brought delicacies to her every evening. She was a good listener and every night he would relive his doings of the day with her. If nothing exciting had happened he would relate old stories about the birth of the Movement, the Gikuyu break with the missions, and about the Harry procession. Mukami would often rebuke him for his vanity, but enjoyed every episode that told of her man's strength and courage.

Warui's main disappointment in life lay in his three sons. They had been conscripted to fight for Britain in the Second World War. The eldest died in active service; the other two came back, overwhelmed less by the actual hardships and violence in the war, than by the strange lands and women they had seen. Both had gone through the Emergency unscathed, escaping forests and concentration camps, by prostrating themselves and cowering before whichever side seemed stronger at a particular time and place. After the Emergency they returned to the Rift Valley to live as squatters on the land owned by the white people. Kamau, the elder of the two, believed implicitly in the power of the British.

'I tell you, if you see an Englishman, fear him,' he would say in a voice suggesting greater knowledge of the whiteman's secrets than Kamau cared to reveal. 'I saw with my own eyes what he did to Hitler. And I tell you the Germans were not boys, either. What do you think Kihika and his men can do with their unpredictable home-made guns, rotting pangas and blunt spears?'

Warui, however, placed his faith in the God of the nation and what he cryptically called the spirit of the black people. He believed, in turns, that people like Harry and Jomo had mystical power; their speeches always moved him to tears; at such times he would tell the story of the 1923 procession and end with the same refrain: 'Perhaps if we had the guns . . .' He had a similar faith in Mugo, he wished his sons had grown to be a man like him, and used the same formula which over the years had made him predict, with a prophetic accuracy that surprised him, the national heroes: you can see it in his eyes, he often told his wife. But now Mukami had died, and his sons had failed him.

After a few inconsequential words, Gikonyo plunged into the subject of his visit.

'Mugo says that he will not lead in the ceremony.'

'What do you say? But I was with him today, this afternoon, and he did not say a thing.'

'Still, he says he'll not lead; he is a strange man, hard to understand.'

'Now that I think about it, he did seem troubled when I talked to him.'

'I've come so that you and I can go there to see him again. Else we shall have to choose another man, and time is short.'

On the way to Mugo's hut, Gikonyo told Warui his disappointment over Green Hill Farm.

'And he did not tell you he had bought it when you saw him yesterday?' Warui asked.

'No, he did not tell me. I could see, though, that he did not want to look at me in the eyes.'

'The gods who rule us,' Warui said with sympathy. He wanted to tell Gikonyo the story of how people once rose against women-rulers who enriched themselves and forgot the responsibility of their office, but only muttered: 'They'll only raise wrath against the hearts of their worshippers.'

Gikonyo did not answer, and nothing further was said on the subject until they were near Mugo's hut.

'It is the old saying come true: Kamwene Kabagio ira,' Warui said.

When a young boy, Mugo once went to the railway station at Rung'ei to look at the trains. He walked along the platform, awed by the goods-train with its many coaches. In some of the coaches were horses, big powerful animals. One of the horses fixed him with its eyes and then yawned, opening wide its strong jaws. Mugo shook with terror and for a time was unable to move. He feared being trampled to the ground by horses' hooves.

Mugo had felt the same irrational terror on leaving Mumbi and General R. He felt pursued from behind, and he could not escape. He wanted to return to his hut, and even quickened his steps to do so. But he was irrevocably drawn to the lives of the villagers. He tried to think of something else – himself, his aunt – but he could not escape from his knowledge of Gikonyo's and Mumbi's lives.

The sun was fiercely hot. Children – there were always children – played in the streets. And yesterday, on Sunday, he had seen these huts as objects that had nothing to do with him. Yesterday, this morning, before Mumbi told her story, the huts had run by him, and never sang a thing of the past. Now they were different: the huts, the dust, the trench, Wambuku, Kihika, Karanja, detention-camps, the white face, barbed-wire, death. He was conscious of the graves beside the trench. He shuddered cold, and the fear of galloping hooves changed into the terror of an undesired discovery. Two years before, in the camps, he would not have cared how Wambuku lay and felt in the grave. How was it that Mumbi's story had cracked open his dulled inside and released imprisoned thoughts and feelings? The weight of her words and the face of General R. dissolved into acts of the past. Previously he liked to see events in his life as isolated. Things had been fated to happen at different moments. One had no choice in anything as surely as one had no choice on one's birth. He did not, then, tire his mind by trying to connect what went before with what followed after. Numbed, he ran without thinking of the road, its origin or its end.

Mugo abruptly stopped in the middle of the main village street, surprised that he had been walking deeper and deeper into the village. Incidents tumbled on him. He stirred himself with difficulty, to cut a path through the heap. He was again drawn to the trench and seemed impotent to resist this return to yesterday. The walls of the trench were now battered: soil had fallen and filled the bottom. Potato peelings, rotting maize husks, bits of white paper, bones and remains of rotting meat were strewn on top and on the banks of what was now a shallow ditch.

Three women, bent double with loads of wood, crossed over the ditch into the village.

Mugo walked along hoping, with a guilty curiosity, to come to the section he himself had helped to dig. Fear and restless expectation raged inside. He would fix his eyes on the scene, and he would not flinch.

The whole scene again became alive and vivid. He worked a few yards from the woman. He had worked in the same place for three days. Now a homeguard jumped into the trench and lashed the woman with a whip. Mugo felt the whip eat into his flesh, and her pained whimper was like a cry from his own heart. Yet he did not know her, had for the three days refused to recognize those around him as fellow sufferers. Now he only saw the woman, the whip, and the homeguard. Most people continued digging, pretending not to hear the woman's screams, and fearing to meet a similar fate. Others furtively glanced at the woman as they raised their shovels and jembes. In terror, Mugo pushed forward and held the whip before the homeguard could hit the woman a fifth time. More homeguards and two or three soldiers ran to the scene. Other people temporarily stopped digging and watched the struggle and the whips that now descended on Mugo's body. 'He's mad,' some people later said, after Mugo had been taken away in a police van. To Mugo the scene remained a nightmare whose broken and blurred edges he could not pick or reconstruct during the secret screening that later followed. He only saw behind the table the inscrutable face of the whiteman, whose cold eyes examined Mugo from head to foot. The voice when at last it came as from a dead body, carried venom.

'You have taken the oath.'

'No, no, Effendi.'

'Take him back to the cell.'

Two policemen pulled him out; they poured cold water on him and locked him in. Strange how often Mugo forgot the hob-nailed shoes dug into his flesh, but always remembered the water on the cement floor.

Mugo looked across to the men and women who worked on the narrow shambas, enclosed by the thick and unkempt hedges that spread from the ditch, once the trench. He seemed to be seeing things as if they were new. Were people always doing this, day in, day out, coaxing the hard soil for food?

Suddenly the curiosity which had driven Mugo back to the trench, died, and he wanted to escape from the trench and the memories drumming inside. He crossed into the village. His hut appeared now the only safe place. He wanted to resume that state, a limbo, in which he was before he heard Mumbi's story and looked into her eyes. The dust he raised as he went back to the hut whirled low behind him.

That was the time Warui had met Mugo in the street. Warui was coming from a small crowd that had gathered outside the old woman's hut. To Mugo, Warui was a particularly irksome apparition at the present time. He despised Warui without being able to say why. Warui's face was troubled with thought, but Mugo did not see this.

'Long ago such things could happen,' he started at once, as if Mugo already knew the subject of Warui's thoughts.

'What things?' They walked slowly in the same direction.

'Have you not heard?'

'Not anything unusual.'

'This one is unusual. Of a truth, such things used to happen, not often, once or twice maybe, but they did occur. When a man or a child died, he was thrown into the forest. When I was young, these, my eyes, saw a man who had come from the dead.'

'What has happened?' Mugo asked impatiently.

'You know the old woman. You know she had a son who from birth could not speak or hear.'

At the mention of the old woman, Mugo became agitated. The nausea he had felt at the sight of Warui disappeared. He could hardly wait for Warui to tell the story at his own pace. Mugo remembered only last Sunday he had almost entered her hut. Had she died?

'And what happens to her son? He was killed. A bullet picks on him, in the heart, during the Emergency. As you can imagine, this was great pain to her. All these years she has not left her hut, and she has not spoken a word to anybody. And then now she begins to speak. Just like that. What does she say? Her son has come back; she says she has seen him twice.'

'It's strange,' Mugo commented.

'Once he went into the hut. And then he went out again, without speaking. So she has kept the door open thus many a day so that Gitogo could come back. She says that he came back recently, stood at the door, and then went away again without speaking. She is talking, talking all the time.'

'It's strange,' Mugo said again, fearing.

'Yes, that's what I say. It's strange in our village, and I cannot stop saying it to myself when I see things that happened one, two, three – many years ago, come to disturb a woman's peace and rest. Those buried in the earth should remain in the earth. Things of yesterday should remain with yesterday.'

When at long last Mugo extricated himself from Warui, he found the incident had disturbed him in a way he could not explain. He wandered through the streets thinking about the old woman and that thrilling bond he felt existed between them. Then he tried to dismiss the incident. But as he went on, he found himself starting at the thought of meeting a dead apparition. Life itself seemed a meaningless wandering. There was surely no connection between sunrise and sunset, between today and tomorrow. Why then was he troubled by what was dead, he thought, remembering the old woman. And immediately he heard Mumbi's voice in his heart and saw General R.'s face looking at him. He stood at an open space in the village. His lower lip dropped: he felt energy leave him. Weak in body, he leaned against a small tree and gradually slipped down on to the grass. He held his head in both hands. It is not me, he whispered to convince himself. It is not me, it would have happened . . . the murder of women and men in the trench . . . even if . . . even if. . . . He was moaning. Mumbi's voice was a knife which had butchered and laid naked his heart to himself. The road from his hut led to the trench. But would it not have happened? Christ would have died on the cross, anyway. Why did they blame Judas, a stone from the hands of a power more than man? Kihika . . . crucified . . . the thought flashed through him, and a curious thing happened. Mugo saw thick blood dripping from the mud walls of his hut. Why had he not seen it earlier, he now wondered, almost calmly, without fear. But he was shaking as he walked to his hut, resolved to find out if the blood was really there.

He saw nothing on the wall. He sat on his bed and again propped his head on both hands. Was he cracking in the head? He started at the thought and again looked at the walls.

It was dark, in the evening, when Gikonyo and Warui called on Mugo.

'I fear I am not well in the head,' he told them. 'I cannot, I cannot face so many eyes.'

'Take Aspro, it will clear your head,' Warui said, unable to penetrate the enigmatic gloom in the hut. 'What does the man sing? Aspro ni dawa ya Kweli.' He quietly laughed alone and then abruptly kept silent, remembering the earlier conversation with Mugo about the old woman.

'Please think again,' Gikonyo told him. Warui and Gikonyo left the hut. Gikonyo was puzzled by the look of terror on Mugo's face. Warui remembered that he had not yet told Gikonyo about the old woman.

'It's only pictures in the head.' Gikonyo dismissed the story, now thinking of Mumbi. Suddenly he felt the urge to beat her, really beat her, and keep her in her place. This time he would not let his mother interfere.

Warui turned to Wambui's place and told her of Mugo's refusal. Wambui and Warui went to a few other huts and told the same story. And so the word passed from one hut to the next. The man who had suffered so much had further revealed his greatness in modesty. By refusing to lead, Mugo had become a legendary hero.

To whom does one turn, Gikonyo mused, as he hurried to vent his anger on Mumbi. He was angry with everybody: the MP (why should these men be elected only to enrich themselves), and Mugo (what does he think he is?), and Mumbi (I had thought marriage would bring happiness). He trembled with excitement outside the house. Nobody would hold him back. He would thrash Mumbi until she cried for mercy.

He pushed the door open, with force, and only stared into Wangari's eyes.

'She has gone back to her parents. See how you have broken your home. You have driven a good woman to misery for nothing. Let us now see what profit it will bring you, to go on poisoning your mind with these things when you should have accepted and sought how best to build your life. But you, like a foolish child, have never wanted to know what happened. Or what woman Mumbi really is.'

In normal circumstances, Gikonyo knew that when Wangari adopted that cool controlled voice, she was angry, or deeply wounded. Now he too was angry and unable to turn into words the many thoughts that passed through his mind.

'Let her never come back,' he shouted, glaring at his mother, including her in the whole conspiracy against his life. Wangari stood up and shook her front right finger at him.

'You. You. If today you were a baby crawling on your knees and eating mud and dust, I would pinch your thighs so hard you would learn. But you are a man, now. Read your own heart, and know yourself.'

She went out and left Gikonyo standing alone inside his new house.

Thirteen

Most of us from Thabai first saw him at the New Rung'ei Market the day the heavy rain fell. You remember the Wednesday, just before Independence? Wind blew and the rain hit the ground at an angle. Women abandoned their wares in the open and scampered to the shops for shelter, soon crowding together in narrow verandahs. Water dripped down the sack and the pieces of clothing with which they covered their heads; little pools formed on the cement floor. People said the falling water was a blessing for our hard-won freedom. Murungu on high never slept: he always let his tears fall to this, our land, from Agu and Agu. As we, the children, used to sing:

> Ngai has given Gikuyu a beautiful country,
> Never without food or water or grazing fields.
> It is good so Gikuyu should praise Ngai all the time,
> For he has ever been generous to them.

It had rained the day Kenyatta returned home from England: it had also rained the day Kenyatta returned to Gatundu from Maralal.

We saw the man walk in the rain. An old dirty basket filled with vegetables and potatoes was slung on his back. He was tall, with broad shoulders, and he walked with a slight stoop that created an impression of power. The fact that he was the only man in the rain soon attracted the attention of people along the pavements and shop verandahs. Some even forced their way to the front to see him.

'What is he doing, fooling in the rain?'

'It is a dumb and deaf man he is.'

'Showing off, if you ask me.'

'Maybe he has a long way to walk, and he fears the night will catch him.'

'Even so be it, he should let the rain break a little, for tell me, what's the profit to him when he arrives home carrying pneumonia in his bones?'

'Or maybe he has something heavy in his heart.'

'That's not anything to make him drench himself ill. Which of us does not carry a weight in the heart?'

The man neared the corner at the far end of Rung'ei shops. Women discussed all the risks people ran by exposing themselves to water. Soon the man disappeared, lost behind the shops.

'What prevents him from taking cover?'

'Mugo is a strange man,' Wambui said reflectively.

Mugo had gone to the market to buy some food. As he pushed his way among the people, between the columns of sitting women, he felt himself watched and regretted coming to the place at all. Then suddenly the sun seemed to die prematurely; the country and the sky turned dull and grey. A cold wind started to blow carrying with it bits of white paper, pieces of cloth and grass and feathers whirling in the air. Clouds were fast collecting in the sky. A few flashes of lightning were followed by a faint rumbling thunder. And abruptly the rain fell. Mugo had another frightening sensation of re-enacting dead scenes come to life. He remembered the women's devils at the Indian shop long ago, and took flight.

Somewhere, a woman started the song of the trench, at one time the village anthem. Others took up the thread.

> And he jumped into the trench,
> The words he told the soldier pierced my heart like a spear;
> You will not beat the woman, he said,
> You will not beat a pregnant woman, he told the soldier.
>
> Work stood still in the trench
> The earth too was silent,
> When they took him away
> Tears, red as blood, trickled down my face.

Mugo's name was whispered from ear to ear. Mysterious stories about him spread among the market women. This would not have happened on an ordinary market day. But this was not just another day. Tonight Kenya would get Uhuru. And Mugo, our village hero, was no ordinary man.

Wambui put it in his way: Independence Day without him would be stale; he is Kihika born again. She went around the market place determined to put her secret resolve into practice. Women had to act. Women had to force the issue. 'And, after all, he is our son,' she told women at the market place at an impromptu gathering after the rain. Wambui's fighting spirit had never died.

She believed in the power of women to influence events, especially where men had failed to act, or seemed indecisive. Many people in old Thabai remembered her now-famous drama at the workers' strike in 1950. The strike was meant to paralyse the country and make it more difficult for the whiteman to govern. A few men who worked at a big shoe factory near Thabai and in the settled area, grumbled and even said, so the rumours went, that they would not come out on strike. The Party convened a general meeting at Rung'ei. At the height of the proceedings, Wambui suddenly broke through the crowd and led a group of women to the platform. She grabbed the microphone from the speakers. People were interested. Was there any circumcised man who felt water in the stomach at the sight of a whiteman? Women, she said, had brought their Mithuru and Miengu to the platform. Let therefore such men, she jeered, come forward, wear the women's skirts and aprons and give up their trousers to the women. Men sat rigidly in their seats and tried to laugh with the crowd to hide the inner discomfort. The next day all men stayed away from work.

Now the women decided to send Mumbi to Mugo. Mumbi the sister of Kihika. They would confront Mugo with sweet insistent youth – youth not to be ignored or denied.

So Wambui went home to pass on the message to Mumbi. And there she found Mumbi had left her husband. But Wambui sought her out.

'This matter concerns all Thabai,' she impressed upon the young woman. 'Forget your troubles in the home and in the heart. Go to Mugo. Tell him this: the women and the children need him.'

Mumbi had found it difficult to tell her parents why she had left her husband. She had never told her own mother or father about the tension in which she lived: how did you go telling people that your husband had refused to sleep with you? Might they not think he was impotent and spread damaging rumours? Anyway, because they did not know the full story, her parents did not welcome her back with open arms. A parent did not encourage a daughter to disobey her man. Wanjiku had even ridiculed Mumbi's feeble explanation.

'The women of today surprise me. They cannot take a slap, soft as a feather, or the slightest breath, from a man. In our time, a woman could take blow and blow from her husband without a thought of running back to her parents.'

'Don't you care about me any more? I cannot stay in his house again. Not after what he said – I cannot, I cannot.'

'Ssh! Don't you talk like a foolish woman.'

'No, mother, if you don't want me in this hut, tell me at once, and I with my child will go to Nairobi or anywhere else. Yes, I'll not go back to that house. I may be a woman, but even a cowardly bitch fights back when cornered against a wall.'

Wanjiku felt with Mumbi. But hers was a delicate task of mending that which was torn.

'We shall talk about it, my child,' she said in a softened voice.

Another thing plagued Mumbi. Even in her grief, she could not forget what General R. had said. Karanja would be killed for his part in Kihika's death. Should this be done in the name of her brother? Surely enough blood had already been shed: why add more guilt to the land? She woke up in the morning with the problem still unsolved. But luckily for her, Wednesday was a market day in Rung'ei, attended by people from the eight ridges around Thabai. She accidentally met a man going to Githima and quickly made up her mind. She got a piece of paper (she had been taught by her brothers to read and write) and scribbled: Don't come to the meeting tomorrow. She addressed it to Karanja and gave it to the man. She felt relieved.

And now Wambui and the women had turned to her for help. At first Mumbi flinched from interfering in matters involving the husband she had left. But as Wambui spoke, a defiant streak in Mumbi grew stronger: she would not let Gikonyo think her lonely and miserable. What if she succeeded where he had failed? The thought thrilled her; she contemplated the mission with satisfaction.

The thrill sharpened as later in the evening she set out for Mugo's hut. The day had been dull and misty; the night seemed darker than usual; Mumbi felt like a girl again, braving the dark and the wind and the storm, to meet her lover. What if Mugo should – she left the question and the answer in abeyance. The possibility that Gikonyo might catch her talking with another man nagged her. But she was free, she told herself, prop-words to her fear. Let him find her then, she repeated defiantly. Nevertheless, her steps faltered and her heart beat wildly as she stood outside Mugo's hut.

At first blood warmed in her veins, fear was mixed with pleasure when she saw Mugo at the door. But Mugo barred the door awkwardly, as if he expected an explanation. She grew a little apprehensive.

'Are you not inviting me in?' she said, with a false lighthearted tone.

'Oh, sorry – come in.' She could not see his face, but there was an unmistakable tremor in his voice. In the light, she noticed the restlessness about Mugo. His proud distance had diminished, his dark eyes had that debauched look one sees in drink-addicts. He sat away from her, carefully, as if he was afraid of her. He was handsome and lonely, she bit her lower lip to steady herself. She looked around the bare hut whose walls were barely lit by the oil-lamp.

'It is a little empty,' he said brusquely, breaking into her thoughts.

'It is all right for a man. An unmarried person has few needs.' She laughed uneasily. She was puzzled by his unfriendliness and fear, a violent contrast to the excitement in his eyes yesterday. Yet she allowed irrelevant thoughts to capture her fancy; if he should want me – If he should—

'You know why I have come,' she asked gropingly, hoping to break his unnerving obduracy.

'I don't know – unless – unless about what you were saying to me yesterday – what I mean is – I did not know what you wanted—'

'Oh, I wanted you to speak to my husband. He would have listened to you. You see, since he returned from detention, he has never once entered my bed. And he has never said a word about the child. What was in his heart was hidden from me, until yesterday. It was hard, hard, hard. . . .' She had started in a matter-of-fact tone and ended in a state. She remembered the day Gikonyo returned home from detention. She had wanted to talk to him, to make him understand by a word, a glance, but no words formed in her mind. His appearance seemed to have crushed her into a stupid unfeeling silence. Yet how she had wanted to reach him, then, there, as she stared at the opposite wall, wondering what he would do to her. She checked herself, and there was a sad pause before she recovered and came back to the present. 'Anyway, that is not important now. I quarrelled with him last night – and returned to my parents.'

'No!' he said feelingly, in an unguarded moment.

'It's true. But that is not why I came to see you in the night. The women of Thabai and Rung'ei area sent me to you. They want you at the meeting tomorrow.'

'I cannot,' he said decisively.

'You must,' she answered, warming up to the challenge.

'No, no.'

'You must – all these people are waiting for you. People want you.'

'But – but – I cannot.'

'They cry for you.'

'Mumbi, Mumbi,' he cried in a tormented voice.

'You will, Mugo, you will.'

'No.'

'I then beg you,' she said firmly, with new strength and authority. She looked at him in the eyes, now reaching out to him, desiring to open his heart, for a minute, at least, unlock the secrets of his power over men and fate. And she held him balanced at her fingertips, and suddenly knew her power over him. She would not let him go.

'Do you understand what you ask?'

'Is it the camps?' she asked, a little relenting.

'No – yes – everything.'

'What?'

'Me.'

'It was hard. They beat you in the camps. We heard about it.'

'Did you?'

'Yes. What happened?'

'Nothing, except that I saw men crawl on the ground, you know, like cripples because their hands and feet were chained with iron.' All the time, he spoke in a subdued voice, like a child. 'Once bottlenecks were hammered into people's backsides, and the men whimpered like caged animals. That last was at Rira.' He paused, as if coldly contemplating a scene distant and yet near. Then he leaned forward a little, conspiratorially, and whispered a child's secret. 'When I was young, I saw the whiteman, I did not know who he was or where he came from. Now I know that a Mzungu is not a man – always remember that – he is a devil – devil.' He paused again to gain breath, and resumed his subdued voice. 'I saw a man whose manhood was broken with pincers. He came out of the screening office and fell down and he cried: to know I will never touch my wife again, Oh God, can I ever look at her in the eyes after this? For me I only looked into an abyss and deep inside I only saw a darkness I could not penetrate.'

Tears formed on Mumbi's face. She desired to reach out, to right the wrong, to heal the wounded.

'Then, Mugo,' she appealed through tears, 'you must speak tomorrow. Not about my brother, he is dead and buried. His work on earth is done. Speak to the living. Tell them about those whom the war maimed, left naked and scarred: the orphans, the widows. Tell our people what you saw.'

'I saw nothing.'

'Even that, Mugo, anything,' she said, feeling him slip away. She fought to hold him and saw that he was shaking.

'About myself?'

'Everything.'

'You want me to do that?' he asked, raising his voice. The change of voice, like a groan from an animal about to be slaughtered, startled her.

'Yes,' she assented, fearfully.

'I wanted to live my life. I never wanted to be involved in anything. Then he came into my life, here, a night like this, and pulled me into the stream. So I killed him.'

'Who? What are you talking about?'

'Ha! ha! ha!' he laughed unnaturally. 'Who murdered your brother?'

'Kihika?'

'Yes.'

'The whiteman.'

'No! I strangled him – I strangled him—'

'It is not true – Wake up, Mugo – Kihika was hanged – listen and stop shaking so – I saw his body hang from a tree.'

'I did it! I did it! Ha! ha! ha! That is what you wanted to know. And I'll do it again – to you – tonight.'

She tried to cry out for help, but no voice would leave her throat. He came towards her, emitting demented noises and laughter. She bounded to the door; but he was there before her.

'You cannot – run away. Sit down – Ha! I'll do it to you—' He was shaking and his words came out in violent jerks.

'Imagine all your life cannot sleep – so many fingers touching your flesh – eyes always watching you – in dark places – in corners – in the streets – in the fields – sleeping, waking, no rest – ah! Those eyes – cannot you for a minute, one minute, leave a man alone – I mean – let a man eat, drink, work – all of you – Kihika – Gikonyo – the old woman – that general – who sent you here tonight? Who? Aah! Those eyes again – we shall see who is stronger – now—'

She tried to scream; again no voice would come out. He closed in on her, one hand on her mouth, the other searching her throat. She panted and whimpered horribly. She looked into his eyes. Even later, she could not explain the terror she saw in them. And all of a sudden she ceased struggling and submitted herself to him.

'What is it, Mugo? What is wrong?' she sobbed.

*

Those of you who have visited Thabai or any of the eight ridges around Rung'ei (that is, from Kerarapon to Kihingo) will have heard about Thomas Robson or as he was generally known *Tom*, the Terror. He was the epitome of those dark days in our history that witnessed his birth as a District Officer in Rung'ei – that is, when the Emergency raged in unabated fury. People said he was mad. They spoke of him with awe, called him Tom or simply 'he' as if the mention of his full name would conjure him up in their presence. Driving in a jeep, one Askari or two at the back, a bren-gun at the knees, and a revolver in his khaki trousers partially concealed by his bush jacket, he would suddenly appear at the most unexpected times and places to catch unsuspecting victims. He called them Mau Mau. He put them in his jeep, drove them into the edge of the forest, and asked them to dig their graves. He asked them to kneel down. Sometimes he broke the prayers with a bren-gun. More often with a revolver. But occasionally he would pardon a man even though he were kneeling at the edge of the grave. So that until the last moment the victim would not know what to do; whether to run away and risk a bullet, or wait and see if Tom would change his mind. They said he was everywhere. Rumours spread. One man had seen Tom here; another had seen him there. Some village men saw his jeep in their dreams and screamed. He was a man-eater, walking in the night and day. He was death. He was especially brutal to squatters who were repatriated from the Rift Valley back to Gikuyu-Ini.

That was in 1954.

His activities came to a climax in May 1955. One evening, driving from the Rung'ei to District Offices, he saw a lone man walking on the tarmac road. The man shrank close to a hedge by the road. Tom shouted at him. The man came towards the jeep faltering, his knees seemed to be knocking together. Near the jeep, his teeth could be heard chattering and clicking, so that Tom was forced to laugh. 'Usiogope Mzee,' he called jovially as if to reassure the man. 'Tom will not eat you.' Suddenly the old man straightened himself, whipped something from his pocket, and two quick shots thudded into Tom's body. Before the frightened policemen could do anything, the man had jumped across the hedge, towards the Indian shops. The policemen shot into the sky. Tom did not die immediately. It is said (he is a legend in the village) that he drove himself to the hospital where he died three hours later without uttering anything coherent except the one word: brutes.

Within hours the villages were besieged by soldiers; official word went round, later to be headlined by newspapers; a District Officer had been senselessly murdered by Mau Mau thugs.

On that day – the villagers to this day talk about it – Mugo had as usual gone to his strip of land near Rung'ei Railway Station, revelling in the dreams he loved, dreams which often transported him from the present to the future. He had come to see in them a private message, a prophecy. Had he not already escaped, unscathed, the early operations of the Emergency? Kenya had been in a state of Emergency since 1952. Some people had been taken to detention camps; others had run away to the forest: but this was a drama in a world not his own. He kept alone, feeling a day would come when horns, drums and trumpets would beat together to announce his entrance into the other world. He often heard men talk as they built huts in the new Thabai; but their words did not touch him: what did it matter to him that women were doing men's work, that children were maturing too early? Had he himself not started fending for himself at an early age? Mugo was among the first to finish their huts within the given time. He had done the work, erecting the hut, thatching the roof, mudding the walls, without help from anybody. The hut was his first big achievement. After moving into it, he resumed his daily life: he looked after the crops, his eyes fixed to the future.

This day, this Friday evening, he came home from the shamba tired. He carefully placed the jembe and the panga against the wall before opening the door, warming inside at the touch of the padlock. He often fussed over pushing the key into the lock, delaying the final act; the operation gave him pleasure; the hut was an extension of himself, his hopes and dreams. He entered, sat on the bed, and admired the walls (the mud was not yet dry) and the cone-shaped roof, from which bits of grass and fern stuck out. Soon darkness crept into the hut. He lit the oil-lamp, whistling to himself as he did so. He then made a fire and fried a mixture of maize grains and beans over the three hearthstones. This was his only meal of the day. He always boiled maize grains and dry beans in large quantities and then, for days afterwards, fried a little at a time, enough for a meal. After eating, he walked to the door to make sure it was securely bolted. Again he lingered over the bolt admiringly. He was only twenty-five. He possessed nothing, but the future was in his hands. He stretched flat on the bed: it was always good to lie in bed after a hard day's shamba. He massaged his stomach, and belched, vaguely satisfied. Outside the hut were curfew laws. Again these laws did not affect Mugo since, even before 1952, he rarely went out. He had trained himself to enter a twilight calm whenever he lay on his back, in bed, or in the shamba. At such moments his heart dialogued with strange voices. And the voices faded into one voice from God calling out, Moses, Moses! And Mugo was ready with his answer: Here am I, Lord.

It was at this stage in his dream when he heard whistles, shouts, and a patter of feet. The whistling rudely tore the night and Mugo's thoughts. There was always such whistling whenever the Forest Fighters attacked a village or killed an important person. But there had been a long lull in Thabai; the last time there had been such a hubbub was the week the Rev. Jackson Kigondu and Teacher Muniu were killed. The whistling increased in volume, then it would fade, as if it came and went with the wind. Then it stopped. The village was thrown into a profound silence. As suddenly, the silence was again broken with the fire of guns. There were shouts, and Mugo heard distant screams from women. The gunfire was now nearer the hut and the whistling became urgent, insistent. A man shouted: Robson. Mugo rested in bed on his right elbow, and his heart beat uneasily at the nearness of the fire and shouting. Again the general noise ended. Mugo heard a man moaning and protesting; I was just going home. Truly, I was only going home. When stillness reigned again, Mugo lay back on the bed and sunk into a half-asleep state. Mugo was among the lucky few who knew not the terror of a police search in their huts at night.

He could not tell how long he was in this state; but he was certainly woken up by a knock at the door. He opened his eyes, startled, and sat up. Who could it be? The knocking was repeated. Mugo moved forward, cautiously, halted, moved forward and again halted. He hit against the lamp. It went out. The sudden darkness alarmed him even more than the tapping of the door. He fumbled for matches around the stones. And at the back of his mind was the urgent question: should he open the door? A third tapping, more continuous, more insistent, made him jump to the door. He stepped aside for the homeguards to enter; at the same time, he resumed his fearful search for matches.

'Let me light the lamp,' he mumbled, stealing a glance at the silhouette of the man at the door.

'You don't need it,' the man said in a low voice. 'The fireglow will do.'

'Who are you?'

'Sssh! Don't shout, and – and don't be afraid.'

'Who are you?' Mugo repeated in desperation, faintly recognizing the voice. The man laughed a little nervously, and Mugo felt the room suddenly turn chilly. He stumbled on a box of matches and was about to strike the box when the man whispered, secretively.

'Don't – the homeguard and the Police are everywhere—He is dead!'

'Who?'

'The District Officer.'

'Robson?'

'Yes – I shot him. I've been wanting to finish him – all these months.'

And there were tears in that whisper. The box of matches fell from Mugo's hands. He had to retrieve it; but his mind was not in the act. A cold fluid had slipped into his belly at the man's words; countless needles pricked his flesh.

'Let me light the lamp,' he said in a voice not his own.

'If you like – perhaps it is better so – mark you, I am used to darkness – do you think they will search all the huts tonight?'

At last Mugo lit the lamp. He looked at his visitor.

'Kihika!' he gasped, involuntarily.

Kihika wore a torn, dirty coat, the khaki sort that soldiers wore in the last big war (now such coats were worn by old men) and muddy once-white tennis shoes. His short wild hair gave severe lines to his face. Mugo edged backwards and leaned against a post near the bed.

'I – I did not know it was you.'

'Must forgive me,' Kihika said, his eyes rolling round the hut. 'I did not want them to follow me into the forest. Besides I wanted to visit you – I have always wanted to speak to you.'

'There – there is a chair.'

'Oh. I am used to standing. For days and nights you are on your feet. Standing. Or crouching.'

'Why?'

'You dare not sleep.'

'Do you want to kill me? I have done nothing,' Mugo appealed.

But before Kihika could answer, there was another blast of whistling. Kihika whipped out a pistol and scrambled under the bed. Mugo collapsed on a stool and felt he would cry. He would be caught red-handed, housing a terrorist. Then he suddenly remembered the lamp and blew it out. The hut was again steeped into darkness. The whistling died down. Kihika wriggled out of his hiding place and stood near the fireplace. Mugo was aware of the man's silhouette above him.

'We don't kill just anybody,' he started speaking as if there had been no interruption. 'We are not murderers. We are not hangmen – like Robson – killing men and women without cause or purpose.' He spoke quickly, nervously, and paced about the fireplace. Could this be the man who had burnt down Mahee? Could this be the man who had once spoken at a public meeting and made women pull and tear at their hair and clothes?

'We only hit back. You are struck on the left cheek. You turn the right cheek. One, two, three – sixty years. Then suddenly, it is always sudden, you say: I am not turning the other cheek any more. Your back to the wall, you strike back. You trust your manhood and hope it will keep you at it. Do you think we like scuffling for food with hyenas and monkeys in the forest? I, too, have known the comfort of a warm fire and a woman's love by the fireside. See? We must kill. Put to sleep the enemies of black man's freedom. They say we are weak. They say we cannot win against the bomb. If we are weak, we cannot win. I despise the weak. Why? Because the weak need not remain weak. Listen! Our fathers fought bravely. But do you know the biggest weapon unleashed by the enemy against them? It was not the Maxim gun. It was division among them. Why? Because a people united in faith are stronger than the bomb. They shall not tremble or run away before the sword. Then instead the enemy shall flee. These are not words of a mad man. Not words, not even miracles could make Pharaoh let the Children of Israel go. But at midnight, the Lord smote all the first-born in the land of Egypt, from the first-born of Pharaoh that sat on the throne unto the first-born of the captive that was in dungeon. And all the first-born of the cattle. And the following day, he let them go. That is our aim. Strike terror in their midst. Get at them in their homes night and day. They shall feel the poisoned arrow in the veins. They shall not know where the next will come from. Strike terror in the heart of the oppressor.'

He spoke without raising his voice, almost unaware of Mugo, or of his danger, like a man possessed. His bitterness and frustration was revealed in the nervous flow of the words. Each word confirmed Mugo's suspicion that the man was mad.

'You think we don't fear death? We do. My legs almost refused to move when Robson called out to me. Each minute, I waited for a bullet to enter my heart. I've seen men piss on themselves and others laugh with madness at the prospect of a fight. And the animal groan of dying men is a terrible sound to hear. But a few shall die that the many shall live. That's what crucifixion means today. Else we deserve to be slaves, cursed to carry water and hew wood for the whiteman for ever and ever. Choose between freedom and slavery and it is fitting that a man should grab at freedom and die for it. We need—'

He suddenly stopped speaking, pacing, and for the first time seemed aware of Mugo. Mugo sat rigidly in his seat, staring at the ground, sure that the homeguards would get him tonight. Kihika was mad, mad, he reflected, and the thought only increased his terror.

'What do you want?' Keep him talking. A mad man was not dangerous as long as he was talking.

'We want a strong organization. The whiteman knows this and

fears. Why else has he made our people move into these villages? He wants to shut us from the people, our only strength. But he will not succeed. We must keep the road between us and the people clear of obstacles. I often watched you in old Thabai. You are a self-made man. You are a man, you have suffered. We need such a man to organize an underground movement in the new village.'

Mugo winced at every word from Kihika.

'I – I have never taken the oath,' he protested, weakly.

'I know that,' Kihika said. 'But what is an oath? For some people you need the oath to bind them to the Movement. There are those who'll keep a secret unless bound by an oath. I know them. I know men by their faces. In any case how many took the oath and are now licking the toes of the whiteman? No, you take an oath to confirm a choice already made. The decision to lay or not to lay your life for the people lies in the heart. The oath is the water sprinkled on a man's head at baptism.'

Other considerations rushed through Mugo's mind. He remembered the door was not bolted. He stood up, walked past Kihika, and listened at the keyhole. He thought of running out or shouting for the homeguards and then remembered that Kihika had a gun. And that gun had just killed a man. He secured the door and went back to his place. He was walking in a nightmare. It was not true that the man who had burnt down Mahee, the man who had just killed Robson, was actually in the hut. He felt a tired desire to speak but could not think of anything to say or do. By now the village was deathly still: the whistles and the gunfire were things that happened in years past. But Kihika was there, no longer panting, or pacing nervously, apparently composed. He was real.

'I will meet you in a week's time,' Kihika was saying triumphantly. Mugo nodded his head. Kihika carefully arranged the place of their next meeting at Kinenie Forest.

No sooner had Kihika finished talking than the stillness was torn for the third time, with distant screams and shots. The screams and the shots rose intermittently and this time did not cease. (The following day Mugo learnt that a number of men, Mau Mau suspects, had been taken from their homes in connection with Robson's death. Two men from the village shot down in the night were later described in newspapers as being members of the gang that had set upon a barely armed District Officer whose service to the District was widely known.) Kihika went to the door and listened. Again Mugo thought of grappling with Kihika and shouting for help.

'I must go – perhaps they will search the houses,' Kihika said in whisper. His nervousness had come back; he was again a man on the run. He opened the door and then quietly shut it.

'Remember our meeting,' he said, before slipping out into the dark, to disappear as suddenly and quietly as he had come.

Mugo stood, still, in the middle of his new hut for a few minutes. The ground below his feet was not firm. Then he ran to the door, flung it open, half-hoping to shout for help. He gazed into the night. For the third time he bolted the door. But why bolt the door? Why should he? It was better to be without a door rather than that it should be there and yet bring in cold and danger. He unbolted the door and slowly walked to bed, where he sat and held his face in his hands. He took out a dirty handkerchief to wipe his face and neck; but half-way in the act, he forgot about the cold sweat; the handkerchief slumped back to his knees. He had once heard noises in the wind, long ago, and had been unable to pick one consistent note; now the noises were in his head.

A few minutes ago, lying on the bed, in this room, the future held promise. Everything in the hut was in the same place as before, but the future was blank. He expected police or homeguards to come, arrest him or shoot him dead. He saw only prison and death. Kihika was a man desperately wanted by the government especially after the destruction of Mahee. To be caught harbouring a terrorist meant death. Why should Kihika drag me into a struggle and problems I have not created? Why? He is not satisfied with butchering men and women and children. He must call on me to bathe in the blood. I am not his brother. I am not his sister. I have not done harm to anybody. I only looked after my little shamba and crops. And now I must spend my life in prison because of the folly of one man!

Mugo woke up the next day surprised that he was not yet in prison. He tried not to think of the encounter in the night. It was only a dream. I have had such nightmares before this. Night exaggerates everything – our fears, misery and despair. Bush and trees appear like men. Ha! Ha! Ha! But his ill-attempts at self-comfort could not undo reality; Kihika's face was indelibly engraved in his mind; the unkempt hair, the shifting eye, banished comforting illusions and made Mugo shiver in spite of daylight. Imagine a man who has been walking through a twilight and feels security in his isolation. Then suddenly darkness descends; and he finds he is in danger of breaking his leg because he is walking on a road that will end, any time, in a deep pit. For the next few days Mugo wandered between his hut and the shamba, every second expecting a policeman or a homeguard to tap him on the shoulder. Whenever he saw a soldier or a homeguard, sweat would suddenly form on his face, his legs felt weak. And not once did he forget Kihika's shadow behind him, waiting for an answer. What shall I do, he asked himself. If I don't serve Kihika he'll kill me. They killed Rev. Jackson and Teacher Muniu. If I work for him, the government will catch me. The whiteman has long arms. And they'll hang me. My God, I don't want to die, I am not ready for death, I have not even lived. Mugo was deeply afflicted and confused, because all his life he had avoided conflicts: at home, or at school, he rarely joined the company of other boys for fear of being involved in brawls that might ruin his chances of a better future. His argument went like this: if you don't traffic with evil, then evil ought not to touch you; if you leave people alone, then they ought to leave you alone. That's why, now, at night, still unable to solve his dilemma, Mugo only moaned inside, puzzled: have I stolen anything from anybody? No! Have I ever shat inside a neighbour's courtyard? No. Have I killed anybody? No. How then can Kihika to whom I have done no harm do this to me?

Jealousy, he decided, unable to find another answer to his own question. The reflection revived his old hatred of Kihika now so strong it almost choked him. Kihika who had a mother and a father, and a brother, and a sister, could play with death. He had people who would mourn his end, who would name their children after him, so that Kihika's name would never die from men's lips. Kihika had everything; Mugo had nothing.

This thought obsessed him; it filled him with a foamless fury, a tearless anger that obliterated other things and made him unable to sleep. The fatal day, Friday, therefore, caught him undecided on a course of action. As was his custom, he took a jembe and a panga and walked in the direction of his shamba. To avoid meeting people, Mugo chose an unused path across the fields towards Rung'ei. It was early and all the fields were deserted. Here and there the fields were littered with broken sites where not a week before stood homesteads that made up Old Thabai village. Mugo's heavy eyes discerned nothing. And his mind was a white blank dazzling the eye like the sun at midday. He was in that stage of exhaustion that comes from an accumulation of sleepless nights, heated, ceaseless, and directionless thoughts – that stage in which a man is irritable, ready to break at the slightest provocation without he himself realizing his danger. His feet brushed against the dew-ridden hedges and soon water, in broken lines, ran down his feet. His lower lip dropped; whenever he was agitated Mugo's lip always fell. He shook everywhere. The trembling and the depression increased the further he walked. By the time he reached the Indian shops, he was very weak, and could not walk. So he dropped his jembe and panga near a mound of rubbish at the back of a shop and sat down to regain strength. At the back of every shop was such a mound from which came a stench of decaying rubbish. Indian children and sometimes men shat there. African children often rummaged through the heaps, turning over newly thrown rubbish with their feet, looking for bread or forgotten coins. Their feet would dig into the 'small loads'. The boys would swear horribly and occasionally would throw stones at the Indians in revenge. Once three African boys were caught holding an Indian girl to the ground, just behind the heap, beside which Mugo now sat to rest. They were accused of raping the girl. Because of their age, the magistrate only sent them to Wamumu Approved School. Mugo was not thinking of these sordid details in the shop's past. He just held his head in his hands and over and over again moaned: 'why did he do this to me?'

Suddenly a small wind blew dust and bits of rubbish into the air. Mugo covered his face with both palms to protect his eyes against the sand. The bits of paper spiralled up higher and higher in a cyclic cone. This storm that so whirled dust and rubbish into a moving cone-shaped pillar was said to be possessed of women's devils. Normally it only lasted for a few seconds and disappeared as suddenly and mysteriously as it had come. But now it went on and on increasing in vigour and threw things very high into the sky. At last the wind stopped. Mugo watched dust and rubbish slowly fall to the ground. Somehow this act relieved him of his shaking and depression. He took the panga and the jembe and continued his journey to the shamba. He was almost calm.

But only for a time.

After walking a few steps from where he had sat, Mugo saw a strange spectacle. He stared at the corrugated-iron wall. His hair pulled away at the roots. He felt shocked pleasure in his belly. For Kihika's face was there, pinned-framed to the shop, becoming larger and more distorted the longer he gazed at it. The face, clear against a white surface, awakened the same excitement and terror he once experienced, as a boy, the night he wanted to strangle his aunt. There was a price on Kihika's head – a – price – on – Kihika's – head.

Mugo walked towards the District Officer, hazed with suppressed wonder and excitement. God called upon Abraham to offer an only son Isaac for a burnt sacrifice upon a mountain in the land of Moriah. And Abraham built an altar there, and laid the wood in order, and bound Isaac his son, and laid him on the altar upon the wood. And Abraham stretched his son, and laid him on the altar upon the wood. And Abraham stretched forth his hand, and took the knife to slay his son. And Isaac, lying there, waited for the sword to sever his head from the body. He knew the sword would surely fall – for a second he was certain of death by a cold panga. And suddenly Isaac heard the voice of the Lord. He wept. Saved from death. Saved from death, Mugo repeated to himself. He walked in this vision. And in his dazed head was a tumult of thoughts that acquired the concrete logic of a dream. The argument was so clear, so exhilarating, it explained things he had been unable to solve in his life. I am important. I must not die. To keep myself alive, healthy, strong – to wait for my mission in life – is a duty to myself, to men and women of tomorrow. If Moses had died in the reeds, who would ever have known that he was destined to be a great man?

These lofty sensations were mixed up with thoughts of the money reward and the various possibilities opened before him. He would buy more land. He would build a big house. He would then find a woman for a wife and get children. The novelty and the nearness of the scheme added to his present thrill. He had never before considered women in relation to his man's body. Now pictures of various girls he had seen in the village passed through his mind. He would flash his victory before the eyes of his aunt's ghost. His place in society would be established. He would be half-way on the road to power. And what is greatness but power? What's power? A judge is powerful: he can send a man to death, without anyone questioning his authority, judgement, or harming his body in return. Yes – to be great you must stand in such a place that you can dispense pain and death to others without anyone asking questions. Like a headmaster, a judge, a Governor.

He arrived, almost too soon, at the offices. The offices had been built recently as a base from which the surrounding villages could be quickly reached. Two rifled policemen, in black polo-necked sweaters, guarded the entrance. In his present state, Mugo felt impatient with these unreal things that stood in his path.

'Can I see the DO?' he asked, attempting to walk past them dwelling on the vision within.

'What do you want?' One of the policemen pulled him back by the shoulder.

'I – I want to see him alone,' he said, surprised.   •

'With a jembe and a panga? Ha! ha! ha!'

'I say what do you want here.'

'I cannot – not to you.'

The two policemen laughed and jeered at Mugo's answers. They took his panga and jembe and threw them on the ground.

'Can't! Can't! Do you hear that? Hey, farmer, what do you want?'

'I must – it is – it is important.' Fear started creeping into him. They searched him all over, roughly pushing him about.

'He ought to remove his clothes.'

'Such a tall man – his thing is probably as long as a donkey's penis.'

'How do you manage women? eh?'

'Women? You are joking. Even a fat prostitute would run away at the sight.'

'Maybe he does it with sheep – or cows. Some people do, you know. At night. Ha! Ha!'

'Ha! ha! Or with old women – bribe them, or force them. Ha! ha! ha!'

'Ha! ha! ha!'

John Thompson, the District Officer, came out and shouted at them to stop the laughter. They told him about Mugo, and he told them to let him in. Mugo was almost short of breath as he bounded into the office; grateful to the whiteman who had rescued him from shame and humiliation. And now that he was in, he did not know how to begin. It was the first time he had ever confronted a whiteman at such close quarters. He fixed his eyes on the opposite wall determined, if possible, not to look at the whiteman's face.

'What do you want?' The voice startled Mugo.

'Kihika – I came to see you about him.'

Thompson sat up in his chair at the mention of that name. Then he stood up, his hands reaching for the edge of the table, as if for support. He peered at Mugo. The two men were almost the same height. Mugo resolutely refused to meet the other man's eyes. The whiteman sat down again.

'Yes?'

'I know—' he gulped down saliva. Panic seized him. He feared the voice would fail him.

'I know,' he said quietly, 'I know where Kihika can be found, tonight.'

And now the hatred he had felt towards Kihika rose fresh in him. He trembled with a victorious rage as he blurted out the story that had tormented him for a week. For a time he experienced a pure, delicious joy at his own daring, at what he suddenly saw as a great act of moral courage. Indeed, for him, at that moment, there was a kind of purity in the act; he stood beyond good and evil; he enjoyed the power and authority of his own knowledge: did he not hold the fate of a man's life in his head? His heart – his cup – was full to overflowing. Tears of relief stood on the edge of his eyes. For a week he had wrestled with demons, alone, in an endless nightmare. This confession was his first contact with another man. He felt deep gratitude to the whiteman, a patient listener, who had lifted his burden from Mugo's heart, who had extricated him from the nightmare. He even dared to look at the whiteman, the new-found friend. A smile spread over Mugo's face. The smile, however, froze into a grin that appeared like scorn, when he met the whiteman's inscrutable face and searching eyes.

The DO again stood up. He walked round the table to where Mugo stood. He held Mugo by the chin and tilted his face backwards. Then quite unexpectedly he shot saliva into the dark face. Mugo moved back a step and lifted his left hand to rub off the saliva. But the whiteman reached Mugo's face first and slapped him hard, once.

'Many people have already given us false information concerning this terrorist. Hear? Because they want the reward. We shall keep you here, and if you are not telling the truth, we shall hang you there, outside. Do you hear?'

Mugo was back in his nightmare. The table, the white face, the ceiling, the walls moved round and round. Then everything stopped abruptly. He tried to steady himself. Suddenly the ground where he stood gave way. He was falling down. He thrust his arms into the air. The bottom was so far away he could see only darkness. But he knew that there were stones jutting out, sharp, at the floor. He was nothing. Tears could not help him. With a choked cry, his body smashed on to the broken stones and jutting rock, at the whiteman's feet. The shock of discovery was so deep it numbed him. He felt no pain, and saw no blood.

'Do you hear?'

'Yes.'

'Say Effendi.'

'Yes—'

The word stuck, blocked the throat. His open mouth let out inarticulate noises. Foam had collected at the corners of his mouth. He stared at the whiteman, a watery glint in the eyes, without seeing him. Then the table, the chair, the DO, the white-washed walls – the earth – started spinning, faster and faster again. He held on to the table to still himself. He did not want the money. He did not want to know what he had done.

Verily, verily I say unto you, Except a corn of wheat fall into the ground and die, it abideth alone: but if it die, it bringeth forth much fruit.

St John 12:24
(verse underlined in black in Kihika's Bible)

And I saw a new heaven and a new earth: for the first heaven and the first earth were passed away.

Revelation 21:1

Fourteen

Kenya regained her Uhuru from the British on 12 December 1963. A minute before midnight, lights were put out at the Nairobi stadium so that people from all over the country and the world who had gathered there for the midnight ceremony were swallowed by the darkness. In the dark, the Union Jack was quickly lowered. When next the lights came on the new Kenya flag was flying and fluttering, and waving, in the air. The Police band played the new National Anthem and the crowd cheered continuously when they saw the flag was black, and red and green. The cheering sounded like one intense cracking of many trees, falling on the thick mud in the stadium.

In our village and despite the drizzling rain, men and women and children, it seemed, had emptied themselves into the streets where they sang and danced in the mud. Because it was dark, they put oil-lamps at the doorsteps to light the streets. As usual, on such occasions, some young men walked in gangs, carrying torches, lurked and whispered in dark corners and the fringes, really looking for love-mates among the crowd. Mothers warned their daughters to take care not to be raped in the dark. The girls danced in the middle, thrusting out their buttocks provokingly, knowing that the men in corners watched them. Everybody waited for something to happen. This 'waiting' and the uncertainty that went with it – like a woman torn between fear and joy during birth-motions – was a taut cord beneath the screams and the shouts and the laughter. People moved from street to street singing. They praised Jomo and Kaggia and Oginga. They recalled Waiyaki, who even before 1900 had challenged the white people who had come to Dagoreti in the wake of Lugard.

They remembered heroes from our village, too. They created words to describe the deeds of Kihika in the forest, deeds matched only by those of Mugo in the trench and detention camps. They mixed Christmas hymns with songs and dances only performed during initiation rites when boys and girls are circumcised into responsibility as men and women. And underneath it all was the chord that followed us from street to street. Somewhere, a woman suggested we go and sing to Mugo, the hermit, at his hut. The cry was taken up by the crowd, who, even before the decision was taken, had already started tearing through the drizzle and the dark to Mugo's hut. For more than an hour Mugo's hut was taken prisoner. His name was on everybody's lips. We wove new legends around his name and imagined deeds. We hoped that Mugo would come out and join us, but he did not open the door to our knocks. When the hour of midnight came, people broke into one long ululation. Then the women cried out the five Ngemi to welcome a son at birth or at circumcision. These they sang for Kihika and Mugo, the two heroes of deliverance, from our village. Soon after this, we all dispersed to our various huts to wait for the morning, when the Uhuru Celebrations would really begin.

Later in the night, the drizzle changed into a heavy downpour. Lightning, followed by thunder, would for a second or two red-white-light our huts, even though it only came through the cracks in the walls. The wind increased with the rain. A moaning sound, together with a continuous booming which went on all night, came from swaying and breaking trees and hedges as the wind and the rain beat the leaves and the branches. Some decaying thatched roofs freely let in rain, so that pools collected on the floor. To avoid being drenched, people kept on shifting their beds from spot to spot, only to be followed by a new leakage.

The wind and the rain were so strong that some trees were uprooted whole, while others broke by the stems, or lost their branches.

This we saw the following morning as we went into a field near Rung'ei, where the sports and dances to celebrate Uhuru were to take place. Crops on the valley slopes were badly damaged. Running water had grooved trenches that now zig-zagged all along the sloping fields.

Uprooted potato and bean crops lay everywhere on the valley floor. The leaves of the maize plants still standing were lacerated into numerous shreds.

The morning itself was so dull we feared the day would not break into life. But the rain had stopped. The air was soft and fresh, and an intimate warmth oozed from the pregnant earth to our hearts.

The field had been chosen by the Party's Uhuru Committee because it was the most central to all the ridges around. The field sloped dangerously towards the Rung'ei shops; the white-chalked athletic tracks rose in sharp bumps and fell into holes and shallow ditches.

First came the school sports and races. Children had turned out smart in their green, blue, or brown uniforms. Each school had its own group of supporters and all was noise and cheering as the children ran and fell and rose again to continue the race. There were two youth bands who, armed with bugles and drums, entertained people in between the races, with victory and military tunes. The bands belonged to the youth-wing of the Party. The school sports and races were followed by traditional dances. Uncircumcised boys and girls delighted the crowd with vigorous Muthuo; they had painted their faces with chalk and red-ochre and tied jingles to their knees; younger men and women did Mucung'wa: older women, in Mithuru, Miengu and layers of beads, danced Ndumo. All that morning, Gikonyo ran from place to place, from group to group, seeing that things ran smoothly. This was his day, he gloried in it, and wanted to make it a resounding success.

The crowd of spectators was not so large as Gikonyo had anticipated. And, contrary to what might be expected on an Uhuru day, a gloom hung over the morning session, that is, over the sports and dances.

But suddenly towards the end of the morning session, something happened that seemed to break the gloom. A three-mile race – twelve laps round the field – was announced. Old and young, women and children could all take part in the event. This spontaneous arrangement (the race had not been on the programme) revived and heated the gathering. Everywhere people shouted and argued, exhorting one another to enter the race. Whenever a woman came forward, she was greeted with appreciative laughter and clapping. The biggest clap was occasioned by Warui, when the old man, blankets and all, came forward for the race. Mumbi, who sat next to Wambui, wept with laughter as Warui jingled across the field to the starting point. Children strutted up and down, around the aged participants.

'Let us join the race,' Mwaura said to Karanja.

'My bones are stiff,' Karanja protested, shifting his eyes from Mumbi to the motley runners.

'Come, man. You were once a great long-distance runner. Remember those days at Manguo?'

'Are you taking part?'

'Yes – against you,' Mwaura said, and pulled Karanja by the hand.

Karanja's sudden appearance startled Gikonyo who, to avoid looking at Karanja, moved to where Warui stood and talked to him animatedly. Karanja was also hesitant; it had not occurred to him that Gikonyo might take part in the race. Then contempt for the carpenter filled his heart; he would not give up the race, he resolved, remembering their old race to the train. The unfinished drama was going to be re-enacted in front of Mumbi, and only a few yards from the same railway station. Perhaps this time he would win the race and Mumbi together. Why else had she written that note, he reasoned with anxious optimism, as he bent down to unlace his shoes. Mwaura was talking to General R. and Lt Koina and seemed to be emphasizing a point with his right forefinger. The competitors, quite a small crowd consisting of women and men and schoolchildren, were now alerted. The whole field was suddenly hushed a second before the whistle went. Then a tumult of shouting from the spectators accompanied the pandemonium of the starting point. The runners trod on one another. A boy fell to the ground and miraculously escaped unhurt from the trampling feet.

Warui dropped out almost immediately. He went and sat next to Wambui and Mumbi.

'You? I'll never trust your strength again,' Mumbi teased him. 'You have shamed all your faithful women.'

'Let the children play,' he said, and slowly shook his head. 'In our time, we ran for miles and miles after our cattle stolen by the Masai. And it was no play, I tell you.'

Before the end of the first lap, many runners had followed Warui's example and dropped out. Only one woman completed the third lap. It was at the end of the fourth round when many people had opted out of the race, that Mumbi suddenly noticed Karanja's presence. Her clapping abruptly stopped; her excitement slumped back to memories of yesterday. The sight of Karanja and Gikonyo on the same field embarrassed her so that she now wished she had stayed at home with her parents. Why had Karanja come, anyway, despite her warning note? Or did he not receive the message? Seeing General R. in the race, she was reminded of what the General had said two days before this. The irony of his words now struck her with her fuller knowledge of the situation. Circumstances had changed since she wrote that note. Then she had not known that the man who had actually betrayed Kihika was now the village hero. How could she tell this to anybody? Could she bear to bring more misery to Mugo, whose eyes and face seemed so distorted with pain? She recalled his fingers on her mouth, the others awkwardly feeling her throat. Then the terrible vacuum in his eyes. Suddenly at her question, he had removed his hands from her body. He knelt before her, a broken, submissive penitent.

'Mumbi!' He gulped. He half-stretched his hands, limp, then unexpectedly hid his face in them. All these abrupt changes in mood and gesture deprived her of words. Despite her fear, she laid a trembling hand on his shoulders.

'Listen, Mugo! I saw my brother die. The District Officer was there and the policemen.'

'You have eyes and ears. Don't you know who betrayed your brother?'

'Karanja! You were there. General R. told us.'

'No!'

She recoiled from him. In his hollow cry, in his look, she knew.

'You!'

'Me – yes – me.'

He had not looked at her. His voice had touched her, begged her. But she could not help her loathing and her trembling. She moved to the door, away from the immobile figure of the village hero. She had no words. No feelings. Nothing. Mechanically but quickly she had opened the door. A dark night. Seemed she walked and ran simultaneously. The darkness. Not even the silhouettes of houses and things. Rain drizzling. And the voices of men and women who sang Uhuru songs reaching her in the drizzle seemed to come from another village, far away.

In the morning she told Wambui: 'Mugo does not want to take part in these ceremonies: can't we leave him alone?' The knowledge she carried inside her involved her in a new dilemma; either Karanja or Mugo. But she did not want anybody to die or come to harm because of her brother. She wished she could talk to Gikonyo, who might find a way out. Why had Karanja ignored her note, she wondered again. Suddenly she grew vexed with herself: what did she care about him, who had ruined her life?

'What is the matter?' Wambui asked.

'Nothing,' Mumbi replied quickly, and started clapping, wildly.

As he ran, Gikonyo tried to hold on to other things; the half-familiar faces in the crowd; the new Rung'ei shops further down; the settled area across. Would Uhuru bring the land into African hands? And would that make a difference to the small man in the village? He heard a train rumbling at Rung'ei station. He thought of his father in the Rift Valley provinces. Was he still alive? What did he look like? He traversed the wide field of his childhood, early manhood, romance with Mumbi; Kihika, the Emergency, the detention camps, the stones on the pavement, the return home to betrayal passed through his mind in rapid succession. How Mumbi had dominated his life. Her very absence had almost unarmed him and made him break down. He angrily jerked his head, compelling himself to concentrate on the present race. He and Karanja were rivals again. But rivals for what? For whom were they competing? Karanja is only mocking me, he thought. He seethed with hatred as he panted and mopped sweat away from his forehead. He ran on, the desire to win inflamed him. He maintained his place close behind Karanja. His aim was to keep a certain pace, reserving his energy for the last lap or so, when he would dash forward, trusting his muscles would obey his will.

Mwaura was leading in the seventh lap. A few yards behind him followed Karanja, then General R., Gikonyo, Lt Koina and three other men, in that order. Most of the other competitors had dropped out. Around the field, spectators stood and cheered now this man, now that. Carry on, carry on, they shouted. Long-distance races had always been popular at Thabai. People despised short distances, regarding them as children's races. Even those who had private grief against Karanja, the former government chief and leader of the homeguards, now lost their bitter feelings in the excitement of the moment. They cheered him on.

And Karanja was remembering a scene, long ago, at the Railway Station, when he stood there fighting his knowledge that Gikonyo and Mumbi were left behind, alone. How he had yearned for the woman! Lord, how the guitar had moaned for Mumbi in the forest! If only he had not been hesitant, waiting upon tomorrow, he might have won her. Later when he proposed to her, she refused him – with a smile. And that refusal irrevocably bound him to her. He waited for his chance. When Gikonyo was taken to detention, Karanja suddenly knew he would never let himself be taken away from Mumbi. He sold the Movement and Oath secrets, the price of remaining near Mumbi. Thereafter the wheel of things drove him into greater and greater reliance on the whiteman. That reliance gave him power – power to save, to imprison, to kill. Men cowered before him; he despised and also feared them. Women offered their naked bodies to him; even some of the most respectable came to him by night. But Mumbi, his Mumbi, would not yield, and he could never bring himself to force her. Ironically, as he thought later, as he thought now, she only lay under him when he stood on the brink of defeat. He had felt a momentary pang of intense victory which, seconds later, after the act, melted into utter isolation and humiliation. He had taken advantage of her. For this, so he thought, she despised him. He could not face her – not after that shoe which caught him in the face and provoked blinding tears. He had always wanted Mumbi to come to him, freely, because he was important to her, irresistible. And now he was running for her. Had she not herself given him a second chance? Her note had rescued him from terrible despair. The Thompsons had gone, the whiteman would go. As long as the Thompsons were there, Karanja believed that white power would never really go. Perhaps it was because Thompson was the first whiteman Karanja had seen and met? For Thompson, the DO, appeared to people at Thabai, before the Emergency, the symbol of the whiteman's government and supremacy. White power had given Karanja a fearful security – now this security, already shaken at the foundation, had crumbled to pieces. He walked in dark corridors. He could not see the sun. And then the letter had come. It warned him not to attend the ceremonies today. Why? Mwaura had already asked him and, in his despair, he had refused to attend. Her letter made him think again, throughout the night. And every moment had sharpened his curiosity to see Mumbi. Thabai was, after all, his village: who dared say Karanja could not go home? Somewhere, in a corner of his heart, Karanja trusted his physical power over Mumbi. Had she not, after all, mothered his child? He did not take her warning seriously. It was a woman's way of doing things. And this view was confirmed when he and Mwaura arrived in Rung'ei, where he learnt that Mumbi had left her husband. Her message had gone sharp into his heart. All my life, I've run for her, he reflected bitterly. But only for a moment, though. He must not let such reflections deflect him from present victory. This was his last race. If he got Mumbi, his life would be complete. Uhuru and its threats would not, nothing would ever touch him, ill. So now he increased his pace. He must catch Mwaura at the tenth round. He must shake off Gikonyo, who stuck like a tick so close to his heels.

For now Gikonyo had passed General R. and held the third place. He clenched his teeth with determination. He knew that Mumbi was watching; he did not want to be humiliated, in front of her, by her lover. She had come to mock him, he thought. She had come to show that she was now independent. Twice he had gone to the place where she sat, to speak to Wambui about something, and he had resolutely ignored her presence. This had made him appear foolish, and angered him all the more. He saw Karanja increase his pace and he did the same. So far, nobody had broken the order established at the eighth round, but the crowd caught the heat and the tension.

Even Mumbi now forgot the burden in her heart, carried away by the moment. She wanted Gikonyo to win, and also prayed that he might lose. She criticized his ungainly running, but followed his progress anxiously. She cheered General R. and Lt Koina who trailed behind Gikonyo. Carry on, carry on, her heart panted, as she waved a white handkerchief. Whenever Karanja passed her she felt embarrassed, and she could not control this feeling.

General R. ran with ease. Before the Emergency he used to run in all long-distance races. He had even developed a theory about such races. 'They test how long you can endure hardship,' he used to say. 'You say to yourself: I will not give up: I will see this to the end.' His body had a beautiful rhythm. As he ran, he rehearsed his part in the scene that was to take place that afternoon. He had been asked to speak in place of Mugo. He was determined not to fail Kihika, whose soul would reign over the meeting, in triumph.

His mind would not dwell in the act. Without warning, he was back in Nyeri. That was where he was born. School and learning: that had been his child's dream, and expectation. He recalled how he used to do odd jobs and hired himself out as a labourer to cultivate other people's fields. His father had graduated from an ordinary colonial messenger into a petty assistant chief. He contributed nothing to the home except violence. He even extorted money from both his wife and son. He was also a man of the horn and would come home drunk to drum the boy's mother with fists. She whimpered and cried, like an animal in a cage. Muhoya – for that was the General's original name – would cower or rush out. He hated himself for his size and lack of courage. But he would not cry like other children – not even when his father laid hands on him. One day I'll get him, he swore inside. He never told his plans to anyone – not even to his mother. He would one day kill the tyrant – his mother would cry with gratitude although she had never complained about the drudgery around her or the fists that rained on her. As he grew, the desire for vengeance became faint. He postponed the day of reckoning to a vague future. But unexpectedly the day arrived. Muhoya, a young man newly circumcised, had come home and found his father at his favourite game. Suddenly the young man felt the moment had come. 'If you value your life,' he cried, 'don't touch her again.' At first the father was so surprised that his hand became numb in the air. Had he heard aright? He fell into a lion's rage. He lifted his hand to strike the boy, but Muhoya caught his father by the arm. The years of hatred and fear made him delirious with a fearful joy. Father and son were locked in a life-and-death struggle. The son did not see a father, but a perpetrator of unprovoked violence, a petty colonial tyrant who would extort money from even his closest relatives. And his father saw not a son, but a subject who had refused to be a subject. But Muhoya had not reckoned with a slave's treachery. The woman took a stick and fought on her husband's side. It was Muhoya who now turned numb with unbelief. 'He is your father, and my husband,' she was shouting as she felled a blow on his shoulder. Muhoya ran out of the house. For the first time, he wept. I don't understand, I cannot understand it. He was glad when the British conscripted him into their war. But he never forgot that experience. Never. It was only later when he saw how so many Kenyans could proudly defend their slavery that he understood his mother's reaction.

He heard Mumbi cheer him on. This roused him to the present. He acknowledged her cheers by increasing his pace. Soon he outdistanced Lt Koina. He ran furiously. He did not want to think about the past. He would never want to live through a similar childhood.

So the drama gathered speed. Koina made a bid to bridge the gap between him and the General. But somehow he could not summon his will to the race. He felt low. He had been like that for two days now. He could not understand it. He had seen much during the Second World War and in the War for Independence. These should have taught him to expect the unexpected in life. He had for instance been quite proud of having been a cook during the Second World War. After the war, he proudly talked about it, until constant unemployment frustrated him and half-opened his eyes. Koina was to become one of those people who ran into trouble with employers because he was forever demanding his rights. He would cite his services to the whiteman during the war and claimed that this entitled him to better treatment. In a shoe-factory near his home, he once told the boss in front of the other workers: 'I want more money. I want a decent house and enough food, just like you. I want a car like yours.'

He was kicked out of the factory. This sobered him a little. It was after this that he went to work for the woman. He had liked her dog. As a boy he had owned a pack of dogs which he used for hunting antelopes. How he would have loved to take her well-fed dog for a real chase of hare and antelopes in the forest! It seemed to please her that he and her dog got on so well. She gave him presents. Every Christmas. Then he started thinking. The amount of steak the dog ate could have fed a whole family. The amount of money spent on the dog was more than the total wages of ten Kenyans. The dog had its own room in the house, with a bed and sheets and blankets! And what about the woman? She had no husband, no children, no extended family. Yet her big house could easily have sheltered many families. How could all this be? Why should he live in a shack while this woman and her dog lived in such opulence and luxury? He became restless. How glad he was when he took the oath to join the Kenya Land and Freedom Army! He had seen the way. Independence, when finally won, would right all the wrongs, would drive the likes of Dr Lynd and her dogs from the country. Kenya after all was a blackman's country.

The day he waited for came: he would now enter the forest to join the Freedom Army. But he was going to enter the forest in triumph over Dr Lynd. He led the men into her house and they took her two guns and a pistol. 'Let me never see you again in this country,' he told her as he felled her dog with panga blows, 'Do you hear? Let me never see your face in Kenya again!'

In the years of hardships and deaths on the battlefield he had almost forgotten the incident, until the other day when he went to Githima to see Mwaura about plans to lure Karanja into attending Uhuru celebrations. And there in front of him was Dr Lynd and her dog. She stood there as if she was mocking him: See me, I have still got the big house, and my property has even multiplied. Githima had not in fact changed much. The exclusive white settlement seemed to have grown bigger instead. Why was she still in Kenya? Why were all these whites still in Kenya despite the ringing of Uhuru bells? Would Uhuru really change things for the likes of him and General R.? Doubts stabbed him. Dr Lynd's unyielding presence became an obsession. It filled him with fear, a kind of premonition. He had tried to share those thoughts with General R., but he could not find the words. . . . Even now, as he ran, the thought of the unexpected encounter made him shudder. The ghost had come to eat into his life; the cool Uhuru drink had turned insipid in his mouth. General R. was now many paces ahead of Koina. Koina stirred himself with difficulty. There was a roar from the crowd: this instilled new strength in Koina's limbs. Only the struggle, only the struggle, he panted.

At the start of the eleventh round Gikonyo dashed ahead of Karanja. A new wave of shouting and screaming acknowledged this break in the pattern. This wave gave Karanja strength as he too made a desperate attempt to regain the lead over his rival. Soon Gikonyo caught up with Mwaura, who fought hard, in vain. Karanja also came and passed him. Mwaura lost heart and was soon passed by everybody. The battle was now between Gikonyo and Karanja. Few knew that there were hidden motives and passions behind this battle; the crowd merely felt its peculiar ring and tension. In the last lap, the two were running shoulder to shoulder. At one point it seemed Karanja would pass Gikonyo. But Gikonyo seemed possessed of a devil. Indeed, there was something reckless about the way the two ran. People strained on their toes.

It was at this time that something unexpected happened. As Gikonyo ran down the hill, his foot caught against a tuft of grass, which brought him down, trapping Karanja in the process. The field went silent. General R. followed by the others came, passed and ran to the finish. Then the field broke into feverish confusion. People rushed to the place where the two men had fallen into a heap. When Gikonyo fell, Mumbi dropped the handkerchief she had been waving. 'Ngai,' she cried, and ran across the field to him. She knelt down and examined his head carefully. Gikonyo was so exhausted and angry that he did not know what was happening. Karanja was the one who first recovered and pulled himself up on to his left elbow. At the sight of Gikonyo's head in Mumbi's hands, so delicate the hands seemed, his eyes lost life and he sank back to the ground. People buzzed around. Seeing that Gikonyo was not hurt, Mumbi remembered their estrangement. Embarrassed, she pushed her way through the crowd and went home before anybody could talk to her. The crowd also broke away arguing and speculating: who of those two would have won the race? Some came out for Karanja; others were on Gikonyo's side. As they disappeared, few noticed that Gikonyo had not yet risen. He sweated profusely; his face was contorted with pain. He tried to rise, groaned a little, and sat down again. It was only after he had been rushed to the hospital that people learnt that Gikonyo had broken his left arm.

And this ended the morning session.

In the afternoon the sun appeared and brightened the sky. The mist which in the morning lingered in the air went. The earth smoked grey like freshly dropped cow-dung. The warming smoke spread and thinned upwards into the clear sky. The main ceremony to remember the dead sons and bless foundations for a new future was to be performed in the afternoon. It seemed that everybody had been waiting and making themselves ready for this occasion. Except for the old women and a few other people who were ill or lame, most people from our village came to the meeting. This was Kihika's day; it was Mugo's day; it was our day.

Other people from Ndeiya, Lari, Limuru, Ngeca, Kabete, Kerarapon, came in lorries and buses, and filed out into Rung'ei market place. There were the schoolchildren in their khaki uniforms of green, red, yellow – of every colour in the rainbow; the village children in tattered clothes with flies massed around their sore eyes and mouths; women, dressed in Miengu and Mithuru, with beads around their necks; women in flower-patterned calicos that showed bare their left shoulders; women, in modern frocks; women, singing Christian hymns mixed with traditional and Uhuru songs. Men stood or talked in groups about the prospects opened up by Uhuru. There were those without jobs, who wore coats that had never come into contact with water or soap; would the government now become less stringent on those who could not pay tax? Would there be more jobs? Would there be more land? The well-to-do shopkeepers and traders and landowners discussed prospects for business now that we had political power; would something be done about the Indians?

We sat down. Githua, whom we playfully called our 'monolegged champion', freely wept with great joy.

The crowd made a harmony: there's something beautiful and moving in the spectacle of a large mass of people seated in an orderly disorder.

A tree was planted at the spot where Kihika once hung. Near it, and tied to a stone, were two black rams, without blemish, for the big sacrifice. Warui and two wizened old men from Kihingo village had been chosen to lead in the sacrifice after tributes to those who had died in the struggle had been concluded. Mbugua and Wanjiku occupied two prominent chairs near the platform. Chairs for the main speakers and leaders of the celebrations were arranged around the microphone that stood on the raised platform. Mumbi, who in the village heard about Gikonyo's broken arm, had gone to the hospital.

We waited.

Again there was the breathless expectation that had hung over our village since the night. It seemed that most people still expected that Mugo would speak. They wanted to see him in the flesh and hear his voice. Stories about Mugo's power had spread from mouth to mouth and were mainly responsible for the big turnout. It would have been impossible to deny the many conflicting reports that overnight turned into stimulating legends. In any case, nobody, especially from our village, would have taken any denial seriously. Some people said that in detention Mugo had been shot at and no bullet would touch his skin. Through these powers, Mugo had been responsible for many escapes from detention of men who later went to fight in the forest. And who but Mugo could have smuggled letters from the camps to Members of Parliament in England? There were those who suggested that he had even been at the battle of Mahee and had fought side by side with Kihika. All these stories were now freely circulating in the meeting. We sang song after song about Kihika and Mugo. A calm holiness united our hearts. Like those who had come from afar to see Mugo do miracles or even speak to God, we all vaguely expected that something extraordinary would happen. It was not exactly a happy feeling; it was more a disturbing sense of an inevitable doom.

★

The secretary of the Party stood in place of Gikonyo. Nyamu was a short man, heavily built, who during the Emergency was caught, redhanded, with bullets in his pockets. It is said that his rich uncles (they were loyalists) bribed the police, and this, together with his youth, for he was only seventeen, saved him from a death sentence, the way of all those caught with arms and ammunition. Instead, he was imprisoned for seven years. Nyamu now called upon the Rev. Morris Kingori to open the meeting, with a prayer. Before 1952, Kingori was a renowned preacher in the Kikuyu Greek Orthodox Church, one of the many independent churches that had broken with the missionary establishment. When these churches were banned, Kingori went without a job for a long time, before he joined the Agriculture Department during land consolidation in the Central Province, as an instructor, a job he still holds to this day. As a preacher, he used to sing and dramatize his prayers; he raised his voice and eyes to heaven, then suddenly lowered them. Often, he would beat his breast and pull at his hair and clothes. Protest alternated with submission, meekness with anguish, warning with promise. Now, he stood on the platform, a Bible in his hand.

Kingori: Let us pray. Lord, open thou our hearts.

Crowd: And our mouths shall show forth thy praise.

Kingori: God of Isaac and Jacob and Abraham, who also created Gikuyu and Mumbi, and gave us, your children, this land of Kenya, we, on this occasion ever to be remembered by all the nations of the earth as the day you delivered your children from Misri, do now ask you to let your tears stream down upon us, for your tears, oh Lord, are eternal blessings. Blood has been spilt for this day. Each post in our huts is smeared not with blood from the ram, but blood from the veins and skins of our sons and daughters, who died, that we may live. And everywhere in our villages, in the market place, in the shambas, nay, even in the air, we hear the widows and orphans cry, and we pass by, talking loudly to drown their moaning, for we can do nothing, Lord, we can do nothing. But the cry of Rachael in our midst cannot be drowned, can never be drowned. Oh God of Isaac and Abraham, the journey across the desert is long. We are without water, we are without food, and our enemies follow behind us, riding on chariots and on horseback, to take us back to Pharaoh. For they are loth to let your people go, are angered to the heart to see your people go. But with your help and guidance, Lord, we shall surely reach and walk on Canaan's shore. You who said that where two or three are gathered together, you will grant whatsoever they shall ask, we now beseech you with one voice, to bless the work of our hands as we till the soil and defend our freedom. For it is written: Ask and it shall be given unto you; knock and it shall be opened; seek and ye shall find. All this we ask in the name of Jesus Christ our Lord, Amen.

Crowd: Amen.

People started singing, led by the youth band with drums, guitars, flutes and tins. Again they recreated history, giving it life through the words and voices: land alienation, Waiyaki, Harry Thuku, taxation, conscription of labour into the white-man's land, the break with the missions, and, oh, the terrible thirst and hunger for education. They sang of Jomo (he came, like a fiery spear among us), his stay in England (Moses sojourned in the land of Pharaoh) and his return (he came riding on a cloud of fire and smoke) to save his children. He was arrested, sent to Lodwar, and on the third day came home from Maralal. He came riding a chariot home. The gates of hell could not withhold him. Now angels trembled before him.

Nyamu read apologies from the MP for the area and from members of the Regional Assembly, all of whom had gone to Nairobi to represent Rung'ei area in the national celebrations. He did not mention Mugo's absence.

Next came the speeches. Most speakers recounted the sufferings of the Emergency, or else told of the growth of the Party. They were proud of Kihika, a son of the village, whose fight for freedom would never be forgotten. They recounted his qualities of courage, humility and love of the land. His death was a sacrifice for the nation.

At the end of each speaker, the crowd cheered or sang, even if the men or women had only repeated points already made. Githua's voice, as he cried, cheered and shouted, drowned that of those who sat near him. All the time most people expected Mugo to speak. Whenever a speaker sat down, they thought the next on the list would surely be Mugo himself. But they waited patiently because the best dish was always reserved to the last.

In the end, Nyamu announced that General R., the man who had fought side by side with Kihika, would speak, in the place of Mugo. Circumstances outside anybody's control had prevented Mugo from coming to the meeting. This announcement was met with silence. Then from one corner, a man shouted for Mugo. The demand was immediately chorused from different parts of the field, until the meeting seethed with Mugo's name in a threatening unison. Then the unison broke into undisciplined shouting and movement; people stood up, groups formed, and they all argued, gesticulated, protested, as if they had been tricked into the meeting. Nyamu consulted the elders. They decided to make one last appeal to Mugo. It took time for Nyamu and the elders to bring the gathering back to order with a promise that a delegation of two would be dispatched immediately to fetch Mugo. The two elders were asked not to take 'No' for an answer. Meanwhile, would the people sit and hear General R.'s words? They settled down again with the song of the trench.

> And he jumped into the trench,
> The words he told the soldier pierced my heart like a spear;
> You will not beat the woman, he said,
> You will not beat a pregnant woman, he told the soldier.

Below the words was the sound of something like a twang of a cord, broken. After it, people became deathly quiet.

General R. stood by the microphone, and his red eyes tried to penetrate the faceless crowd. He cleared his throat, twice. He knew what he wanted to say. He had rehearsed this act, word for word, many times. But now, standing on the edge of the precipice, he found it difficult to jump or fix his eyes on the scene below. Compressed into a single picture, his life in the forest flashed through his mind. He saw the dark caves at Kinenie, the constant flights from bombs in Nyandarwa forest, thirst, hunger, raw-meat and then their victory at Mahee. Tell them about this, a voice in him insisted. Tell them how you and Kihika planned it. This picture and the voice disappeared. Now it was the face of the Rev. Jackson Kigondu that stood before him: Jackson had consistently preached against Mau Mau in churches and in public meetings convened by Tom Robson. He called on Christians to fight side by side with the whiteman, their brother in Christ, to restore order and the rule of the spirit. Three times had Jackson been warned to stop his activities against the people. 'In the name of Jesus, who stood against the Roman colonialists and their Pharisee homeguards, we ask you to stop siding with British colonialism!' But Jackson became even more defiant. He had to be silenced. It was the same Jackson who now stood before him, mocking him, 'We are still here. We whom you called traitors and collaborators will never die!' And suddenly General R. recalled Lt Koina's recent misgivings. Koina talked of seeing the ghosts of the colonial past still haunting Independent Kenya. And it was true that those now marching in the streets of Nairobi were not the soldiers of the Kenya Land and Freedom Army but of the King's African Rifles, the very colonial forces who had been doing on the battlefield what Jackson was doing in churches. Kigondu's face was now transformed into that of Karanja and all the other traitors in all the communities in Kenya. The sensation of imminent betrayal was so strong that General R. trembled in his moment of triumph. He clutched the microphone to steady himself. He was suddenly aware that the crowd had stopped singing and were watching him. This threw General R. into a panic. Could everybody see the face or was it only in the mind? General R. wondered in his panic. He looked straight ahead, and addressed the face that mocked him.

'You ask why we fought, why we lived in the forest with wild beasts. You ask why we killed and spilt blood.

'The whiteman went in cars. He lived in a big house. His children went to school. But who tilled the soil on which grew coffee, tea, pyrethrum, and sisal? Who dug the roads and paid the taxes? The whiteman lived on our land. He ate what we grew and cooked. And even the crumbs from the table, he threw to his dogs. That is why we went into the forest. He who was not on our side, was against us. That is why we killed our black brothers. Because, inside, they were whitemen. And I know even now this war is not ended. We get Uhuru today. But what's the meaning of "Uhuru"? It is contained in the name of our Movement: Land and Freedom. Let the Party that now leads the country rededicate itself to all the ideals for which our people gave up their lives. The Party must never betray the Movement. The Party must never betray Uhuru. It must never sell Kenya back to the Enemy! Tomorrow we shall ask: where is the land? Where is the food? Where are the schools? Let therefore these things be done now, for we do not want another war . . . no more blood in my . . . in these our hands. . . .'

General R. found it difficult to continue. Looking at these people, his doubt fled, he knew they were behind him, that in asking for change he had spoken their word. The mocking face of the Rev. Jackson disappeared. Now he resumed his speech in a calm, confident voice.

'We want a Kenya built on the heroic tradition of resistance of our people. We must revere our heroes and punish traitors and collaborators with the colonial enemy. Today we are here to honour one such hero! Not many years ago today, Kihika was strangled with a rope on a tree here. We have come to remember him, the man who died for truth and justice. We, his friends, would like to reveal before you all the truth about his death, so that justice may be done. It is said, I am sure this is the story you all know, that Kihika was captured by security forces. But have you ever stopped to ask yourselves a few questions? Was he captured in battle? Why was he alone? Why was he not armed? Shall I tell you? On that night Kihika was going to meet somebody who betrayed him.'

He paused to let his words sink. People looked at one another, and started murmuring. The drama was even more exciting than they had imagined.

'Go on!' someone shouted.

'We hear you,' several voices cried out.

General R. continued.

'Maybe he who betrayed Kihika is here, now, in this crowd. We ask him to come forward to this platform, to confess and repent before us all.'

People looked this way and that way to see if anybody would rise. General R. waited, enjoying the tension, the drama was now unfolding as he had envisaged. Though he could not see him, he knew where Karanja sat. He had told Mwaura and Lt Koina to keep him in sight.

'Let him not think he can hide,' General R. went on. 'For we know him. He was Kihika's friend. They used to eat and drink together.'

'Speak his name,' Githua stood up and shouted.

'Toboa! Toboa!' more people cried, severally, almost thirsty for revenge.

'I give him a last chance. Let him come forward as a sign of repentance.'

People suddenly stopped rumbling and shouting. They sat tensed-up, eyes turned in the same direction, to see the man who was standing. He was tall, imposing, but those near him could see his face was agitated. Nobody had seen Mugo come to the scene. He wore a dirty coat and sandals made from an old lorry tyre. It is Mugo, somebody whispered. The whisper spread and became louder. People clapped. People shouted. At last, the hermit had come to speak. The other drama was forgotten. Women cried out the five Ngemi to a victorious son. General R. was angry with Mugo for ruining the climax of the other drama. Would Karanja escape? He did not show his anger, in fact, he immediately left the microphone to Mugo. People waited for Mugo to speak.

'You asked for Judas,' he started. 'You asked for the man who led Kihika to this tree, here. That man stands before you, now. Kihika came to me by night. He put his life into my hands, and I sold it to the whiteman. And this thing has eaten into my life all these years.'

Throughout he spoke in a clear voice, pausing at the end of every sentence. When he came to the end, however, his voice broke and fell into a whisper. 'Now, you know.'

And still nobody said anything. Not even when he walked away from the platform. People without any apparent movement created a path for him. They bent down their heads and avoided his eyes. Wanjiku wept. ('It was his face, not the memory of my son that caused my tears,' she told Mumbi later.) Suddenly Githua rose from his corner and followed Mugo. He laughed and raised one of his crutches to point at Mugo, and shouted: 'A liar – a hyena in sheep's clothing.' He denounced Mugo as an imposter and challenged him to a fight. 'Look at him! Look at him – the man who thought he would be our Chief. Ha! ha! ha!' Githua's laughter and voice only sharpened the profound silence at the market place. People sat on with bowed heads for a minute or so after Mugo and Githua had gone. Then they rose and started talking, moving away in different directions, as if the meeting ended with Mugo's confession.

The sun had faded; clouds were gathering in the sky. Nyamu, Warui, General R., and a few other elders remained behind to complete the sacrifice before the storm.

Karanja

But the rain when later it fell, did not break into violence. It drizzled continuously, varying neither in speed nor in volume. The country, it seemed, was going to plunge into one of those stinging drizzles that went on endlessly. On such days the sun never said good morning, or else good night. Without a watch, you could never guess the time.

At his mother's hut in Thabai, Karanja crammed a few clothes into a bag.

'You'll not let me make you a cup of tea?' his mother asked again. She sat on a stool near the fireplace; her right leg bent at the knee, resting on a hearthstone. She was bowed double, leaning forward, so that her chin and hands rested on the bent knee. Wairimu was wizened, with hollow eyes and protuding jaws. Her eyes now watched the silent movements of her son at the door.

'No,' Karanja said, after a pause, as if words and speech cost him pain.

'It is raining outside. A cup of hot tea will warm you inside – since you say you'll not stay here for the night.'

'I've already said I don't want tea – or anything,' he said, his voice raised with obvious irritation. The irritation was directed less at Wairimu than at the bag he handled, the smoke-ridden hut, the drizzle outside, at the life and things in general.

'Hii, I was only talking,' Wairimu said in a withdrawing voice.

It was never easy to tell the relationship between Karanja and his mother. She was the third of the four wives that Karanja's father had acquired by paying so much bride price in goats and cattle. He acquired them, yes, and then left them to their own resources. He built his hut a mile away from his wives, maintaining equidistance in emotions and help from each of the wives and their children. He visited each woman in turn, sprung a child at her and then retired to his hut. Wairimu's children died at birth; Karanja was the sole survivor, the only living evidence of her man's surprise visits to her bed. Wairimu had expected much from her son. She looked up to him as the man who would take care of her in her old age. From an early age Karanja had, however, shown tendencies that were not the normal attributes of a hardworking son. He sang, played the guitar, and ran after women.

'You must stop playing that thing,' Wairimu had complained. 'You must do some useful work,' she often said, threatening to break or burn the guitar. They often quarrelled. But in rare moments when son and mother came together, she would gently tell him a story to illustrate the fate of every idle person. It was in this story that Karanja often remembered his mother and in time of agony it made him long for her.

'Once, long ago,' she would begin, 'there was a poor woman who had only one son. Njoki, for that was her name, wanted her son to realize that they were poor and could only get enough to eat by working hard. Every morning her son woke up and polished his shoes and ironed his clothes carefully and then went to his playmates in the shops and streets. In the evenings he would come back with a crowd of young men and women, and would ask his mother for food. Njoki was a generous woman and liked young people in the house. She would give them food and tell them stories. But every day she grew sadder because her son would never take a jembe or a panga to the shamba. Because she did not want to embarrass her son, she always hid her sadness whenever there were people in the house. Njoki was a woman with a good heart and people always praised her generosity and hard work. This pleased her son, because he was really proud of his mother and people called him son of Njoki.

'One day he brought home three great friends from a distant village. He had visited them many times and was always lavished with food and drinks. He in turn talked about his home and had often promised them a similar treat should they ever visit him. That is why he now asked his mother to treat them to a feast. Njoki lit a good fire. She laid a clean cloth on the table. She brought plates and spoons and wiped them clean. Then she went back to the kitchen. Her son was very happy and talked about his mother and her cooking. Njoki came back from the kitchen with three plates and on each plate was a pair of shining shoes. She put the plates and the shoes on the table.

'"I am afraid today I did not go to the shamba," she said. "I spent the whole day polishing these shoes, and so this is all there is to eat."

'Her son could hardly talk for shame. The following morning he took a panga and a jembe and never left the field until sunset.'

'Aah, that is meant for me,' Karanja would say. 'All right, tomorrow I shall come to the shamba with you.'

During the Emergency, Wairimu disapproved of her son becoming a homeguard and a Chief and said so.

'Don't go against the people. A man who ignores the voice of his own people comes to no good end.'

Although ashamed of his activities, she stuck by him, for, as she said, a child from your own womb is never thrown away.

Karanja finished packing things into the bag. Then, as an after-thought, he turned to his mother.

'Is my guitar still here?'

'Look in that heap at the corner.'

Karanja had forgotten his guitar until now. During the Emergency he had stopped playing it altogether. He rummaged through a pile of broken pots and calabashes until he fished out the instrument from the bottom. The wood was cracked, was covered with dust and soot, and smelt of smoke. The strings were loose and two were broken. He tried to dust off the layer of dust and soot, then gave up the effort. He fastened one or two of the loose strings. He strummed a little; the instrument produced a rumbling noise as dust fell into the hole. He walked to the door. Outside, it was still drizzling.

'Where are you going in the rain?' Wairimu asked. Karanja stopped at the door as if shocked by the question. He slowly turned round; his dull eyes flickered slightly, his chest heaved outwards. He was going to say something when a wisp of smoke entered his eyes, he coughed a little, and stepped aside. His eyes glistened with tears. The moment was gone.

'I don't know,' he said. 'I am going back to Githima,' he continued with decision. He went out, his bag and guitar slung on his back. Wairimu did not stir from her huddled position near the fireplace.

The drizzle tapped, drummed the guitar and the bag. Soon the dust and the soot soaked and started to slug down. He walked towards the bus stop at Thabai Trading Centre, through the greying mist, looking neither to the right nor to the left. A bus arrived at the stop, dropped passengers and then went away. Karanja walked in the steady pace of a person not in a hurry to reach his destination. He saw Mumbi (she must have come out of that bus) cross the road into the village, shielding her head from the drizzle by a Gikoi. His heart beat suddenly rose from near paralysis and quickened at the sight of Mumbi. Caught in the mist and the drizzle, she appeared more beautiful than ever before.

But how could he forget the deep concern on her face as she bent over Gikonyo, after the fall? This had thrust Karanja back into pain and despair. If she had only glanced at him, ever so slightly, he might have hoped. But she had seemed unaware of his existence.

Still Karanja's heart beat. Mumbi did not see him until she was very near him. She gave a cry of surprise.

'How is Gikonyo?' he asked, without thinking much about the question. He guessed she had gone to the hospital because he had not seen her at the meeting.

'He is all right. The nurses told me he might be out soon.'

'I looked for you at the meeting. I wanted to see you. I wanted to thank you for the note.'

'It's nothing. It cost me no effort. In any case, you ignored it.'

'Then I had not known what the warning was all about. I'd thought you wanted to see me.'

'No.'

'Never?'

'Never again.' They spoke hurriedly because of the drizzle.

'Anyway, thank you,' he said after a small pause. 'They wanted to kill me?'

'I don't know.'

'I know. Mwaura told me.'

'Who is Mwaura?'

'He works with me. When Mugo came to the meeting—'

'Mugo, to the meeting?'

'Yes. And confessed—'

'Confessed?'

'Haven't you heard? He came to the meeting and in front of us all said it. He seems to be a courageous man.'

'Ye-es!' She agreed, recovering from the shock, and starting to edge away from Karanja. 'It's raining. I must go home,' she said.

'Can't I . . . may I not see the child . . . last time?'

'Can't you be a man and leave me alone, Karanja?' she said with passion, and immediately turned away. Karanja watched her go until she was swallowed by the mist and the village huts.

'Ye-es. He is a man of courage,' he repeated in her direction. 'He even saved my life: for what?'

Karanja resumed his walk. His head and clothes were drenched with water. Two buses arrived, one after the other. NARROW ESCAPE was leading, closely followed by LUCKY ONE.

'Nairobi?' inquired a turn-boy, already taking his luggage.

'Githima!' he said and clutched his luggage more firmly.

'Then take them inside, quick.' Even before Karanja found a seat, the turn-boy whistled and NARROW ESCAPE started to move. Then LUCKY ONE behind it, came and passed. The two buses raced for customers at the next stop.

'Step on the oil and let it burn,' the turn-boy egged the driver. Each bus wanted to reach Nairobi first, because of people returning home from the Uhuru celebrations in the city.

Within a short time the bus reached the Githima stop. Karanja got out and the bus ran on, already about half-a-mile behind its rival. Karanja went into an eating-house by the road. The place was crowded with people sheltering from the rain. He put his bag and guitar against the wall, in a corner, and sat down at a small deserted table. When the waiter came round, Karanja ordered tea and a chapati with beef stew. He rested his head in his hands, elbows on the table, and stared at nothing. Flies crowded the cracks in the table which were filled with the heavy ooze of darkened sugar, oil, bits of meat and rotten potatoes. The food came and the smell of the steaming stew made him want to vomit. He pushed it aside. Then he sipped a little tea. Again he stared at the table, without noticing the flies or the deposit along the cracks. At the door, people buzzed about Uhuru, Jomo, and the rain. In his mind Karanja was turning over the confusion of the day's events, grasping at now this, now that, anything that would give them some sort of coherence.

He vaguely remembered the nightmare he had undergone at the meeting when General R. called for the traitor to go to the platform. Mwaura sat next to Karanja. Lt Koina sat a few yards away. The two darted surreptitious glances at one another and then at Karanja. It was then that he realized the words of General R. were aimed at him, and he immediately connected them with Mumbi's warning. If he walked to the platform, people would claw him to instant death. He had a momentary picture of all those hands tearing at his flesh. Was this not what he had feared would happen when Thompson departed from the land? He was scared of black power: he feared those men who had ousted the Thompsons and had threatened him. He thought of standing up and publicly denying any guilt in Kihika's capture. But fear nailed him to the ground. Then that man, Mugo, had appeared with a confession which relieved Karanja. Mwaura turned to Karanja with eyes tense with malice. 'He has saved you,' Mwaura said, and swiftly moved away.

Thinking about this, Karanja involuntarily shuddered at the thought of what would have happened to him if Mugo had not arrived on time. As a boy, once, Karanja saw dogs tear a rabbit. They tore its limbs and each dog ran with blood-covered pieces. Karanja now saw himself as that rabbit. But why am I afraid of dying, he asked himself, remembering the many men, terrorists, he and other homeguards led by their white officers, had shot dead? Then, somehow, he had not felt guilty. When he shot them, they seemed less like human beings and more like animals. At first this had merely thrilled Karanja and made him feel a new man, a part of an invisible might whose symbol was the whiteman. Later, this consciousness of power, this ability to dispose of human life by merely pulling a trigger, so obsessed him that it became a need. Now, that power had gone. And Mumbi had finally rejected him. For what, then, had Mugo saved Karanja? He sipped another mouthful of tea. It had gone cold, and he pushed it aside. Life was empty like the dark and the mist that enclosed the earth. He paid for the meal he had not eaten, collected his bag and guitar and walked towards the door.

'Here,' the waiter called him back, 'here, you have forgotten your change.'

Karanja turned round, took the money, and without counting it, went out. And she won't even let me see the child, he thought sadly, as he took the road to Githima. Why did I want to see the child today? He had never felt such a desire before. A car rushed past and just missed him. He moved aside, still closer to the bank, almost brushing against the kei-apple hedge, without being conscious of his action. Thompson has gone, I have lost Mumbi. His mind hopped from image to image, following no coherent order. Incidents in his life would pop up and then disappear. What if Kihika was alive, and appeared to him, now, on the road? Karanja started, afraid of the hedge and the dark. The rain had dwindled to thin, straying showers. Karanja's clothes stuck heavily to his body. He had gone to see Kihika hang from a tree. He had searched his heart for one has pity or sorrow for a lost friend. Instead, he found only disgust; the body was hideous; the dry lips over which a few flies played, were ugly. What is freedom? Karanja had asked himself. Was death like that freedom? Was going to detention freedom? Was any separation from Mumbi freedom? Soon after this, he confessed the oath and joined the homeguards to save his own life. His first job was in a hood. The hood – a white sack – covered all his body except the eyes. During the screening operations, people would pass in queues in front of the hooded man. By a nod of the head, the hooded man picked out those involved in Mau Mau.

It's the hooded self that Karanja now vividly saw in front of him, in the dark. He could almost touch the slits through which the man inside the hood saw the world. It's only in the mind, he reassured himself. He was now near the railway crossing. He heard a train rumble in the distance. He remembered the race to the train. The rumbling was becoming nearer and louder. One day people were collected from villages in Rung'ei Station for screening. One by one they went past him, and Karanja inside the hood recognized many people and knew with pleasure that none of them could see him. The scene shifted to the meeting in the afternoon. 'He seems to be a man of courage,' he thought. And she had agreed with this. The picture of Mugo at the platform, like a ghost, rose before him, merging with that of the hooded man. Karanja stood near the crossing, contemplating the many eyes that had watched Mugo at the meeting. The train was now so near he could hear the wheels screeching on the rails. He felt the screeching in his flesh as on that other time at Rung'ei Station. He was conscious too, of many angry eyes watching him in the dark. The train was only a few yards from the crossing. He moved a step forward. Then it swished past him, the lights, the engine and the coaches, so close that the wind threw him back. The earth were he stood trembled. When the train disappeared, the silence around him deepened; the night seemed to have grown darker.

Mugo

Mumbi wanted to run and walk, and surrender her body to the drizzle, all at the same time. She trotted, panting under the pressure of a load she could not put down. The news of Mugo's confession came on top of what, for her, had been a trying afternoon. At Timoro hospital, Gikonyo had not spoken a word or shown any awareness of her presence. 'He thinks I am bribing him to take me back,' she reflected with pain, on seeing him shut his eyes and turn his head away in pretended sleep at her approach. 'But I will not go back to his home, not if he kneels before me,' she had resolved. Arriving home drenched, Mumbi found Mbugua and Wanjiku drowsing by the fire, without talking; the child slept on the floor. The warmth in the hut was a welcome contrast to the mud, mist and the showers outside. Mumbi changed into dry clothes without a word, her limbs making an effort she barely willed.

'How is he?' Wanjiku approached, cautiously, after Mumbi had sat down.

'I will not visit him again,' she burst out, in a tone that included her mother and father in things that constantly thwarted her in her search for peace among broken pots, and ruins. 'Not even if I hear he is dying.'

'Step gently into the road,' Wanjiku retorted, her word edged with sarcasm. 'Such words should not be spoken in his house. Remember that he'll always be your husband unless he demands back his bride-price.'

'My husband? Never.'

'Sssh!'

Gradually Wanjiku soothed her spirits, and Mumbi agreed to look after Gikonyo for as long as he was in the hospital.

'A sick man is never abandoned in hospital. Even an enemy is often rescued from danger. Besides, you need not go to Timoro alone. There is Wangari, a woman unequalled anywhere, in her industry and warm heart.'

Mumbi felt wanted again. She listened to Wanjiku, who told her about Mugo and the meeting, in detail. Mbugua went on nodding at the fire, an old man who, these days, rarely talked except when Kariuki came home during the holidays. Mumbi heard the story and felt that she ought to do something. What can I do, she countered the feeling with a question she knew nobody would answer for her. The fire made her drowsy. She was struck with exhaustion; the weariness came into her limbs, over her shoulders, into her head and heart, warming itself in every joint. She longed to curl against her aged mother and be comforted. What can I do, she asked again. Listening to the muffled noise of rain falling on the grass-thatched roof, she abandoned herself to that weariness which possessed her as if to rescue herself from the need to act. Mumbi remained in her seat, her body and spirit passive before a disaster she sensed with her eyes and ears. 'I'll see Mugo tomorrow. Besides he was present and so he knows,' she persuaded herself in bed, on the floor, beside her child. 'The night is dark and it is raining.'

She and Wangari rose early and went to the hospital together. Gikonyo sat up in bed. His arm had been plastered.

They told him about the meeting and Mugo's great confession. He listened to the story with head slightly bowed.

Wangari and Mumbi saw Gikonyo tremble so that the blankets that covered him shook.

'What is the matter?' his mother asked, thinking of the pain in his arm. Gikonyo did not seem to have heard. He stared at the opposite wall, at something beyond the hospital. After what to them seemed a long silence, Gikonyo looked at the two women. He was more composed. His hard face had changed, almost softened. The scowl was gone. His voice when he spoke was small, awed, almost tinged with shame. 'He was a brave man, inside,' he said. 'He stood before much honour, praises were heaped on him. He would have become a Chief. Tell me another person who would have exposed his soul for all the eyes to peck at.' He paused and let his eyes linger on Mumbi. Then he looked away and said, 'Remember that few people in that meeting are fit to lift a stone against that man. Not unless I – we – too – in turn open our hearts naked for the world to look at.'

Hearing him speak thus, Mumbi felt herself lifted to the clouds and then pulled back to the earth by a tremendous fear. 'I should have gone to him before coming here,' she thought.

As soon as she got back to Thabai, Mumbi rushed to Mugo's hut and pushed open the door. Everything was set as she had left it the other night. The fire had clearly not been made for a day or two. The bed was not made. A worn-out blanket with bristles sticking out, hung from the bed on the floor. Mumbi shut the door behind her and hurried to seek out General R. in his hut. She found it locked. 'All right, I shall come back in the evening.'

In the evening she went back and found no light in Mugo's hut. She groped her way in the dark, and then, frightened, called out: 'Mugo.' There was no answer. 'Where has he gone? Where has everybody gone?' She looked about her, retreating to the door. She wanted a witness, any witness, to contradict the answers that stormed into her – like innumerable echoes shouting back her words and fears, in the dark. She opened the door, more frightened, and ran all the way, through the drizzle, across slithering paths, to her parents' home.

Though not conscious of the fact, Mumbi had re-enacted the same movement as on the night she went away from Mugo. Only then there had been light in the hut and Mugo was able to see what he translated as scorn and horror on her face. He remained standing, staring long at the seat she had just left. Later he shut the door, put out the light and went to bed. He lay on the bed, aware that he had just lost something. Many times, the scorn on Mumbi's face flashed through the dark, and a shuddering he could not control thrilled into him. Why was it important to him now, tonight, what Mumbi thought of him? She had been so near. He could see her face and feel her warm breath. She had sat there, and talked to him and given him a glimpse of a new earth. She had trusted him, and confided in him. This simple trust had forced him to tell her the truth. She had recoiled from him.

He had lost her trust, for ever. To her now, so he reasoned, saw and felt, he was vile and dirty.

And then suddenly he heard the village people around his hut singing Uhuru songs. Every word of praise carried for him a piercing irony. What had he done for the village? What had he done for anybody? Yet now he saw this undeserved trust in a new light, as the sweetest thing in the world. Mumbi will tell them, he thought. He saw the scorn and horror, not on Mumbi's face alone, but on every person in the village. The picture, vivid in his mind, made him coil with dread.

That night, he hardly closed his eyes. The picture of Mumbi merged with that of the village and detention camps. He would look at Mumbi and she would immediately change into his aunt or the old woman.

He woke up early and strangely felt calm. He remained calm. He remained calm all the morning. The torturing images of the night before had gone. This surprised him; why could he feel calm when he knew what he was going to do?

Nevertheless, when the moment came, and he saw the big crowd, doubts destroyed his calm. He found General R. speaking, and this reminded him of Karanja. Why should I not let Karanja bear the blame? He dismissed the temptation and stood up. How else could he ever look Mumbi in the face? His heart pounded against him, he felt sweat in his hands, as he walked through the huge crowd. His hands shook, his legs were not firm on the ground. In his mind, everything was clear and final. He would stand there and publicly own the crime. He held on to this vision. Nothing, not even the shouting and the songs and the praises would deflect him from this purpose. It was the clarity of this vision which gave him courage as he stood before the microphone and the sudden silence. As soon as the first words were out, Mugo felt light. A load of many years was lifted from his shoulders. He was free, sure, confident.

Only for a minute.

No sooner had he finished speaking than the silence around, the lightness within, and the sudden freedom pressed heavy on him. His vision became blurred at the edges. Panic seized him, as he descended the platform, moved through the people, who were now silent. He was conscious of himself, of every step he made, of the images that rushed and whirled through his mind with only one constant thread: so he was responsible for whatever he had done in the past, for whatever he would do in the future. The consciousness frightened him. Nothing would now, this minute, make him return to that place. Suppose all those people had risen and dug their nails and teeth into his body?

In his mind, this thought turned into fact. He did not enter his hut. He heard Githua's laughter and felt himself pursued. He did not want to die, he wanted to live. Mumbi had made him aware of a loss which was also a possibility. He lingered outside his hut and peered around him, into the village, at Kabui Trading Centre and the road which went beyond. Would people rise and come for him? He saw the clouds gather in the sky. Maybe he ought to run away from the village before rain fell. He started walking towards the road. He went for a few yards and then thought he might meet with people coming from Rung'ei. He would go the other way, through the village, and join the other road to Nairobi. There, he would start a new life.

Strong in this resolution, he hurried along the main village street, which he had always taken on the way to the shamba. But already people from the meeting had started to stream into the village. The streets and the huts would soon be alive with people and he would not get away. He quickened his step. Now he faced the hut that belonged to the old woman. A thrill burnt him. He felt an uncontrollable desire to enter the hut, to see the old woman, this once, for the last time. But he decided to go on before the rain and the darkness fell.

The first few drops of rain, however, caught him before he had moved more than a few steps. He'd better take shelter from the rain, he thought. If the old woman was in, couldn't she, in any case, hide him until the hour of dark when he could get away secretly? He retraced the steps, crossed the street, and suppressing a high voice that urged him to go away immediately, entered the hut. The old woman sat near the empty fireplace, her feet buried in the ashes. At his entrance, she raised her head slowly. Her eyes in the darkish hut had a strange glint.

'You – you have come back!' she said, her face contorted by a half-frozen smile into something not of this world.

'Yes,' he said, his body aflame with a desire to escape, which he again suppressed.

'I knew you would come, I knew you would come to fetch me home,' she seemed grotesque in her happiness. She attempted to rise and staggered back into her seat. Slowly she rose again.

'All these years I've waited for you – I knew they had not really killed you – These people, do you know they didn't believe me when I told them, when I tell them I have seen you?'

She walked towards him. But Mugo was not listening to her wild muttering. For suddenly her face had changed. Mugo looked straight into the eyes of his aunt. A new rage moved him. Life was only a constant repetition of what happened yesterday and the day before. Only this time she would not escape. He would stop that oblique smile, that contemptuous glint in the eyes. But before he could move, the woman staggered back into her seat. The smile still lingered on her face. She did not move or make the slightest stir. And suddenly he knew: the only person who had ever claimed him was dead. He buried his face in his hands and stood thus for a few seconds.

Later, he shut the door behind him and went into the drizzling rain. He did not continue with his earlier plans. Instead, he walked back to his hut. In the hut, he lit the oil-lamp and sat on the bed. He did not remove his wet clothes. He stared at the wall, opposite. There was nothing on the walls: no visions of blood, no galloping footsteps behind him, no detention camps, and Mumbi seemed a vague thing in a remote past. Occasionally he tapped the bed frame, almost irritably. Water dripped from his hair, down to his face and neck in broken lines; water dripped from his coat, again in broken lines, down his legs and on to the ground. A drop was caught in his right eyelashes and the light from the lamp was split into many tiny lashes. Then the drop entered his eye, melted inside, and ran down his face like a tear.

He did not rub the eye, or do anything.

There was a knock at the door. Mugo did not answer it.

The door opened and General R., followed by Lt Koina, came in.

'I am ready,' Mugo said, and stood up, without looking at his visitors.

'The trial will be held tonight,' General R. pronounced, gravely. 'Wambui will be the judge. Koina and I will be the only elders present at the hearing.'

Mugo said nothing.

'Your deeds alone will condemn you,' General R. continued without anger or apparent bitterness. 'You— No one will ever escape from his own actions.'

General R. and Lt Koina led him out of the hut.

Warui, Wambui

Warui gazed out, avoiding the dull vacancy in Wambui's eyes.

'It has been going on for two days, this drizzle,' he commented, prompted to say something by the unease he felt in Wambui's hut. He sat, huddled near the door, with hands and feet buried under the blanket; his neck, ringed with wrinkles, and his grey head, were the only uncovered parts of his body. Wambui crouched, opposite him, her vacant eyes now and then resting on Warui before straying to the mist, and the rain, outside.

'Such drizzling can go on for many days,' she said with a dull voice. They both relapsed into silence, making a picture of bereaved children for whom life has suddenly lost warmth, colour, and excitement. There was no fire in the hearth. Bits of potato peelings, maize-husks and grass lay strewn on the floor as if the hut had not been lived in for a day or two. Under different circumstances, this would have surprised Warui or any visitor, because Wambui's hut was one of the tidiest in the village. She swept the floor at least twice a day and cleaned utensils immediately after use. In the hut every utensil, every piece of equipment had its own place in various racks built against the walls. As for the mud walls, they were smeared with white ochre she bought from Weru, and she often checked to see that every crack was immediately filled and worn-out areas restored. 'A man has nowhere else but where he lays his head,' was the cryptic rejoinder to the many compliments on her tidiness. Warui had not seen her since the day of the big sacrifice. For the last two days people in Thabai had more or less kept to themselves, avoiding, by general consent, public discussions on the events of Uhuru day. There were things that puzzled Warui, questions for which, in vain, he sought answers in the heart. Failing, he had come to see Wambui. Yet they now conversed, as if they did not know what the other was talking about, as if they were both ashamed of certain subjects in one another's presence.

'Perhaps it is this cold that killed her,' he tried again.

'Who?'

'The old woman.'

'Ye-es!' she said, irrelevantly, and sighed. 'We all forgot her on that day. We should not have left her alone. She was old. Loneliness killed her.'

'Why on that day, I keep on asking myself. She used to live alone, or is that not so?'

'Then, life was around her. The smoke and the noise of children. On that day, all of us went to the meeting. All of us. There was no smoke anywhere, and there were no cries or laughter of children in the streets. The village was empty.' She spoke as if building up a case in an argument.

'But why on that day?' Warui persisted in his doubt. He, too, seemed engaged in an argument, in the heart.

'She was lonely, can't you hear? Her son came for her. Gitogo fetched her home on that day,' she finished with impatient irritation.

'Yes. Things started changing in our village the day she started seeing visions of the dead.'

Wambui looked at him. This time she did not say anthing.

'And that day,' Warui went on, 'that day! First Gikonyo breaks his arm.' He stopped unexpectedly and turned to Wambui. She was looking at the showers outside, indifferent to his words, to the questions in his heart. Looking in the same direction, he saw Mumbi suddenly emerge from the mist, a few yards from the door. Mumbi came into the hut, her feet wet, bespattered with mud. Water dripped down the sack with which she covered her head and back. She removed the sack, and shook it a little, before hanging it on a rack. Wambui gave her a seat near the door.

'It's cold,' Mumbi said, holding herself together, making a hissing sound as she sucked in air through her closed teeth. 'I am not in luck today. My mother is just making a fire at home, so I run away to this place because you always have a ready fire. See what I find.'

'Did you go to the hospital today?' Wambui inquired.

'Yes, I was there with my mother-in-law. I go there every day.'

'How is the arm?'

'It is not badly broken, only cracked. He will be out soon.'

'Something went wrong . . .' Warui started again, slowly following his own thoughts. 'Everybody gone. And a minute before, the field was covered with so many people, like in the days of Harry, you know, at the procession. Then in the twitching of an eyelid, all gone. The field was so empty. Only four (or were we five?) left. We slaughtered the rams – and prayed for our village. But it was like warm water in the mouth of a thirsty man. It was not what I had waited for, these many years.'

'You say that, and it was the same with me, with everybody. I'd never once suspected that he . . . that Mugo had done it.' With effort Wambui had mentioned the one name she and Warui had been avoiding. Mumbi did not say anything for a while.

'He has not been found,' Mumbi at last said in a changed voice.

'Nobody has seen him since that day,' Warui answered, as if Mumbi had asked a question.

'Maybe he has bolted himself inside the hut,' Wambui said.

'I went there last night. The door was not locked, or bolted from the inside. I found nobody in.'

'Perhaps he has left the village,' Warui observed.

'Or maybe he was in the latrine when you went in.'

'But I went back to the hut this morning before I went to the hospital.'

A small breeze blew rain-showers into their faces. Wambui rubbed the water from her face with the back of her hand. Warui bent his head and rubbed his face against the blanket. Mumbi tilted backwards as if to move back her seat, and did nothing. They all retained their places near the door.

'Perhaps I could have saved him. Perhaps I could if I had gone into the hut that night,' Mumbi lamented.

'Who are you talking about?' Wambui asked quickly, and turned her eyes away from Mumbi.

'Mugo.'

'There was nothing to save,' Wambui said slowly. 'Hear me? Nobody could have saved him . . . because . . . there was nothing to save.'

'But you did not see his face, Wambui, you did not see him,' Mumbi said in a heated voice. Then she lowered it and continued. 'I mean the night before the meeting. When you sent me to see him – his face changed as with pain in the heart – I mean – his face was different as he told me about—'

'What?' Wambui and Warui asked together. This news seemed to have captured their interest.

'About Kihika, my brother.'

'You knew?'

'Yes. He told me.'

'Maybe you should have told us this before the meeting,' Wambui said accusingly, and lost interest in the news.

'I did not want anything to happen. I never knew that he would later come to the meeting.'

'That's true,' Warui agreed and resumed his thoughts in a puzzled, almost disappointed voice. 'I was deceived by his eyes. But I ask myself: Why did he do all that in the trench and in detention?'

Mumbi was the first to recover from this mood of introspection. She said:

'I must go now. I'm sure the fire is ready at home. Perhaps we should not worry too much about the meeting . . . or . . . about Mugo. We have got to live.'

'Yes, we have the village to build,' Warui agreed.

'And the market tomorrow, and the fields to dig and cultivate ready for the next season,' observed Wambui, her eyes trying to see beyond the drizzle and the mist.

'And children to look after,' finished Mumbi as she stood up and took her rain-sack ready to leave. Then suddenly she turned round and looked at the two old people, as at aged wisdom which could tell youth the secrets of life and happiness.

'Did any of you see General R. on the night of the meeting?'

Wambui looked up at her with startled fear in her eyes. Warui was the first to answer without turning his eyes from the rain.

'I have not seen him since he spoke at the meeting.'

'Neither have I,' Wambui also said in a tone that rejected all responsibility in face of possible police inquiries.

Mumbi went out. Soon Warui followed her out, still muttering to himself: 'Something went wrong. I was deceived by his eyes, those eyes. Maybe because I am old. I am losing my sight.'

Wambui sat on and watched the drizzle and the grey mist for a few minutes. Darkness was creeping into the hut. Wambui was lost in a solid consciousness of a terrible anti-climax to her activities in the fight for freedom. Perhaps we should not have tried him, she muttered. Then she shook herself, trying to bring her thoughts to the present. I must light the fire. First I must sweep the room. How dirt can so quickly collect in a clean hut! But she did not rise to do anything.

Harambee

Wamumu was Gikonyo's last detention camp. He was kept there for a year. The detainees in this camp worked on a new irrigation scheme on the Mweya plains in Embu. They were converting the dry plains into rice-growing fields. As he dug canals, Gikonyo often looked across the flat plains and saw the Mbere and Nyambeni hills that cut Embu from Ukambani. He knew the land beyond belonged to Wakamba. Yet Gikonyo always imagined home and Mumbi as lying behind these hills.

One clear morning he saw Kerinyaga; its snow-capped tops just touching the sky in the distant horizon moved him to tears. Not that he had a particular feeling for landscape. But the sight of the legendary mountain, its head thrust into the mist, somehow softened him in that way.

This experience now stood fresh in Gikonyo as he convalesced in Timoro hospital. The medicine-smell in the hospital reminded him of the marshy-decay along the Tana river. It was at Mweya, on the same day, that he again seriously thought of carving a stool from wood, a wedding gift to Mumbi. The idea gradually took concrete shape as he worked in the sun amidst the river-decay and the muddy earth. He would carve the stool from a Muiri stem, a hardwood that grew around Kerinyaga, and Nyandarwa hills. The seat would rest on three legs curved into three grim-faced figures, sweating under a weight. On the seat he would bead a pattern, representing a river and a canal. A jembe or a spade would lie beside the canal. For days afterwards, Gikonyo thought about the carving. The men's faces kept on changing; he altered the position of their shoulders, their hands or heads. How could he work a river in beads? Shouldn't he replace a jembe with a panga? He puzzled over little details and this kept his mind and heart away from the physical drudgery. He hoped to work on the stool as soon as he left detention.

Lying in hospital, Gikonyo was again possessed by a desire to carve the stool. He had been in Timoro for four days. For the last three days he thought of Mugo and the confession. Could he, Gikonyo, gather such courage to tell people about the steps on the pavement? At night he went over his life and his experiences in the seven detention camps. What precisely had all these years brought him? At every thought, he was pricked with guilt. Courage had failed him, he had confessed the oath in spite of vows to the contrary. What difference was there between him and Karanja or Mugo or those who had openly betrayed people and worked with the whiteman to save themselves? Mugo had the courage to face his guilt and lose everything. Gikonyo shuddered at the thought of losing everything. Every morning Mumbi and Wangari brought him food. At first he tried not to speak to Mumbi; he even found it painful to look at her. But after Mugo's confession, he found himself trying to puzzle out Mumbi's thoughts and feelings. What lay hidden behind her face? What did she think of Mugo and the confession? He increasingly longed to speak to her about Mugo and then about his own life in detention. What would she say about the steps that haunted him? Another thought also crept into his mind. He had never seen himself as father to Mumbi's children. Now it crossed his mind: what would his child by Mumbi look like?

It was on the fifth day that he recalled Mweya and his desire to carve a stool. He stirred in the hospital bed, careful not to lie on the plastered arm. At first it was a small flicker, the sort he used to feel at the sight of wood. Then, as he thought about it, he became more and more excited and his hands itched to touch wood and a chisel. He would carve the stool now, after the hospital, before he resumed his business, or in-between the business hours. He worked the motif in detail. He changed the figures. He would now carve a thin man, with hard lines on the face, shoulders and head bent, supporting the weight. His right hand would stretch to link with that of a woman, also with hard lines on the face. The third figure would be that of a child on whose head or shoulders the other two hands of the man and woman would meet. Into that image would he work the beads on the seat? A field needing clearance and cultivation? A jembe? A bean flower? He would settle this when the time came.

On the sixth day, Mumbi did not appear at the hospital. Gikonyo was hurt, and also surprised to find how much he had looked forward to the visit. All day he remained restless and wondered what had happened to her. Had she stopped coming altogether? Had she reacted against his obdurate silence? He anxiously waited for the dawn, the following morning. If she did not—

But she came, alone. Normally she and Wangari visited him together.

'You did not come yesterday,' he told her, accusingly. Mumbi sat on the bed and took her time before answering.

'The child was ill,' she said simply.

'What – what is wrong with – him?'

'Just a cold – or 'flu.'

'Did you take he – him to the dispensary?'

'Yes!' she said almost curtly. Gikonyo tried not to look at her. Mumbi appeared impatient and wanted to go.

'When do you leave hospital?' she asked.

'In two days' time.' Now he turned to her and just caught her eyes. She was not looking at him. He was surprised to find that tiredness in her eyes. How long had she been like this? What had happened to her over the last few days?'

'I am going now,' she said. 'I may not come tomorrow – or the next day.' She started to put things in the bag determinedly. He wanted to say: don't go. But he suddenly said: 'Let us talk about the child.'

Mumbi, already on her feet, was surprised by these words. She sat down again and looked at him.

'In here, at the hospital?' she asked, without any excitement.

'Now, yes.'

'No, not today,' she said, almost impatiently, as if she was now really aware of her independence. Gikonyo was surprised by the new firmness in her voice.

'All right. When I leave the hospital,' he said, and after an awkward pause, added: 'Will you go back to the house, light the fire, and see things don't decay?'

She considered this for a while, her head turned aside. Then she looked at him, directly, in the eyes.

'No, Gikonyo. People try to rub out things, but they cannot. Things are not so easy. What has passed between us is too much to be passed over in a sentence. We need to talk, to open our hearts to one another, examine them, and then together plan the future we want. But now, I must go, for the child is ill.'

'Will you – will you come tomorrow?' he asked, unable to hide his anxiety and fear. He knew, at once, that in future he would reckon with her feelings, her thoughts, her desires – a new Mumbi. Again she considered his question for a little while.

'All right. Maybe I shall come,' she said and took her leave. She walked away with determined steps, sad but almost sure. He watched her until she disappeared at the door. Then he sank back to bed. He thought about the wedding gift, a stool carved from Muiri wood. 'I'll change the woman's figure. I shall carve a woman big – big with child.'

Weep Not, Child

ISBN 978-0-14-310669-2

Two brothers, Njoroge and Kamau, stand on a garbage heap and look into their futures: Njoroge is to attend school, while Kamau will train to be a carpenter. But this is Kenya, and the times are against them—in the forests, the Mau Mau is waging war against the white government, and the two brothers and their family need to decide where their loyalties lie. For the practical Kamau, the choice is simple, but for Njoroge the scholar, the dream of progress through learning is a hard one to give up.

Petals of Blood

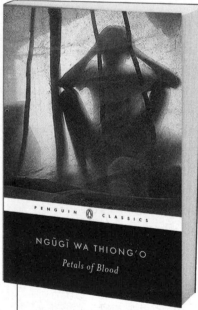

ISBN 978-0-14-303917-4

The puzzling murder of three African directors of a foreign-owned brewery sets the scene for this fervent, hard-hitting novel about disillusionment in independent Kenya. As the intertwined stories of the four suspects unfold, a devastating picture emerges of a modern third-world nation whose frustrated people feel their leaders have failed them time after time. First published in 1977, this novel was so explosive that its author was imprisoned without charges by the Kenyan government.

PENGUIN
CLASSICS